FUGITIVES IN A NEW UNITED STATES

The First Book in the series of a Dystopian Future United States

T. Ó Domhnaill

Self-Published by Crann na Beatha Ltd. USA

Self-Published By Crann na Beatha Ltd.

Midlothian, VA 23441

www.crann-na-beatha.com

ISBN-13: 979-8-9889157-5-1

United States Copyright Registration number TX-9-343-976

Cover design by: Robin Locke Monda

Cover Image: iStock Photo

Author's Image: Company Logo

Printed in the United States of America

This series is dedicated to all of the people around the world who are fighting to make the human race one big happy family. And also, to all of those fighting against governments who would take our basic human rights away from us to make themselves richer at our expense.

Table of Contents

Prologue

By the year 2031, the United States is no longer the superpower it used to be. It has been taken over by an autocratic, theocratic government, which threw out the original constitution. They've instituted a national religion, shut off all immigration and all non-whites, immigrants or any who refuse to accept the new national religion, are encouraged to leave the country or be forced into labor camps. Millions have migrated to other countries, leaving a vast labor shortage and economic ruin. What's left of the country is on the brink of total collapse. In some regions, It already has.

FUGITIVES IN A NEW UNITED STATES

Chapter 1

In the Beginning

Doctor James Naismith is on the run with a bounty on his head. He is of Pakistani origin; his parents having immigrated to the United States in 2007 when he and his sisters were very young, and immigration for well-educated people was relatively smooth. James and his sisters grew up in a moderate neighborhood. He went to college and medical school at a semi-prestigious university and had become an OBGYN doctor in a state that had allowed abortions until 2029. His father had also been a doctor and had been in high demand.

That was the year that the United States became a failed democracy and reverted to an autocratic theocracy run by white Christian nationalists. The old Republican political party had succumbed to its base and has been taken over by the evangelicals. In 2024, the U.S. elected a hardline conservative president who slowly eroded civil rights for anyone not of the White Anglo Saxon Protestant faiths.

The new president had the majority of the congress and most of the supreme court justices on his side and between them all, starting in 2025, he started stripping away women's rights, voting rights, and many other freedoms originally granted by the Bill of Rights and subsequent amendments to the constitution.

Freedom of the press became a laughable joke. Independent news media companies were shut down and foreign journalists were banned from the country. Immigration was shut down entirely by 2027 and all non-natural born citizens were either deported or rounded up and moved to camps reminiscent of what the U.S. did to the Japanese in WWII. This act included all naturalized citizens and green card holders. Visas and green cards were revoked as well. Caucasian naturalized citizens were given some preferential treatment but if any had brown or dark skin, they were just given somewhat better jobs than the green card holders by the work camp managers.

Any white, native-born citizens, who refused to practice the nationalized Christian faith were also rounded up and given the choice to leave the country or be put in the camps. It didn't matter what country they went to; they had to go or be forced into the work camps with all the other undesirables.

Dr. James, as he is fondly called by his patients, was raised a Muslim by his parents, along with his two sisters, who are either dead or in a camp in northern Virginia now.

Islam is outlawed in the new country as is any other religion other than their version of protestant Christianity. Catholics are tolerated but only as second-class citizens. Churches and associated school properties across the country now belong to the new government. The same for the Mormons and any other Christian offshoots. They were all strongly encouraged to convert to the new evangelical religion of the country or become second-class citizens. All of their church-owned properties were forfeited to the new government as well.

Any Christians who were not white were given a choice, leave the country or end up in a work camp. White Christians who had been members of any offshoot churches not tolerated by the new government were strongly encouraged to convert to their brand of Protestantism or leave but it was not mandated like the other undesirables. They were just told that they could not practice their old faith openly or risk the camps.

Needless to say, to be of any Christian faith other than the officially recognized religion in the new country led to a life of extreme prejudice and poverty. Those of other Christian faiths were not allowed to own property and were banned from any decent paying work.

It was in this nationwide chaos that Dr. Naismith continued taking care of his patients for as long as he could, even though it had been against the law to perform abortions in the United States since 2026.

Once the law passed, he kept at it, always in the shadows and always on the move. He carried a minimal kit with him so he could travel light. Whenever he treated someone, he left immediately afterwards to get as far away as possible before the local militias and secret police came looking for him.

He had some close calls these last few years but he managed to stay hidden for now. He was lucky because there is a strong underground network of people around the country who still believe that this new government is wrong and are in rebellion against it.

This rebel group runs an underground transfer network that helps people like Dr. Naismith and others move from place to place to avoid the government and the new secret police forces under The Department of Homeland Security.

Chapter 2
The Good Doctor

Dr. James had just left a neighborhood makeshift women's clinic in an industrial backend area of Brooklyn, NY, where he had been helping several women hiding in abandoned buildings. Most of them were from central and south America originally and had come across the southern border in the early 2020's during the height of the immigration surge back. Now they were on the run to avoid being rounded up and sent to the nearest work camp.

Their families, or what was left of them anyway, were also there. Like Dr. James, they were constantly on the move to avoid the authorities. Dr. James would always do his best with what he had, but sometimes, he had to turn away the worst cases because he didn't have what he needed to treat them; clinics with imaging equipment, surgery rooms, etc. He had just his medical bag, actually a medical back pack, and a few medicines bartered off the black market.

He had most of what he needed and occasionally the help of a nurse, who was usually also on the run, to do simple DNC's or minor baby health checkups but, with no lab facilities available, it was all he could do. In the first months after the coup, he had access to closed clinics provided by the underground but as Homeland Security started to step things up, they were all but demolished across the country now. When he had access, he was able to perform C-sections and small surgeries but that was rare now.

Such is his life after 2029. He knows that someday his luck will run out and they will probably shoot him when they catch him, but he accepts that. His parents died during the initial roundups of those deemed undesirable in the United States. He is also on the list to be deported or picked up and he went into hiding as soon as he found out.

His parents were supposedly killed while resisting internment in the local work camp; at least, that's what he'd been told. Dr. James blamed himself for not being there to protect them, but he had been living in another part of the country at the time and couldn't get back to them. His two sisters had been picked up and were now reported to be in a work camp in northern Virginia.

With his persona non-grata status, he had no way to travel publicly without being picked up by authorities. Dr. James did try to reach his sisters but stopped when they managed to sneak a letter out and told him to stay away and run. He has been on the run ever since.

Living the life of a fugitive was not what he had envisioned when he graduated from medical school.

Dr. Naismith had been accepted for a residency at a good hospital in California and had moved to Los Angeles to start his new career before things got bad. While he was there, the country fell apart before he tried to find a way back to the east coast. He would never forgive himself for being so selfish and not being there to protect his parents and sisters.

It wasn't too hard to get hooked up with the local underground network in southern California once he went on the run. A doctor with his skills was considered a valuable commodity. His stay there didn't last very long because the Western regions of California, Oregon and Washington state, although some of the last holdouts against the Christian coup of the government in D.C., didn't stand long against the large National Guard offensive sent to bring them into line.

A large portion of the white population in this region had supported the takeover and helped the soldiers anyway they could during the rebellion. Especially when it came to rounding up all the undesirable peoples and transporting them to the new work camps.

Dr. James had seen the work camps from a distance and they were squalid. Hundreds of people living in tents and makeshift wooden buildings, water and food supplied by the government. All able-bodied people of working age, 14 years and up, were transported and guarded every day, except Sundays, to work on construction projects, domestic jobs for the rich white citizens or whatever else the new government wanted them to do. If they refused, they were punished by beatings, loss of rations, and other cruelties. Some were outright killed as there were no longer any laws being enforced regarding the treatment of the detainee's outside of the cities. If someone was killed, the perpetrators were lauded as heroes in the rural communities. Sanitation was bad and disease was frequent but the new white rulers didn't care as long as nothing left the confines of the camp. Medical services were nearly non-existent, leading to a lot of suffering and death.

Dr. James had, by now, traveled the length and breadth of the country trying to stay ahead of the authorities in the last couple of years and he was getting tired. It is hard to live and help people when you always have to look over your shoulder and around every corner every minute of your day. He never knew when he would have to move. Anytime day or night, word would come that they were close and he needed to go.

Off he would go in some sort of transport if he was lucky, or if not, he would have to head out on foot. He was always on the lookout for anyone or anything suspicious.

That was the other part of the new government's policies. They offered cash rewards for information leading to the capture of any fugitives or undesirables by the authorities. Depending on the fugitives, the reward could be substantial and Dr. James's bounty was very high now.

Such was the life for all of those on the run in the new United States. Hounded by nearly everyone and never truly knowing who you could trust. Dr. James had gotten to know a handful of people he could count on during his travels. Word travels on the grapevine in the underground, especially regarding people like him. Dr. James was usually welcomed wherever he went and taken care of as best as they could with what little they had so he would want to return whenever possible.

That was another byproduct of this coup. When the new government took over in 2029, they tried to continue bullying other countries around the world like before but, very few would have much to do with them anymore and nearly all the corporations who wouldn't support the new government left the country and took everything with them. They relocated to more business-friendly countries and never looked back. While this was happening, the U.S. became a pariah around the world and the economy bottomed out.

The United States had transformed from a manufacturing powerhouse in the mid to late 20th century into a service economy by 2020's and did not have the capacity to take care of its people when the crash came in 2029. Now, most of the white citizens who weren't working for the government, were out of work and blaming the undesirables in the work camps. But they still wouldn't step up and do any menial work that required them to get their hands dirty. That was what the undesirables were for.

Agriculture officials in Washington D.C. have been working on getting the heartland back up and running to provide food for the people but it is going slow. Manufacturing is also starting slowly as there is no more money to invest in the infrastructure, start up new factories or rebuild the old ones. Hence the labor camps. The government is desperate to get the economy back up to where it used to be at any cost.

The world has condemned the United States for its human rights abuses, comparing them to China and Russia but they don't care. It's all about the money for what's left of the wealthy class and government officials.

The wealthy Christians who inherited the mantle of government are without any support from other countries outside the U.S. and not enough supporting taxpayers to cover the expenses of running a country.

Chapter 3

Meeting old friends

Dr. Naismith had finished up a couple of hours ago and was now in the care of the local resistance in Brooklyn. The rebels were trying to get him out of the city by way of the subway tunnels, most of which weren't being used anymore.

As the small group traveled through the old tunnels, the nurse who had been helping Dr. James stopped long enough to shake his hand and wish him good luck. She was headed in a different direction and would be traveling down a different tunnel now.

He also wished her good luck and safe travels as she headed down the other side tunnel, soon lost in the dark, murky light. His group leader motioned for them all to hurry up. They had a rendezvous to keep in order for him to make it out safely in the next leg of his journey.

After about another hours' worth of walking, dodging rats and muck, the group reached their destination. A man stepped out of a side tunnel and gave the correct call sign. As the group walked over to greet him, he quickly waved them into his tunnel out of sight. He needed Dr. James and anyone else who was going with him to come quickly now to avoid being seen.

Dr. James was traveling alone as he was wont to do most of the time, so he stepped out and quietly said, "Thank you" to the group for helping him again. He didn't know when or if he would be back so he just waved good bye and walked behind his new guide. Dr. James didn't know this man but as he knew the right call sign, he felt like he could trust him to a degree. Just in case, he kept a hand on his long belt knife as he walked down the tunnel.

Dr. James had killed people while defending himself from those who had tried to capture or kill him because of his skin color and religion.

He hated the thought that, as a doctor, he was supposed to save lives, not take them. All he ever wanted to do was help people. Now he was on the run, trying to help those he could while trying to stay alive. His major concern was for his two sisters living in a labor camp in northern Virginia that he had vowed to rescue as soon as he could.

The man kept up a brisk pace as they continued through the current tunnel. Dr. James wanted to ask how much further but gleaned that this man did not want to chitchat, so he kept quiet and followed as close as he dared so as not to lose sight of his guide in the murky light.

Pretty soon, the murky tunnel started to get brighter ahead and he breathed a little sigh of relief but was still wary of his guide and what may lay ahead. The man continued without a word towards the light. Since there was no change in the man's body language, Dr. James kept his hand on the hilt of his knife just in case of an ambush.

They reached the end of the tunnel and the man let out a bird whistle from the old train platform they were on. Another whistle came back from the dark and a small handful of people came out onto the platform from the other side. Dr. James recognized a couple of them from his previous trips up here.

One of the women he knew smiled at him, and James relaxed a little bit, then walked over to greet her. His guide up to that point stood aside without another word, and Dr. James wondered just how safe was he? Had he been compromised by this man? As he greeted his friend, he kept an eye on his guide for anything else that might give him any worry.

When he finished pleasantries with his friend Deanna, he asked her "Who is he?"

She told him, "We found him wandering the tunnels a little while back and he has turned out to be a very reliable, quiet person that won't talk about his past. He's proved himself trustworthy by guiding expeditions to scavenge for useful things and scout for any Homeland

Security incursions. He is also a good fighter and so far, hasn't given us any reason to doubt him." She looked over at the man and chuckled, "He is a little spooky though."

Deanna asked, "Are you ready for the next leg of your journey out of the city?"

Dr. James replied, "Yes, more than ready." He thought to himself, "I don't like tunnels and dark, enclosed spaces so the sooner we are out of here the better." She waved everyone together and they headed down the next tunnel towards the lights.

As they headed out, Dr. James looked back and saw the quiet spooky man bringing up the rear. The man didn't smile but he did nod his head in greeting so he felt a little better but decided that he would remain vigilante until he was somewhere he felt safer. Hopefully soon.

Dr. Naismith was trying to get to upstate New York, or what was left of it. From there, he could travel relatively safely over to New Hampshire where he knew some people. Once in upstate New York, he could refresh his supplies and get some rest before figuring out how to get there safely.

The landscape changed constantly with regard to how and where Homeland Security was operating. They were getting more organized now after a couple of years of fits and starts while rounding up all of the easy captures. Now that they were concentrating more on the stragglers and fugitives, Dr. James had to be more careful and gather as much intelligence as he could about where they were operating before making any decisions about where to go next. Those choices were becoming less and less available as time went on.

He had decided a little while ago that it was time to regroup up in the known safe havens in Northern New England. He knew a lot of places he could hide for a time with more people ready to assist him.

Some of the local folks had started out helping refugees get across the Canadian border right after the new government took over. That became harder as Homeland Security started increasing patrols and searches around the border regions. They wanted to be in control of who was allowed across the border, usually after a stint in a labor camp.

The underground groups worked to assist people across the border without being seen and provided safe havens wherever they could. Especially since the Canadians had closed their borders to the United States and only traded with Europe, Asia and Africa now. Alaska was given to the Canadians during the trade wars of the late 2020's. The United States had been forced to cede the state and its military bases over to them in exchange for desperately needed humanitarian aid and to prevent the Russians from establishing a foothold in North America.

If anyone is caught trying to cross into Canada illegally, they are likely to be shot on sight by the U.S. border patrol. The Canadians will just arrest you, which is a far better prospect than remaining in the U.S.

Dr. James's ultimate plan is to rescue his sisters in Virginia and find their way up north into Canada without getting caught. He would rather they be arrested and jailed in Canada than killed in the United States, or in the case of his sisters, likely something even worse than death. He has tried not to think about the cruelties his sister's may already have been subjected to.

He was thinking about all of this again as they trudged up the tunnel. They were headed upwards now so he knew they were close to the end of the tunnels and maybe some fresh air. He would take a gloomy wet night outside rather than being stuck in these tunnels any longer.

Soon, they came to the end of the tunnel. A scout was sent ahead to see if anyone was waiting for them unexpectantly. As they waited, Dr. James started to get more nervous and fidgety. Deanna grabbed his hand and tried to calm him down a little as they waited.

She was a single woman he had met over two years ago as part of the resistance network set up to move people across the border. When he showed up, he had provided some medical treatments for them and some refugees, after which Dr. James became a very welcome sight whenever he came through again.

She was a Wiccan as were most of her group. They had practiced their faith quietly in the mountains around upstate New York for decades before the crash. Now they were outlaws for not converting to Christianity and labeled as witches. A sure death sentence if caught by Christian fanatics or a labor camp with mandatory Christian indoctrination classes if caught by Homeland Security.

Dr. James was single and rather dashing when cleaned up, so he was welcome here in more ways than one. Not that he took advantage of that blessing but he didn't turn down a clean bed and a warm woman to keep him company when offered.

Dr. James was not a practicing Muslim anymore because of all of the trauma he had endured since his parents were killed. He had given up on God out of frustration with everything that was happening to him and the good people he met in his travels. He lived life one day at a time and took what little kindness and pleasures that were offered when they were offered because as he told himself every morning, "This this might be my last day."

The scout returned and reported that it looked like the coast was clear but the strongest should lead the way just in case of trouble. Deanna agreed and the spooky guide stepped up from the rear to join the lead group. The non-fighters, along with Dr. James, waited a little more and followed behind in single file bringing up the rear.

Once they all cleared the tunnel, clean air assailed James's senses and he slowed to take a breath. As he did, there was a commotion from the leaders up ahead. Lookouts had spied a small patrol of Homeland Security police in the area where they had intended to pass, so they needed to plot a new route out of the city.

Deanna was a part of that planning committee so she left him to join the others. Dr. James decided that a sit down on a rock in the outside air would feel good right about now and he found the nearest concrete block at the end of the tunnel to wait. He was pretty nervous, but it wasn't like this was the first time he'd had to change course in one of his journeys. He decided it would be best to rest while he could and wait it out.

Chapter 4

The escape from the city

As Dr. James rested on the block, he took stock of where he was and where he needed to go. Right now, this subway tunnel came out in an urban area on the north side of New York City. The tracks ran by a little park and across the street was a row of brownstones. Everything had a very rundown look to it and he didn't see any people in the streets. Which was probably a good thing for them, he thought, even though it was pretty late at night by now.

While Dr. James waited for his friend Deanna to return from her meeting with the leaders, he started to think about his future. Obviously, anything he planned would involve his sisters once he rescued them. Rescue being the key word. He just wasn't sure how he was going to accomplish that part yet.

How he planned to rescue his sisters get them across the border into Canada remained to be seen. First, he had to rest and resupply before heading south to Virginia. He chided himself, saying "Baby steps James, baby steps. All will come," he thought. He just had to have faith that things would work out. As he shook himself back into awareness, he said "In sha'Allah" quietly to himself and looked around once again.

Everyone else was taking advantage of the respite as well while they were waiting for the next move. Some were laying down taking cat naps. Others were sitting together chatting with one another. As far as they knew, Dr. James was just another refugee so they left him alone.

Very soon Deanna returned to say that they had worked out an alternative route to get them to safety. It would take a little longer but it should be safe, for now. They had to get moving quickly as they needed to be out of the city before sunrise.

With that, everyone started rousing to get ready for the next leg of their journey. The folks who looked like militia fighters took the lead with a small rear guard. Dr. James, Deanna, and the few other non-combatants made up the middle of the column.

They headed out of the tunnel area into the small street park, trying not to bunch up too much to arouse suspicions if anyone were looking out their windows this late at night. No one had seen any lights in any of the windows yet, but extreme caution was the word now until they got past this residential area.

Everyone wore dark, non-descript, camouflage clothing of one kind or another, which helped them blend in with the trees and bushes in the little park. As they headed out, they stayed as far away from any working street lights as possible. So far, so good.

As they all passed through the park and the next few blocks, the neighborhoods started to become more suburban. The group stuck to the alleyways as much as possible on their way through. They were all on heavy alert now for the slightest odd noise or lights. Some of them had been through here before but that didn't make it any easier.

If anything, it made it more stressful because someone might spot them and note that they have seen groups of people passing through here before. The next thing you know, the police would be all over them. As the group continued on, they maintained their spacing and kept each other within sight so as not to lose anyone in the dark.

Eventually, they passed beyond the little borough and made it out to the old thruway. Now they could pick up the pace and travel a little faster. Running alongside the old freeway system towards upstate New York offered a little more openness and security. The farther north they traveled, the less people they had to worry about spotting them, especially during the witching hours, as Deanna liked to joke about.

They all ran at a slow jog to make time. Stopping every little while to drink some water and catch their breaths. 10 minutes and they were at it again. This was the life for fugitives. A very physical life of running and hiding from the authorities. No one could afford to be a slacker. Slackers ended up in the camps or dead somewhere. The oldest in this group were in their early forties and very fit for their age. They had to be in order to do this kind of work.

Dr. James remembered reading in college that native tribesmen were noted runners and could run all day due to their stamina. Slow trots like they were doing now were sustainable as long as you stayed hydrated and stopped for protein occasionally. Now this group was emulating those indigenous people in order to stay alive and remain free.

The group trotted on into the early morning until the sun started to rise. As light started to blanket the countryside, they veered away from the sides of the highway and headed into the woods. There were paths in the woods that were familiar to the leaders so they continued north until the big city was nothing but a glow on the horizon to the south.

Chapter 5

Getting Reacquainted

They were largely out of danger for the moment and needed to take a break before changing course for the mountains in the north east. Everyone gathered around into a clearing in this particular patch of woods and broke off to use the bathroom and grab some rations from their rucksacks. The militia leader told them all to stay close and take a twenty-to-thirty-minute break before they moved on again.

Dr. James settled down on the ground next to Deanna and grabbed some protein bars and water from his bag. While he was eating and resting, he asked, "How've you been since the last time I was up this way?"

She talked about a couple of her acquaintances who had been caught a bit ago and sent to the camps and she was sad about that, as she would be for any of them. No one had been killed since the last time they had seen each other so that was a good thing. They chitchatted some more before it was time to get going again.

They gathered up their gear and prepared to head out. As she was shouldering her pack, Deanna stepped close and gave Dr. James a coy smile, quietly saying, "You are welcome to stay at my house again once we arrive".

He smiled and replied "I would love to." He remembered the times they had spent together before on previous trips up here so he wasn't too surprised about the invitation. He was just glad that she hadn't taken up with anyone else since he had visited last. That could be awkward and he didn't do awkward.

Dr. James had always been a bit of a loner, which was why he hadn't gotten married before. His parents had been dismayed by his solitary lifestyle as, like all parents from the old country, they wanted to have grandchildren to take care of.

With all of the chaos in the country and across the world now, he didn't think he would ever settle down. Maybe someday if he ever found a safe place to live with his sisters but that was way off into an imaginary future right now.

The group made it to a parking lot in a deserted area of a small town and loaded themselves into a commercial truck that had been parked there waiting for them. This afforded them some cover and speed to reach their destination in the mountains. There weren't supposed to be any checkpoints on the highway to worry about, yet.

After a few hours, they arrived at their drop off point at a secluded highway rest area. They trekked back out into the woods again, only now in a more northeasterly direction away from any main roads. With it being broad daylight, they needed to stay hidden from sight as much as possible. Heading in the direction they were going, that wouldn't be nearly as hard as it was in the city. There were a lot more forests to travel in now going upwards into the Adirondack mountains.

Up in the far remote areas of the Adirondack's, this resistance group lived scattered amongst the mountains, lakes and rivers of far northern New York state and the western Vermont border areas. All the while helping people cross the border or to get elsewhere safely without the authorities catching them. They felt that this was their mission in life and would continue until they couldn't anymore. Hopefully passing this on to their children and so on.

All afternoon they traveled the paths through the woods heading into the mountains. The scouts kept reporting all clear and they continued on until just after sunset. As they settled down to take another thirty-minute break, everyone was bone tired. They all looked like they were near the end of their endurance. Dr. James made the rounds to see if anyone needed him for anything but everyone was fine, just tired.

He came back to sit alongside Deanna once again and asked, "How are you holding up?

She replied "I don't think I have it in me to make these kinds of trips anymore. I'm going to see about changing positions in the group when we make it back home. I want to work at helping people cross the border instead of helping with rescues in the cities," she said with a tired smile.

Dr. James agreed with her, "Maybe it is time to find a safer vocation and I am also thinking about my future." He had told her about his sisters before but now he told her that he was going to concentrate on rescuing them and bringing them up north to cross the border once and for all. He just had to come up with a plan to get that done.

She smiled knowingly, and said "I will support you anyway I can once we get home and you have a chance to research a plan." As they continued talking about it, the call came around to head out again. Everyone grabbed their gear and continued up the trails ahead. As pitch darkness started to fall around them, they went back to walking in single file and keeping in sight of the person ahead and behind.

They had long since left any cities or large towns behind and the trails were getting steeper as they climbed further up. They finally arrived at a large lake about eleven pm or so and skirted around the east side until they could continue north.

Most of the people in this area lived on the west side of the lake closer to the interstate so they were relatively safe going this way. They traveled through the night once again but by this time, James was getting pretty tired after having no sleep for the last two days. He told himself, "I can't continue this lifestyle for much longer as it will eventually kill me at an early age. If not by getting caught, by sheer exhaustion from trips like this one."

They continued walking until the word was passed back that they were almost home. Just another couple of hours. Everyone started to lighten up. People were starting to relax and chat with each other when the leader passed back for everyone to be quiet. They weren't home yet and anything could go wrong. James echoed that sentiment in his head. You were never safe in this new world. He had found that out the hard way in other places he had been around the country.

Dr. James never relaxed entirely. He knew that you could not afford to let your guard down for even a minute these days. Homeland Security was getting better at finding people every year and punishing them when caught. This was another good reason to get out of this God's cursed country now before he became another casualty. He knew it was only a matter of time.

Before long, as he was musing about all of the misery and death, they arrived at their destination point. Everyone would be splitting off into smaller groups of twos and threes now to find their way to their homes up in the mountains. Dr. James waited for his cue before following Deanna and another young lady in the group. As they started out, James realized that he was so tired from the trip and no sleep, he had lost track of time. They had been on the road for two days solid now and he would be glad for a shower, a good meal and a clean, soft bed to sleep in for a few hours.

Chapter 6

The Raid

As folks started to head off into the woods, a local perimeter watch ran up the path from town and told everyone to stop. He said, "Grab anyone that just left and bring them back as I have really bad news to tell everyone."

As everyone gathered around, he told them, "While you were gone, Homeland Security raided the area with a large contingent of troops and grabbed everyone they could find for interrogation and possible relocation to work camps. A lot of the houses were burned to the ground and it isn't safe anywhere near the area now. The troops are still going house to house up in the more remote areas looking for possible fugitives. Those either on the list of wanted people or those they suspect maybe harboring fugitives. Anyone found not listed on the national database of registered people in the area are being arrested and sent to a camp, along with any undesirables."

"No one in your small group is safe now. All of you are known collaborators with the rebels and you will be arrested if found."

His advice was for everyone to scatter to anywhere but this part of New York State until things settled down. If anyone had relatives in Vermont, Massachusetts, or anywhere east of here, this would be a good time to pay them a visit. For others, what remained of the resistance would try to get them out of here to another safe area of the country.

Dr. James looked at Deanna and quietly asked her, "What do you plan to do?" He knew that she didn't have any family around anymore. Her husband had left years ago over religious differences and her kids were gone as well. They had gone with their dad when he divorced her. The other young lady also didn't have anyone here because she had originally arrived on the run from an abusive boyfriend and stayed. She had been too afraid to start another relationship after that episode in her life.

Everyone started talking at once amongst themselves. Some had family members up here and wanted to know their status. Others were wondering where they were going to go. As the noise started to get louder, their leader once again, told everyone "Quiet down. We don't need to attract any attention to ourselves."

He told everyone to separate into groups. Those who had family here and were worried about them, step to one side. Those who had family that they could go to outside the area fall out to different group. For those who had no one and nowhere to go, stay put until they could sort out what to do next.

Deanna wanted to know if they had raided her small house up in the mountains and the young man didn't know. He just repeated what he had said earlier. All he knew was that Homeland Security was searching every house they could find and no one was safe anywhere around here anymore.

Deanna looked at Dr. James and asked him, "What do you think?" He said "It wouldn't be a good idea to take any chances. We need to get somewhere out of sight quickly before someone gives us away under extreme coercion." That meant torture but he didn't want to tell them that. He had seen the results of Homeland Securities intense interrogations and it hadn't been pretty. He had treated patients at other places that had been tortured by them.

What to do was the question. James needed rest before he could go too much farther but now, he had nowhere to go. It was beginning to look like his rest would be somewhere deep in the mountains before heading east to northern New England. Maybe he could scare up a good meal but even that was looking iffy.

Then there was the matter of the Deanna and Theresa, the young lady he barely knew. Now they didn't have anywhere to go either and James wasn't sure he was up to taking care of them, not that they needed much from him. They were pretty capable on their own but still, he felt a little responsible. After all, he was the reason they had made this trip to the city. Although, he reasoned, if they hadn't made this trip, they might have gotten captured in the initial raid. Maybe "Allah" was looking out for them.

As they were discussing what to do, the young man recognized Dr. James and came over to say hello. He seems that the doctor had treated him for a cut on his last trip and he remembered him. He asked the doctor, "What are your plans?"

Dr. James told him, "That's what we are discussing. I'm not sure what my next step is going to be and the other two are working that out."

The kid said, "I know somebody who could help you and any others here who don't have anywhere else to go. If it's alright, I can sneak back down the mountain and bring him up to meet you."

This raised an immediate alarm bell with James. With his already paranoid nature, this was a red flag given what was going on right now. He started to say no when the group militia leader came over to see what was going on. He asked if they had made a decision on where they were going to go yet.

The young watch guard repeated what he had told Dr. James's little squad and the militia leader asked him "Who are you talking about?" When the young man told him, the militia leader gruffly asked him, "where is he right now?"

The young man said, "I can take you to him." At this, the militia leader said "No, it isn't safe enough. As for bringing him up here, maybe, but me and a couple of my trusted soldiers will go with you just in case of trouble."

When he heard this, the young man started to get nervous, which James's thought was a dead giveaway that this kid was a bounty hunter. He was looking to cash in on them. The militia leader apparently noticed the change as well and told him, "Stay here and help keep watch, me and my most trusted men will go find this man and bring him here, if we can. It will give us a chance to recon the area to see if we can find out how many troops we are up against."

The young man looked dejected but agreed to stay behind and help provide security, not that he was being given much choice. The militia leader went over to talk to his men and in a couple of minutes, three of them stepped out and got ready to hit the trail. The others gathered around the young man and escorted him out to a perimeter spot where they could keep an eye on him.

One of the men going down the trail was the spooky man from the city tunnels. When he looked up at Dr. James's little group, he nodded his head again, only more pronounced than the last time, as if to say, "I got you, I will take care of you." Then they headed down the trail towards the little village in the valley below.

As they left, the people in the other group who had somewhere else they could go, gathered up their gear and started heading out. They came by and wished Deanna and Dr. James good luck as they walked off into the woods. It was getting close to daybreak by now. Dr. James was beyond tired by now and needed to find a place to rest. He asked one of the militia guards if he could lay down somewhere while they waited for the others to return. The man told him, "Sure thing Doc, just tell me where you'll be so we can keep an eye on you. You are a little bit of a celebrity up here and we want to take good care of you."

He asked Deanna and Theresa, "Have you decided what you want to do?" Deanna looked at Theresa and then back at James and said "Not yet. I want to wait until Mike (the militia leader), returns, or not, before I make a decision." James nodded and excused himself to find a place to lay down for a power nap.

Deanna asked, "May I come with you?" Theresa wasn't sure what to do but asked to tag along too until a better idea came up.

The three of them went over to a small spot under a tree and scraped away the pine cones and sticks to lay down. Dr. James had a small blanket that he carried for just such situations and spread it out under the tree. It was just large enough for two.

Deanna asked, "Can I lay down next to you for a little while?"

Dr. James replied "Sure, no problem."

Theresa also had a poncho that she broke out and laid down on the other side of them. Dr. James waved at the militia guard to let him know where they were and laid down with Deanna curled up next to him.

Theresa cuddled up along her other side for warmth and they all took a little nap together. Dr. James went out like a light but not before he listened for Deanna's breathing to slow down as she went to sleep on his shoulder. His last thoughts before nodding off were how much he liked having Deanna this close after being so alone so much.

Chapter 7

On the Run

Dr. James had been asleep for a little over an hour when the militia member walked over and gently nudged his foot. It startled him from his deep sleep and as he looked up with eyes wide, the man said, "Mike is back and he wants to talk to you guys."

James started to stir, which woke up Deanna, who then shook Theresa. They got up, shook off their exhausted sleep and Deanna said, "I need to use the bathroom," which seemed like a good idea for all three of them.

After they returned, they grabbed their gear and walked out to the little clearing where the militia members were gathered around another stranger. Deanna recognized him and started to walk up to him but the man shook his head no slightly as if to tell her, "You don't know me." She stepped back and grabbed Dr. James's arm to wait quietly for further developments.

The man introduced himself as "Mr. Smith," an obvious false name, but James didn't care as he understood the reason for subterfuge. With everything that was going on here locally, this man wasn't taking any chances.

The man proceeded to update them on the situation in the area. As they already knew, Homeland Security was raiding their village in the valley, going store to store and house to house in residential neighborhoods and outlying homes in the mountains around the whole valley. The nearby rural farms and homes would be next.

If they suspected anyone, they were tossing the homes for information and burning some as a lesson to others. They had information that people in the area were part of the resistance against the new government and anyone was to be arrested if the slightest evidence were found in any of their homes and businesses.

Those who could, were fleeing to the mountains with whatever they could carry on their backs. All roads were now blockaded with checkpoints. Some of the troops were now starting to follow the trails up into the mountains to try and catch any who have fled.

"My advice is for everyone here to head east now before they find this clearing. The militia members will cover your backtrail and try to lead the troops away in a different direction." He explained, "We don't have the weapons or manpower to take on this many government troops, so we will try to draw them off to allow as many as possible to escape and then scatter ourselves."

Deanna asked, "Has my house had been discovered yet? "If not, would it be safe to head over there to pick up some supplies before leaving?"

Mr. Smith said "No, there are no safe places anymore. The woods and areas around the village are crawling with Homeland Security troops. Best to go now and try to find supplies along the way. Warnings are already going out ahead of you on the secure channels of our short-wave radios and the Ham radio stations before we shut down. All of those who have already fled are passing the word along as they can."

Dr. James was taking this all in and remaining quiet. He had seen this before and knew what to expect. He was sort of prepared. He just needed some more water and food for the trail. A clean change of clothes would be nice but, maybe he would get lucky on the way. Sympathetic people had been helpful to him in the past so all he could do was pray for a little deliverance.

He looked at Theresa and asked her, "What do you want to do?" He knew Deanna would probably go with him to show him the way across the mountains.

Theresa hesitated for a minute, then asked "Would it be all right if I come with you guys?"

James looked at Deanna who replied, "Absolutely, you're more than welcome to come along. You will have to keep up though. We will have our hands full getting across the mountains"

Deanna turned back to talking to Mr. Smith while Dr. James started discussing a little of what to expect on the trip. Deanna turned back around and told them, "Mike's crew will share their water and some trail food with everyone to get us all started but that will have to last until we find some more along the way. Given our situation, I have no idea when that might be. Everything in this part of the country is in absolute chaos with this sudden raid."

Deanna knew the back trails out of here as she had lived up here all her life. She assured James and Theresa that she would be fine to lead them out and over to safety across the Adirondak's. She did ask around if anyone had any recent weather reports as sudden storms were notorious this time of year, especially up in the high country.

"It is late May right now and it can still be chilly up there at night." She asked Dr. James and Theresa, "Do you both have any warm clothing as you will likely be needing some?"

James did but Theresa did not beyond what she was wearing and that might be a problem. No one here had any to give her either. Deanna said "We'll just have to deal with that as needed."

There was no way they would remain free if they tried to get anything from down in the valley. Mr. Smith told them all, "I barely made it up here myself without being discovered".

Mike agreed, "It won't be safe to go down to the village until the storm troopers have left. But they are sure to leave a small contingent behind and leave the checkpoints up for a few weeks as well."

"Once the majority of the troops have left, we will try and sneak back into town to grab some food and other necessities but until then, we are all on the run up here in the woods."

Mike's people had caches buried around the area that they could tap into but these stashes just held food, water and ammunition for the most part. Not much help for any of fugitives like Deanna, Dr. James and Theresa.

The militia members stepped up to share what provisions they could amongst the remaining fugitives with apologies that they didn't have more.

Deanna told them, "It's okay, I understand." She had known most of them since they were kids, so she knew how they felt. She said "I hope to be able to return home someday soon. I will make it up to you with a big feast once you have chased all of the 'Storm Troopers' out of our valley." They all laughed and told her they would do their best to get rid of them for her.

Chapter 8

Over the mountains and through the woods

Once the three of them were all set to go, Deanna waved good bye to her friends and neighbors, then set off down what was little more than a deer trail through the trees and brush. As it was nearly mid-morning now, she needed to set a fast pace without exhausting them too badly. She knew that Dr. James was just about at his end with little to no sleep in the last couple of days, not that she and Theresa had that much more. That little power nap they had this morning wouldn't last them too long.

Right now, she needed to guide them as far east as she could before they could afford to take any breaks and rest. She was also worried about food as they didn't have anything more than trail food and protein bars to last a couple of days. But right now, getting as far away from here as possible without a trace was first and foremost.

Deanna led off at a brisk pace on the little narrow trail. She told them both to try watch their steps so as not to step in any mud or soft earth to make it harder to track them. She thought to herself, "If can teach them how to leave as little trace as possible, we just might fool any city cops. Hopefully there won't be any really good trackers following us but I don't want to take any chances."

She taught them how to wind through the trees and brush and to gently push away any small branches rather than breaking them off as they passed through. Broken branches were easier to spot for anyone with any tracking skills. She did her best as quickly as possible along the way to teach them how to evade average trackers.

As they kept going, James could feel his energy levels ebbing pretty low and wondered if he would be able to keep up for much longer. He noticed that Theresa, who was walking ahead of him, seemed to be faring better than he was. She was a few years younger than him and he admired her stamina. He also wondered how Deanna was doing? He thought she was close to his age, but he wasn't really sure just how old. They hadn't spent much time talking about details like that the last time he had been up here. She seemed to be doing okay though as she maintained a steady pace without seeming to flag.

They kept going until about noontime until they came to the opening of a mountain canyon with rock walls on both sides. Deanna called a halt and told them, "Let's take a break here and eat something now because we might have to break into a run up ahead once we get into this canyon. I didn't want to take any chances of someone seeing us in the canyon from above." She advised, "Stay close to the walls and move as fast as you can without stirring up any dust or make any loud noises. There are more deep woods to hide in further into the valley once we reach the other side of this canyon."

While they were taking their small break, Theresa asked Deanna, "How do you know about all of these trails through the mountains so far from your house?"

Deanna replied "My Wiccan coven made it a point to travel all through the mountains around here before the crash as part of our religion. We believe in living with nature and learning as much as possible about the natural world around us. My friends and I went on many camping trips hiking all through the mountains around here."

As she was getting them ready to go again, Deanna asked them "Are you all okay?" She was looking at Dr. James as she asked.

James replied "I am fine for now. But I would like to make camp early today, if it is safe enough. We need to eat and get as much sleep as we can if we are to make it through the day tomorrow. We will need to set up a night watch though."

Given how tired they all were, he suggested no more than two-hour shifts to avoid falling asleep while on watch. The women agreed and they started out again.

Within minutes they came up on the canyon opening Deanna had told them about. It opened up into a wide chasm with sheer granite walls on either side all the way to the top. She motioned for them to stay close to the wall on the right and to be very quiet. She whispered, "Run as fast as you can while trying to step softly. Any loud, sudden noise can trigger a rock slide, which would alert anyone above us that we are down here."

They started their run down the canyon, looking up whenever they could. No one wanted to be caught by a falling rock or Homeland Security at this point. Deanna kept the lead and continued to look for anything amiss ahead of them such as strange tracks, rocks out of place, dust up ahead or pebbles falling from above. She wasn't too worried about her charges behind her. They weren't too bad for city people, although Dr. James did have some experience being on the run. She admired him for keeping up as well as he had so far, given that he had traveled farther than she and her group had when they picked him up in the city a couple of days ago.

Deanna reminisced a little while she was trotting down the canyon path. When Dr. James had visited their village the last time, he had been brought in from the west, first by boat across Lake Erie and then through the countryside below Buffalo, New York to their village near the Canadian border. When he arrived, it had been by car and he was well rested and ready to go to work helping the women around the area who needed his special skills. He also had basic medical skills so he stitched up a few cuts, diagnosed a few other maladies as best as he could and dispensed medicines as he had available.

As a lifelong resident of her village, and living alone in her cabin up in the woods, she didn't have to think too hard about inviting him to stay with her while he was attending to everyone. She didn't get too attached during their time together as she knew that once he left, she likely would never see him again.

"But he is a looker and I have fond memories of our time together," she remembered with a small smile.

She had been very surprised when the word came around last week, that a volunteer party was needed to go down and rescue their favorite doctor from the city. They had made this trip a few times before for other people so she was one of the first to volunteer when she heard that it was for Dr. James.

Now, as they were on the run together, she realized that she didn't want to lose him again. She thought to herself, "I will do whatever it takes to make sure we make it somewhere safe together." Deanna was pretty sure that once they reached a safe haven, Theresa would go her own way and then it would be just her and James to figure out what came next.

They stayed in the shadows whenever possible, working their way through the canyon. Everyone was doing their best to stay as quiet as they could. Deanna had told them that the way through was almost a mile long. Since it was near midday, Deanna was more concerned about being spotted by any Homeland Security troops that may know about this canyon than anything else.

They were nearly through when some gravel fell down from above and Deanna raised a closed fist to stop and remain still. As they stopped even breathing at this point, she waited to see if she could see or hear anything more. They waited for what seemed like an eternity before Deanna gave them a hand wave to motion them forward again, but at a dead slow pace so as not to make a sound. She slowly put one boot in front of the other between breaths and listened for any strange sounds. Every couple of steps, she would stop, look and listen.

After moving about twenty feet, Deanna spied the woods ahead. She decided to hide in case they were walking into a trap. If there was going to be an ambush, it would likely be there at the edge of the woods. She came up behind a large outcropping in the wall of the canyon and motioned for them to hug the wall and get down on the ground using hand gestures. She wanted to wait and see if she could discern any movement in the trees ahead. Maybe some inexperienced trooper would accidently move a tree limb to give himself away.

As they waited in the semi-shade of the big rocks, nothing moved other than the insects. Deanna saw some birds flitting about and watched to see if anything spooked them. So far, nothing. No more gravel falling either. They didn't have any weapons beyond belt knives for camping that wouldn't be much use against guns. After about twenty minutes, with still no movement and the birds behaving as if there was nothing wrong, Deanna decided to take the chance. She rose up to a crouch and worked her way forward around the outcropping, expecting any second to hear a shot ring out or troopers come pouring out of the woods yelling and screaming as they did. Still nothing. As she worked her way towards the trees, she signaled the others to follow at a distance and to keep low.

Deanna reached the first line of trees and dived behind the first big trunk she could find. As she lay down under the tree, she looked out to watch the other two make their way to her position. "So far, so good," she thought. She realized she was actually scared for the first time in her life. Before, she always had a healthy respect for nature and the dangers out in the back country. She had learned her woodland skills from her father and brothers, who had been avid hunters and Army combat veterans. Her father had been in the Army during Desert Storm and her brothers had been in the Army and Marines during the twenty-year wars after 9/11. Her two older brothers had completed multiple tours to Iraq and Afghanistan.

As she watched, Dr. James and Deanna crouched low as she had told them to as they made their way to her. At the last stretch, she watched Theresa jump up and run into the woods behind her while Dr. James came near to stepping on her as he made it into the edge of the woods. Theresa quietly made her way over to them as Dr. James lay down next to Deanna.

As they regrouped under the trees, Deanna quietly told them "Keep a watch out for anything making any unusual noises or movements in the woods around us. I have a bad feeling about this place and want to get out of here as fast as possible."

She took the lead again but this time, she stayed in the deepest part of the woods not following any path, just heading east. As they walked single file through the thick trees trying to be as quiet as possible, Deanna kept thinking that something is wrong. Then she realized it was too quiet here. Despite the insects buzzing and walking about, there were almost no birds or small wildlife running around under the trees.

Now she was really paranoid. She whispered to her companions, "I think there may be bad guys in the woods or on top of the mountains around here so keep a sharp eye and ear out for anything at all." She continued to lead them single file through the woods walking through the fir and spruce trees using the needles to cushion their steps. She warned them, "Stay away from any small saplings that might make a noise if your clothing brushes against them."

They continued silently through the heavy woods until late afternoon. As the sun started to set in the western sky behind the mountain peaks, Deanna told them, "Take a break. If there are any troopers or hunters out here, we may have eluded them for now."

They sat down under a tall spruce tree and broke out their water bottles and trail bars. It was good to rest for a few minutes. Deanna didn't let her guard down though. As she sat down next to Dr. James, she kept an ear out for any strange sounds or lack thereof. It was still a little too quiet in these woods to suit her but maybe she was just a little too paranoid after the canyon.

Chapter 9

The trap and the camp

As they ate and drank, she shushed them and whispered her fears. James immediately came to attention and whispered, "I'm sorry for not paying more attention. I'm so very tired and it is starting to make me shut down a little."

Theresa whispered tiredly, "I promise to pay more attention too." They ate in silence after that and quicky prepared to continue on.

Deanna figured if they could just make it until darkness, they had a good chance of making it out of here. She led them off into the woods again heading east as much as the woods would let them. Deanna hoped that they didn't get lost out here trying to outrun her fears. She knew the path coming out of that canyon but she had been afraid to take it earlier for fear that the bad guys also knew about it, and were lying in wait for them to come walking right into a trap.

Deanna thought to herself, "Maybe I'm wrong but it's better to be paranoid now than fall right into their hands. After dark, we can try to find the trail again. Maybe we have passed far enough east and bypassed any trap laid for them." She could only hope. "Worst case scenario, we spend a cold night under the trees and find the trail in the morning at sunrise."

As the sun continued to settle down behind the mountain peaks, the woods started getting darker and it was becoming very hard to see through the trees now. If they were going to find the trail, they needed to find it before it got any darker.

Deanna veered right heading south towards the mountain on their right. As they moved closer to where Deanna thought the trail might be, they all paid close attention to every sound and movement in the woods around them. Moving with their heads on a swivel as her brothers used to say. She missed them more than ever right now. They were way far away and could offer no help now. She would have to use every skill her family had ever taught her to get them out of this mess.

After a few minutes, Deanna started recognizing certain rock formations ahead. As they got closer, she slowed them down like before. One slow step at a time to listen for anything out of place. As she got closer to the trail, she heard a noise over to the west. She held up her fist to stop everyone and listened again.

As she crouched down behind a small fir tree, the other two lay down and crawled under other trees to stay out of site. As she listened, she heard it again. It sounded like a small radio. Sure enough, the voices came faintly through the trees back down the trail towards the canyon exit where they had been. The ambush had been set about a quarter of a mile east of the canyon and would have nailed them for sure if her instincts hadn't made her more paranoid than usual.

She determined their relative position to them and figured that she had guessed right. They were behind them now and, if they were extremely quiet, they could slip down the trail without them knowing they were there. Not that she was going to brazenly step out on the trail. She planned to stay inside the woods parallel to the trail where she could follow it without too much trouble.

She stepped back and motioned for Dr. James and Theresa to follow her. As it was near dusk now, she didn't want to go too much farther tonight. She knew of a spot down the trail a little further that she thought would keep them reasonably safe tonight. No fire though. As they were passing through the trees, she whispered to them, "We will have to set up a cold camp tonight and do as Dr. James suggested, set two-hour guard shifts and a quick jump off down the trail in the morning at the first hint of sunrise."

She knew that they were on their last legs and wouldn't last much longer. This place she knew of was just a few more minutes east off the trail. Deanna and her friends used to camp there whenever they were out this way so she knew right where it was. She figured she would have no problem finding it in the dark. Which was good for them. They needed all the help they could get right now.

Deanna was not much of the praying sort. She would attend Wiccan rituals with her friends on the holidays and honor her ancestors and the ancient Gods of the woods. But praying for miracles, she left that to the Christians.

James had been silently praying ever since the first alert from Deanna in the canyon. He promised God that he would be more pious if he would look after them during this trip. Of course, he knew in his heart that this was not true. His current life didn't give him time to stop and recite his prayers five times a day as required in the Quron but he hoped God understood.

As he brought up the rear, he kept praying for Deanna to lead them to safety soon as he truly was about finished. He mused about what a life with her might be like as they walked silently through the trees in the dark. He asked himself, "I wonder if a Muslim and a Wiccan can manage our cultural differences." He also prayed no one got hit by a low hanging branch in this darkness tonight. They didn't have the time to stop so he could tend to any wounds right now.

Within 10 minutes, Deanna found her hidden camping spot off the trail in the woods. She thought she could still smell the faint tinge of old charcoal in the air here and knew they were in the right place, even though it was near pitch dark out now. Maybe it was just her imagination about the charcoal but it still felt welcome for the first time in days.

She whispered, "We are here. We will set up camp with what little we have. Hopefully it won't get too cold tonight without a fire." They had a blanket and each other to keep warm with, although she didn't know how comfortable Theresa would be snuggled up next to her while James stood his night watches. I guess they would find out, if it got cold enough.

They laid out the blanket and Theresa's poncho, then ate a quick meal. Theresa volunteered to stand the first watch. As Dr. James and Deanna rolled up together in the blanket, she worried about Theresa standing guard. "Will she be able to stay awake? Will she be able to tell if someone is sneaking up on her in the dark?" She was so worried that she had trouble settling down. Dr. James was already asleep, out cold from exhaustion.

She quietly got up and came to sit next to Theresa, who was sitting a few feet away in the dark. Theresa was a little cold and trying hard to stay awake so she was glad for the company. They talked a bit about the troopers back down the trail and Deanna reassured her that only a handful of people knew about this hideaway camp spot. It was doubtful that the troopers had come this far east scouting for anyone yet. Deanna reminded her of what to listen for and gave her a rhyme to recite to help her stay awake in the dark. If she heard anything, or got scared, come wake her immediately.

Theresa assured her. "I can stay awake for the next couple of hours. Go to bed. I'll be fine."

Deanna crawled back into the blanket next to a warm James and felt reassured enough now to be able to sleep. As she drifted off, she dreamt of her late father being there with her as she slept.

The watches through the night were quiet. They all got much needed rest and some troubled sleep, but sleep nonetheless. At the first sign of daybreak above the mountains, Deanna, who had taken the last watch, quietly woke everyone up to start the next leg of their journey. She figured that the troopers wouldn't rouse until full light so they might have a couple hours to scoot down the trail to try and get ahead of them. As she grabbed a quick drink and bite to eat, she said a silent prayer to the Gods of this wood to protect them and guide them in their escape.

Chapter 10

The runaways

The trio hit the trail going east as quickly as they could get ready. The stars were still out, bright with the morning chill with a trace of the coming sunrise on the eastern horizon. As Deanna led the way once more, she set a quick pace to try and put as much distance between them and those behind them. She just hoped that they weren't all that smart to post a watch further down the trail.

She figured they would deal with that if it came up but right now, it was "move, move, move", as her brother used to say, when they had to go somewhere quickly. He had been a sergeant in the Army once upon a time.

Dr. James brought up the rear again like before. This time, he kept a close watch on their backtrail to make sure they weren't being followed. He had taken his woodsman training seriously in the last couple of days, learning as much as possible from Deanna. James had been a little embarrassed yesterday when she started teaching them basic survival and trail skills. He thought he had been pretty good at it until then. Admittedly, he had been exhausted and not thinking too clearly but that was still no excuse.

As the trail meandered east through the valley, they kept going until the sun was well above the mountain peaks before Deanna called a break. James reported "I haven't seen or heard anything from behind us so maybe we have made it far enough to relax a tad?" Deanna agreed. If they hadn't heard or seen anything by now, they had made it safely past that checkpoint back at the canyon.

That didn't mean that they where safe by any means, just that they had cleared their last situation. Deanna hoped that her militia friends back home were still okay. She was worried that they might get into a firefight with Homeland Security and someone she knew ended up hurt or dead. No use thinking about that too much now. She needed to concentrate on getting them all to that safe refuge in Vermont that she knew of and hoped that the old resort was still operational.

During their short break, Deanna told them about this place she knew of just across the border in Vermont. She and her friends had stayed there before and had heard the owners were passing refugees through with supplies after the crash. The underground network had placed them on the list of people that could be relied on to help travelers when needed.

This would be their first stop on the way east to New Hampshire. She wasn't sure how far away they were right now but, she might be able to give a better estimate as they continued down the trail. Right now, she advised Theresa and Dr. James "Keep a close watch for anything different, such as fresh shoe tracks, trampled grass or broken tree limbs alongside the trail. Also listen to the birds and insects. If things get quiet all of a sudden, or if a flight of birds suddenly takes off nearby, motion with your hands for everyone to get off the trail and get to cover."

The two of them nodded and said, "okay" as they grabbed their gear. Deanna led off at a slow jog to make better time. She told them to do their best and if they needed to slow down, to let her know so they could take a break.

After about an hour, Deanna recognized where they were by some familiar trees and bends in the trail from her previous trips. She whispered back to Theresa, "By my memory, we are about five to six hours from the Vermont border and that old resort. If we can keep up our current slow jog, we should make it before dark."

They took another short break a couple hours later and Deanna said, "I am a little concerned about possible Homeland Security forces at the border so we need to be a little more cautious from here on out. Pay attention to every detail as we get closer to the border. We can't afford to relax until we have reached our destination and learned what is going on."

She stepped out on the trail again and kept a watch on the sun. She didn't want to be out on this trail after dark again tonight, especially trying to sneak across the border. She hoped they wouldn't have to sneak across but she wasn't willing to take any chances. She knew that it was better to think of the worst-case scenario and prepare for it, then hope it never came to pass.

By mid-afternoon, they took another short break for water and food, just long enough to drink, eat and use the bathroom. As they started out again, Deanna heard and watched a flock of sparrows break from some trees up ahead and raised her fist to stop everyone. She motioned them off the trail into the trees to see if anything else happened.

As they waited in the shadows, Deanna tried to see if there was anything on the trail up ahead. She noticed a small dust cloud about fifty feet ahead of their position. It looked like something was stirring things up over there. She motioned for them to stay low and proceed slowly behind her as she decided to check things out. She didn't think it was Homeland Security troops as they were not likely to be stirring up dust like that. But it could be something like an animal in distress or worse, some inexperienced people out bounty hunting.

Bounty hunters were more likely to shoot first and worry about any consequences later. She was worried about being shot by idiots, plus the sound of gunshots was sure to bring unwanted attention to the area. As they crept closer to where they had seen the dust, she slowed down using the trees and small bushes alongside the trail to hide in.

Dr. James stepped ahead of her and told them, "I will sneak over to take a look and be right back."

James got down on his belly and crawled through the low bushes until he could see around the bend in the trail. As he peered around a tree, he saw a young man and woman by the trail with the man kneeling next to her as she sat on the ground. The young woman looked hurt. The young man was trying to help her and that was what was stirring up the dust. James kept watching for a few minutes to see if the man had a gun anywhere near him but didn't see anything. Just two people with back packs, one of them a young woman who looked like she needed a doctor.

Dr. James decided to take a chance and show himself. He slowly stood up and raised his hands where the young man could see them, announcing himself very quietly so as not to startle them. The young man immediately stood up preparing to defend the woman on the ground. He didn't have a weapon in his hand so James thought he should be relatively safe for the moment. As he slowly approached, he introduced himself, "I am Dr. James and I am a medical doctor, may I help?"

He assured the young man that he just happened to be on the trail heading east and hearing the noise, wanted to know if he could help.

The young man, who introduced themselves as Ben and Stacy, adding that they were recent newlyweds, said, "You can approach but I will hurt you if you try anything funny."

As Dr. James slowly walked up, he asked, "What happened?"

Ben replied, "She tripped over a rock and hurt her ankle."

Dr. James suspected a simple turned ankle at this point and kneeled down to check. Sure enough, that was all it was, a minor sprain. A simple diagnosis and treatment.

He asked Ben, "Do you have anything to wrap her ankle with to try and stop the slight swelling?"

Ben looked in his bag and pulled out some duct tape and a tee-shirt. Dr. James took the shirt and tore into strips and using the duct tape, wrapped Stacy's ankle tightly. He told them, "She shouldn't put any weight on it for a couple of days" and asked Ben to look for a forked branch he could make a crutch out of.

As Ben went into the woods to look, Dr. James asked Stacy, "What are you folks doing way out here?"

She softly told him "We are running away from where we used to live because the towns people became very angry with us after we got married by a justice of the peace a couple of weeks ago."

She explained that her parents had disapproved of Ben because he didn't come from a prominent family and had tried everything to stop them from being together. Her father had arranged for her to be married to the son of one of the leading members of their town because "It was the proper thing to do in this, now, Christian nation." According to her father, arranged marriages have been around since before Christ and he had made a deal with the intended boy's father. Her family would pay a dowry price for her to be married into this prominent family.

Stacy told Dr. James, "I didn't want to be married off to someone I didn't love for money, so I convinced Ben to sneak away with me in the dead of night and marry me in front of a Justice of the Peace. We have been running east for a few days now, not sure where to go."

Dr. James helped her to her feet while they waited for Ben to return. He didn't say anything about his two companions yet, and decided to wait a little longer, if at all, before revealing them. He still wasn't sure enough about them yet to trust them too much. He wanted to be sure they wouldn't tell anyone about them before he allowed Deanna and Theresa to approach. He was sure they were watching all of this, from where he had left them. For the moment, all these people needed to know was that he was a traveling doctor who just happened to be on the same trail. If the authorities were looking for them, they were looking for three people, two women and a man. Dr. James thought it best to keep quiet until he learned more.

He kept the conversation going while they waited, using his best bedside manner. As he asked more seemingly innocent sounding questions about them, he learned that the small community they had come from were ultra-conservative white patriarchal Christians. They were all huge believers in the new government and didn't like outsiders interfering in their business. They just wanted to start a new life together without their elders, especially her parents, telling them how to live their lives.

They heard Ben returning through the brush and trees as he had never really made any attempts to be quiet while he whittled out a makeshift crutch. He was not very talkative like Stacy was and watched Dr. James with a suspicious eye as he adjusted the crutch length for her. Once she started limping around on the crutch, Ben asked her, "Do you think you can make it now?"

She replied, "Maybe with some padding on the top of the crutch where my arm is resting. I think I can manage as long as we don't have to travel to much father today."

Ben looked back at Dr. James and said, "Thanks for the help. I will try to repay you somehow when I can." He then asked where Dr. James was heading and James hesitated just enough to catch Ben's attention. Dr. James replied, "I am heading east just like you folks."

Ben looked at him with that suspicious look again as he and Stacy started slowly heading down the trail ahead of the doctor. James spoke up again, "Do you know where you are planning to stay tonight?"

Ben replied, "We have heard of a place just across the border that might provide us some supplies and rest before we head further east."

Right away, an alarm bell went off in James's head. He didn't trust Ben quite yet and the last thing his party needed was to run into them at this supposed refuge up ahead. Ben would obviously recognize Dr. James and might be able to identify Deanna and Theresa to the authorities if they showed up with him.

Dr. James told Ben, "I am also heading to what sounds like the same place but I have never been there. If you don't mind, I would like to tag along. I just need to retrieve my backpack and I will be right back, if that is, okay?"

Stacy smiled and said, "You are welcome to come along doctor," eliciting a jealous stare from Ben. James walked back around the bend in the trail to find Deanna and Theresa.

As he came up on their hiding spot, Deanna stepped out, startling James. He recovered quickly and asked if they had observed the couple.

Deanna said, "Yes we have and we agree that they should not be trusted yet." They decided the best thing to do was for Deanna and Theresa to follow out of sight and figure something out once they got to the resort. She told James, "Go ahead with them and try to learn more about what Homeland Security is up to around here and we will follow along quietly out of sight."

With a plan of action, James hurried back down the trail with his pack and caught up with the young couple. He walked behind them and tried to engage them in pleasant conversation asking about what was going on around the area. He explained that he had never traveled this way before and wanted to know about the local places and the people a little. Stacy had no problem telling Dr. James all about the town they came from and some of the more famous, in her mind, local folks.

They both told him, "We haven't seen anyone from the new government up here in quite a while, not since the government representatives had come around telling everyone about the new government a couple of years ago."

With that bit of news, James felt a little easier about things but he still worried about the young couple letting on that they had seen three strangers out here, a man and two women. He would have to figure something out as they really needed the food, rest and fresh clothing before continuing east. As they kept walking, Ben started to feel a little more at ease and talk a little more.

He told Dr. James what he thought would happen if he and Stacy were caught and brought back to the little town they had escaped from. As he listened, James realized that they had as much to lose as he and his friends did if anyone recognized them. He started to formulate a plan that might strengthen their chances of getting to a place he thought was safe in New Hampshire.

Dr. James knew some people in the local refugee network over there. He had worked with them before and knew that, if they were still there, most of his worries would be over. They just had to get there safely. And now, that just might include these two runaways.

 He kept up a running conversation with them while they walked down the trail, learning more about them as they talked. It became obvious that they were very much in love with each other and Ben would do anything to protect her. He came from a farming family and she was the daughter of a local retailer. Stacy was eager to start a new life with him, away from their parents, and he just wanted what she wanted. Ben's plan was to find a farm and hire himself out until he could start his own farm, living happily ever after with Stacy and any children. No one telling him how to live his life. He just wanted a peaceful life on a farm away from all of the chaos.

Dr. James hated to disabuse him of his dreams as he knew that in this new country, the chances of the government leaving him alone were slim to none. But he left that alone. Let them have their dreams while they could. He had been a dreamer once but not anymore. Reality had kicked him hard when his parents were killed and his sisters taken to a camp.

It was also obvious that they were Christians so James didn't even think about discussing religion. It might lead to unpleasantness between them if he let on that he was a Muslim. He was already a little worried about what they might be thinking about his darker skin tone as it was.

Chapter 11

New Friends and a Recon

Just before dusk, Ben, Stacy and Dr. James saw some lights coming from a large house up ahead and off to the side of the trail situated on the side of a mountain with a big lawn out front.

It looked like it had once been a hunting lodge or a resort. He slowed down and advised caution before just walking in like tourists. He asked them, "Have either of you ever been here before?"

Ben replied, "No, we just heard about the place from some people we knew where we came from."

Dr. James decided to make a command decision as it didn't look like he had much choice right now. He asked Ben and Stacy to sit still for a few minutes as he thought he may have dropped something in the trail behind them.

Ben said, "Sure, I will stay with Stacy to keep her safe until you return, but hurry as I don't want her on this makeshift crutch any longer than necessary."

James left them standing there and walked back down the trail to find Deanna and Theresa. Within a couple of minutes, he spied them and walked up. As he approached, Deanna asked, "What is going on?" with a worried expression.

Dr. James explained, "Ben and Stacy are also on the run and have every reason to steer clear of any authorities as much as we do. They are just young and Ben is very protective but naïve. They are waiting for me up ahead as I came back here to 'find' something I dropped. That something being the two of you."

James told them a little of their story, where they were headed, sort of, and that they lacked much of a plan. He asked them, "Do you trust me enough to know whether these two young runaways are lying to me or not?"

Deanna wasn't sure and Theresa said, "I will abide by whatever you guys decide."

James asked "Would you be comfortable enough to come with me and let me introduce you?"

Deanna replied, "I'll go along since I trust you, but I will be ready to run at the first sign of trouble."

James replied, "Fair enough."

They walked back up the trail together and as soon as the two women came into view, Ben started and moved Stacy behind him. Dr. James held up his hands and assured them that his friends were very safe and were refugees just like them. Deanna and Theresa came up with their hands showing at their sides trying not to show any ill intent.

Dr. James asked Ben, "What did you think when I first come up on you back on the trail? Do you remember how distrustful you were? I felt the same way about you and wanted to make sure you weren't someone other than who you said you were before introducing my friends."

At that, Ben backed down and said, "I guess I didn't think about it like that, I'm sorry." With that, Deanna and Theresa introduced themselves. Stacy was ecstatic about having other women to talk to.

She said, "Although I love Ben dearly, he isn't the most conversational person" and they all chuckled a little. Even Ben smiled a bit, although it was just an upturn of his mouth.

Since they were now all friends, sort of, Deanna explained a little bit about Homeland Security to them. She told them, "They are not our friends and we all need to be very careful about approaching strange places before we decide if it is safe to enter. We have to know who is there first as not everyone may be friendly."

As she was explaining this to them, Ben started to get a look like he was wondering just who these people were. He didn't want to get into any trouble with the authorities. He just wanted to get east as far as he could so that no one would think to come looking for them. He didn't want to get involved with anyone else's problems. But he decided to keep listening in case he heard something useful.

Stacy listened quietly and also started to wonder a little but about who these new strangers were. They seemed friendly enough and didn't sound like they had any malicious intent but she was starting to get a little apprehensive over this talk of government and Homeland Security. She just wanted a warm bath and a soft bed to sleep in to rest her ankle for a couple of days. She didn't care about anything beyond running away with Ben to start their life together away from their parents.

After listening to her, Ben finally decided that Deanna seemed to know what she was talking about. Her plan to check out the lodge or hotel or whatever it was up ahead seemed like a good enough idea. They were still close enough to their former town for someone they knew to be waiting to take them back. Ben would do anything to stop that and that would definitely cause a ruckus. He asked Stacy to step away for a minute to talk about it, then agreed to follow with caution and let the more experienced folks lead the way. Dr. James offered to help with Stacy and for that, Ben was grateful. It was a lot of work trying to help her walk with that wooden crutch.

Deanna led the way down the main trail towards the hotel lodge but stopped short in the woods before walking down the side trail to the lodge. It certainly looked like an old tourist hunting lodge with a wraparound porch on the front and what looked like maybe a big kitchen in the rear. There were a handful of soft outdoor lights on around the outside but not overly bright like spotlights.

Deanna told them, "I want to check around the area to see if there are any signs of other guests. If you want to follow, stay hidden and be very quiet," looking at Ben as she was saying this.

Dr. James said, "I offer to stay with Stacy if Ben wants to go?"

Ben looked at Stacy as if to ask if she was okay with that. She looked back at him and nodded her head, then looked at Dr. James to mouth a thank you.

Deanna, Theresa and Ben skirted the front lawn, staying in the woods around the lodge to see what they could see. Deanna was looking for tracks and other sign on the ground, while Theresa watched the house for any sign of movement in the windows. Ben had no idea what to do so he figured he would just follow along and keep an eye on their surroundings in case he spotted anything else.

As they silently walked around the perimeter towards the back, Deanna noticed signs of foot traffic leading away from the back door of the house. The tracks went back and forth down a trail headed into the woods behind the house. She decided to check it out in case there were any surprises down there. They followed the trail for a bit and came to a small clearing. Deanna crept closer to see if there was anything there worth worrying about.

She found a spot under a tree that she could crawl under to get a good look at the clearing without being seen. She motioned the other two to keep watch behind them in case someone from the house decided to come down the trail.

Looking out from her spot, all she could see in the near dark, were a couple of small storage buildings and some tarp covered objects out in the middle of the clearing. She didn't feel like going out there to see what was out there. They didn't look too terribly dangerous, although the little storage buildings looked pretty new as did the tarps. There was no one else there and that was her main concern for the moment.

She slid back out from under the tree and rejoined her companions. Deanna relayed what she had found and said, "We should get a better look at the house before announcing ourselves."

They retreated back up the trail towards the house and continued walking around the perimeter without seeing anyone, not even inside near the windows. That worried Deanna a little and she wondered if something might be wrong in the house. Are the owners being held against their will inside?

Deanna decided to take a chance and sneak a peek into one of the windows to see if anything was amiss.

Theresa told her, "This doesn't sound like a good idea. Maybe we should just wait a little more to see if anyone moves around inside."

 Deanna replied, "We can't afford to wait too much longer. We don't want to be out here after dark and Stacy needs medical attention." As she mentioned Stacy, Ben immediately felt guilty for thinking more like someone out of an action movie instead of a caring husband.

They went around back and found a place where the trees were closest to the back of the building. Once there, they found a thick stand of trees to hide in, and Deanna crept out into the twilight to sneak up to a window. As she kept low, she continually looked for anyone walking by any of the windows. Still nothing. She made it to the wall under a window near the back door and waited to see if she could hear anything from inside. Still nothing. She decided it was now or never. She was scared but knew that there was no other way.

She stood up and peeked into a corner of the window ever so briefly and didn't see anything at first glance. She decided to take a little longer look. As she looked inside and held her gaze for a minute, she saw someone in the other room beyond the wide kitchen entrance. A man was sitting on what looked like a sofa talking to someone she couldn't see. They didn't look distressed so she kept checking with furtive looks in the window. She wanted to find out how many people may be inside.

She didn't see anyone else. Just the same person on the sofa talking to someone with a TV on. Deanna decided that she needed a better look inside. The kitchen was nearly dark without any lights on and it looked pretty clean. She stayed against the outer wall and crept around the house continuing to look into windows. The rest of the house was dark inside so not much to see. She came around to the front corner and stopped. There were too many outside lights on for her to feel safe in creeping up on the porch. She thought, "Now what?" She crept back around to where the other two were hiding and told them what she did and didn't see. They decided to go back to where Dr. James and Stacy were waiting to make a decision.

Once they arrived it was discussion time. Deanna was all in favor of waiting to see if the lights went out at bedtime and Dr. James said, "Stacy needs to get off her ankle soon." Ben just wanted to do what was best for Stacy and Theresa just wanted to follow the majority.

 Then James had an idea. "Why don't I just walk up and knock on the door by myself? I doubt anyone would hurt me straight away as I am a doctor and I can get an idea if it is safe or not."

Deanna said "no" right off as being too dangerous but James insisted that this was all that was left for them to do.

"Sneaking looks in the front windows will not win us any friends," he said.

She finally agreed but told him to run for the woods if he saw just one Homeland Security uniform.

He replied "I will be careful, don't worry."

Chapter 12

Rest and respite?

Dr. James stepped out and walked across the front lawn. As he stepped up on the porch, he noticed that there was no dog barking. He thought that seemed a little odd for a place so far out of the way. He knocked on the door and waited. In about a half minute an older man asked "who is it" from behind the door. Dr. James introduced himself and said, "I am looking for a place to rest and resupply before continuing east and I have heard of this place from some special friends."

The man opened the door a little bit to get a look at the doctor. Seeing no immediate threat, he stepped out onto the porch with a shotgun under his arm. He looked Dr. James up and down for a minute and asked him "Is there anyone else with you?"

He didn't sound too friendly nor did he sound outright hostile so James told him "Yes, there are four others, one of whom is injured."

The man introduced himself as Mr. Polk and said, "My wife and I have lived here for nearly 35 years. With everything that is going on these days, you can't be too careful living this close to the border right now. Bring your friends out so I can take a look at them."

James stepped out to the edge of the porch and waved. Everyone then stepped out of the woods in front of the house and started walking towards the porch. As soon as Mr. Polk saw Stacy, he stepped back into the house and hollered for his wife. When she came out on the porch and saw them, she ran out and grabbed Stacy's arm to help Ben bring her inside.

Mr. Polk let the rest step in and welcomed them to their, once upon a time, hunting lodge. He explained, "We used to get a lot of guests up here before the government changed hands but now, not so much. No one has any money for frivolous activities like trophy hunting anymore. But we do accept donations from the underground networks working to help people who don't need any attention from the authorities on occasion. I suspect your group falls into that category", he said with a wry smile. "Not to worry," he told them, "I have a reputation to maintain and I won't abuse that for anyone. I never liked the government anyway, even before the change."

He asked them, "When was the last time any of you have eaten?"

 Deanna replied, "We have been eating nothing but trail rations for the last three days."

Ben said, "We ran away with little to no food and that ran out sometIme yesterday."

Mrs. Polk said, "Not to worry, I have plenty of venison in the kitchen and some canned vegetables from the garden. I can whip up a good meal for you. If you want to go upstairs and take showers before dinner, you are welcome to." The mister, as she called him, would show them where the clean towels and spare rooms were while she cooked. "We have some clothes left behind by other travelers if you need to replace anything not fit to wear anymore. Just let us know and we will rummage around to see if we have anything you can use."

For Deanna's trio, this was a true blessing. Deanna wanted to light a candle and offer a prayer to the Gods of the woods after they had showered and eaten. James planned to find a quiet room so he could offer his prayer of thankfulness. As for the rest, it was all about getting cleaned up, food and rest too.

Before heading upstairs, Dr. James asked Mr. Polk, "Do you have any Ace bandages? I want to rewrap Stacy's ankle after she has had her shower or, preferably, a hot bath to take the load off her ankle."

Mr. Polk said, "Sure, give me a few minutes to find something. Meanwhile, take her upstairs and I will be up in few to with the medical kit and show everyone where to find the towels. There are bathrooms at each end of the hallway. You are all welcome to hang out until I get back."

Deanna could hear Mrs. Polk rummaging around in the kitchen and it was a comforting sound. She felt safe enough to go upstairs and get ready for a much-needed shower. She could tell that Theresa was right there with her. Dr. James would follow after helping Ben carry Stacy up the stairs.

As they gathered in the hallway, Mr. Polk came up the stairs with a medical kit and told Dr. James, "I had doubts about you being a doctor when you first introduced yourself on the porch tonight. Now I see that you were telling me the truth. You behave like a doctor who cares for his patients and knows what he is doing. Welcome again doctor. It is good having you here."

He looked at the rest of them with a mysterious look and said, "I am looking forward to hearing your stories in the morning over coffee." He then showed them the linen closet and told them, "Help yourselves. Everything else is in the bathrooms. Holler if you need anything. I will be down in the kitchen helping the missus get some food ready for you after you have cleaned up."

After everyone finished their showers and Stacy her bath, they changed out of their well-worn clothing into spare clothing from their back packs and returned downstairs. Stacy came down with Ben, her ankle freshly wrapped, and they gathered in a large dining room just off the kitchen. They all sat down to the best meal any of them had had in several days. Everyone was very grateful for the hospitality and expressed their gratitude several times during the meal.

After they finished, Deanna and Theresa offered to help wash the dishes but Mrs. Polk shooed them away after they helped clear the table. She said, "I appreciate the help but I am only going to dump the scraps and rinse the dishes for the night because it's getting late. I'll wash them in the morning." She told them, "Get upstairs and get some sleep before you all fall out of these chairs. I am too old to be carrying anyone upstairs to bed" and they all laughed.

As everyone headed to their rooms, Deanna went to see James and found him sitting on the edge of the bed deep in thought. She stepped inside the door and asked him, "Are you all right?"

He replied, "Yes, I am fine. I am just meditating before prayers."

 Deanna replied "I'm sorry, I didn't mean to disturb you" and started to turn away.

As she did, James called her back and asked her, "Will you stay a minute?" Deanna turned back towards him and sat down on the bed next to him. He quietly told her, "My plans have changed because of that last near miss in New York. It is time for me to go after my sisters before it's too late." He told her a little about his friends in New Hampshire and his plan to make his way to them from here before heading down to Virginia.

He asked her, "What are your plans once we leave here?"

Deanna said, "I don't know yet. I haven't thought that far ahead. All I've been concerned with up until now, was getting us this far. I need to think about it some more. We can talk tomorrow after a good night's sleep." She stood up to leave and James grabbed her hand. As he stood up, he pulled her to him and kissed her softly. At first, she was surprised and then she leaned into him and returned the kiss.

As they came up for air, she asked him softly, "Would you like to come to my room after your prayers?" He replied with a little smile, "I would like that, thank you."

Deanna returned to her room and lit the candle Mrs. Polk had given her. She couldn't help but feel a little flutter in her stomach over the prospect of sharing her bed with James again. As she tried to settle down and pray to Cernunnos, the ancient God of the woods, all she could think about was Brigid, who came to her whenever she thought about being with a man. She felt like she was being blessed now and felt a warmth of acceptance in her choice of being with James.

She finished her prayers and had just slid between the clean sheets, when she felt more than heard James enter the room and slip into bed beside her. Now she felt complete as if her life was right where it should be. As she reached for him, he kissed her again with a lot more passion this time, despite his exhaustion. As everyone in the house settled down for the night, everything that happened in the last few days seemed to melt away like a bad dream for the moment.

Chapter 13

Suspicions

Deanna woke up in the bright sunshine coming through the window. She felt every one of her muscles this morning but knew she had to get moving. She would feel better once she got cleaned up and started walking around. She reached over and found that James had already woken up before her and had quietly left. She wondered if he woke up for morning prayers, or at least she hoped that was all it was.

She heard the others starting to stir so she got up and headed for one of the bathrooms hoping she wouldn't have to wait for an open one. She walked down to the end of the hall and was in luck. After finishing in the bathroom, she went by James's room and when she didn't see him, figured he must be downstairs. She could hear voices down there but nothing louder than a mumble.

As she finished getting dressed and headed down herself, she caught Ben coming out of his room. She asked him, "How are you doing?"

 He replied, "fine," with a puzzled look.

Deanna motioned for him to come closer so she could ask him something. She lowered her voice and asked "How long do you plan on staying?"

Ben replied, "We aren't sure but we want to stay a couple of days until Stacy's ankle gets better." He whispered, "Why are you asking?"

Deanna told him, "I have a funny feeling about this place," and asked Ben to talk to Stacy about their story on how they met on the trail. She asked him, "if you would be willing to tell the Polk's that we all came from the same area of New York state, it might make things less suspicious for all of us. Just let me know what you decide before we sit down to the table."

Ben said, "Okay, I will talk to Stacy."

Deanna went downstairs to the dining room where she found Dr. James and Theresa already at the table waiting for everyone else. Theresa had some coffee and Dr. James was drinking, what looked like, tea. Deanna sat down next to James and grabbed his hand for a quick squeeze. He smiled back at her with a quizzical look in his eye. She shook her head no slightly to say not yet. She told everyone out loud "We should wait for Ben and Stacy before eating." As she said that, Mrs. Polk came out of the kitchen and asked, "Are they on their way? The food is going to get cold."

"They should be down shortly." Deanna replied with tight smile that didn't reach her eyes.

As they chatted, Deanna grabbed a cup of coffee from the pot on the table and asked Dr. James and Theresa to "Step out on the porch while we're waiting." They both gave her a look that asked, "what is going on?" As they stepped out, Deanna asked, "Have you seen Mr. Polk this morning?"

Dr. James answered, "I haven't seen him yet this morning and I've been up since sunrise for morning prayer." Deanna smiled and thought, "I was right and I have nothing to worry about with him." Dr. James gave her a knowing smiled in return.

Theresa asked, "What do you want to talk to us about?"

Deanna lowered her voice and told them, "I still have that feeling from last night that something isn't quite right here." She asked them, "How long do you guys feel like staying before we head out? I don't see anything out of place but something feels wrong. The sooner we put this place behind us, the better I will feel."

James replied, "I am ready whenever you are, just say the word."

 Theresa nodded and said, 'Sure, whenever."

Deanna said in a low voice, "Let's keep a close eye on our hosts without being too conspicuous. Act like everything is just a vacation in the outback of upstate Vermont," she said with a wry smile.

As they walked back inside, Ben and Stacy came downstairs and joined them in the foyer. Dr. James asked Stacy, "How does your ankle feel this morning?" She replied, "Much better, thank you."

Ben stepped over next to Deanna and quietly told her, "We can be ready to leave by tomorrow, if that is, okay?" Deanna replied softly, "I will let you know what we decide a little later."

With that, everyone sat down at the dining room table and Mrs. Polk came in and started putting bowls of eggs and plates of bacon and pancakes on the table. As she put the first ones down, Theresa got up and offered to help. They both came back with steaming plates of food and everyone starting to dig in. Mrs. Polk came back out with a fresh pot of coffee and offered refills to all who wanted.

Conversation died down to muffled groans of appreciation for the good food and the occasional "pass me" something until everyone had their fill. As they sat around finishing their tea and coffee, Mr. Polk came in through the back door of the kitchen and asked everyone, "How is breakfast?" Of course, everyone praised Mrs. Polk for putting out such a great feast. He smiled, filled a cup with coffee and sat down with them.

After he settled into his chair, he looked at each of them and asked, "Do you remember what I asked you last night?" Most everyone nodded or murmured yes. He turned to Deanna, who was sitting the closest and asked, "Tell me your story."

Deanna hesitated a bit and told him a story about coming from over near where Ben and Stacy were from and just happened to meet them on the trail. As she was talking, she looked over at Ben and Stacy, then returned her gaze to Mr. Polk. As she finished her tale, Mr. Polk looked at Ben and asked him, "Now what's your story." He knew they were newlyweds but he wanted to know why they were headed east.

Ben, never one to talk much, looked at Stacy and repeated the story they had told Dr. James about the bias towards them from their kin and neighbors in their home town and how they decided to leave and start new life east of there. He also confirmed meeting the other three on the trail.

"It isn't actually a lie, other than the sin of omission," Ben thought. Maybe God will forgive him. He and Stacy had discussed what Deanna had asked him to say earlier and Stacy told him, "We can do this one little favor for them for all they have done for us."

Mr. Polk took another sip from his coffee cup and looked at them for a moment before smiling, "You're all welcome to stay a day or so to rest up. We have a little food we can spare for you when you get ready to leave." With that announcement, it seemed the atmosphere suddenly got lighter around the table but Deanna watched Mr. Polk's eyes when he made the offer and she didn't see any real welcome there. Her intuition about this place just got worse.

Dr. James could sense her nervousness and whispered, "Are you okay?" When Deanna didn't reply, he waited a moment watching everyone while sipping his tea. Theresa was already out in the kitchen helping Mrs. Polk and he knew she would go along with whatever they decided.

After a couple of quiet moments, he asked Deanna, "Would you like to take a stroll around the yard to walk off some of that breakfast?" She looked at Mr. Polk for a reaction but he just continued to sip his coffee as if he were somewhere else at the moment.

Deanna replied, "Sure." She got up and headed towards the front door with Dr. James following right behind her. When they stepped off the front porch into the grassy lawn, she walked out far enough where she knew they couldn't be heard. As they slowly walked around the perimeter of the lawn, she told James, "I am getting a really bad feeling about this place, especially after that morning coffee conversation." James kept quiet and just listened as they walked. When she had finished, he waited a moment before answering.

He asked her, "What do you want to do? It will look rude and suspicious if we pack up quickly this morning."

She agreed and told him, "I want to get a look under those new tarps we saw out in that small clearing last night, if we can manage it somehow. That might resolve some of my suspicions or not."

James wasn't sure how they could manage that in broad daylight and said so. They continued walking and brainstorming ideas for a possible distraction that would allow her to slip back out to that clearing.

Then she looked at him and said, "What if you offered them a free checkup while you are here? Who knows when another doctor might get out this way."

Dr. James thought about it for a minute and replied, "I will ask. If they agree, you will have to go out there by yourself or it will draw attention." She agreed to be careful.

With a plan in hand, they walked back to the house. Dr. James wanted to look at Stacy's ankle this morning anyway and rewrap it for her. That would give him his opening see if the Polk's would like a medical checkup.

When they reached the porch, Deanna went to sit down in one of the porch chairs and asked James, "Would you please bring me another cup of coffee?" James replied, "No problem, I'll be right back."

James returned with the coffee and sat with her for a moment looking out at the mountains and woods. He was nervous too. He wanted to get east as soon as he could for a different reason than everyone else. The sooner he got to his friends in New Hampshire, the sooner he could get resupplied and head south to Virginia.

After a couple of quiet minutes, he got up, excused himself and went to find Ben and Stacy. Dr. James found them in the front parlor room, sitting on the couch together chatting about something when he walked up. They looked up and stopped talking as if they had been caught talking about something they didn't want him to know about. He asked, "May I examine Stacy's ankle and rewrap it?" Stacy replied, "Sure doc, go right ahead."

Dr. James went to work and as he was checking her ankle, Mrs. Polk stepped in and asked, "Does anyone need anything else?" Dr. James looked up and asked, "Would you and your husband like me to give you a health checkup while I am here?" She said, "I will ask the Mr. and get back to you." She thanked him and left.

 Dr. James finished wrapping Stacy's ankle and told her, "You will probably be fine by tomorrow, but you should still take it easy for another week or so. We can try you out with a cane instead of crutches, if you like?"

Stacy thanked him and looked at Ben, who had been sitting there quietly the whole time. Ben thanked him also and softly asked him, "Have you guys decided when you want to leave yet?"

Dr. James replied quietly, "I will know more by midday." He smiled with his doctor smile, stood up and walked out to the kitchen to find Mr. and Mrs. Polk.

They were in deep conversation by the kitchen sink when he walked in and they stopped talking when he walked through the door. Mr. Polk told him, "I think the free checkup would be very nice and we want to know if the offer still stands?"

Dr. James replied, "Yes, I can take a look at you both in a few minutes if you want? I just need to get my bag from upstairs and I will meet you in the parlor. We can go where ever you would be comfortable with for the checkups."

Dr. James briefly went to the front door to give Deanna a hand signal that all was a go, then went upstairs to get his things. As he walked up, he said a silent prayer to keep Deanna safe.

Chapter 14

The Discovery

Deanna waited on the porch for James to come back downstairs. When she saw him come down the stairs through the front windows, she walked around back to find that trail in the woods she had found last night. She gave Dr. James a couple more minutes before walking into the edge of the trees towards the path. Once she was out of sight of the house, she made her way to the trail and walked carefully so as to not leave any discernable tracks as best as she could.

She hurried down the trail and veered off into the trees when she spied the clearing ahead. She returned to her spot under the tree again and waited a minute to make sure it was all clear. Not seeing anything moving, she crouched low and headed out to the first tarp covered object and tried to look underneath. She couldn't see anything right away under the tarp, so she had no choice but to peel one back a little bit.

She found a wood and metal box that looked military grade. Dark green with white writing on it identifying something but she didn't know enough about military stuff to understand what she was looking at. Just the fact that this was definitely military in origin was enough for her. She put the tarp back as close to original as she could and took a quick look at a couple of the other piles. Without lifting the tarps, she could tell that they were more of the same. The small locked storage buildings were too new to belong to the lodge, so likely held more military grade supplies. Maybe ammunition?

Deanna had seen enough. It was time to get back and make a plan to get out of here without arousing suspicion. They needed to leave today, if they could. She made her way back the porch the same way she arrived, down the trail and through the edge of the woods. She sat back down in her chair on the porch as if she had been there all along, and after a short time, Mr. Polk came out and asked "How are you enjoying the morning sun?"

Deanna replied, "I am enjoying the respite and warm sun a lot, thank you very much. I really appreciate the excellent hospitality you are showing us."

He said "I am glad that you all are resting up. If anyone needs anything, just holler," as he headed back into the house.

She sat there until James came out and sat down next her. She whispered about what she had found under the tarps and told him, "We need to get out of here as soon as possible with arousing any suspicion. I don't think any of that stuff belongs to the Polk's but whoever it does belong to might show up at any minute. I think it belongs to either Homeland Security or some local militia, neither of which is good for us."

James listened as she told him about what she had found and it made him really nervous. He was a wanted man with a bounty on his head. The last thing he needed was to get kidnapped by any local militia group and held for the bounty. Or worse, arrested by Homeland Security. He agreed with her, "We need to leave quickly, within the next hour, if possible."

Deanna said, "I will talk to Theresa and see how things are looking with the Polk's." She also wanted to let Ben and Stacy know what their decision was. Let them make up their minds on what they wanted to do. She knew that Stacy couldn't walk too fast and running was out of the question. Maybe Ben could carry her for a little way?

 Deanna said, "We should try to leave right after lunch."

She went to find Theresa to let her know. She passed by the parlor where Ben and Stacy had been earlier but they were gone now. Deanna hoped they were upstairs. She found Theresa in the kitchen talking to Mrs. Polk and asked if she could talk to Theresa for a minute. Theresa followed her out the back door and when they were a few feet away from the back of the house, Deanna quietly told her everything.

Theresa's eyes got wide. She whispered, "Oh my God" and asked, "What's the plan?" For reasons of her own, she didn't want to be caught by anyone either. She had been on the run before and didn't want anyone to know who or where she was.

They went back into the kitchen. Leaving Theresa there, Deanna went upstairs to find the newlyweds. Ben and Stacy were in their room sitting on the bed together as Deanna walked up to the door. She asked, "May I enter?" Ben nodded yes. Deanna explained what she had found and what that meant for them.

She looked at Stacy, "The three of us are going to try and leave right after lunch today and you can come if you want?"

Ben asked, "What about Stacy's ankle?"

Deanna asked him, "Do you think you could carry her if we have to leave in a big hurry?"

Ben thought about it for a minute and said, "I think so, as long as it won't be too far."

Deanna told them to think about it and let her or Dr. James know as soon as possible, one way or another. She returned downstairs and went back to the front porch. She found James and Theresa sitting there talking quietly. Dr. James said, "We are discussing a plan, what there is of it." He said, "The checkups went well and the Polk's are pretty healthy. No issues that I can find." Then softly in the next breath, "How do you want to handle this?"

He told them, "Our hosts appear to be just normal folks and maybe they are just letting whoever store the stuff out there without knowing what it is."

Deanna didn't think the Polk's were all that innocent, as least not Mr. Polk anyway.

Whatever was going on, they needed to go this afternoon. Deanna told them, "I've talked to Ben and Stacy and we should have their answer soon. Meanwhile, separately go upstairs and pack your stuff so we can go quickly."

Theresa said, "I'll go first." After she left, Deanna looked at James and asked him, "Do you feel rested enough to make a run for it, if we have to?" He replied, "I'm good." He understood the need and was anxious to get to New Hampshire anyway.

Chapter 15

On the run again

When Theresa returned a few minutes later, Deanna went upstairs to pack her kit. She didn't have much out so it only took a couple of minutes to get her bag ready and put it by the door. As she got to the bottom of the stairs, James passed her on the way up with a knowing smile. She decided to go to the kitchen and see how their hosts were doing. As she came through the archway, Mr. Polk was nowhere around but Mrs. Polk was there puttering around the kitchen.

She looked a little startled when Deanna walked in but looked up with a smile. She asked, "Can I help you with anything?"

Deanna replied, "Could we have an early lunch as we are thinking of taking off afterwards to start heading east down the trail?"

At this announcement, Mrs. Polk became agitated and started looking around. She hesitated a bit and said, "No problem, I'll get right on it." Deanna thanked her and decided that this woman needed to be watched. She walked out to find Theresa.

Theresa was still sitting on the front porch when Deanna told her about the encounter in the kitchen. She told Deanna, "I'll offer to help with lunch and keep an eye on her." As Deanna went back in the house, Ben met her at the bottom of the stairs.

He told her, "Stacy is okay with us leaving with you. I just hope we don't have to leave in too big of a hurry."

Deanna smiled and said, "I hope so too."

Deanna went back upstairs to see what James was doing as he had been gone for quite a while. She went up to his room and found his bag all packed and sitting by the door next to hers but he was nowhere to be found.

Deanna went back downstairs worried about where he could be. They didn't need complications right now so she looked around all of the common areas and there was still no sign of him. Now she started to get worried. He didn't normally just take off without telling someone.

She went out to the front porch to see if he was outside on the lawn somewhere. There was still no sign of him. As Deanna walked around the side of the house, she heard someone talking in an angry tone. She continued walking towards the back and when she rounded the corner, she spotted Dr. James and Mr. Polk in a heated argument. She decided to try and sneak up quietly without being seen to find out what it was all about.

They were arguing about them leaving. Mr. Polk was trying to convince Dr. James to stay until tomorrow morning. He was telling him, "You won't make it to another hotel before dark tonight. It will be a rough camp in the woods if you all left this afternoon." Deanna stayed out of sight and let James explain to Mr. Polk, "I meant to tell you after lunch and I am sorry you had to find out without us telling you yet."

Mr. Polk continued to raise his voice, calling them rude and inhospitable. He seemed like he was saying anything he could to convince Dr. James to change his mind and it was starting to look like James might need a little backup. Deanna stepped out of hiding and approached them. When Mr. Polk noticed her, he quieted down, mumbling under his breath about ungrateful people as he walked off.

Dr. James looked at her and shrugged his shoulders. He explained, "I don't know how he found out but Mr. Polk confronted me upstairs, then asked me to come out here to have it out with him."

That was the last straw for Deanna. It was obvious that he was doing everything he could to stall them from leaving too soon. That meant that someone was probably on their way and likely not very friendly.

She told James, "Go upstairs, grab our bags and bring them down to the front parlor. I'll go in through the back door and let Theresa know that the gig is up and we need to go now. No time for lunch. For Ben and Stacy, it is now or never."

Deanna entered the house and just glanced at a somewhat traumatized looking Mrs. Polk. She was tempted to interrogate her but knew they couldn't afford the time. For all she knew, whomever Mr. Polk had been talking to might well be on their way now and could be here any minute. They couldn't afford to take any chances.

Deanna met James by the staircase with their bags. She grabbed hers from him and slung it over her shoulders as they headed out to the front porch. She told James on the way out, "Be on the lookout for Mr. Polk as he still has a shotgun somewhere."

James smiled and said, "Not anymore." Deanna gave him a look but didn't ask. Theresa was already on the porch waiting but Ben and Stacy were nowhere to be found yet. Deanna asked, "Has anyone seen them?" James said, "I think I heard them upstairs in their room."

After a couple of minutes, the two of them came down with their bags. Ben said, "I'm also worried about who might be coming and I don't want any attention drawn to us. If it's okay, we would like to come with you until we get to New Hampshire."

With everyone on the porch now, Deanna led off across the lawn towards the main path that they had come in on. Just as they all started out across the lawn, Mr. Polk came out of the house and glared at them with a mean look in his eye.

Deanna was worried about being followed and having enough food. They had skipped lunch and hadn't gotten any extra food from the lodge due to the riff with the Polk's. They would just have to make do and try to pick something up along the way. "The border is only a couple of days travel", she thought.

Deanna headed out and everyone fell in behind her, nearly running for the trail. At the end of the path to the lodge, she found the trail heading east and starting walking as fast as Stacy could manage. She had to admire the young lady's spunk; Stacy was doing a pretty good of keeping up. Of course, Ben was right there helping her as much as she would let him.

Deanna told everyone, "I want to get as far east as possible today and scout for a place away from the trail to camp for the night." She outlined setting up a night watch, like they had done back in New York and, maybe a camp fire, if it felt safe enough. They nodded and said "no worries." Dr. James felt pretty sure Ben would help with guard duty when the time came.

The little party continued through the afternoon with Dr. James dropping back to bring up the rear, in case Stacy needed anything and to watch their back trail. Ben was too preoccupied with taking care of his wife than paying attention to anything else.

Taking water breaks every so often, they kept up a good pace and managed to make it to late afternoon without anyone coming after them. During one of their little water breaks, Deanna asked James, "Did Polk say anything that might have given you any indication that someone would be arriving soon?"

Dr. James spoke up so everyone could hear, "He didn't say anything directly but, from how he erupted over finding out about our plan to leave, he acted like he needed to keep us there until the next morning." James speculated, "Maybe that was when he had been told someone would be there and he was to hold us."

Deanna asked him about the shotgun, and James said, "I found the gun in a room off the parlor when giving the Polk's their checkups. I spiked it after the checkups were finished. Likely Mr. Polk found out about it after storming off from our argument and realized that he had no way to keep us without it. Which is probably why he was glaring at us when we left," he said with a wry smile.

Everyone else just smiled back and nodded. They all realized the close call they had just had and that this was serious business. There were people out there looking for them for different reasons and none of them sounded like friendlies.

They walked hard until the sun started to go down in the late afternoon. Deanna started looking for a place that looked like it would offer them some security for the night. As they continued down the path, she spotted a deer path crossing the main trail heading off into the woods and down a slight hill. Deanna thought there might be some fresh water down there and a place to set up camp. She stopped everyone and pointed it out to them. She asked Ben, "Do you think Stacy can make it down that path?"

Ben asked, "Why do you want to get off the trail?" She explained about needing to hide for the night. Ben didn't like it and wanted to keep on going.

Deanna told him, "You are more than welcome to keep going but there is safety in numbers if we stick together." She asked him again, "Do you think you can follow us down this narrow trail in the woods?" Ben appeared scared but not willing to admit it to anyone.

Deanna looked at James and Theresa for a minute, let out a sigh and said, "let's go." The three of them started into the woods. Stacy cried out, "What about us?" Deanna looked back and said, "You need to make up your minds right now as we are running out of time. You either follow us or head out on your own."

Stacy looked at Ben and asked him, "What do you want to do?" Ben looked back at Deanna and said, 'okay," grudgingly. They fell in behind the trio and started following them. Dr. James stayed in the middle so he could keep an eye on Ben and Stacy, just in case. With Ben in a sullen mode, like a child who has been told no, he didn't want to take any chances on him doing something stupid out of spite.

Deanna followed the trail slowly as she knew from experience, that following an animal trail could have pitfalls underfoot. She reminded them of trying not to break any branches and leave tracks, if they could help it. Dr. James passed that on to the younger ones behind him. He showed them how to step without leaving much of a trace and to avoid breaking branches on their way through the small brush. Ben, being a hunter, just followed along but Stacy tried to listen attentively.

After about twenty minutes, Deanna heard what sounded like water moving. As she continued downhill, Deanna started to see a small creek ahead through the trees. She discovered quickly that there wasn't much open space to set up a camp site anywhere but they would figure something out once they got down by the water to look around.

When they arrived by the small stream, they discovered that it wasn't much more than a few feet wide, fairly shallow and flowing pretty steady down through the woods to the east. It had a sandy, rocky bottom so that meant the water would be fairly clean. Deanna wondered if they might be able to catch a couple of brook trout or something to supplement their meager trail rations. The bank area was full of small trees though. No clearings to make a good camp.

Deanna gathered them around and explained, "We will need to find some comfortable spots between the trees as best as we can and if we want a fire, it will have to be small and only for cooking, to be put out quickly when dinner was finished." She also explained that the smoke should be disbursed enough through the trees to not be seen but the smell of a wood fire could linger long enough for someone to track them if they kept it going all night. "We will drown the fire with water so we won't have to worry too much about the wood smoke smell afterwards. Everything has to be kept small and try not to mess up the ground too much tonight."

Ben offered to go fishing, saying he had a little experience with hand fishing. Only Deanna knew what that was and wished him good luck. Meanwhile she helped everyone else find comfortable spots under the trees and bushes. She advised them to not get too close the bank as the ground could give out under them and they would get pretty wet, not to mention cold as the water had quite a chill to it still.

With everyone setting up their sleeping spots, Deanna wandered over to the stream to see how Ben was doing. As she watched, he reached into the creek and quickly threw a trout up into the grass next to her. There were already two more laying there waiting to be eaten. Deanna didn't want to disturb him so she went back to find James. She found him laying out their blanket under some small saplings as she walked up. He looked at her and asked, "Is this spot, okay?" She replied, "Anywhere next to you will be fine by me." James smiled and finished up.

As everyone came back over from setting up their little sleeping spots, Stacy asked about Ben. Deanna told her about the fresh fish for dinner tonight and everyone brightened up. James wanted to help but Deanna said, "Let him be, he needs to feel like he can contribute in his own way. He'll be along soon." She reached into her bag and got out some tinder, then asked James and Theresa to help her find some dry firewood. She asked Stacy, "Stay sharp and keep a watch on the hill we just traveled down and help Ben when he returns with the fish. They will need to be cleaned before eating."

They fanned out into the surrounding woods and started gathering twigs and broken branches to make the small fire with. Deanna also looked around for anything like animal tracks or any other sign as well. She didn't need any large animals finding them tonight, like a black bear for instance, but all she could see were the occasional deer tracks and evidence of squirrels and chipmunks so she felt a little better about their choice for the night.

Once they had their arms and hands full of wood, they headed back and she told them, "I haven't seen any signs of anything to worry about tonight." She laughed and said, "Let's go feast on fresh fish and maybe some wild herbs, if we can find any." They all laughed and headed back to camp.

As Deanna started the fire, Ben and Stacy walked up with four trout hanging from a forked branch. They weren't really big but big enough to make a decent meal along with the rations from their bags. Theresa had been scrounging the creek bank and had found a small handful of wild mushrooms to season the fish with. Once the fire got going, they rigged a spit and set the fish on to cook.

As the fish cooked, everyone chatted about what might lay ahead for them. Deanna was worried about what might be behind them still, but Theresa, Ben and Stacy started talking about their futures. It turned out that Theresa had been a hair dresser and wanted to find a place to start again. Ben and Stacy described the farm they wanted someday, with kids to raise and an idyllic life together.

Deanna listened but didn't say much as she still wasn't sure what her future was yet. She was pretty much convinced that whatever lay in store for her would be with James, if he wanted. She had no family to speak of. Her ex-husband and their two children were living in 'enemy' territory in a Christian town in central Pennsylvania. Her parents had passed on and her brothers were living several states away.

Dr. James also didn't have much to say as his future was very much in doubt. He knew what he was going to do and, so far, only Deanna knew what that was and he wanted to keep it that way. Maybe she would like to go along but, no matter what, he was going after his sisters as soon as he could get resupplied and organized. He needed a lot of intelligence to formulate a plan before even thinking about starting out on that adventure.

Once the fish were ready to eat, the feast was on. Everyone ate heartily until there was nothing but bones left, which Deanna told them, "Drop the bones and leftovers in the stream and make sure it all goes downstream or at least in the creek bottom. Don't leave anything for any animals to come scrounging around the camp for tonight and any humans to find later. When you have to go to the bathroom, go downstream from the camp as far as it is safe to do so and bury any solid waste. Don't pee near the camp. Hopefully, there will be minimal trace of our little camp once we've left and nature will cover our tracks before any humans find this place."

When they were all finished, Dr. James grabbed some water from the creek and put out the fire. It smoked a little but went out pretty quickly. Once the ashes cooled, he scattered the charcoal around the area to help bury it in the grass. He knew It would take an experienced tracker to find evidence of them being here after a couple of days.

The night watch shifts were set up and everyone understood what to do in case of any emergencies. They sat around until darkness settled in and Deanna said, "it's time to set the first watch and for everyone to get some sleep." As they rolled into their blankets, James and Deanna snuggled up on his blanket and kissed good night. She let him put his arm around her as they drifted off to sleep with the wildlife settling down with them.

About 1:00 in the morning, James heard something and woke up. Ben and Stacy were quietly trying to wake them up. They had heard something coming from up on the trail above them. James got up quietly, trying not to disturb Deanna, and softly walked over to where they had been sitting. As he stood quietly, he heard a faint noise up ahead of where he was looking. As he waited, he saw a couple of deer walking down the trail munching on leaves along the way. Dr. James slowly put his finger to his lips and motioned for them to stand very still. As they watched in the faint moonlight, the deer meandered down, and when they passed by the makeshift camp, they gave a few sniffs and jumped the creek to disappear into the woods on the other side.

When they passed out of sight, James smiled and told them, "It's okay, you did a good job as night watches. I'm going to turn back in but don't hesitate to wake me again if you hear anything else." He left them there and walked back to the blankets. Deanna asked him about it in a whisper and he told her what they saw. She smiled and said, "I'm glad that was all it was," and they went back to sleep.

After a mostly, uneventful night, daybreak arrived and Deanna started waking everyone up. Once again, they were leaving right at the crack of dawn to get ahead of any possible pursuers. They got up, took care of personal business and ate a small cold breakfast to get them going. As they were heading back up the hill towards the trail, Deanna took one last look around to make sure they didn't leave much behind to track them with, other than some trampled grass. She brought up the rear until they made it up to the main trail. Dr. James had been scouting around and told her that it all seemed to be clear for now.

Deanna took the lead once again as they had just enough light from the breaking dawn to see the trail going east. With everyone set to go, she set off on another fast pace, Stacy dependent. Although she was doing much better this morning and it looked like she would be able to maintain their pace. Deanna wondered how much farther the New Hampshire border was from here.

She knew that wouldn't stop Homeland Security but, she didn't think that they had much to worry about from them right now way out here. She was more worried about any local militias that may be bounty hunting. She knew about the bounty on Dr. James but there was likely one out on her and Theresa as well now.

Chapter 16

The Militia

They headed down the trail as quickly as they could in the early morning hours. They were all worried about being followed today. Dr. James brought up the rear again to allow Ben to keep helping Stacy. There hadn't been any sign of anyone behind them but Deanna was now focusing on what may lie ahead. She knew that with radios and phones, they could just as easily be waiting for them up ahead somewhere.

She kept them going with hand signs and water breaks like before. This time, Dr. James did the hand sign class for Ben and Stacy. After trekking along all morning, Deanna decided it was time for a lunch break. All they had left were a handful of trail rations. They would need to ration their food until they could find more. She had everyone break out what they had and distribute it evenly amongst the group.

They were all nervous so the small talk was minimal. They quickly ate and continued on. They kept this pace up, avoiding towns, staying off the main roads, scrounging up small bits of food from convenience stores without drawing too much attention and hitching occasional rides from local farmers whenever they could. All the while, camping in remote spots to avoid detection.

After a few days, they finally started getting close to the New Hampshire border. As they arrived close to the border about mid-day, Deanna heard a flight of small birds suddenly take off from some trees in front of them. She stopped everyone and waited. She didn't hear anything more but she knew that didn't mean much.

She motioned everyone off the trail and waved for Dr. James to come up to her. When he arrived, she told him what she heard. He volunteered to scout ahead to see if there was anything to worry about. "Let me check things out."

Deanna squeezed his hand and nodded, "Okay, be careful."

James crouched low and stayed off to the side of the trail, keeping as quiet as possible. As he slowly moved forward, he started to hear people talking in low voices up ahead on the trail. James got down and crawled ahead through the brush, moving very slowly so as not to make any sounds. As he crept closer, he started smelling a camp. The smell of unwashed bodies was pretty rank, and that was saying something compared to how they had been living on the trail since leaving the lodge.

As he peered through the small bushes and ferns, James found the source of the voices and smell. There were three very scruffy looking men camped out about fifty feet in front of him. They appeared to be standing guard over the trail at the border crossing and bored by the looks of things. At the moment, they were standing around chatting together and laughing at some joke told by one of them. The worst part was that they were armed and looked dangerous. Dangerous as in they would probably shoot anyone they didn't know on site.

James slowly worked himself back out of his hiding spot and returned to his companions. As they gathered around, he told them what he had found. Deanna asked, "What type of guns did you see?"

He replied, "They look like semiautomatic rifles and pistols mostly." Since all any of them had were camping knives and only a couple of those between them, it was obvious that attacking them was going to be out of the question.

They discussed their options. Going around them through the woods like they did in New York wouldn't work this time. The undergrowth was too thick and, she reasoned, "If these are local yocals guarding the trail, there are likely some more down in the woods waiting to back up the road guards as needed."

They were effectively blocked from crossing the New Hampshire border unless they could figure out a way through.

Deanna asked James, "Did you notice any other details that might help us?". All he could tell them was that they were very dirty, smelly and didn't have any military discipline like Homeland Security agents.

Ben spoke up and said, "We can make that work for us." Everyone looked at him with surprise as he had never spoke up without being asked before. He explained, "If these guys are that lazy, they will likely bed down early right after dark and if they do set a watch, the watch likely won't be too alert." He explained that he had seen guys like this before. They were out here at a boring guard post and didn't like it so they would be spending their time complaining and not be very disciplined.

"We can probably slip past them in the wee hours after midnight if we can be quiet enough." Ben looked at Deanna and Dr. James with a grim look in his eyes.

Deanna thought about this and told them all, "It's worth a try because we don't have any better ideas right now." She told everyone to stay off the trail and find a place to hide until it was time to go. "If anyone needs to get up and go to the bathroom, let someone know in case something happens."

Everyone found a spot amongst the trees and settled down to wait. Stacy was restless and tried to talk to Ben but he kept shushing her. He knew how to hunt and being on the defensive didn't sit right with him so he was a little short with her.

As Stacy started to sulk, Theresa came over to sit next to her. She told Ben, "I will keep her company and you can go do something constructive over by Dr. James and Deanna, if you want?"

Ben frowned and crept over by Dr. James to sit down. James looked at him but figured it was none of his business. He had bigger things to worry about than Ben and Stacy's squabbling. He was trying to think of a way to make their shoes quieter when they tried to slip through the other camp tonight. He told Ben what he was thinking and Ben knew straightaway what to do. He told Dr. James and Deanna, who was sitting on the other side of Dr. James, "If we can sacrifice a couple of shirts, we could cut them up to make shoe covers. This will soften our footfalls when we creep through the little camp tonight."

They thought this was a great idea and set to work gathering shirts from those who had something to spare and used their knives to cut foot covers for everyone. With the roll of duct tape, they could make this work.

Ben explained how to make them and added, "They also have an added benefit in that there won't be any tread marks from our shoes either, just impressions in the dirt. Given how lazy these guards seem to be, they won't even know we were here, provided we can sneak by quietly."

Ben also suggested that everyone take some soft green fern leaves and rub the leaves over themselves to mask their body odors. They could also make a paste from the leaves and rub it over their clothing and put some around their waists.

Deanna added to that by suggesting, "We can use plants to make face paints as well to keep our skin from shining in the night or camp fire." Something she learned from her brothers.

As they set to work on their new project, the afternoon passed by quickly. When darkness arrived, Dr. James suggested that he creep back over to see what the guards were doing.

Ben said, "I'll go this time. I need to feel more like I am contributing some." Stacy told him, "I am afraid, I don't want you to go," but Ben looked at her and replied, "I need to do this, I can't just sit around and wait for things to happen."

Dr. James looked at Deanna and she shrugged her shoulders. "Let him go," she said.

Ben crouched low and slipped into the woods off to the right of the trail. His plan was to try and circle around the guard post to see if he could find a way through tonight. Ben carefully crept forward and when he heard the voices off to his left, he crawled the rest of the way on his belly. It was just as Dr. James had described. A makeshift camp with three very unkempt dudes. One standing up and the other two lounging around a small campfire next to the trail. They weren't making any attempts at concealment and it looked like they didn't care to.

Ben took a closer look at their weapons and it did look like a couple of AR-15 style rifles, semi-auto pistols in leg holsters and maybe a deer rifle with a scope next to a tree by the fire. It was getting close to sundown and becoming a little harder to see without getting closer. Something he didn't dare to do right now. Ben watched for a little while longer until the sun hit the horizon. The only other thing he noticed was that it looked like they were passing around a bottle of something and it didn't look like water. If it was what he suspected, by the way they were passing it around and laughing, it was probably something stronger. He thought to himself, "That's a good thing and gives us another advantage when we slip through tonight."

Ben returned to where the others were hiding and reported his findings. All they could do now was wait and keep watch for anyone trying to sneak up on them. So far, it looked like no one knew they were here and they wanted to keep it that way.

Deanna asked, "Is everyone ready for tonight?" They all replied "Yes we are." She advised everyone to try and get a nap and rotate a watch to make sure no one crept up on them. She wanted to get going between midnight and 1:00 in the morning.

Dr. James took the first watch and everyone else settled down in the brush to take naps as best as they could. They rotated every couple of hours with Ben and Stacy standing watch together. At just after midnight, Deanna woke up, not that she had been really sleeping anyway, and woke everyone else up. They put the paste on their skins, the ferns in their clothing and, this time, Ben led the way. He said, "I know the best way through the camp from my last scouting mission and I can lead us through." Dr. James went right behind him in case there was any trouble and Deanna put Stacy between herself and Theresa who was providing rear guard.

They all had their makeshift shoe covers on, taking it slow and easy through the brush and small trees. Ben walked very slow to prevent any noise and stopped when he could see their campfire. He whispered for everyone to stay there while he crept up to recon the camp. Ben crouched down and gently eased up to where he could see into the camp. Sure enough, they were all asleep. Two in their blankets and the guard asleep, sitting with his back against a tree and head on his knees. His rifle was leaning against the tree next to him. Ben was tempted to sneak over there and take the gun.

As Ben continued to watch for a few minutes, all he could hear was snoring. He decided to try and work his way around to the tree where the guard was sleeping and take his rifle. Ben slowly crept around the edge of the little camp, staying out of the light from the campfire and not looking directly at the fire so he wouldn't lose his night vision. He slowly made his way behind the guard and crept up to the base of the tree. He could just see the rifle leaning there and all he had to do was slowly reach out and take it.

Ben quietly crouched behind the tree and reached around to grab the rifle, slowly lifting it so he could pull it around to his side. Just as he did, he heard the guard shift and mumble something. Ben held his breathe and prepared to run. The guard just went back to sleep and Ben pulled the rifle to him. He slowly stood up, took two steps back and returned into the trees from where he had come in. He kept up his silent mode until he finally made it back to where he had left everyone. Dr. James was very relieved when Ben finally ghosted out of the woods from the direction of the camp. He wanted to ask where he had been but they were in a no talking zone. Then James noticed the rifle on Ben's shoulder and he knew.

Ben took point again and led everyone quietly past the sleeping guards. As they passed through, it became more obvious that these men were part of some local militia unit. Whether they were on the lookout for them specifically or just here as border guards was unknown, and obviously no one was going to ask.

The five of them passed by the ugly camp site and continued on into the early morning hours before dawn. What Deanna and her Wiccan friends used to call the witching hours, "Which seems like another lifetime ago," she thought as they ghosted down the trail.

After walking quietly down the trail for a while, they stopped to take off the shoe coverings and ferns. They needed a water break and Deanna told everyone, "We should be close to the border crossing now." She took the lead from Ben and they set out once more.

Just as the sun started to show light on the eastern horizon, Deanna noticed a weathered sign off to the side of the trail. It read, "Welcome to New Hampshire, The Granite State." It looked like it had been mounted by the state park service a long time ago. She wanted to shout with happiness but she kept silent and just pointed out the sign to everyone. There were a lot of weary smiles as they walked by.

Deanna also knew that they weren't safe yet. Most militias didn't care much about what state they operated in up here. They would travel the same trails they did with little resistance from any locals. Most people were afraid of standing up to the groups of heavily armed militia members anyway.

Now they just had to make it to Dr. James's friends. She whispered to James, "Do you know the way to our destination from here?"

James said "I will know more once the sun comes up and I can figure out where we are. It's been a while and I've never come overland on this trail before. I just know what town we're looking for and I should be able to find my friends from there."

He also thought, after they started off again, "We may have to find some motor transport to finish the trip. I don't think we will make it on foot without being seen but I'll address that issue once we take a break at sunrise."

Chapter 17

New Hampshire

After another hour of walking, the sun had come up enough for them to try and see where they were. As none of them had ever been in this part of New Hampshire before, it was time to get off the trail and try to figure out how to get to the little town Dr. James knew about. None of them had a map so they would have to do it the hard way, by seeing if they could find a friendly face and ask for directions.

They finished their breakfast break and set off to see if they could find any civilization up ahead. Deanna wanted to find some high ground to try and see the area to the south. She figured that would be the most likely direction to find any sign of human habitation. Even a gas station along a back road would serve right now.

She was leery of just walking up to a strange house out here looking the way they did right now. The homeowners might just shoot them or call the police, neither of which would be good. They walked a little further and Ben spotted a small hill with a bit of a clear view of a valley below. They would have to get off the trail to get to it though. Deanna stopped and looked where he was pointing. She looked at everyone and asked, "Do you think we can all make it to the hill?"

 Everyone said "Sure," Stacy grabbed Ben's arm and said "Let's go."

They threaded their way through the woods to the hill and looked out from around the trees. Down below was a large farm. Lots of fields and some cattle but no sign of anyone out and about yet, at least from this vantage point. Deanna wanted to stay put for a bit to see if there were any people down on this farm but Ben and Stacy wanted to go now to ask for food and directions.

Deanna warned them about possible militia members or sympathizers and tried to get them to be patient. Stacy started to get loud and Ben had to shush her again. She started pouting and looked about ready to cry, mumbling, "I am just very hungry and dirty and I want to feel normal again."

As Ben tried to reassure her, Deanna kept looking out over the farm below. Soon she spotted someone coming out of the barn heading for the house. She couldn't see well enough from so far away to determine whether he had a weapon or not but it didn't look like it. He looked like just an ordinary farmer. Deanna didn't want anyone to see them and she figured that if they could make it out to the road, they could walk down the road a little to see if they could figure out where they were.

After discussing options, Dr. James warned them, "From my experience roads can be dangerous if we stay on them too long. The longer you walk along the side of a road in strange territory, the better the chance of someone not very friendly seeing you and calling it in." He told everyone, "New Hampshire is a mix of folks on one side or the other, politically. You never really know who is who until you've reached a known safe haven. It would be best if we find our location quickly and get off the road until we can secure some transportation."

Deanna started down the hill, staying close to the trees. She planned to circle the field to try and find a way down to the road without being seen. They all fell in behind her with Dr. James bringing up the rear this time. He was worried that Stacy might break and run for the house down there and he didn't think he could depend on Ben to stop her. In fact, Ben might try to stop him and that would be bad. Dr. James didn't want to hurt him and Ben also had that rifle. It might be best to keep an eye on them and hope for the best.

They made it to the edge of the field and walked to the corner of the fence. Deanna could see the dirt farm road alongside the field and a rock pile bordering the other side of the tractor path. She went over to the rocks and stepped over the old rusted barbed wire fence strung between some small trees, mostly cedar, along the fence line.

The rest followed as she led them down towards the farm trying to keep under cover of the trees.

After a few minutes Deanna stopped and looked around. Mostly she just listened. She wanted to listen for any cars on the road nearby. If she could hear one car pass by the farm, she could gauge how far away and which direction the road was. As they waited, Stacy started fidgeting again. Deanna looked at her with a glowering look and she stopped. A couple of minutes later, she heard it, a car on the road out in front of the farm. She listened to it pass and figured out its direction. She waved everyone up and they started out towards the road where she heard the car.

Soon, they were standing in a tree line next to a small two-lane country road. There weren't any signs, so far, telling them the name of the road so Deanna started walking alongside the road in the direction she had heard the car going earlier. She reasoned that since it was early morning, someone was likely commuting to work somewhere which usually meant some kind of civilization nearby.

She told everyone, "Keep a close eye out for any cars that may be coming and get off the road to avoid being seen." All was quiet so far. Apparently, there weren't too many commuters around here this early in the morning but it was only a little after six am now. Just as she was thinking that, Dr. James heard a car coming from behind them so they all ducked behind the trees on the side of the road. They watched the pickup truck go by and looked at the driver. He seemed pretty normal looking so they went back out to the road once he passed around the curve.

After a couple of miles, they saw a gas station sign poking above the trees ahead. Deanna called a halt and they had a discussion about how they wanted to handle this. Dr. James wanted to check it out closely before just walking up to the door.

Theresa offered to go, saying, "Since I am fairly young and ordinary looking, I think I can manage to scout around without anyone taking much of a second look at me. Does anyone have a couple of dollars so I can look around and buy something small to avoid suspicion?"

Ben offered her a 5-dollar bill and told her to "bring back the change" before James could say anything so he let it go.

They walked up a little farther and stepped back into the trees to wait for her. Theresa stepped out and walked across the road to the store. At first, she looked for any cars at the gas pumps and there wasn't any right now. Then she stopped to look in the front windows for any signs of other people. All looked normal so far. As she walked in the door, she looked at the young man behind the cashier's counter as she headed into the aisles. While she stood looking at the snacks, she glanced surreptitiously around the store to see if anything looked off. So far, so good. She picked up a Hostess cake and walked up to the cashier. As she laid the 5-dollar bill on the counter, she asked, "Do you have any road maps of the area?

The young man, who seemed to be taking a little more than normal interest in her in a slightly creepy way, said, "There are some maps in a rack by the door."

As she walked over to the rack to look, the young man kept looking at her with a small smile as if he were undressing her in his mind. She found a road map of New Hampshire and asked, "How much?"

The man kept looking at her body instead of her face and said "$1.99."

The little cake was $2.99 so she said, "I will just take the map, thank you." Theresa was anxious to get out of there as quickly as possible.

She thought, "So much for me thinking I'm ordinary looking." Theresa was of average height and slim build, with an ordinary looking face and long, straight, dark brown hair that she kept up in a tail with a scrunchy. After paying for the map, she looked at the young man who kept staring at her like he hadn't seen a girl in a long time. Theresa thought about flirting with him just to make him squirm, then thought better of it and left. Once outside, she walked out towards the main road first, to give the young man the wrong idea about which direction she was going. Theresa walked out far enough so that he couldn't see her anymore, then she veered back down the side road to find her friends. She told them about the creepy kid inside. At this, Ben growled under his breath like he wanted to go after him.

Theresa took out the map and they all looked at it to see where they were. There were highway signs at the intersection out in front of the gas station so they knew where they were now, sort of. Now to find it on the map. Deanna found their location quickly enough so she asked Dr. James to point out where they were heading. Dr. James studied the map for a couple of minutes and pointed to a small city down near the south western Vermont border and Massachusetts. "Here."

There was no doubt now that in order for them to get there, they would have to find some transportation. James outlined another plan. "What if we can find an old-fashioned pay phone?" Everyone looked at him as if he were from another planet.

Deanna laughed, "A phone booth in this day and age? No way."

He looked at them and said, "All I need is access to a land line and I can try to call my friends to see if they might come up here and get us."

It took a minute for that to register with everyone in this age of mobile phones, none of which anyone had right now. Deanna being a few years older than the rest, was the first to make the connection. Land lines were so out of date now, that the chances of them being monitored by the government were slim. She asked Dr. James, "Will your friends actually come and get us?" James then told them about his friends.

Dr. James's 'friends' were part of a regional network of safehouses, underground spies and informants across New England and down into the mid-Atlantic states. They assisted in small domestic terrorist acts, and provided other support wherever they could. Dr. James was well known to them as he had treated quite a few of their people when they had gotten hurt during some of their 'protests' the last time he was here.

He explained, "This is my destination and you are welcome to come along, as one of the other things this group does is to take care of refugees from Homeland Security and the government. They can help find a place for you, even provide someone a new name and documents, if you want, or help you get where you want to go without any government tracking. All I need is a land line."

Theresa spoke up, "I didn't see anything like a pay phone anywhere around the outside of the gas station. Nothing inside either, as far I could see. Although, I was distracted by that creep who leered at me when I was inside."

Deanna volunteered to return to the gas station this time to take another look. She smiled at Theresa and said, "I doubt he will stare at my backside when I go inside" and they all laughed. Deanna was wiry looking, about five foot, eleven inches tall, with short light brown hair and had a look that said "You better not mess with me." Being an avid outdoors enthusiast all her life, she was pretty strong for her size and had a tanned complexion from all of her time spent in the woods and mountains.

James smiled, telling her. "Be safe. I'll walk you to the corner of the store in case there are any complications."

 Deanna left her pack with Theresa and walked over to the gas station with James following a little behind, keeping to the shadows alongside the building.

When she walked around to the front, she started scouting for any sign of a pay phone. Nothing outside, so she walked in and started browsing the store. The same young man who had leered at Theresa gave her only a cursory glance as he took care of a customer at the counter. Deanna walked towards the back of the store and found a short hallway leading to the bathrooms and storerooms. That's where she found the phone. It was a derelict looking old pay phone booth hanging on the wall in the back of the hallway.

She turned down the hallway like she needed to use the lady's room. As she walked towards the bathroom door, she looked at the phone and determined that, despite its battered look, it still looked functional. She discretely picked up the receiver and heard a dial tone, "Bonus" she thought, as she went into the lady's room to wash up, just to make things look normal.

When she finished, Deanna walked back out front and looked around a little more. She noticed that the young man running the cash register had a look of disinterested boredom, and would probably be glad for anything to entertain him. Deanna decided to see if she could solicit any information from him about the local politics and people around here. Anyway, she was spoiling for a little fight after what Theresa told them about him.

She sauntered up to the counter and looked at him. "How you doing?"

The man looked at her with a disinterested look and said, "Can I help you?"

Deanna started asking him about the local churches and if any farms might be looking for helpers. The young man replied, "There are lots of churches around here, do you have one in mind? Then he asked with a sneer in his voice, "Are you a Catholic?"

That was enough of a red flag for Deanna. If this young man felt emboldened enough to talk to her like that in public, then he obviously was one of the new government's avid supporters.

She didn't give him an answer. She thanked him for his time and walked out. There was a mirror next to the front door to enable the cashier to watch parts of the store that couldn't directly be seen from behind the counter and Deanna watched the man's reaction to her in the mirror as she left. He was behaving like the type that might make a call to report suspicious behavior to someone after she left the store.

She walked by the front window and around the corner of the building where she met James and told him about the phone and the kid's behavior. James listened as they walked back across the road. As they gathered around, Deanna waved everyone into the trees to avoid being seen. She was worried that they might have company soon.

Dr. James wanted to go right away to use the phone before anyone showed up looking for her. Deanna remarked, "With your dark complexion, you will stand out quickly and likely draw some racist remarks or worse."

Ben offered to go with him as a backup. He said, "Maybe with me along, it might not look quite so bad. If things do get out of hand, we can deal with it together."

Deanna advised him, "If you go, leave the rifle here with us to keep things low key." Ben looked at Stacy and then gave the rifle to Deanna to hold while they were gone. Dr. James and Ben walked across to the store and went inside. James kept glancing at the young man behind the cash register as they continued towards the back. The young man watched them closely when they turned down the hallway. Ben walked behind him and kept turning to glare at the young man up front as if daring him to say anything. Once Dr. James picked up the phone receiver, he kept watch so Dr. James could make his ever so special phone call.

With his back to the doctor, Ben watched the store, especially the front door. They didn't want to get trapped in this store by more people than they could handle, which wouldn't be more than one or two at this point. He listened with half an ear as the doctor made his call. Dr. James kept his voice low and asked for someone by name when the phone was picked up. After a couple of minutes, he started talking to someone about what happened in New York and where they were right now.

When Dr. James finished explaining their predicament, Ben heard someone on the other end faintly sounding very excited and a bunch of conversation he couldn't hear. Dr. James acknowledged the caller and said "We need to stay out of sight." Then Ben heard some more mumbling and Dr. James told his friend that they would try to find "it" and be waiting. With that, he said good bye and hung up.

Dr. James said, "Let's go". They slowly walked back out towards the door. As they walked by the coolers, Ben decided to buy Stacy something cold to drink. He told Dr. James, "I'll be right out."

James headed outside to wait but remained where he could see the cashier's window. As he waited, he looked around at his surroundings.

There was the usual half a dozen run down looking gas pumps and the smell of urine and gasoline. Surrounding the gas station here on this lonely corner of roadway, was all open farm land with a few trees marking the fence lines and the sides of the roads at this intersection. He was looking for anything out of place in this idyllic farmland. As he mused and looked around, Ben came out with the cold drink. He smirked about how much the young man in there seemed intimidated by him. Ben, who was in his early twenties, a stocky six-foot two, longish dark hair and beard with the broad shoulders of a farmer and outdoorsman. Stacy, by contrast, was a petite, five-foot three-inch blonde cheerleader type who looked like she was still in high school.

They walked back to where everyone was hiding in the trees and Ben gave Stacy the cold drink. Stacy looked at Ben in surprise and said with a bright smile, "Thank you." She took the can and stood off to the side where she could sip it while waiting for someone to decide where they were going next. She didn't care right now where they went as long as it had a shower and a hot meal.

Dr. James told them a little about the phone call. He didn't mention the man's name just that his friend told him, "We need to find a particular church and wait there for someone to pick us up."

He had told his friend that there were five in his party, then he paused, looked at Ben and asked, "You still want to go, right?"

Ben stepped next to Stacy, looked down at her and asked, "Do you want to continue on with them or strike out on our own now?"

She didn't care, she just wanted to go somewhere where she didn't have to look over their shoulders anymore. Ben looked back at Dr. James and said, "Is it true what you said earlier, that we can get new identities from your friends?"

Dr. James replied, "Yes, if you want? It might take a little while, if you're willing to wait for them."

Ben shrugged his shoulders and said, "Okay, we'll follow you to your friends place and figure things out from there."

Dr. James asked to see the map again. He wanted to know where the closest town was to their current location. He didn't think it would be very far from this gas station.

As he looked, he pointed to a spot and said, "There. This was where we're going. Supposedly, there is a minister in a certain church there who is a good friend to the people where we are going and he should be able to offer us food and shelter until my friend arrives tomorrow. We just have to make it over to this church without being seen."

His friend had told him that there isn't much Homeland Security presence up here but that is because of the bounty hunting militias running around, like the ones they had snuck around last night. They all started walking across the road to go around the gas station from the back side. There was no doubt that the young man inside would report a group of strangers walking up the road if he saw them together, especially if he recognized any of them as being in and out of the store today.

They walked over to the fence behind the store and looked across the big field. It was still early in the growing season, so nothing was very high yet. Little green shoots coming up and that was about it.

Deanna also noticed that there wasn't any room between the fence and the back of the store due to the trees there so they would have to climb over the fence and walk along the field. They would be in the relative open, but if they hurried across, they could get into the woods on the other side in a few minutes, hopefully without being seen from the road.

They climbed over the barbed wire with Dr. James and Ben holding the top wire down for the women and then stepping over to bring up the rear. They quickly ran down the track next to the field to get to the woods, once again climbing over some barbed wire. Once inside the woods, the little group meandered through the trees keeping the main road in sight walking towards town. Every time they would come to another field, it was the same, cross the fence and run across as quickly as they could to avoid being seen by any cars or farmers.

Chapter 18

The Church

As they entered the outskirts of town, they did their best to hide amongst the buildings and back streets searching for the church that Dr. James had been told about. Finally, over on the other side of this little town, they found it. Deanna halted everyone next to a Big Lots Store in a run-down shopping plaza across the street to check things out.

As they all lined up against the side of the store, Deanna began looking at the church. Ben and Dr. James kept a watch out for anyone that might be paying a little too much attention to them while they waited.

After a few minutes, she advised caution, "We need to straggle across the street in ones, and twos." She took off across the parking lot to cross the street to the church. It didn't look like much, just a non-descript, non-denominational church with service times and a piece of scripture on a bulletin board out front. Deanna walked up to the front door and found it locked. She waited until everyone had crossed over and told them to follow her around to the back so as not to arouse suspicion by hanging around the front. They all trooped around to the back of the church where they found a car and an unlocked back door.

Deanna suggested that Dr. James go in by himself as it was his friend that had recommended this place. James agreed and slowly opened the door. The rest kept out of sight as he stepped inside. He was met by a middle-aged minister standing in a little office with an older woman sitting at a desk. The minister looked up, smiled and asked, "Can I help you?"

Dr. James introduced himself as just James and said, "My friend Robert recommended this church as a place where we can wait safely until he can arrive tomorrow to pick us up. He then said a code word his friend had given him and the minister got a serious look on his face.

The minister looked at his secretary and excused himself. He quietly asked James where his companions where and James said, "Just outside."

The minister, Dr. Hammond, told him, "Quietly bring them in and I will find towels and a washroom to start with." When James hesitated, Dr. Hammond told him, "Don't worry about Mrs. Moody, she has been here for years and she is used to this by now."

James returned to the door and brought everyone in. When the other four came in, he introduced them to Dr. Hammond, who was waiting next to Mrs. Moody, who barely looked up from her desk. She looked up and smiled a little at them, then went back to work. They followed Dr. Hammond through a set of doors, around the church alter area and through another set of doors back to some classrooms and bathrooms. Dr. Hammond told them all, "Make yourselves at home and I'll be right back with some clean towels."

Everyone just stood around quietly, anxiously waiting for the minister to return but he was only gone a couple of minutes before returning with a handful of towels. He then said, "I will be down the hall in the last classroom when you're finished."

They all went and cleaned up in the gender separate bathrooms and brought the towels down to the classroom where Dr. Hammond was waiting. He asked them all to sit down so he could find out what they needed. He looked at them and asked, "Is anyone hungry?" Everyone enthusiastically replied all at once, "Yes please, we can all use a hot meal for a change, if that is possible?"

Deanna spoke up over the rest and asked the minister about the local politics. When Dr. Hammond gave her a quizzical look, she explained that they were refugees from New York state and were trying to avoid any trouble from the local townsfolk. She had heard stories about how some small towns didn't care much for strangers these days.

Dr. Hammond reassured them, "You are safe here in this church" and he proceeded to explain. "I've been here for the last 3 years and my secretary, Mrs. Moody, has been here all of her life and is from a long line of Quakers. I had been the pastor of a small church out in the mid-west before 2024 and I watched my congregation tear itself apart over the divisions in the country. I tried not to take sides but when the government nationalized a version of protestant Christianity, I knew I could no longer remain on the sidelines. Once I became active in this disagreement with the government's policies, my congregation pushed me out. So, I came up here and reopened this church as a front for my other activism, which is helping religious fugitives and other refugees on the run from the new government."

"This was why the underground doesn't hesitate to recommend this church to people in need as a place to lay low until they can be transported too somewhere safe." Dr. Hammond continued, "This church is a safe haven for anyone who needs it. I can provide some refreshments, showers, some small articles of clothing and a place to lay down for a while as needed."

Deanna wasn't feeling comfortable here and kept asking nervous questions. Finally, James reached over to try and calm her down but she couldn't relax.

Dr. Hammond looked at her, and asked, "Why are you uncomfortable here?" She replied, "I haven't set foot in a Christian church in over 20 years and I am not a Christian believer, so does this make me exempt from your hospitality?"

Dr. Hammond laughed and replied, "All are welcome here, as it says in the bible. I don't ask about a person's spiritual or political beliefs; I just minister to the needy as Jesus did."

That eased some of Deanna's tensions but she remained on high alert nonetheless. As she was talking to the minister, Ben and Stacy gave her a long look when she admitted to not being a Christian but remained quiet.

Dr. Hammond looked at all of them and repeated, "You have nothing to worry about here." Then he looked at Ben and said, "if you need a place to put that rifle, I have a small closet where you can store it until you get ready to leave."

Ben turned a shade of red and sheepishly replied, "In all of the rush to get here and take care of Stacy, I had forgotten about it. If it's okay, I would like to hang onto it for a little longer until we get settled."

Dr. Hammond said, "That's fine. Just be careful with it. We don't want any accidents in here."

He asked if anyone else had any questions and everyone shook their heads no. With that, he asked them to follow him down to a small dining area that had a kitchen off to the side. He gave them a little tour and said, "You can use it as long as you clean up afterwards. There is food in the refrigerator and the pantries, and you can help yourselves. If you need anything else, just ask me or Mrs. Moody and we will try to help."

Dr. Hammond left them to take care of themselves and went back to his office. Theresa started looking around the kitchen and said, "I can set up a meal for anyone who is hungry." Stacy offered to help so the two of them started gathering things from the cupboards and the fridge. Pretty soon, the smell of food cooking started making everyone's mouth water.

As they were making a mid-afternoon meal, the others sat down at one of the tables in the dining area. Deanna asked James, "What's the next part of the plan?"

He told them, "We need to lay low here until my friend arrives, either tomorrow or the next day for sure. Likely tomorrow. Today, we eat a hot meal, relax as best as we can and try and get a good night's sleep. Maybe the church has a TV room or at least a radio to listen to for news of the outside world?"

The two young ladies served up a wonderful hot meal and everyone filled up. As they were eating, Deanna said she wanted to look in the food pantry to see if there were any food they could take with them on the next leg of their journey. Theresa said, "I didn't see any but I wasn't really looking either. I just grabbed the first things I could find to make a quick meal."

Deanna wanted to relax after their meal so she said, "I'll take a look around later."

After they finished eating, and everyone was cleaning up their paper plates and trash, Stacy shyly asked Deanna, "If you aren't a Christian, what faith do you believe in?"

Deanna turned to her and replied, "I am a Wiccan and we believe in nature and the old Celtic Gods of pre-Christianity," then turned away to put her trash in the bin.

Stacy stood there for a minute while putting her trash in the bin then walked slowly back to where Ben was sitting as if deep in thought. Ben asked her, "What's the matter?"

She sat down without saying anything, and after a minute she told him about Deanna. Ben frowned and quietly said, "It's none of our business and you should never have asked. Just leave it alone."

When Deanna sat down with James, she whispered to him about what Stacy had asked. She told him, "Be careful around her, especially about your Muslim faith."

He assured her, "I had already thought about that back on the trail as soon as I knew where they came from. Not to worry." He told her, "We will likely be saying good bye to them soon anyway as I don't think they want anything to do with the underground."

Deanna thought about that and decided to keep a closer eye on them until they were well away from here. She wasn't too worried about Ben but Stacy, on the other hand, was becoming unpredictable. She said to James, "I hope your friend gets here quickly tomorrow."

James agreed, as he was anxious to get started on his plan for Virginia but he also worried about the two newlyweds.

Dr. James decided to stretch his legs a little bit with a walk around the inside of the church and asked Deanna, "Do want to join me?"

She replied, "No thanks, I think I want to hang out here for a little while." James knew it was to keep an eye on Ben and Stacy so he turned to Theresa and asked her.

Theresa said, "Sure, just as soon as I am finished cleaning the kitchen." Stacy jumped up and went to the kitchen to help, leaving Ben, Deanna and Dr. James at the table.

Deanna asked Ben, "Have you made any other plans yet now that we're in New Hampshire?"

Ben replied, "Yes, we want to take you up on your offer of new identities and then start looking for work once we have them."

Dr. James answered, "You're welcome to come as before but that rifle might make some people nervous."

Ben said, "I'll think about that but for now, I don't want to part with it just yet." As a signal that this conversation was over, he pulled the rifle around, put it on the table and started breaking it down for a little cleaning. He looked like he knew what he was doing so they left him alone.

After a few minutes, Theresa came over and said she was ready to go. James excused himself and they went to find Dr. Hammond. James exited out of the hallway where they had come in and went around to see if they were still in the office out back. When they entered, Mrs. Moody was still there but Dr. Hammond was not. James said, "Hello, is Dr. Hammond around? I have some questions I would like to ask."

She replied, "He stepped across to his residence and he will be back in a few minutes, is there anything I can help with?"

Dr. James decided to see how trustworthy she might be and asked "May I have a small area for my evening prayers? I would like a quiet place, if that is possible."

She looked at him and asked, "Are you a Muslim?" and Dr. James replied. "Yes, I am."

She said, "I completely understand and I will ask Dr. Hammond as soon as he returns. Is there anything else I can help with?"

Dr. James asked, "Do you have a TV or a radio somewhere that we can turn on to get the news? It's been a long time since we have heard anything."

Mrs. Moody replied, "Yes, there is a TV in the conference room near the kitchen and you're welcome to use it as long as you keep the volume down. We don't want to let anyone outside the church know that we have overnight visitors."

Dr. James thanked her and they walked back to find the others. Theresa went to find the TV room and James returned to the kitchen, only to see Deanna explaining to Stacy and Ben about Wicca and Islam. As he walked in, they looked up and stopped their conversation.

James told them about the TV room and remarked, "Theresa is already down there checking it out, if you want to go?" Ben said "Sure", and helped Stacy up to go find the TV room. James didn't say anything but gave Deanna a look that was a question in itself.

Deanna shrugged and said, "Stacy started asking me questions about Wicca and Islam after you left. It seems she genuinely wants to learn. I also told Stacy that in full disclosure, you are a Muslim. So far, so good. I didn't detect any bias from her and I am not worried about Ben." Deanna got up and they walked down to the TV room where Theresa had figured out how to turn on the TV.

She had found a cable news channel and everyone was listening trying to catch up on the news they had missed since leaving New York. Mostly it was about how the new government was continuing to root out domestic terrorists and how the legislators were consolidating their power to more closely align with the teachings in the bible and so on. James had heard all of this before. Nothing seemed to have changed much since the last time he had listened to a broadcast.

Then towards the end of the show, there was a segment about the raid in upstate New York that got everyone's attention. The newscaster reported about how the raid had been successful in rooting out a group of non-Christian believers that had failed to register with government and eliminating members of a rebellious militia that had been carrying out treasonous acts of terrorism in the region. The newscaster said, "They killed or captured the majority of them but Homeland security was still on the lookout for a small handful that had escaped into the mountain wilderness."

Everyone sat straight up in their chairs with anxious looks. On the screen were older pictures of Deanna and Theresa, likely taken from their homes in New York, said to be traveling with an unidentified man. The news anchor said these people were terrorists and anyone spotting them could be rewarded with a bounty payment if captured and their identities confirmed.

Ben and Stacy looked at the three of them and started to ask questions. "What happened. Why are you considered terrorists. Who are you Dr. James?"

James let Deanna and Theresa do the talking. He just sat there and listened. As Deanna started to tell their story, Dr. Hammond walked in and sat down in a chair behind them, quietly listening until she was finished. James looked up when he came in and passively kept an eye on him. He didn't want to make the reverend nervous.

When Deanna and Theresa finished telling their stories, Ben and Stacy sat in silence for a minute while they processed everything.

Stacy finally spoke up, "This doesn't change my mind about what I think of you." She told them, "I know what we've been through together and I rely on that, rather than the liars in the news. Everyone who has ever watched the news lately knows that the media only says what they are told to say by the new government anyway." She reached over and gave Deanna a big hug, which surprised Deanna, to say the least. Dr. James just smiled and looked over at Dr. Hammond to see his reaction.

The reverend smiled and said, "That is good story and I'm glad you all made it this far safely." He looked at James and said, "I have your quiet place ready for you whenever you want. It is two doors down from here on the right." Then he smiled at the rest and said, "if you want to see where you will be sleeping tonight, come follow me and I will see that you get settled in."

Everyone followed him out and down the hallway. The reverend walked down to the end of the hallway towards the back of the church building and opened a door to a small dormitory like room with several twin beds inside. He said, "I'm sorry that I don't have accommodations for husbands and wives."

Ben said, "We'll make do." Deanna smiled at James and said, "I'm sorry." After looking inside, they went back to the kitchen to grab their packs and get settled in for the night.

As Dr. Hammond started to leave, he said, "Mrs. Moody is heading home now and I will be in my residence behind the church if you need anything. Please try to only come get me if it is an emergency as there is no cover between the back door of the church and my little house out back. If you absolutely need me, try to come over after pitch dark to avoid prying eyes in the local community." With that, he left them to enjoy the rest of their evening.

The little group set up their beds and went back to the TV room to see if they could learn more about the hunt for the fugitives. After a little while, everyone hit the showers and it was lights out for a good night's sleep, or at least a more restful one than any they had endured since leaving the resort. Tomorrow would be an interesting day and everyone was anxious as they crept into their beds.

James left them to settle in and went to the quiet room set aside for his evening prayers. As he pulled out his prayer rug and started his meditations, he tried to put away his anxieties and let 'Allah' take over to clear his thoughts. When James finally finished and made ready to leave, he felt a little easier about the days ahead. As he entered the little dormitory and made it over to his bed next to Deanna's, she smiled up at him in the darkness and asked, "Do you feel better?"

James replied, "I do indeed feel a little more at ease and I think I can sleep a little now." He reached down and kissed her good night then crawled under his blankets.

Deanna was also a little more relaxed. She wasn't worried about the newlyweds any more, they were just young and learning about the new world beyond their cloistered village where they had grown up. She just didn't trust their good fortune in making it this far. She knew that she would be restless tonight trying to sleep but it was still better than what they'd had on the trail. She chided herself and thought, "It's time to try for a little sleep and worry about tomorrow when it arrives." She planned to sleep with an ear out for strange noises tonight though and her camp knife was under her pillow as she still didn't believe in being complacent yet.

Chapter 19

The Escape

Deanna woke up with a start and surreptitiously looked at her watch. Something had startled her out of her light sleep. It was a little after four am and she lay there in the dark, listening without moving, looking around with just her eyes. She didn't hear anything moving in their little room so she pulled herself up a bit as quietly as possible so as not to disturb anyone.

Then she heard what sounded voices outside in back of the church muffled by the walls. She decided to take a look just in case. She slid out of bed as quietly as possible, and started slipping on her clothes. As she was pulling her shirt on, she noticed James had woken up also and as he started to ask what she was doing, she looked at him with her finger across her lips to keep him quiet. He quietly slipped from his bed and starting getting dressed as well.

As James was getting dressed, she looked around and spotted the rifle standing against the wall next to the head of Ben's bed. She padded over in her stocking feet, picked it up and slung it over her shoulder to hang in front of her. She quietly walked over and listened through the door for any strange sounds, especially for any early morning unwanted visitors. When she didn't hear anything, she cracked it open just a sliver to look down the hallway. The hallway was nearly pitch dark with only the exit signs above the doors offering any light. With no one in sight, she went out into the hallway to put her shoes on. As she was tying her shoelaces, James slipped out beside her and did the same.

Deanna whispered that she had been awakened by what sounded like, voices out back. She wanted to have a look around to make sure they were still safe. Her idea was to go to one of the classrooms and sneak a peek out a window. First though, she wanted to have a listen at the back door in the hallway that led to the parking lot. She tiptoed over and put her ear to the door. She could hear faint muffled voices through the door so she motioned James over and told him, "Go quietly wake the others and get them ready to leave."

As he left to take care of this, she went to an open classroom door, got down on her hands and knees to crawl in and look out a window. As she peered out, she could see what looked like flashlights shining from the parking lot of the church where the good reverend's little residence was. She didn't see anything on this side of the building but there was likely someone watching the front doors of the church. She scooted back across the classroom floor to the hallway to wait on the others.

As she stood there thinking, Ben came out carrying his boots and whispered, "What is going on?" Deanna made hand motions telling him to be quiet and whispered that someone was out in the parking lot of the church right now. Ben took the rifle from her, slipped it across his shoulder while they waited for the others without another word, for which Deanna was grateful. She needed to think of a way out of here and quickly.

The others all stepped out of the little dormitory and Deanna kept her finger across her lips to stop any questions for the moment. As they looked at her, she pointed towards the door going out into the congregation area and motioned for them to follow her. Once at the doors, Deanna quietly walked up and listened at the door before cracking the door open. Seeing nothing around the pews and front stage area, she slipped through the door and Ben followed her closely. Deanna told the others to stay put until they returned. As they moved across the front of the church, Ben kept the rifle pointed out across the pews towards the front doors.

Deanna went up to the door going into the back-office area and checked for sounds once again while Ben walked over to the stain glass windows to see if there were any lights flashing around outside. He crouched low to avoid showing a silhouette and peeked out from a window sill. Nothing so far but he waited until Deanna gave him the all clear before moving in behind her again. As she cracked the door open, Ben stuck the rifle barrel inside the door as she opened it to slip through.

They glided across the floor to the outside exit and Deanna listened again. This time she heard muffled voices coming from the parking lot not too far from the door. It sounded like only a couple of them. Someone was arguing about something and she could make an educated guess about what that might be. She backed away from the door and motioned for Ben to stand guard while she went and told the others.

Deanna quickly walked back around to where Dr. James and the girls were waiting to give them the news. She told them, "I don't know if we have been found but I don't want to be trapped inside this building if they come for us." She wondered, out loud, "Maybe we can escape through one of the windows in a classroom?"

James said "I'll go check and be right back." As they waited, Stacy and Theresa looked shaken up. Stacy especially. Theresa had her arm around her trying to reassure her that everything was going to be okay.

Dr. James returned and said, "The windows are all locked from the inside but we can slip out if we need to."

Deanna told them all to wait and she would go get Ben. She went back to the office and asked Ben if he had heard anything more from outside?

Ben whispered, "No, things have quieted down," but he looked worried. He was thinking he would rather they, whoever they were, continue to argue so he could tell where they were. Deanna motioned for him to come and they quietly headed back around to where everyone was still waiting.

Deanna told Ben about the windows as they were quietly walking back. Ben offered to go find the best window to slip through and come get them once he found it. James volunteered to be his backup just in case. They slipped into the first classroom to check the windows. Just like Dr. James said, they all had window locks on the inside. Ben peered out through the bottom of the window to prevent a silhouette again and didn't see anything moving outside. He waited a few minutes to see if he could see anything but there was nothing so far.

Ben figured they were going to have to take a big chance here. First, getting everyone through the window quietly without being discovered would be the first hurdle. Then, it was going to be figuring out where to hide until their ride showed up. He thought about that for a minute and crawled back out of the classroom. Dr. James met him at the door and they walked back to the others.

Ben whispered to Dr. James and Deanna that he had just thought of something important. "If we have to leave, how were we going to tell Dr. James's friend where we are, once we have escaped from the church? If we miss this guy, who knows what will happen to us."

Dr. James thought about it and wondered out loud, "Maybe there is a landline we can use in the church office." He wanted to find out. He told them, "I can try to make a quick phone call and set up a different rendezvous place." The question is, he thought, could he do it quietly enough to avoid being heard from outside the office?

James said, "There is only one way to find out." He asked Ben to keep watch while he tried to make the call. Ben nodded his head yes. Dr. James and Ben made their way back the office and sure enough, there was a land line on Mrs. Moody's desk. James went over and picked up the receiver to check for a dial tone. It sounded good. They likely used it a lot here. Ben was over listening by the door and waved to him that he could go ahead and make the call.

Dr. James dialed the number he had memorized and waited for someone to pick up. As he waited, he watched Ben nervously in case he needed to drop the phone quickly and run. After about four rings, someone picked up the phone and a woman answered. James asked for his friend and she asked who was calling. James gave her the code word he had been given the day before, then she told him she would be right back.

James waited for what seemed an eternity before his friend came on the line. He told him about their predicament and asked, "Do you have a backup plan for coming to get us?"

His friend replied, "I have one but it might be a little difficult for me to get there this time of night."

James didn't care right now. He told his friend, "We need to get out of this church right now and we need a place to go where you can find us."

His friend gave him a place where they could go and James hung up the phone. Ben motioned him over to the door and had him listen. They heard voices again coming from the parking lot and they didn't sound very friendly. Both of them backed away from the door and went back to the others.

Dr. James told everyone, "We're out of time. It is now or never."

They all went to the classroom, got down on their hands and knees to crawl to the windows. Ben peered over a sill again and waited. If he craned his head around to look towards the back of the church, he could see a faint light coming from parking lot. He whispered to them, "I will go out first. Someone hand me the rifle as soon as I hit the ground outside."

Ben reached up and slowly opened the window latch. He was worried it might be old and squeak once he turned it but all he heard was a small rasping noise. Once the latch was open, he grasped the bottom of the window and inched it up until he could crawl through. He knew that this was where he would be the most vulnerable to detection so he crawled out and immediately dropped to the ground next to the wall under the window to stay in the shadows. He waited a minute and when he didn't see anyone, he stood up and asked for the rifle and his back pack.

Once Ben was secure outside, the others helped Stacy get through next. Ben helped her down and told her to get flat on the ground close to the wall to wait for everyone else. The other three worked their way out and James, being the last one out, did his best to close the window behind them without making any noise. Ben stood guard with the rifle pointed towards the back of the church until they were all outside with their gear.

Dr. James pointed across the street as the direction they needed to go but there were street lights to contend with. Ben decided he wanted to have a peek around the back of the building to see who was back there. Deanna shook her head no, emphatically, but Ben was insistent. Deanna reluctantly agreed to let him go. As they waited, Ben hugged the wall and crept back to the rear corner of the church.

As he approached, he could hear voices but they weren't arguing this time. He thought he recognized the ministers voice among them and decided to take a look around the corner. He lay down in the grass with the rifle at his side and poked his head around just enough to see who was talking. He saw Dr. Hammond talking to two men who looked like they were hunters. They were dressed in jeans and hunting clothes as if they had just returned from a deer hunt. Since their weapons were slung and pointed at the ground, Ben decided to pull back to listen to their conversation for a minute.

He listened as Dr. Hammond kept telling them that there was no one in the church and the leader of the two men kept insisting that they needed to check inside. They had heard from someone in town that a group of strangers had been seen heading this way and they had been sent to find them by going from building to building in this part of town.

Dr. Hammond argued quietly, "If you could wait until sunrise, I will be more than happy to let you in for a look around but not at four thirty in the morning."

The man tried to argue a bit more but finally agreed to wait. He told Dr. Hammond that his group wants to maintain good relations with the people of this town and they didn't need the reverend telling everyone that they had ransacked his church in the middle of the night. They would go get some breakfast and be back after sunup.

Ben quickly crawled back from the corner and crouched low at a near run to get back to the others. He waved at them to find a hiding spot quickly. As they all scrambled away from the building and into the bushes around the church, headlights came on in the parking lot. A truck drove out to the street and turned down the other way. They all waited for the tail lights to disappear into the dark before running to the parking lot.

Chapter 20

Waiting to be Rescued

Dr. Hammond was just unlocking the back door when they ran up, startling him badly. As he calmed down, he started to explain but Ben told him, "I already know as I have been listening to you."

Dr. Hammond shook his head and told them all to get inside quickly before anyone else spotted them. Once inside, they all gathered around him and he said, "Go clean up any trace that you have been here as you don't have much time before they return."

Deanna led them all back the to the kitchen and said, "Scrounge around for any kind of travel food and one of you go make sure that window is closed tight and locked again."

They all walked quickly to cupboards and shelves to grab what they could as James stepped out to take care of the window they had crawled out of. They all returned to the dormitory to make sure they hadn't forgotten anything and made the beds to look like no one had been there. Within twenty minutes, everyone was ready to leave.

Dr. Hammond looked out the back door for any other visitors or watchers. When he didn't see anything, he waved them outside. He whispered, "I am sorry that this has happened and I wish you luck and God's blessings." He asked, "Do you have a plan yet?"

James replied "I called my friend and all is arranged, I hope." When the reverend raised his eyebrows, Dr. James told him about the phone call, apologized for using his phone.

Dr. Hammond told him, "Don't worry about it, unless they are tapping my phone lines, which I doubt, no one will know. I don't want to know where you're going for safety reasons and I don't want to have to lie about it either. It's enough that I covered for you tonight." They all smiled a bit over that last remark.

Deanna said, "Let's go."

Dr. James led the way across the church parking lot and looked down the street. They needed to get across the street away from the street lights. As James looked, he saw a place down the street where there were a lot of trees on both sides that blocked the one street light nearby.

As they hurriedly walked across the parking lot, Theresa waved good bye and Dr. Hammond waved back, then headed into his little house. When they reached the trees, James looked around to see if there were any houses nearby or buildings in general. He saw some a little way off with no lights coming from them so he led off across the street at a run and quickly reached the other side with everyone following close behind.

As Dr. James ran across the street into a little patch of woods, he stopped to wait for everyone to catch up. Once they were all across, he started walking through the trees towards the shopping plaza where the Big Lots store was on the other side. Dr. James skirted the parking lot to try and stay out of the street lights then went around to the back of the stores.

He told everyone, "There is supposed to be an empty store on this side of the strip mall that we can hide in, according to my friend, and we are to wait for him there. He will be up to get us as soon as possible later today."

James led them to a rundown looking back door that belonged to a store with a faded sign overhead. He put his ear to the door and waited. When he decided it was relatively safe, he reached down and moved a loose piece of cinder block by the door and found a key, which he then used to unlock the back door. Dr. James motioned for Ben to point the rifle at the door as he entered, just in case.

Once Ben was ready, James slowly opened the door and peered inside. It was very dark so he headed inside to poke around. Ben followed with the rifle at the ready as they tried to maneuver around the back storage area of this long-abandoned store. There were old boxes everywhere and trash on the floors so it was all they could do to walk around without walking into something in the near pitch dark. Dr. James decided that there was nothing in here but rats and they should be safe enough for a few hours as long as they stayed away from the front of the store.

Once everyone was inside, James closed and locked the door from the inside and they settled down to wait. The floor was so dirty that no one wanted to lay down so they pulled up some boxes and an old broken chair and tried to rest. No one felt like talking right now so everyone just kept to themselves while Ben kept watch at the archway leading out to the old sales floor in order to see out of the front windows. He wanted to know when those men returned and to keep a watch for anyone else.

Right after sunrise, Ben said quietly, "They're back."

Deanna and Dr. James stepped up to look around him through the front windows. Sure enough, that same truck pulled back into the church parking lot and the same two men got out. Dr. Hammond came out and greeted them. After they talked briefly, they walked over to the church office door and went in.

Ben looked at Deanna and James, then shrugged. He said "They are definitely the same two men I saw earlier." As there was nothing to see anymore and little they could do for now, Deanna and Dr. James went back to the box they had been sitting on. Ben said "I'll let you know if I see anything else."

It was well past sunrise now and the world outside was starting to light up with the morning sun. Ben stayed off to the side of the archway to keep in the shadows of the back room. He remembered the men telling the reverend that they were checking all buildings in this area for them. As he kept watching, the men came out of the church and stood talking in the parking lot some more before getting back in their truck. Dr. Hammond waited until they left before returning to the church.

Ben crouched low to go out to the front window so he could watch which direction the truck went before reporting back to his friends. He told them, "I don't think the men found any trace of us in the church as it looks like they left without any issue." He mentioned that the minister had gone into the church to maybe double check everything.

Dr. James decided to stretch his legs and told Ben he would stand watch for a little while. "You can go ahead and rest with Stacy."

Everyone was getting a little itchy waiting for their rescuer to show up so Deanna said, "Maybe we should take a breakfast break while we are waiting. That might ease some of the tension." They all grabbed their bags and rummaged around for some cold breakfast food.

As the rest ate, James watched patiently out the front windows. So far, all he had seen were a few store employees from the stores next door coming to work. They looked like restaurant workers coming in early to prep food. Suddenly he had an idea.

Dr. James walked back and asked, "Would anyone like to have a take-out breakfast?" They all looked at him like he was a little crazy. James told them, "One of you can take the orders and quickly go down to one of the restaurants here and bring us something back, I'm buying."

Deanna wanted to know if anything was open this early in the morning and James replied, "I don't know but someone can go look. One person can go without arousing suspicion. Obviously, you will need to keep an eye out for anyone suspicious looking but it is doable. Who wants to go?"

Stacy volunteered to go as long as Ben went with her. Everyone said "no", at the same time. As they realized they had all responded so quickly together, everyone laughed. Deanna said, "It has to be just one of us to avoid problems."

Ben said, "I'll go." He explained, "I can pretend I am part of a work crew since I look the part right now." Stacy pouted a little bit but agreed.

Dr. James told Ben, "Look for any doughnut or coffee shop that might be open. There won't be any Starbucks here but maybe a local mom & pop store you can charm your way into. It would be best not to order anything memorable, just coffee and doughnuts to go." He then gave him a twenty and opened the back door for him.

Ben cracked the door and looked into the alley area before heading out. He carefully walked around the building to the front and looked around the corner at the parking lot for anyone suspicious looking. "So far, so good," he thought. Ben then walked down the sidewalk in front of the stores and looked for a restaurant that might be open. After he walked about four stores down, he saw a sign that read "Mollie's Coffee Shop." Ben walked up to the front door to look inside. This little shop was just what he was looking for. A local coffee shop that catered to working class people. Just what he looked like in his rough looking clothes and unshaved face.

Ben stepped inside and looked around. There were a small handful of people in work clothes sitting or standing around waiting for orders, and a counter area with signs that said, "Order Here," and "Pick Up." He moved off to the side once inside the door and watched for a minute. It was all just an ordinary day and he looked like one of them. He walked up to the counter and placed an order for five coffees and a dozen doughnuts to go. When the young girl asked him what kind of doughnuts he wanted, he replied, "Nothing fancy, give me half dozen plain and the other half dozen with some blueberries in them."

Ben stepped away from the counter to wait. As he stood around, he watched folks pick up their orders and leave. A few other folks sat down at the little tables, drank their coffee and ate their doughnuts while chatting with friends. No one paid Ben much attention, which was good. Pretty soon his order was ready. He paid and left. As he stood just outside the door, he looked around the parking lot again and this time, he noticed a small faded red pickup truck over by the Big Lots store at the end of the strip mall. There were two men inside watching people exit the stores. Ben took note of the make, model and color of the little truck and casually walked back towards the other end of the mall.

He didn't want to just duck around the corner with those two watching so he walked a little slower and kept glancing over his shoulder at them. It looked like they hadn't paid much attention to him so far, so he continued to head towards the last store. By the time he arrived, the truck was still sitting in the same place so Ben quickly ducked around the corner and walked at a near run to the back door of the empty store. He knocked in the prearranged signal and Dr. James cracked the door. Ben pushed through quickly and as he was handing out the coffee and doughnuts, told everyone about the two men in the pickup truck.

He said, "I don't think they noticed me enough to pay me any mind but I can't go back out there without arousing interest."

Deanna thanked him for the coffee and food and said, "If everything goes well, no one will need to go back out anyway." With that, everyone dug into the coffee and doughnuts and ate like it was the best breakfast ever.

By this time, half the morning was gone. Dr. James was still watching the front windows when Ben walked up to describe the little truck.

James said, "I will be on the lookout for it," and just as he said that, the little truck cruised by the windows of the empty store. Ben and James instinctively ducked back out of site and peered around the corner of the window to watch them. It was still dark enough in the store to mask them from sight but they warned everyone to get away from the doors and be quiet.

Dr. James watched the truck roll slowly by as if they were looking for someone. He paid close attention to the man on the passenger side trying to peer into the empty windows as they drove by. The driver turned up a parking lane and parked in a space out in front. As James watched, the man in the passenger side got out, walked over to the front window and peered in. James motioned for absolute quiet and for everyone to remain still. As he turned back to watch, the man walked back to talk to his partner.

Ben's heart rate was double what it had been a few minutes ago. He watched the man walk over and look in the windows. Since he didn't look all that excited, Ben thought the man would just go back and they would move on. When the man went back to talk to his partner, he waited to see what they would do next. As Ben watched, they closed the doors to the truck and walked around to the back of the mall.

James motioned that the two men were headed towards the back. Everyone cleared the door area and tried to find darker areas to hide in. As they waited, they started to hear the men talking and checking door handles. Pretty soon, the door handle to their hiding place rattled. Everyone held their breath until they heard the two men continue on down the line.

As the two men walked down out of hearing range, Deanna whispered, "That was close." She looked at James as if to ask, how soon can we get out of here? James shrugged his shoulders and, whispered, "soon now."

Ben kept watching through the front window and after about twenty minutes, he saw the two men return to their truck and leave. He went back for more doughnuts and told everyone the news. As he went back on watch, doughnuts in hand, he thought about their close calls this morning and he realized just how dangerous this all was. He was just now coming to understand what he and Stacy had gotten themselves into by running away from their families and community. He wondered if this was all worth it? Then he reasoned that it was too late to turn back now. They would just have to tough it out until he and Stacy were finally safe somewhere.

Chapter 21

Off to the Hideout

They waited and waited until the tension was so thick you could cut it with a knife. Just as everyone was starting to get really edgy, a discreet knock was heard at the back door. They were using the knock code Dr. James had been given in that phone call early this morning. James mimed quiet and went to the door. He slowly unlocked it, keeping his foot against the bottom, and cracked it open. His friend quickly said, "Let me in" and James opened the door enough to let him in, then quickly shut and locked the door behind him.

The man looked at everyone and when Dr. James came up beside him, he introduced his friend as Robert, just Robert, no last name for security reasons.

Robert smiled and asked them, "Are you ready to go? There is a 7 passenger SUV outside but we need to go now. We heard on the underground network that the local militia is out in force looking for you in this area." Dr. James confirmed this and told him about their misadventures this morning.

Robert said, "All the more reason to go right now. The SUV is right outside. We should go one at a time and get in as quickly as you can. We will leave as soon as the last one gets out, which will be me." As he watched the front windows, everyone grabbed their gear and started for the car. Theresa was the first one out the back door, and spotted the cream-colored GMC Yukon sitting right in front of her. She ran for the side door and jumped in quickly.

The driver was a youngish looking woman, with short cropped, dark hair who introduced herself as Mona, "Robert's partner in crime," she said with a laugh. Next in was Deanna, soon followed by Ben and Stacy, with Dr. James and Robert jumping in last.

As Robert got in, he told Mona, "Go, but not too fast in case we are being watched around front." This sizable SUV had tinted windows and a powerful engine as they noticed when Mona put it in gear and headed out around the corner of the mall.

When she drove around to the side of the building, she stopped and Robert got out to look at the parking lot. Dr. James had told him about the two men in the little pickup truck and what it looked like. Robert didn't see anything so he returned and they slowly drove down the edge of the parking lot towards the street. Everyone sitting in window seats was looking out for that little truck or anyone else that might be taking an interest in them.

As Mona stopped at the exit from the parking lot, Ben saw the little red truck still sitting in the parking lot over by the Big Lots store. He pointed it out to Mona and Robert as they turned left onto the street. As they watched, the truck didn't seem to notice them and fugitives sighed with relief.

Dr. James asked Robert how things were for him and his family and Robert replied, "All is as good as it can be but we surely missed you and your medical skills. We have had quite a few mishaps and more pregnant refugees have arrived since your last visit so we need you badly." Robert asked Dr. James, "How long will you be able to stay this time?"

Dr. James replied, "As long as you need me for."

With that, James introduced his friends and told him about their adventures, starting with the story about the raid in New York and their trip across the mountains.

When he got around to talking about Ben and Stacy, Stacy interjected and said, "We just want to find a safe place where we can raise a family and help out other people like us." This caught Ben by surprise. He had no idea that Stacy was thinking like that. All he wanted to do was disappear into obscurity to work a farm somewhere safe and take care of his family. He didn't want to get involved with anyone, especially after all that they have been through so far but he kept quiet and let Stacy do the talking, with a mental note to ask her what she was thinking, later when they were by themselves.

As they were talking, Mona was quietly driving through town, maintaining speed limits and keeping a close watch for any possible trouble, like someone following them.

During a quiet moment, Mona said, "I have always been a driver of one kind or another. I am former Army and have driven all kinds of vehicles on deployments and then for Homeland security while I finished my reserve time. That was when I decided that I didn't want anything more to do with the Army and the new government. As soon as I was discharged from the Army, I looked up the underground network and reached out to offer my services. I have been there ever since."

Robert told them, "I have been an activist since before 2024 and now I am considered a domestic terrorist. As a young man, I was a member of a group called Antifa and I participated in a few protests back in the Trump presidency days. After the Republicans won the 2024 election and slowly took apart the old democratic government, I went into hiding and worked with a new group that morphed into this national underground network. My family had helped some but, I mostly kept them separate from my work for safety reasons. The less they knew, the better for them. I have participated in and have been in charge of some pretty dark things through the years but I never wanted my wife and kids to know about any of that."

Mona finally made it out of town and onto the state highway going south. No one from town was following them so far, so she kicked it up to the speed limit and set the cruise control on for a few minutes. She told everyone, "There are some small snacks in the back that you can munch on while we head for home.

At that, Ben reached in the back and grabbed the first bag he could find, bringing it up over the seat back. He placed it on the floor and reached in to see what was there. He pulled out some small sandwiches, water bottles, a handful of cookies and some crackers. Ben let Deanna pass things out as he took some for himself. He thought to himself around bites, "Now things are starting to look up."

While they were eating, Robert explained, "We're not out of the woods just yet. There are still lots of militia soldiers running around out here and we still need to be very careful for quite a few more miles." He warned, "Sometimes they set up road block checkpoints, illegally of course, and a pain in the butt to get through. If we hear about one, we'll try to work something out ahead of time."

Deanna asked, "How will you know ahead of time?"

Robert replied, "We have a special cell phone with us with a special chat app we use to get information about things like that. We also have a regional network of people in three states that pass off intel as we travel around. Anything we learn is passed on to everyone listening in, and continuously updated."

Deanna was impressed. She looked at Dr. James with a new admiration for what he was involved in and his broader network of friends. She had no idea of the scope until now. She had always thought her little group in upstate New York was just a regional network, not part of any national resistance. As she sat there eating a sandwich, she wondered about her future even more. Would James still be interested in staying with her after this? He was obviously more important to the national resistance than she thought. She decided that this would be a conversation for a later time when they were safe.

Theresa dug into the sandwich that Deanna had given her and also pondered her future. All she knew how to do was office administration and women's hair styling, which she had learned on the fly after running away from her abusive boyfriend a couple of years ago. She didn't know if that was even a needed skill anymore. She wanted to learn something new but decided she would wait until she was somewhere safe first before making any decisions about that.

James munched on a sandwich in the middle seats and conversed with his long-time friend. As they talked, Robert brought him up to speed on what had happened since he had last seen him and it sounded like he was going to have his hands full once he got settled in. Robert said there were lots of people needing medical attention, especially pregnant women on the run from the religious arm of Homeland Security.

~

This branch of Homeland Security was responsible for making sure that women seeking abortions were arrested, and doctors performing abortions were punished. The new government had set up an agency to take care of pregnant women who couldn't afford to take care of their babies, plus all of the other religious and political aspects of promoting the birth rate.

Populations around the world have been on the decline for a long time and it's been getting worse every year. Countries are pushing hard for women to have more children but it isn't working and governments are screaming in the news about the fall of mankind if they don't get the birth rate back up above the death levels. The baby boomers from the last century are nearly all gone now and the vacuum in the work force has been a serious issue since the Covid-19 pandemic of 2020.

In the U.S., this had hit the labor markets really hard in the mid-2020's. They lost a huge portion of their population during the years when the baby boomers died off and so many other people opted to immigrate out of the country during the protestant reformation after 2028. This loss caused a major economic recession. All of the non-Christians and a large percentage of the Christians that disagreed with the new government, left the country to immigrate to more religiously tolerant countries, devastating the work force and economy.

Something which the new government has yet to overcome. The more they persecuted the remnants of those non-conformists, the more other countries around the world stopped doing business with the United States over human rights abuses. Now the U.S. is having a lot of trouble paying their debts and people are starving in the more rural areas around the country.

This is what the United States has become now. A land of religious persecution and labor camps, if they were lucky, for any dissidents. For the poor and hungry Citizens, food banks and government shelters were the only sources of food and shelter anymore, unless they went on the run. Which is why there are so many people around the country trying to hide, seeking help and why people like Dr. James are so valuable.

~

All of this was mulling around in their minds as they traveled down the road that afternoon. What is their future going to look like? None of them had ever imagined that they would be forced out of their somewhat, comfortable lives before all of this. Now they were all part of the general dysphoria of displaced peoples trying to escape the national police and a theocratic government.

The large SUV continued down the highway for a couple more hours and the tired fugitives drifted off into cat naps after their small meal. Dr. James stayed awake talking to Robert and Mona, whom he didn't recognize from his last trip up here. She must have joined up after he left a couple of years ago. As they were chatting, Mona suddenly interrupted to let them know that the cell phone just pinged and a message arrived about a road block up ahead.

They were traveling down interstate 89 south right now and almost to the Sutton East exit. According to the message, the checkpoint was located at exit 8 and they had blocked off the highway.

Mona said, "We will have to get off the interstate and go over route 103 west to 114 south to try and get around them and hope they aren't looking for us over there."

In about another mile, they reached exit 9 and Mona turned off to head west. After a few miles, she turned south onto the 114 towards Henniker. With the afternoon shading into evening, Mona kept a real close eye on the road ahead in case of surprises. That, and she had her earbuds in listening for more information about any authorities in the area.

She wasn't in any hurry, just another leisurely drive in the country as far as anyone could see as they drove by. The new plan was to stay on the 114 south until it transitioned into the 77 south and then turn off on the 136 west towards Peterborough. From there they would travel west on the 101 to Keene and then into the mountains to the Pisgah State Park. With Homeland Security out looking for them, she didn't dare attempt state highway 202 west. It likely had checkpoints on it like the interstates also. She thought it best to stay on the rural roads until they reached Keene.

Mona updated Robert and Dr. James as things rapidly changed. With things getting more intense, the others woke up to ask what was going on and Dr. James caught them up on the new developments as Mona focused on the surrounding countryside and the side roads they were passing.

It was getting harder to get more information from their sources as they continued through the countryside. No one was out scouting this part of their route so Robert and Mona did their best to keep a lookout for anything out of place as they kept moving south and west. The reports kept coming in about the checkpoint on interstate 89 and, now a possible report of one on state highway 202. Mona was glad she opted out of that route way in advance. Now all they had to worry about was a random local cop stopping them for something, anything at all, and radioing it in.

They reached the 101 west in the early evening and there was a little more traffic. Mona stayed clear of any other vehicles, staying just under the speed limits, not getting too close and not letting anyone else get too close. Mona was getting tired from the stress of trying to maintain a safe distance between their car and everyone else without looking suspicious. Robert didn't want anyone getting too close to be able to see inside their car, even with the tinted windows.

Dr. James kept watch from the side window where he was sitting and now, everyone else was awake and looking out the windows as well, especially behind them.

So far, they had seen nothing but commercial trucks and commuters. No one that looked like they were giving them any additional attention other than a cursory glance as they passed by. Mona made sure to stay in the slow lane, when there were two lanes, and to maintain whatever speed everyone else seemed to be doing to keep a low profile. There had been one car who had gotten stuck behind her and beeped their horn at her. They sped out from behind her when an opening occurred. Everyone watched nervously as the car sped down the highway in front of them.

They finally arrived in Keene and Mona mixed with the traffic going through town. Now they had to really watch for any authorities that may be parked on any of the side streets and roads. This wasn't a large city but Robert was sure that the word was out, even over here. Robert commented, "There's likely a multi-state search going on for you guys by now so we need to get up into our mountain retreat as quickly as possible and lay low for a few days."

"Out of sight, out of mind," he quipped.

Robert continued, "Eventually the search will dwindle and fade away like they usually do and Dr. James will be back in his former status, although," Robert turned in his seat to look at Deanna and Theresa, "You two apparently, have become wanted fugitives as well for some reason," he said with a grin.

"It's nice to be famous," Deanna replied sarcastically.

Mona finally made it through town traveling a few more miles south before turning off. She headed west before turning on another road that led up to a very narrow country road going up to a mountain top. Deanna could see the mountains ahead in the moonlight and wondered what kind of accommodations they might expect from folks likely living off the grid up here.

Chapter 22

Refuge?

 Robert told them, "This is the last leg of the trip. We're headed up to an old ski resort that has been closed down for years called Crotched Mountain, that we moved in to and took over. This place closed down due to lack of snow and not enough money to make their own snow anymore. There just weren't enough people with spare money to throw away on ski vacations after the crash, much like the rest of the vacation and tourism industry in the country."

Mona kept going up the mountain and soon, they arrived at a small resort town that had seen better days. It was apparent that this had once been a thriving little resort village once. Now, it was dark and gray, with buildings looking sad and forlorn. There were no people about but there were a handful of lights on in some of the buildings. Nothing bright, as if they were using lanterns and candles.

Mona pulled the car up under the overhang in front of an old hotel and stopped. She stayed seated and listened to her cell phone for a minute and when she looked at Robert, she said, "Homeland Security has put out an all-points bulletin on three of our passengers, two whom have been identified as Deanna and Theresa, traveling with an unknown dark-skinned male."

Robert barked, "Everyone out and into the hotel now." He explained, "Sometimes they fly helicopters over this mountain. As far as everyone in this area is concerned, this is a ghost town and I mean to keep it that way. This car will be a liability if it's seen from the air."

Once everyone was standing inside the doors with their packs, and Ben carrying the rifle, Robert led them towards the front lobby area and then down a hallway to an old banquet room. He told everyone, "Make yourselves at home and I'll be right back." He asked Dr. James "Come with me please" in a low voice as he looked at the others.

When they left, Deanna turned around and looked at Theresa with a slight smile, "How does it feel to be a wanted fugitive?"

Theresa looked terrified with all of these new revelations and asked, "What's the plan now?" After being involved with the refugee network in New York, she knew what would likely happen to them if they got caught. They would probably be made to 'disappear' like so many others she had heard about.

Deanna was also worried and wasn't sure about trusting their new benefactors just yet. They seemed nice enough but there was something a little off. Maybe it was just nerves but she had learned to trust her gut instincts before, it had saved her from trouble then, and now, she was getting that strange 'Spidey Sense' again. Deanna looked over at Ben and Stacy and asked, "How are you guys doing?

Stacy replied, "I'm a little scared right now" and Ben just glowered at her with a narrow-eyed expression. Deanna noticed that he had the rifle pulled around to his lap now and that was how she knew how nervous he was. She tried to reassure everyone that things were going to be fine but it sounded hollow.

After a few quiet moments, Deanna said, "I think I want to go check things out instead of sitting around waiting for a squad of storm troopers to come through the doors." She stepped over to the door and Ben stood up to come with her. She explained, "All I want to do is take a look through the doors and if we don't see anything, go out and check the lobby area."

Ben said in a low voice, "I'll come with you in case of trouble."

She opened the doors and looked down the hallway, then looked out towards the lobby. She didn't hear anything so they ventured out to look around. She went behind the front counter first, but there was nothing but empty shelves and dust. The cupboards behind them were also empty. They walked out to the lobby and checked around the chairs and little tables for clues about who their hosts might be. They walked around to the elevators and stairs going up. There were no lights on at the elevators so they apparently were not being used. The stairway looked like it had been used recently though.

Deanna and Ben returned to the conference room to check on Theresa and Stacy. Just as they sat down, Robert and Dr. James returned. Robert told everyone that accommodations in this old hotel had been set up. "If you will please follow me, I will take you to your rooms."

They all looked at each other and hesitated at which Dr. James spoke up and said, "It's okay, there is nothing or anyone to be afraid of. This is a very safe place."

Deanna got up thinking, "I need to trust someone and James hasn't let me down yet. Maybe things will be okay for now." When she walked over to James, the rest followed and Robert led them over to some stairs at the end of the hallway. He took them up to the third floor and gave each of them a room key, telling them, "Go get settled in and cleaned up. Someone will be up shortly to get you when dinner is ready."

When they all started to split up to find their rooms, Deanna looked at James and asked, "Which one is yours?"

James looked back, smiled at her and said, "These rooms probably have queen sized beds, do you want to share a room with me?"

That was all she needed to hear. She melted into his arms and kissed him there in the hallway before following him to his room a couple doors down. Ben and Stacy turned away, feeling a little embarrassed, as they found their room and went inside.

Theresa also turned away feeling a little envious. She felt all alone and started thinking about her future again. She was pretty sure Deanna and Dr. James wouldn't just abandon her here but she couldn't help but feel scared now that she was a wanted fugitive. She found her room and decided to watch and see how things went at dinner tonight in case she needed to make any changes to her plans.

Ben and Stacy were married and now that it looked like Dr. James and Deanna were a couple. She wondered if that was going to change the dynamics between them as she locked her door and prepared to take a long, hot shower for the first time since they had left the resort in Vermont, in what seemed like an eternity ago.

About an hour after Robert had left them to settle in, a young man went around knocking on their doors informing everyone that dinner was waiting for them in the banquet room downstairs. They all responded and said they would be down momentarily.

The young man waited at the end of the hallway leading downstairs until they all came out looking for him. Ben and Stacy came out of their room last and they all followed the young man down to the banquet room. Someone had set up a couple of tables with paper plates, cups and disposable cutlery on one end of a table with a handful of trays with sandwiches and soup on the other end. Condiments were at the other table for anyone who wanted anything.

They all got in line and started to serve themselves. Deanna remarked sarcastically, "At least they aren't planning on starving us for now." Dr. James looked at her sideways but remained quiet. No one else paid her any attention as they walked down the table filling their plates.

Once everyone sat down and started to eat, Robert came back in and asked, "Did everyone find everything all right in their rooms? How is the food? I am sorry but it is the best we can do this late and on short notice. Tomorrow will be better, I promise," he said with a smile. He looked more like a hotel concierge instead of the leader of a regional network of domestic terrorists.

Deanna replied, "Everything is fine. We're just happy to be here after everything that's happened in the last couple of weeks." Ben, Stacy and Theresa nodded in agreement and kept on eating. James stared at Deanna a little longer as if pondering something, then went back to his food.

As he continued to eat, James started thinking about Deanna's sarcastic remarks about their hosts and hospitality. "Have I placed my trust in someone that might have issues with my friend?" He thought that this might bear some more scrutiny before he made anymore commitments to her going forward.

When everyone had finished eating, they cleaned up and sat down to talk about their plans for the future. Dr. James already knew what his plans were so he kept quiet and let everyone else talk.

Ben and Stacy, again, talked about how they wanted to find a farm to buy, once they had enough money put together.

Theresa said, "I'm not sure what I want to do now that my old life is gone. I need to find something different in order to feel needed again. I need a purpose."

Deanna also didn't have much to say as she was waiting to have a one on one with James before she made any decisions. As they talked a little more, a couple of young men came in to clean up. They decided it was time to head for bed. As they all went upstairs to their rooms, it was all "good nights" and "sleep tights" as they went into their rooms.

When James and Deanna entered their room, she said, "I need to talk to you."

 James looked at her and replied, "All right, I need to ask you about some things as well. You go first."

Deanna sat down in a chair and told him to sit also. "She is looking pretty serious," he thought. "That can't be good."

Deanna asked, "What are your immediate plans while we are here?"

 James sat there for a minute and said, "My plans are to provide whatever medical assistance is needed here and gather intelligence for my trip south. I don't know how long that will take but I don't want to take too long as I am worried about my sisters in that camp."

She looked at him and said, "Does that include me in any way? I need to know where I stand in your plans to rescue your sisters."

James replied, "You are welcome to stay with me for as long as you wish, provided I can count on your support for my work and plans to go to Virginia. I am a little concerned about your feelings towards my friends here though. Is there something bothering you that you wish to tell me?"

Deanna looked at him again and with a straight face, told him about her feeling that something wasn't right since getting in the car with his friend Robert. She explained, "This instinct for trouble has gotten me out of scrapes in the past and I have learned not to ignore it. I can sense it right now and I want to know what you think."

James was taken aback. He knew all about gut instinct and sixth sense intuitions when it came to dangerous situations. He had felt similar instincts in the past that had warned him of impending danger.

James asked, "Do you have any idea what may be bringing on your sense of something wrong?"

Deanna replied, "Not yet, just a strong feeling so far. How well do you trust Robert after being gone for so long," she asked?

James thought for a minute and told her, "I used to think I could trust Robert with my life but I did notice a subtle change today. I didn't think much about it until just now. I guess I was too caught up in trying to reach this place without getting caught that I ignored my own instincts."

Deanna smiled, "I get it, really, I do. You've known this friend for a long time and it's easy to slip back into old comraderies like you've only been gone a short time. I have been there but we need to pay attention to our instincts and not get complacent for one minute. We have a couple of other people we have taken some responsibility for now and we have to honor that."

James sat there for another minute then grinned, "I knew there was something about you that made you different from anyone I have ever been with before. Now I figured out what it is. You are my other half, my voice of reason. That, and you make a great survival partner" He laughed, then leaned over and kissed her softly.

Deanna held him and said, "I think I could fall in love with you Dr. Naismith. Why don't we go to bed and talk about it some more," she said with a low, sexy voice.

James didn't need an engraved invitation. He started taking off his clothes, following her into the bedroom. He would worry about the shadowy things tomorrow. Tonight, it was all about being with Deanna, whom he also thought he was falling in love with.

Chapter 23

The Masks Come Off

The next morning, with bright sunshine coming through the windows, everyone started drifting downstairs for breakfast and whatever else the day was going to bring. James and Deanna came down to find Theresa already there with a cup of coffee from one of the urns on the table.

Once again, the meal was buffet style in trays on the table and everyone was to help themselves. Deanna walked over, grabbed a plate and utensils, plastic of course, and passed a plate to James. As they were putting food on their plates, Theresa watched with envious eyes and waited for them so sit down.

Once they had their food, James and Deanna sat down across the table from her and started to eat. In between mouthfuls, James asked Theresa, "Did you sleep well last night?"

Theresa nodded and kept sipping her coffee. Staring at them for a minute or two without responding. When Deanna looked up with a "Are you okay" look on her face, Theresa started to say something when Ben and Stacy moseyed in and started to fill their plates. Theresa let it go, with a narrow-eyed look, as she watched Ben and Stacy serve themselves.

 When the newlyweds came over and sat down, Stacy noticed the quiet tension in the group at the table and asked, "Is everything all right?"

Deanna looked back at Theresa and said, "I think so" and returned to her meal.

Ben sat down and dug in, not caring about any of the drama. All he cared about today was to try and get set up with new identity papers, then finding a place to move on to as soon as possible. He was anxious to leave the fugitive life behind so he could set up a normal life with Stacy without looking over his shoulder all the time.

Stacy looked at them for a moment longer and settled in to her breakfast. She also started thinking about how fast could they leave and start a clean life somewhere safe. She would follow Ben's lead but she had already decided that maybe it was time to put a little distance between them and their new 'friends'.

As everyone continued eating and Theresa continuing to sip her coffee, the silence became a little thick at the table until Dr. James decided to break the tension, if he could. He stated to everyone, "I'll be working at the little clinic here for quite a bit of my time today and I will be largely unavailable until my patient load gets caught up."

Deanna already knew this because they had talked about it last night. But for the other three, it sounded like this may be where they would part company. Theresa was still thinking about what she wanted to do and wanted to ask Robert about her options, either here or somewhere else, safe from the authorities.

With a bounty on her head, she had fewer options than Ben and Stacy and she didn't want to endanger them. The only things she knew how to do, was being a hairdresser or a secretary. Something she learned when she lived in New York City so long ago. Neither skill had any appeal to her anymore. She wanted to do something she was passionate about, which was helping people.

Theresa knew that she couldn't pursue that idea staying with Dr. James and Deanna as they were going to be heading south after the doctor was finished here and she didn't want to live under the threat of danger anymore. The best time of her life was when she had been helping refugees get over the Canadian border or bringing up others from the city who were on the run.

Theresa wanted to ask Robert if there were any small groups in this part of New England she could join, like the one she had been a part of in upstate New York, but she was afraid to ask on her own. She needed Dr. James to recommend her but she was afraid to ask now.

While she was deep in her thoughts about this, Deanna finished her breakfast and sat, sipping her coffee. She couldn't stand it anymore and decided to make a more direct approach to find out what was bothering her. She looked at Theresa and asked, "Theresa, will you go for a walk with me? I need some female company this morning to sort some things out."

Theresa looked up with a stunned look and hesitated for a minute before answering, "Okay," in a low voice.

Deanna looked at James and said, "We will be back in a little while. Go do what you need to do and I will catch up with you later." With that, she grabbed her breakfast dishes to put in the trash and waited for Theresa to catch up.

When both women were ready, they went out into the lobby to look around for a moment. Deanna said, "I want to take a walk outside in the daylight to get a good look around. Are you okay with that?"

Theresa nodded "yes" and they walked out the front door of the hotel into bright sunshine.

Deanna shaded her eyes and turned around in a circle to look at the resort area they were now living in. All she could see was the front of the hotel and some small buildings across and down the street that looked like they used to be retail store fronts. They were shabby and looked like they may have been converted into living quarters of some kind.

There were no signs anywhere or any sign of life. No people walking around like you would see in any other small village. Almost like a ghost town. Deanna looked back at Theresa and motioned for her to follow as she headed down the small street towards a larger building at the edge of this old ski village.

As they walked side by side, Deanna asked Theresa, "What is bothering you? We have been friends for a long time so you can tell me."

Theresa thought for a minute and told her what she had been thinking about. As Deanna listened, she knew how important this was so she kept quiet until Theresa finished.

Deanna stopped walking and grabbed Theresa by the hand. As she looked directly into Theresa's eyes, she told her, "I'm proud of you for everything you've been through without bailing on me along the way so I will do whatever I need to do for you to see that you're happy. You deserve that much and more." With that, Deanna gave Theresa a big hug and held it for a minute.

Theresa wasn't expecting that so she stood there for a minute with her eyes starting to tear up. She didn't know Deanna thought that of her until now and it changed how she felt about Deanna in her heart. When she saw how Dr. James and Deanna had hooked up back on the trail, Theresa felt sure that she would be left to fend for herself once they reached relative safety. Now she knew different and felt a little ashamed for thinking like that in the first place.

No one had ever treated her like family before and this caught her by surprise. When she was growing up, her childhood hadn't been too good. Her parents struggled to make ends meet and Theresa and her siblings were more of an afterthought than children. They were barely provided for and beaten for the slightest reasons or sometimes, for no reason at all that they could figure out.

Theresa ran away as soon as she was legal and never looked back. She had found a job in a fast-food place and enrolled in a tech college, where she learned how to work in an office. Although sometimes she wondered about her siblings and how they were doing. She didn't even know if any of them were still alive after all this time.

When Theresa wiped her eyes, Deanna felt a little wet around hers as well and smiled. Without another word, they trekked up the street towards the big building. As they arrived out front, Deanna could see movement inside through the front door so she pushed the door open and walked inside.

After they entered, they could see people moving about that they hadn't seen before. Deanna motioned for Theresa to follow closely and proceeded to look around. As they looked into the side rooms off the hallway, there were people using communications devices, looking at maps, reading papers and looking at computer screens.

No one bothered to look up as they walked past as if Deanna and Theresa belonged there. Near the end of the hallway, as they neared a corner, a young woman came bustling around and nearly walked into them while looking down at an iPad.

She looked up when nearly bumping into Deanna, letting out yelp in surprise. Ruth said, "I'm so sorry" then looked up again when she realized who she had nearly run into. Ruth stepped back and asked, "Who are you and what are you doing here? You don't belong here. You need to leave immediately," in a loud voice meant to get attention.

Deanna and Theresa stood there not sure what to do for a minute, then Deanna tried to introduce themselves. Ruth wasn't having any of that. As far as she was concerned, they were trespassers and needed to leave now. With all of the commotion in the hallway, people started to come out of their offices to see what all the noise was about.

At that point, Robert came out of a back office and made his way to the front of the crowd. As he approached the two so-called trespassers, he reached out and grabbed Deanna's hand to shake it and asked, "What are you doing here?

Deanna explained, "We were out for a stroll after breakfast and wanted to look around a bit. Then we saw this place and I decided to check it out. We didn't mean to trespass but there were no signs saying otherwise."

Robert smiled and replied, "You are welcome here but you strolled in at a busy time and there is no one available to show you around right now. Maybe if you came back a little later? I can come down at get you when I have a little free time, if you like?"

Deanna looked at him and smiled, "That'll be fine, we'll wait to hear from you. If it's okay, we'll just head back down and try to stay out of trouble."

Robert smiled again and said, "No problem, I'll see you later" and turned around to head back to his office, as if they had interrupted something very important.

When Robert left, everyone else went back to their offices and Ruth stood there looking a little embarrassed. She started to apologize and Deanna told her not to worry about it, they were just leaving. Deanna turned around and headed out the front door to go back down to the hotel. As they were walking back, Deanna waited until they were a little way from the building before asking Theresa, 'Did you think that was a little odd?"

Theresa replied in a soft voice, "Yeah, that was a little spooky. I wonder what they're hiding?"

Deanna said, "Yeah, I wonder about that too." They walked down the street at a brisk pace, anxious to inform the others of their encounter. As they entered the hotel, they could hear loud voices coming from the banquet room where they had been eating. It sounded like some people arguing so Deanna and Theresa nearly broke into a run to see what all the noise was about.

As they entered the room, they found Ben and Stacy standing near the serving table arguing with a young man from Robert's people. Deeanna saw that Ben was holding the rifle at the ready. Stacy was red in the face and livid about something. As Deanna and Theresa walked up, the young man stopped yelling and stepped back. Deanna asked, "What's this all about?"

Stacy pointed at the young man and said, "He came in here and demanded that Ben give him the rifle because it's against their rules for guests to carry a weapon around here and Ben said no."

Ben spoke up, "I am not giving this up to someone I don't know just because he says so. I'll unload it and carry the mag with me but that's as far as I am willing to go here. If he wants to fight me for it, bring it on."

Deanna looked at the young man in question and asked him, "Who are you?"

He replied, "My name is Steve and I am in charge of security here. This man is breaking our rules and he must obey them for everyone's safety. I demand that he turn over that rifle and ammunition to me or I'll bring more people in and we'll take it from him." Steve stood there looking at everyone with a menacing look as if to dare them to defy him.

Ben looked like he was getting ready to point the rifle at him at any moment and Deanna didn't need to start a war, especially since they just got here. She walked over next to Ben, with Theresa following. They stood there looking back at this 'Steve' who came across as so high and mighty. Deanna thought about it for a minute, trying to come up with a solution that would work for all parties here.

Finally, she asked Ben, "What would make you comfortable here with regard to that rifle and ammunition?"

Ben replied, without taking his eye off Steve, "I'm okay with leaving it in our room while we come down to eat or if we need to go to another building while we are here but I won't let any strangers just come in here and try to confiscate it by force. I don't tolerate bullies."

Deanna looked over at Steve and asked, "Will that work for you or are we going to start a war here and someone gets hurt?"

Steve glowered at Ben and said, "Let me check with the higher ups and I'll be back with an answer ASAP. Meanwhile, you stay here until I get back or else." Steve turned around and marched out ramrod stiff.

Ben looked at Deanna and Theresa and said, "Thank you, I was getting ready to shoot him when you walked in." Theresa walked over and put her arm around Stacy's shoulders as they waited.

 Deanna knew that Steve would probably return soon with reinforcements so she turned to Ben and asked him to go put that rifle in his room before they returned so it would be out of sight and out of mind for now until they sorted this out. Ben looked at Stacy and she nodded her head "yes." Ben hurried out to put the rifle away and get back as quickly as possible. He wasn't about to leave Stacy alone for one minute with all that was going on.

While everyone else was waiting, Theresa asked Stacy, "Are you alright?"

Stacy replied, "I'm okay, I'm just afraid of Ben losing his temper and someone getting hurt. Ben is very protective and not afraid to fight anyone. I know he will protect me with his life and that is what I am most afraid of. I don't want to lose him," and she started to cry a little as Theresa kept holding her.

Theresa was getting a bad feeling about this place but wanted to wait until she had a chance to talk to Deanna after things calmed down. She was also concerned that Dr. James might not be very objective when it came to his old friends and wondered how that might play out going forward.

Deanna's "Spidey Sense" was going off the charts now as she tried to wait patiently for Ben to return. She was dreading the next confrontation with Steve and whomever he brought back with him. She desperately needed some guidance from James but he was at the clinic and probably had no idea what was going on here right now. All she could do was wait and think of some way to diffuse this situation before it escalated even more.

Within minutes, Ben returned without the rifle and told Deanna, "I hid it somewhere where only I know where it is because they likely have a master key to our rooms. They could threaten us at gunpoint in order to retrieve the rifle from our room. I'm not taking any chances with these people. They're coming off as no different than the local militias up north."

After about another fifteen minutes, Steve returned, this time with four more 'soldiers' and they were armed this time. Then Robert followed them into the room but he wasn't smiling this time. He looked at Ben and then at Deanna for a minute, shook his head and asked, "Where's the rifle?"

Deanna just looked at him without replying. Ben stood his ground next to Stacy, putting her in behind him.

Robert looked at Steve and growled, "Go find it."

As Steve approached Ben, the other three militia members took out their pistols and pointed them at the group. Ben stood up straighter and got a look on his face that said, "come on, come get me." Steve came up and walked around the group looking for the rifle, then asked Ben, "Where is it? The more you hold out, the worse it will be for all of you. We don't hold with strangers doing as they please here, especially if it endangers us in any way."

Ben just stood there and kept quiet, trying to shield Stacy as best as he could. Robert shook his head once more and told them, "I have to maintain a strict no tolerance policy for everyone here because of the danger we are all in. This is due to the valuable resistance work we do. Everyone has to obey the rules, no exceptions. Please give us the rifle and I promise I will make sure it is well taken care of. You can have it back when you leave."

Ben looked down at Deanna as if to ask, "Now what do we do?"

Deanna couldn't see any way out of this safely so she whispered to Ben, "Go ahead and give it to them because we aren't being given any choice. We don't want any bloodshed. We don't have anything else to fight back with and I don't know enough about them to judge whether they would cut us down or put us in a cell somewhere."

Ben held his hands up and walked slowly upstairs to retrieve the rifle and magazine he had stashed. As they all waited, two of the soldiers moved out to the hallway with weapons at the ready to wait for Ben to return. The others all watched Deanna's group for any sign of resistance with a look of anxiety as if looking for any excuse to shoot. Robert just stood off to the side trying to stay out of the line of fire.

Pretty soon, Ben came down the stairs holding the rifle out in front of himself with the magazine in his other hand. The two soldiers in the hallway roughly grabbed them and pushed him back into the room, where he returned to Stacy again. As Deanna watched all of this unfold, she was watching Robert's body language the whole time. It soon became obvious that this was not the man whom James talked about so fondly before they arrived here nor the jovial friend in the car on the way here.

Now she started to worry about James, wondering if he was all right. She wondered if he was being held under duress as he took care of the waiting patients supposedly stacked up waiting for him, or was it all a lie?

Chapter 24

The Trap

Dr. James left the banquet room soon after Deanna and Theresa went out for their walk. He thought he knew where the clinic was from his previous trip here so he headed over there with his backpack. As he walked, he thought about last night and smiled in remembrance of their love making and discussions of their future together. He couldn't be happier right now as he sauntered up the street towards a building behind the hotel.

When he arrived, Dr. James was greeted as if he were a long-lost relative returning home and was quickly introduced to the little medical team at this clinic. The nurse practitioner who met him at the door was the same woman with whom he had worked with the last time he had been here so they started catching up right away. As they walked and chatted, James noticed that the other staff looked nervous but he became distracted by his old friend's blissful chatter and dismissed it as paranoia.

 As they arrived at a treatment room, Dr. James was ushered inside and asked to wait for his first patient. His friend, Tracy, said she would bring him in. Dr. James walked in and as soon as he sat down, Tracy left, closing the door behind her, which he thought was odd. There were no medical records or charts waiting for him in this office either. Dr. James decided not to break out all of his medical supplies just yet because he was starting to feel uneasy. After a couple of minutes, Tracy escorted a patient in and asked the man to sit down.

He was dressed in a woodlands camo uniform that had seen better days and had what looked like a bullet wound. He had a large bandage on his thigh that was full of blood and he was in obvious pain. Dr. James looked at Tracy for a half minute and asked to see her out in the hallway.

As soon as they stepped out, he asked, "What the hell is this? Where are the female patients waiting for my OBGYN skills?"

Tracy's face quickly hardened and she replied, "There aren't any. We're at war here. We have battle wounded that need a doctor and you're it. If you don't treat them, I'll call the guards and they'll force you to. Don't bother calling Robert," she said with a sneer, "this is all his idea. So, get in there and get to work, doctor," she said with emphasis on the word doctor.

Dr. James was aghast at what she said. He didn't know what to say for the moment so he walked back into the treatment room and looked at the man's wound. It was infected from not being treated right away so he set about sterilizing the wound and stitching up what was obviously a bullet hole.

As he was taking care of one battle wound after another, from bullets to shrapnel wounds, and other lesser medical issues, he thought about his situation and how to get out of here. He also wondered how the rest of his group was doing. Where they all right? Where they being held against their will, like he was?

After what seemed like hours, nurse Tracy returned again, this time without another patient. She remarked as she entered, "Good job doctor, you've taken care of the worst of the wounded we have for now. You can take an escorted bathroom break and eat a little lunch before the next round of patients this afternoon." Dr. James stood up from the chair and looked out to see an armed guard waiting for him in the hallway. Tracy stepped out and the guard stepped in with his hand on his pistol.

As Dr. James walked down the hallway to the bathroom, he now understood why the staff had seemed so nervous this morning when he'd arrived. It seemed that everyone he knew here had changed attitudes since his last visit and they were in war mode. Against the current government? Likely so, but with such an all-out war footing? That didn't seem like the same Robert he knew from before. While he was thinking, he tried to look around without being too obvious.

Dr. James was now in survival mode and looking for anything that would help him escape this madness.

He noticed that his guard looked like a seasoned veteran and realized that he would have to be very careful not to make any sudden moves. James also didn't see any other staff around as they walked down the hall. They probably had been ordered to greet him to give him a false sense of complacency so Tracy could lull him into thinking it was like old times. James had to admit, it had worked. He'd had that one moment of doubt that got swept away by Tracy's lies when he walked into the clinic this morning.

After his bathroom break, the guard walked him down to an empty lunchroom where nurse Tracy was waiting with a sandwich and a bottle of water. She had set them down on a table in the middle of the room where the guard could watch him with a good field of fire if James tried anything. Dr. James sat down and ate his lunch while watching the guard. Tracy left as soon as he walked over to the table without so much as a word.

Dr. James really did feel like a prisoner now and wondered how long this was going to last. More to the point, what was going to happen to all of them when they were no longer needed? For himself, his medical skills would likely keep him in bondage until they didn't need him anymore. As for Deanna and the rest, they're excess baggage and likely in duress much like he is at the moment.

Would Robert execute them as traitors or prisoners of war? He needed to get out of here and find out. There wasn't much he could do right now with this guard watching his every move but, he would keep a sharp eye on every little detail the rest of the day to see if there were any cracks in this prison.

After he had slowly eaten his sandwich and finished his water, the guard gestured and told Dr. James, "Let's go, time to get back to work." They went back to the same treatment room as before and the afternoon disappeared in a haze of minor medical issues from the people in the local village here. It seemed that everyone here was on a war footing based on the attitudes of his patients. Some were afraid and had been that way for a while. Others were defiant and ready to fight an enemy, any enemy, treating Dr. James like a captured prisoner of war.

When the day was over, nurse Tracy came in and sneered at Dr. James, telling him, "It's time for you to be escorted to your cell for the night," she said sarcastically. Dr. James asked, "What happened to you and everyone else since the last time I was here? Why am I a prisoner now?"

Tracy looked at him with contempt and replied, "We are nearly isolated on this mountain now because of people like you who get to wander around the country free as a bird. We have vowed to go down fighting since they killed Robert's family a couple of years ago, right after you the left the last time. Robert blames you for their deaths, thinking that you gave him away to the feds. Your friends are being held as insurance against your life as long as you behave and take care of our current medical needs. After that, Robert will decide what to do with all of you.

Oh, by the way, he tends to execute prisoners when caught because we can't afford to feed them," she said laughing cruelly as she stepped out to let the guard escort him to the hotel.

Dr. James decided that escape from here was paramount to anything else right now. He knew that he had no way to prove his innocence to his one-time friend so he wasn't going to try. As he waited to be escorted to the hotel, he once again wondered if Deanna and their companions were all right or had they been hurt.

His guard stepped in as he grabbed his backpack to head out. The guard insisted on inspecting the bag before they left so Dr. James handed it over. There was nothing in it except medical supplies and some personal items so it didn't take long to go through it before he handed it back.

It was late afternoon when they stepped out of the clinic. The sun was low on the mountains that surrounded this former resort area. Dr. James walked towards the hotel with his guard just behind him cradling a rifle loosely in his arms. The sling over his shoulder so he could pull it up in a second. They quietly walked down the street to the hotel.

As they walked through the doors and across the lobby to the banquet room, James saw the first militia member standing guard at the door. He figured the others must be inside standing guard. Sure enough, when he hesitated, his escort gave him a push through the door, telling him "Go sit down with the others."

Deanna and the rest of their group had been in here all day under guard since the confrontation that morning. As James walked in, Deanna stood up quickly, startling the guard who raised his rifle towards her in response. As she looked at him, she scowled, "What are you so afraid of? We're pretty defenseless and no threat anymore, so back off and let me have a moment with Dr. James." The young man stood down and walked over by the door to talk to the other guards.

Deanna gave James a hug and whispered, "Are you alright? We heard from your 'friend' Robert," she said his name sarcastically and spit on the floor, "that they pretty much kidnapped you this morning."

 James replied softly, "Yes, they deceived me this morning. The nurse I worked with last time I was here, who had been very nice to work with before, now hates my guts for something they think I did after I left them last time."

Deanna stepped back and looked at him for a moment, "That explains things a little bit. I wondered why Robert was so hostile this morning after you left. He was a regular Dr. Jekyll and Mr. Hyde with us here. So, what's our status at the moment?"

Dr. James looked back at the guards but they looked just looked like any other bored guards at the moment. He put his hand on Deanna's lower back and ushered her closer to the table where everyone else was sitting. As they looked at him, Dr. James softly explained their current situation without telling them what nurse Tracy told him regarding Robert's late family members. When he finished talking, Stacy asked, "Are we hostages now?"

Dr. James replied, "Yes, your insurance for the moment to prevent me from trying to escape or hurt anyone while I administer to their medical needs. I don't know any more than that right now. There are guards everywhere here. We will likely be locked in our rooms every night from now on and be escorted everywhere we go until Robert decides what to do with us."

Ben had a look of simmering anger on his face as he listened and wished he had been able to stash that rifle somewhere before all of this but he knew that they weren't left with much of a choice. They had walked willingly into an elaborate trap and he didn't see much leeway for any escape attempts yet. But he would be looking hard for a way out every moment he could.

Dr. James looked back at the two guards at the door and noticed that only one of them looked like a veteran. The other young man was nervous and looked like he would rather be somewhere else. Neither one of them was over twenty-five, and the one who was always looking around nervously looked like he was only eighteen or nineteen at best. Dr. James was more worried about him than the seasoned guard as this kid would be the most likely to shoot out of fear.

James sat down next to Ben and asked in a whisper, "Have you seen anything we can use to help us get out of here?" Suddenly, the young guard shouted, "shut up, no talking."

They all looked at the young man and the older guard said, "Chillout man, they aren't going anywhere. Relax, the old man will be here soon and you can head out, okay?" The younger man looked angry at being admonished in front of the 'prisoners' as he thought of them so he turned away angrily to walk out into the hall.

The older guard took up his post inside the door again and stared at the group at the table as if to dare them to say anything to him. As he glared at them, Dr. James returned his attention to Ben and asked him again, in a whispered voice, "Have you had a chance to notice anything that might help us?"

Since the table was halfway across the room, his voice would have been just a mumble to the guard at the door and he didn't seem to concerned. This guard appeared a bit arrogant and maybe a little too confident, Ben noticed.

They sat discussing options for about another half hour when Robert returned. As he entered the lobby, the youngest guard came back in the banquet room as if he expected everyone to stand up to attention when their leader entered. The two guards came to attention as Robert entered, which he seemed not to notice. He focused his hate filled gaze directly on Dr. James, walking up to within a couple feet of the table.

"I see you all are getting comfortable with your new status here today. I am not sorry I tricked you all but, I will admit, I was only after the good doctor. I couldn't very well just grab him without arousing your attention and I didn't have time to deal with all of you up north. Nor could I avoid unwanted attention in a snatch and grab, so, here you all are. As you have likely been told by Dr. James, I am using you as hostages to keep him from doing something stupid. I expect everyone to behave or you will be shot. Since you are all on the fugitive list, if you disappear, no one will care."

"We are being actively hunted by Homeland Security for our rebellious activities and they have pretty much shut off all of our supply lines now. We have some stores saved here but there is not enough for everyone for a prolonged period. We are making plans to escape but we needed a skilled doctor to get our wounded well enough to travel. And lo and behold, just as I was thinking we weren't going to be able to get them out, who should call out of the blue, but my old friend Dr. James" he said sarcastically. "How fortuitous for us here."

Robert looked directly at Dr. James and said angrily, "We have unfinished business, you and I, but first, I need you in your medical capacity. Rest assured; we will get to that once you have all of my people patched up well enough to travel."

 "Tonight, you will be fed here like before and then locked in your rooms with guards at each end of the hallway to make sure everyone behaves. This will be your life for now until I figure out what to do with you once we are ready to get out of here. Starting tomorrow, the good doctor will come to work every day at the clinic and the rest of you will be guarded in a less hospitable place than this hotel for security reasons. I can't afford more than one guard to watch over you right now so we have rigged up a sort of jail cell for you."

"Good night, all," he said sarcastically as he turned and left the room.

Chapter 25

Escape and Evade

Deanna looked at everyone and reassured them in a low voice that they would get out of this somehow but Stacy was looking pretty panicked. Theresa wasn't looking so good either. In a few minutes, the guards brought in the food trays again, only this time, it was just some thin soup and homemade bread, with water in an urn.

Deanna smiled and said to everyone, "I guess the vacation is over now," when they went up to grab their meager supper. As they sat eating, Deanna looked at James and Ben, whispering to them, "If we do this right, we can get past those two guards at the door and get out of here tonight. It may be too late if we get locked up in a cell tomorrow."

James looked at her and asked, "What do have in mind?"

Deanna outlined a plan to distract the oldest of the two guards and the way to disable the young, anxious one out in the hallway. She wanted to distract the veteran with some innocuous request and draw the young one inside to take him down without any gunshots. Ben could do the heavy hitting while the rest of the group tied the guards up and took their weapons.

Ben just had one question. "How're we going to distract this guard well enough to take him out without the other one figuring out what is going on? I am thinking this plan needs some more details before we set this in motion."

Dr. James concurred. "What are you going to distract him with because he's not going to be too interested in anyone flirting with him. That would be too obvious. You will need a good conversation starter if we're going to catch him off guard."

Deanna said, "I have a plan, don't you guys worry about that part. We just need to figure out how to jump them once I distract him."

Theresa spoke up and said she had an idea. She said, "Stacy and I could ask the youngest if we can help clean up the supper dishes to show that we're being cooperative and the two guards might relax a little.

Deanna said, "That just might work. I'll try to strike up a conversation with this one about local politics and their military situation to see if I can learn anything useful."

As they finalized their plans, James looked at the guards surreptitiously to see if they were paying attention to their whispered conversations but they appeared more bored than anything else right now. The older one stood over by the door chatting with the younger one while toying with his gear instead of paying any attention to them.

The final plan was for Deanna to engage the older guard in a conversation to distract the younger one in, and once they were both distracted, rush them to disarm and tie them up out of sight. They first had to get permission to start cleaning up the serving table, which would bring them all close enough to make the leap.

Deanna got up from the table to put her bowl and spoon in the trash. As she stood by the trash can, she looked at the guard to get his attention. When he looked over, she smiled in an engaging way. He watched her with a relaxed posture as she played with the spoon for a minute. When she had his attention, Deanna asked, "Could a couple of us help you guys with the cleanup here? It looks like you could use a hand and we want to cooperate despite this little feud going on. This isn't our fight and we don't want to get in the middle of it."

The veteran, Roy, looked at her for a minute, then turned around to the door to ask his partner, "Would you be okay if the ladies helped you with KP duty?" He said with a chuckle. Roy was obviously the senior of the two and, apparently liked to rub it in whenever he could.

The young kid stepped in, looked around, turning red in embarrassment, "Sure, why not. I could use a break." He walked over to the table and looked at Deanna differently than his usual blustery attitude. About that time, Theresa sauntered up near him and smiled at him like a teenage princess. He fell for it hook, line and sinker. As he smiled back at her, Theresa started helping him pick up asking him about his life here. She spun a yarn about being on the run from an abusive boyfriend, which was not too far from the truth.

Dr. James and Ben split up and walked way around them so as not to draw any suspicions by getting too close, letting the women work their magic. Once Theresa had the kid enthralled, Deanna walked around the end of the table and asked Roy about his role here.

Roy smiled and said, "Don't come any closer." He didn't raise his gun up but his eyes narrowed just a little. Roy proceeded to tell Deanna that he was like a corporal around here, at which the younger one looked up with a frown from where he was by the table.

He proclaimed that he was in charge of certain security details and had spent one tour in the Army before coming home and joining a local militia. Then he met Robert, who convinced him and some of his ex-military buddies to join his militia group. "The rewards are better here than with my previous group, with better upward mobility," he said with a smile in the kid's direction. "I get a better share in the loot when we raid a place, if there is any. The higher in rank you get, the bigger the share you receive," he added with another lopsided smile in the kid's direction.

Deanna kept at it, asking him about their future plans, because as she explained, "We are looking for a safe refuge. We know we are prisoners for now but maybe we can be more than that once Robert and Dr. James work out their differences."

Roy was only happy to preen about how good he and his other militia brothers were at doing their jobs and how they were building up quite a war chest that they were going to use for their retirement fund someday.

While he was going on about how good he was at his job, Theresa kept the kid engrossed in talking about life here and lack of girlfriends, as if they were in high school or college together. As Ben looked on, he motioned for Stacy to hang back to avoid getting hurt while he slowly worked his way around Deanna towards the front wall near the door. Ben knew how to stalk so he walked very slowly. Dr. James walked over to the other side of Deanna but not close enough to spook Roy. As if he just wanted to listen to their conversation.

The plan was for Theresa to physically get close enough to the kid to keep him from using his rifle. Dr. James would disarm him, catching him unaware while at the same time, Ben and Deanna would rush Roy while he was distracted and knock him to the floor to disarm him.

As the kid kept smiling and blushing with Theresa, she slowly moved closer to him, while pretending to start picking up stuff from the table. All she really did was move the bowls, spoons and leftover soup towards that end of the table but the kid didn't notice. All he could see now was a pretty, older girl who was taking an interest in him.

Theresa moved to within touching distance to the kid. She picked up the soup pot next to him, gave him a flirty look and 'accidently' tripped, spilling the soup all over the young man. He immediately dropped his hands down to take care of the mess, and Theresa started to help. When she moved in, Stacy stepped up and they tripped him to the floor.

As soon as the soup spilled all over the kid and Roy's attention was diverted, Ben and Deanna quickly hit him hard putting him down on the floor. Deanna sat on him to pin his hands down and Ben put his boot on his neck to keep him from bucking Deanna off.

Dr. James grabbed the guns from the kid and once the two young men were disarmed, they were placed together sitting down against the wall. Ben took the shoelaces from their boots to tie their hands and feet together so they couldn't get loose and Deanna grabbed some napkins from the table to make gags.

Now that they were clear here, they had to figure out how to escape the resort without being seen. One of the first things Ben had noticed earlier in the day was that the guards didn't have any radios or cell phones. He knew that this was the best thing for their escape plans as these two guys had to rely on relief watches or running out for help rather than voice check-ins. Electronics were becoming quite a scarce commodity in the outside world due to the trade issues and apparently that was spilling over into the militias.

Some people still had cell phones, if they could afford them, but that was only a small percentage of the population. Here in this redoubt, Robert probably likely didn't want to take any chances with cell phone tracking so he probably only used hand held walkie talkies that were passed out to a few trusted people. Low-level guards not being on that list.

While things were getting tidied up, Dr. James suggested they all hurry up and grab their gear from their rooms before someone came in to check on these two. Ben offered to stand guard while everyone ran upstairs, to meet back here as quickly as possible. Stacy would get their gear while Ben stayed with the prisoners.

As they all left, Ben grabbed both pistols and rifles and started checking them out. As he started racking the bolts and checking the magazines, the two guards looked even more startled as it was obvious that Ben had a lot of experience with weapons. Once Ben was satisfied, he strapped on one of the holsters and put a pistol in it. The other pistol he reserved for whomever wanted it once they returned. The same for the rifles. He kept the best one and set the other one out of reach.

Pretty soon, everyone returned with the backpacks and rucks. Stacy grabbed the leftover bread from the table to stuff it into their bag. Ben asked everyone, "Who wants the second set of guns?"

When no one answered right away, Deanna said, "I'll take them. I likely have the most experience other than Ben here." She took the pistol and holster from Ben and looked the rifle over, much the same way Ben had earlier. Again, much to the surprise of the two young guards. Apparently, their prisoners were not who they had seemed to be earlier.

Deanna took another look at the bonds on the two prisoners and leaned down to whisper to Roy, "Sorry about this, no hard feelings, okay?" She smiled at them a little as she followed everyone out into the lobby, turning out the lights, then closing and locking the door on her way out.

One they were all gathered near the front doors, Ben slipped out into the foyer to look out the glass front doors. Since the lobby lights were turned down low, he was in near total darkness standing at the doors.

Ben didn't see anyone walking around outside but he continued to look for a couple minutes more. He was looking for window lights that might indicate people who could see them as they exited the hotel. They had discussed going out a back door but didn't want to take a chance that Robert's people had alarms set on them.

Ben slowly opened a door slightly and peered out. As he looked around, he checked up the little street. The nearest lights were pretty far down the street and fairly dim.

All they had for outside light here was starlight from a cool, crisp, New England night and a half-moon on the horizon. Ben gestured for everyone to step out and move along the building away from the lights up the street. As everyone stepped out, Ben kept watch on the street behind them and waited for Deanna to exit. Ben would bring up the rear guard while Deanna would try to lead them to the road headed down the mountain, which was likely being guarded.

The little group stayed to the building and tree shadows as they made their way down to the small road. After about a half mile, Deanna saw the turn to the road going down the mountain up ahead and sure enough, there was a guard posted looking down the road. He wasn't paying attention to anything behind him and he looked bored.

Ben took point and crept up on the young guard. As an experienced hunter, he knew how to avoid walking on things that made noise and to walk ever so slowly. He kept the guard's back to him and crept up behind him. With a light, steady breeze blowing through the trees rustling the leaves, Ben was able to get close enough to hit him in the back of the head with the butt of the rifle. When he went down, everyone ran up to drag him into the woods next to the road. They used his boot laces to tie him up like the others, and used a strip of cloth from the guard's pockets to gag him with. Ben figured he would be out for a little while.

They all started down the road to make their escape. It was only about five miles down to the main road but the guards in the hotel would probably be found before they made it that far. They had to run as fast as they could manage to the end of the road in order to try escape Robert's crew, then try and flag a car down if possible.

Chapter 26

On the Run from Everyone

The fugitives jogged as fast as they could in the dark to try and make it to the main road before their escape was discovered, which might be any minute now. Deanna tried to maintain a pace that would keep everyone together. They couldn't afford to have stragglers. She knew that if anyone got caught by Robert this time, they would most likely be shot on sight.

After trotting for about twenty minutes, Ben signaled for a break. His side was splitting as he was not a big runner. Deanna slowed down to a fast walk and urged everyone to try their best to keep up. After a couple of minutes, Ben caught his breath and said, "Let's go."

Deanna ran slowly staying with Ben and Stacy to make sure no one was left behind.

After another thirty minutes or so, they started to hear traffic and Deanna knew they were getting close to the main road. She asked if everyone was up for a small sprint to try and make it to the road. All signaled "Go" and she took off for the road. Deanna looked back over her shoulder and saw Ben and Stacy lagging a little so she dropped back to try and help. She told James and Theresa "Run as hard as you can and we will be right behind you."

As Deanna slowed down for Ben and Stacy, James and Theresa sprinted off down the road. Deanna asked Ben how he was doing.

Ben said between breaths, "I am about done but I'll make it. You can go ahead and we'll be right there."

Deanna replied, "There is no way in hell I am leaving you two on your own. My brothers taught me to never leave anyone behind and that means you now. I'll stay with you until we reach the road. Let's go."

As they started running as fast as they could, they heard the sound of a vehicle coming down the road from the resort. Ben suddenly found new energy. They took off running as fast as they could. As they came to the end of the road, Deanna yelled out, "They're coming, take cover across the road out of sight!"

As Deanna, Ben and Stacy caught up with the other two, Dr. James grabbed Ben by the arm and helped him across the road. Deanna wanted to set up an ambush but James said, "That would be a bad idea as we don't need a firefight with who knows how many fighters with just two rifles, pistols and a couple of magazines of ammo for each. We need to hide as best as we can."

Deanna grudgingly agreed. They set about making fake shoe tracks that led out to the paved highway while staying off the dirt shoulders to avoid leaving any real tracks to find. It was hard making the jump across the shoulders into the brush without leaving much trace in such short notice but Ben picked Stacy up and almost threw her across into the brush. The rest made running jumps and scrambled into the trees and low bushes just in time.

Just as everyone laid down in the tall grass and covered themselves as best as they could in the dark, a truck and jeep came down the road from the resort and stopped at the intersection. There were about a half-dozen militia members with Robert in the vehicles. Two of them stepped out to look at the road for any traces of their quarry.

As the fugitives watched from the deep grass across the road, the militia members looked around a bit and got back in the jeep. Then both vehicles turned right, headed down the road towards the next town. As they drove off, everyone breathed a sigh of relief but before anyone stood up, Deanna said, "Wait, let's make sure they don't double back. We don't want to get caught out in the open now."

Ben crouched in the grass behind a tree to see if he could hear anything coming. After a few minutes, a car came down the main road from the other direction so Ben ducked back down to let it pass.

After the tail lights disappeared into the dark, Deanna stood up and said, "We've made it this far, now we need a new plan to get away safely as far from here as possible. Any ideas?"

Dr. James got up and told everyone, "I know of another safe haven in southern Maine, if we can figure out how to get there. Right now, we might as well be in California considering where we are in the mountains here. I know where it is and I have a good idea how to get there from here but, so does Robert, and that is going to be the problem. We'll have to figure out how to escape him, dodge Homeland Security and find a way to get to my friends in Maine."

Deanna knew they were in dire straits. They had some food, a little water, and a long way to go to get to possible safety. All with lots of bad guys chasing them through the woods. What an adventure. There was nothing she could do right now to make it any better except urge everyone to keep going and not give up.

Deanna spoke up and talked to everyone about their situation. She said, "The best thing to do now is head down the road in the other direction until we find a highway sign that will tell us where we are, then figure out which way would be the safest way east."

 Everyone agreed and they set out walking, staying on the pavement to keep from making tracks. Deanna told them, "This late at night, we are not likely to see many cars out here on this stretch of road but stay close just in case we have to jump off the road."

They set out going in the opposite direction that Robert and his crew had gone, figuring that this was the safest way off of this mountain. After walking a couple of miles, they saw some lights in the distance. The lights belonged to a handful of houses alongside the road. This road dead ended there and they would need to figure out which direction to go in. In a few more minutes, they came up on a road sign that said state highway 63, north to the right, south to the left.

Dr. James got out that old map they had gotten from that gas station. Although it had only been a couple of days ago, it seemed like a week had passed since they had been there. With only starlight and a pole lamp at the intersection to see by, they tried to read the map. Theresa found highway 63 on the map located on the west side of Pisgah State Park. Now they knew that they had to head north from here, find highway 9, then follow that east to Maine. That would be a very long trek on foot.

With a plan made, they set out heading north into the night all the while watching out for Roberts's crew and any other strangers who may be out this late. Deanna told them as they started out, "We don't know how many sympathizers Robert may have here in the immediate area so we'll have to be very careful until we get clear. If fortune favors us, Robert is headed east towards Keene to look for us so we need to hightail it north as fast as we can."

Deanna knew they had to find some sort of transportation as there was no way they could walk all the way to Maine, much less avoid detection here in New Hampshire. Hiring a car wasn't an option because, one, no one had enough cash, and two, any type of digital transaction, such as credit cards, would automatically get flagged by Homeland Security. Despite their troubles with Robert, they were still considered fugitives and domestic terrorists by the government and they had best not lose sight of that while trying to escape from Robert.

During their first break alongside the highway a couple of hours later, Deanna broached the subject with everyone. Deanna asked, 'Does anyone have any ideas?

Ben quipped, "We can borrow a car from someone and leave a note," he said with a smile.

Dr. James frowned replying, "That would only complicate things even more. We don't need to have local law chasing us for being car thieves now either."

Theresa remarked, "Maybe we can ask someone to give us a ride?"

"Stacy, not wanting to be left out said, "We could ask but we're too close to Robert's hideout right now. We would have to make it a lot farther north in order to attempt anything like that."

Deanna looked at them and said, "Think about it tonight while we trek north. We'll need a solution by daybreak as we won't be able to hide in broad daylight around here. Someone will report us for sure."

Dr. James knew they were pretty much running out of options and he blamed himself for their situation. He'd trusted his relationship with Robert implicitly and look at what that brought them. On the run again, with little food or water and few choices. They had more guns and ammo than before but, unless you robbed someone at gunpoint, they wouldn't be much help in getting them to Maine.

Deanna was thinking also but along different lines. She knew how to hunt, as did Ben, but did they want to take the time to go hunting, and dressing a deer for food? Not likely. Besides, any shots would bring unwanted attention. Mostly they just didn't have the time to spare. So, how to feed and water her little group? They had a few dollars between them so they could buy some food and drinks but transportation, that would be a tougher problem.

After a quiet walk down the road, Ben said he had a possible idea. "Why don't we sneak over to a house and get some water from a water hose? It will be enough for tonight and maybe something else will come to mind."

Deanna thought for a moment and said, "Why not? Just as long as we do it without waking anyone up. Let's find a place." They opted to stay away from any place right next to the road and looked for a place that was set back off the road a bit. After walking for another mile or so, a farm appeared out of the darkness. Ben pointed to it and motioned for everyone to get off the road.

Ben told them, "I'll go take a look. We don't need to stir up any farm animals that could wake anyone up." Everyone agreed, so Ben took off into the dark over the fence. He watched his step, keeping to the grass and walked as quietly as possible. He was looking for cows or horses that might start making noises over intruders. They could be as bad as dogs sometimes.

He went down by the barn to look for a water spigot that maybe served the animal troughs. It would likely be the most remote from the main house and out of sight. Sure enough, he spied water troughs next to the barn wall with a water spigot nearby. He knew that all anyone had, were some plastic travel mugs in their backpacks but they would have to do for now. He returned to where they were still hiding and told them the news.

Everyone followed Ben single file through the field down to where the water spigot was at and they filled their personal containers while Ben kept watch on the house. When everyone had filled up, Deanna stood watch while he filled his. They all walked carefully back up to the road without any problems and continued heading north along the highway.

At least they had water, Deanna thought. It's too dark to see if it's clean enough to drink but, if they're careful, it'll get them through the night. She could tell that all of this running and stress was wearing everyone out. They will have to find some transportation in the morning or they won't make it too much farther.

As they continued to walk, all the while keeping a constant lookout for Robert and his crew of militia members, the physical weariness was starting to take their toll. Lack of sleep and proper food was causing everyone to walk a little slower and take more rest breaks.

Along about five in the morning, they came up on another little village. It was just a small group of houses, with a small gas station and convenience store. The store was still closed but it seemed like a good place to take a nice break and wait for the place to open. Everyone gathered around off to the side of the building in the shadows to sit down and take a cat nap. Ben offered to stand guard but Deanna told him, "We'll take shifts."

Everyone was pretty hungry and very tired from last night so sitting down next to the building wall didn't elicit any complaints about the dirt and smells. As everyone but Ben dozed, their thoughts turned to "What next?"

About seven thirty, a car pulled in and parked out front near to where they were napping, startling everyone, including Deanna who was on watch at this point. She had been lost in thought and half asleep so she didn't notice the car until it slowed down to pull into the parking lot. As soon as the car turned in the driveway, she quickly ducked back around the corner to wake everyone up, shushing them and pointing to the car.

When the driver got out, she looked like a mid to late thirties typical convenience store worker. As Deanna watched from the corner of the building, she went up to the front doors and opened them without even a glance in their direction. Once she was inside, Deanna turned around and said, "Let's give her a few minutes to get situated, then we can trickle inside in ones and twos to get some food and clean water, use the bathrooms to clean up and take it from there."

After waiting about fifteen minutes, Theresa volunteered to go first. She walked up to the door and stepped in to look around. It looked much like the other one up north, from a couple of days ago. Theresa walked in, said "hello" in a quiet voice and looked around for the bathroom. Like the other gas station convenience store, it was in the hallway in the back between the drink and food coolers. Theresa walked back to the women's bathroom and washed up.

When she returned to the store area, Theresa looked around for some food and found some day-old sandwiches in one of the coolers, plus the same old packaged sweet rolls and cakes found in any convenience store anywhere. There were also some ugly looking coffee urns up front that the lady was trying to get set up for the day.

Theresa grabbed a sandwich and a bottle of juice from a cooler and headed up front to pay. The woman came around the counter and rang her up, looking like she had just rolled out of bed not too long ago. Theresa didn't say much, just kept her head down and mumbled "thanks," then walked out.

When she went back around the corner to her friends, she reported what she saw. "Not much to see, just another typical convenience store in Podunk New Hampshire," she said with a tired smile.

The others meandered inside in pairs waiting a few minutes between trips. Cleaning up and bringing back something to eat to tide them over until they could find something better. As they were eating and resting around the corner of the building, a truck pulled in to get some gas. The man went in to the store, likely to pay for the gas. When he returned to his truck and started pumping, he looked up and spotted Ben standing at the corner of the store.

Normally, this probably wouldn't have sparked much attention but Ben was carrying a rifle and he had a pistol holstered on his thigh. That got Ben a long stare as the man finished pumping his gas and got ready to leave. The man, Big John, as his friends called him, was curious about why a heavily armed, young man would be hanging around the corner of his local store.

Chapter 27

The Farm

Big John considered himself a patriot and was an Army veteran. He didn't agree with the current form of government but kept those feelings to himself and his wife. He wanted to be more of an activist but he didn't want to lose everything in the process. So, he kept a low profile and worked his farm quietly. He knew his neighbors and stayed away from any of the radical ones, which kept him in good graces with his friends and his church.

Big John put up the gas nozzle and put the gas cap on. When he finished, he casually sauntered over towards Ben with his hands out in plain sight and asked, "Are you lost? You don't look like you're from around here."

Ben immediately came to attention and Dr. James stepped out from around the building behind Ben.

When Dr. James stepped out, the others followed after. The first thing Big John noticed was Deanna with the other weapons and he stopped where he was. Now he grew concerned that he may have stumbled into something dangerous. Dr. James came out from behind Ben and reaching out his hand in greeting.

He smiled and said, "I am sorry for how we look but, I assure you, we are not in the least bit dangerous. We are travelers and stopped here for a little rest. Is there something we can help you with?"

Big John knew what the young lady's car from the store looked like and didn't see any other cars in the parking lot, so he wondered about their story. Migrant travelers? That didn't add up to what he was seeing. What he observed, was a sort of scruffy looking group of folks, armed to the teeth, with rucks, looking like they would shoot and run at the first sign of a threat.

Big John decided that this was going to be his watershed moment. He had always wanted to help someone in need and this looked like the perfect opportunity to satisfy his desire to help someone. He shook Dr. James's hand and said, "I was going to ask you the same question. Is there anything I can do to help you folks? You sure look like you need a hand right now."

Deanna stepped out from behind James and asked, "May I know who you are? We have to be careful right now as there are some very bad people looking for us. We don't want to run into of them again." She also shook Big John's hand and looked inquiringly at him.

Big John was not real tall but he was bulky and not the overweight kind. He stood about six feet, had a big neck and shoulders from his Army days and working on his small farm. He was older now and losing his hair but he introduced himself and told them, "I have a small farm just up the road and if you want, I'd be happy to offer my assistance in whatever way I can. I don't have much and largely what I have in the way of food comes from my farm. You are welcome to come with me to get a good meal and rest a bit. We can figure out the rest after a spell."

Ben stood back and watched warily. After what they'd just been through, he wasn't taking chances anymore. He turned to Stacy and said, "We can go along here but be on the lookout for anything that looks shady." Stacy nodded her head and hung back with Ben. She was very tired and hungry and just wanted all of this to be over with.

As Deanna and Dr. James negotiated with this stranger who wanted to be their new friend, Theresa was hanging back also. After the last two days, her trust levels were at rock bottom now. She also was just wishing for all of this to be over with, one way or another.

Big John noticed the hesitance in the other three and thought, while talking to Deanna and Dr. James, these folks have been through some rough times lately. He was reminded of his deployments to Iraq and Afghanistan back in the twenty ought's and knew the look. These were refugees of a sort, on the run and looking for a safe haven, although armed and dangerous.

Dr. James introduced them by first names only and didn't offer any details on their travels or misadventures. He thought it best to keep a low profile for now until they figured out their next move. Once the introductions were complete, and Big John had made his offer, James looked at Deanna then turned back to Big John, "Can you excuse us for a moment? We need to discuss your offer of hospitality before we agree to come with you."

Big John replied, 'Sure, I completely understand. You don't know me from Adam and I walk up out of the blue and offer you hospitality without any reservations. I'd be cautious too. Take your time. I'll be over by my truck if you need anything." Big John stepped back to the front of his truck, leaned back and waited.

Meanwhile, Deanna and Dr. James turned and they all walked back around the corner. Deanna kept the man in sight and asked everyone their thoughts.

Ben immediately said, "I don't trust him yet but he sounds sincere. I'd be okay going with him to check things out."

Theresa echoed that but told Deanna, "I have been with you from the beginning and I've learned to trust your instincts so, I'll continue to trust you in this. Whatever you think is fine by me."

Deanna looked at James and asked, "What do you think?"

Dr. James looked at everyone and saw how tired and hungry they were. He replied, "I'm inclined to accept his offer of hospitality. I agree with Ben, he seems to genuinely want to help for some reason we don't know about yet. I think we can trust him up to a point, until we know more. I'll go out and let him know what we've decided and work out transportation."

Dr. James walked out and tried to stay away from the front of the store so the lady inside wouldn't see him. As he walked slowly across the parking lot, he motioned for Big John to come over. Big John stood up from where he was leaning on his truck and walked up. As he approached, he asked, 'Well, what did you all decide?"

Dr. James replied, "We've decided to take you up on your generous offer, if we can work out our security concerns. We need to stay out of sight as much as possible right now so we have to come up with a plan that will accomplish that."

Big John scratched his head in thought and said, "You can all ride in the back of my truck for now. Lay low in the bed as we leave here. My place is just a couple of miles up the road going north here on this road. I can pull out from the pumps and load you up at this corner, then we can go whenever you are ready."

Dr. James smiled, "Great, we will get ready now. We just have our backpacks and guns to bring, as we travel light these days, unfortunately. The guns won't be a problem, will they?"

Big John laughed, and said, "Not to worry, I am an old Army veteran and I understand." He turned around and walked back to get his truck.

Dr. James walked back and told everyone to get ready. He explained that the plan was for them to lay low in his truck until they got past this gas station and up to his place a couple of miles down the road. Dr. James advised, "Let's put the rifles in the back of the truck. Deanna can ride upfront with her pistol, and we can lay down in the back and be ready to jump out quickly if needed. I certainly hope it doesn't come down to that though," he said with a one-sided smile.

Just about then, Big John pulled up to the corner where they were standing. Deanna quickly jumped in the cab and everyone else jumped into the bed of the truck to lay down below the sides as best as they could. When they were set, James knocked on the back window to let Big John know they were ready.

Big John drove out to the road as if he were leaving like he always did when getting gas here. Nice and easy, with a slow foot on the gas, turning left towards his farm. Just another day, except it wasn't. He was acutely aware of his cargo now and his old combat instincts and training were kicking in. The adrenaline rush was heady and making him feel more alive than he had felt since he left the Army.

After the truck drove out of sight of the gas station, everyone in the back of the truck tried to make themselves as comfortable as they could. Everyone was pretty much of the same mind, what if this turned out to be like the other safe havens they had been to? No one was talking, just thinking about their situation and what to do if things went sideways here.

After about three miles, they slowed down for a driveway leading up to a farm a little way off the road. The main house was at the end of the driveway and a barn stood off to the south side with pasture land stretching out behind the barn and way down behind the house, leading into a large wooded area. The older house looked big enough to handle a small group of refugees and had a welcoming, country charm, feel to it.

As they turned down the driveway, Deanna noticed some cows down in the field behind the house and a handful of chickens scattered around the backside of the barn. It looked like something from a postcard or a painting. Big John drove the truck into the barn and stopped just inside. As he and Deanna exited, the others clambered out of the back and gathered their gear, looking at Big John for the next move.

Big John said, "All of you wait here out of sight while I let my wife know we have company for lunch and maybe a couple of days. I also want to make sure everything else is good before I walk you around to the back door."

Deanna walked over to her friends and nodded. She then grabbed the rifle Theresa had been holding for her and pulled the bolt back. She held the gun low but the look in her eyes when she looked up, meant business. Ben followed suit and racked a round in the chamber of his rifle as well.

Big John thought, "Uh oh, these folks are not your typical refugees. Who have I brought home?" He didn't have a gun on him but he dearly wanted one now. He put his hands up and said, "Hey, take it easy, I just need to make sure everything is alright before I introduce you to my wife."

Ben looked at him with narrowed eyes and replied, "Sir, if you knew what we've been through the last few days, you'd understand. We can't take any chances. We'll be waiting right here for you, but if there's anything amiss, we'll be ready."

Big John stepped back away from the truck and walked backwards out the barn door, then turned around to head into the back door to his house. He had to get a grip on himself to keep from running. His instinct right now was to run hard for the house and grab his gun. He also knew that he needed to remain as calm as possible so as not to spook his wife, whom he loved dearly. She was the calming influence in his life and he needed that right now.

Big John jumped up the steps to the back door and entered a little more briskly than normal so his wife, working in the kitchen, was a little startled by his abrupt entry. He took off his ball cap and said, "Honey, we have some unexpected guests out in the barn and we need to be careful. They're on the run from something and appear dangerous but I don't think they're looking for trouble. They just look like they have been through a lot lately. Do you think we could offer them a little hospitality for a bit?"

His wife, Barbara, looked at him. She saw her husband looking excited for the first time in a long time and wondered just who he had brought home. Now she was curious, "Okay, let's take a look at these refugees you're so excited about. I'll go get your pistol just in case of trouble." She walked out of the kitchen and returned a couple of minutes later with a Glock pistol in a belt holster and handed it to him.

Big John asked her, while he was putting the holster on his belt, "Has anybody called or stopped by since I left this morning? We don't need any surprises right now."

Barbara shook her head no, and said, "No calls and no visitors, other than the strays you just brought home," she said with a wry smile. They both stepped outside and walked back to the barn to greet their new guests. When they entered Barbara was met with two rifles pointed at them for a minute, then lowered but not away. These two looked ready to handle anything threatening right now.

Big John introduced his wife and asked them to ease their weapons down. There was no threat here. Ben was looking at the pistol on his hip and declined to put his rifle down just yet. Deanna set her rifle down leaning against the truck and walked around to greet Barbara. They both smiled and it was like they had known each other before. There was an almost instant bond. James introduced himself as Dr. James. And at the mention of that name, Big John recognized him from some gossip he had heard a couple of years ago.

Big John and his wife had heard about the traveling doctor that had been in the area back then and the good things he had done for the local folks while he had been here. They didn't have a need back then so they hadn't gone up the mountain when he was there. Besides, the militia group that inhabited that old resort wasn't the sort of people Big John wanted to know anyway, and he didn't want them to know him. Their reputation before the doctor showed up had been dodgy, then it got worse after the fatal car accident. Everyone for miles around knew about the accident and the aftermath. The leader, whose wife and children had been killed in that accident, went off the deep end and everyone started hearing stories about his activities, and they weren't good stories.

Big John, his wife and their close friends around here stayed clear of all that mess and they wanted to keep it that way. He had a lot to tell his new guests and wondered when would be the best time to sit down with them to give them the low down on where they were. He was sure they also had quite a tale to tell as well.

Barbara took the lead and invited everyone into the house to get cleaned up and have some coffee or something. At that, Ben put the rifle muzzle down and grabbed Stacy's hand. He slung the rifle behind his back on the strap and walked around the truck, with Theresa following behind. Deanna grabbed her rifle and followed Barbara out of the barn and in the back door. As they entered, Deanna and Ben stacked the rifles by the door and took off their shoes, with everyone else following suit. The boots went onto a pan by the door where Big John's other boots were sitting.

Barbara had everyone sit down at the big table and said, "The bathroom is around the corner and down the hall a bit, help yourself. I'll put on some more coffee on and whatever else I have. Does anyone want anything else?"

Dr. James replied, "I'd like some tea please, if you have any? If not, a glass of water will be fine."

Barbara reached up into a cupboard and said, "I just have some Lipton, if that is alright?"

James said, "That will be just fine."

As everyone settled in at the table to wait for their coffee and tea, Big John looked at them from where he stood by the kitchen sink, and asked, "Who are you running from? It's quite obvious and I'd like to know if they might be a threat to us here. Tell me a little bit about who's chasing you?"

Dr. James looked at everyone and Deanna nodded, "Go ahead". Dr. James outlined their trip from upstate New York and what happened at the mountain resort yesterday and last night. He detailed the entrapment, threats and escape and as the story unfolded about Robert, Barbara let out a gasp and held her hand to her mouth.

Big John just shook his head and when Dr. James finished the tale. He said, "I knew he was trouble."

Big John then told them a little about themselves. He had served two enlistments with the Army, deployed three times as an infantryman to Iraq and Afghanistan between 2003 and 2011. He left the Army after being wounded in action and returned home to New Hampshire. He and his wife had inherited this farm from her father and they have been here ever since, eking out a living on his VA disability pension, what little money they made from the farm and her elementary school teaching job. She was out for summer break now so she could help too.

Deanna started to relax for the first time in a couple of days. Theresa also started to feel better. Ben and Stacy were still hanging onto each other as if the world were coming to an end at any moment. Dr. James was as affable as ever, following Deanna's lead at the moment. After a few quiet minutes, as everyone was digesting the stories, the coffee and tea became ready and Barbara broke the ice by pouring cups for everyone.

While sipping their coffee and tea, Barbara asked, 'Would anyone like a slice of homemade bread, or a scone or something?" All of a sudden, the dam broke and everyone started talking at once and they all laughed, except Ben. But Ben was Ben and this was no surprise. He did crack a smile though when Stacy stuck an elbow in his ribs.

As they chatted for a bit, Big John asked the question no one had broached yet, "Do you have a plan?"

Deanna replied," We have a loose plan for now but it's subject to change at a moment's notice. We're trying to get to another safe haven Dr. James knows of in Maine. A place he's been to before where we can resupply and rest for a while before our next adventure. With Robert's crew and Homeland Security looking for us, we're in desperate need of transportation right now."

Chapter 28

Ben and Stacy decide to stay

Big John listened and when she finished, he said, "I think I can help with that. I know a guy," laughing at the cliché. Big John explained that he knew someone who had a couple of old cars that were off the books, sort of. All they needed to do was make contact discreetly and make a deal. "If one of this guy's cars disappeared, it wouldn't raise any alarms. Just don't get stopped for any reason."

Dr. James asked, "What kind of a deal?"

Big John explained, "He likes to barter for things. He only uses money as a necessary evil and likes to trade in goods and services for the things he acquires. Don't ask where he gets 'things', it's better not to know. But he's reliable, for a price," he said with a smile.

Deanna looked at everyone at the table and said, "We are pretty much out of other options right now and would welcome any help, no matter where it comes from. Just let us know what to do and we will do our best."

Ben spoke up for the first time and asked, "Are there any farmers here needing a hand? We want to find a quiet place like this to settle down and start our new life together. I am a good worker and experienced with farm work, having been raised on a working farm back in upstate New York."

Stacy looked on quietly, so it was obvious they had been talking about this recently. Deanna was caught a little off guard but stayed quiet to see how things rolled out.

Big John scratched his chin a little and thought for a moment. He replied, "It just so happens, I am in need of some help here and I also know of a couple of my neighbors who could use a strong young man to help out at times. Would you be interested in sticking around here to find out if that would work out for you? We can pay them a visit tomorrow, if you want?"

Ben's face lit up and he looked at Stacy sitting next to him to see what she thought. She looked excited too so, Ben said "Yes" enthusiastically.

When Big John saw how their faces lit up at the prospect, he knew his feelings about them were bearing fruit. He started seeing Ben and Stacy as the possible children Barbara and himself had never been able to have. In that moment, he started to imagine grandchildren playing out in the yard someday.

Big John looked over at his wife and saw on her face the same thing he was thinking. He loved his wife dearly and he would give his life for her but he always regretted the fact that they were never able to conceive children together.

Deanna looked at Theresa and asked, "Have your plans changed?"

 Theresa replied, "No, not really, I still want to be a part of something like we had in New York. I want to find a new group and do the same with them as we did back there and I think Maine might give me that, as long as they haven't been compromised like Robert's crew," she added, looking at Dr. James with a wry smile.

James looked back at her and chuckled a little. "I will do my best to make sure they haven't before we get there this time."

Deanna laughed a little and looked over at Ben and Stacy. "I always said after we hooked up on the trail, that you could do as you wished anywhere along the way. I am glad to see that you may have found that place you have been looking for and I want to wish you the best of luck."

Ben mumbled, "Thank you." Stacy let go a couple of happy tears and also said, "Thank you. You and Theresa have been like the older sisters I never had and we would never have gotten this far without you." She looked at Ben and said, "We likely would have been caught back in Vermont and returned to my parents if it hadn't been for you guys." Ben looked down and grimaced.

Big John and Barbara stood silently as they were talking and he leaned over to whisper to her, "Let's make them as welcome as we can and work on getting Ben and Stacy settled in." Barbara smiled, nodding her head yes. She was always happiest when she had a purpose and this was probably the biggest thing that's happened to them since her father died and left them this farm.

Barbara spoke up, "I'm going to start setting up the extra bedrooms for you folks. Help yourself to more coffee or tea and I will be back in a little while."

Stacy stood up and replied, "I would love to come give you a hand, if you don't mind? I need something to take my mind off the last couple of days."

Barbara looked at her and smiled, "Come on then, let's get to work."

After they left, Ben looked over at Big John and said, "Thank you," again. He so wanted Stacy to be happy and he had been scared that she would leave him to go back to her parents because of all of the troubles they had run into after running away. And now, it looked like their dreams might get a good jump start right here. He felt a little guilty about leaving their little group but he had to put his and Stacy's needs first.

Dr. James stood up to grab a biscuit and walked out to the front room. He stood in the doorway of the kitchen looking out into their family room. He saw family pictures of older people, likely passed on now, from the age of the pictures but no pictures of children. This confirmed what they had told them earlier. Big John and Barbara were who they said they were, an older childless couple looking for an opportunity to help. If things work out, maybe they will be blessed with grandchildren by proxy. James hoped they wouldn't try to overdo it with Ben and Stacy though. Stacy still loved her real parent's; she just couldn't stand to be around them. As for Ben's parents, Ben never really talked about them much. But it did look like they raised him pretty well.

All of this made James think of his parents and sisters wistfully. He'd finished crying over the loss of his parents several years ago but he still remembered them fondly. Now, he really needed to rescue his sisters. It's been way too long since he's seen them. He turned back to the kitchen and made another cup of tea. Deanna and Theresa had fresh cups of coffee in front of them, sipping them slowly.

Dr. James turned to Big John and asked, "How soon can we get started on that transportation? We really need to get to Maine as soon as possible. I have two sisters down in a northern Virginia internment camp I need to rescue as soon as I can manage. That's all I will say about that, as I don't want you and your lovely wife to get into any trouble over me. The less you know, the safer you'll be."

Big John thought once again that there's more to these folks than they let on. "I can make a phone call after lunch, if that will work for you? If my friend is available, we can make an arrangement this afternoon, providing everything's in order. What do you have to offer for a trade?"

Dr. James responded, "I am a doctor, so I can offer free medical services, for one thing, and maybe we may have something else to trade with, depending on what your friend wants."

Big John stood there for a minute and then said, "I'll be right back." After a minute, he returned with a cell phone and made a call. When the other person answered, Big John told him about a traveling doctor that he had just met and wondered if they would be interested in his services? Dr. James heard an excited voice on the other end and waited. It seemed that his services would likely be in demand soon.

Big John asked Dr. James as soon as the call disconnected, "How soon can you be ready to make a house call? This would go a long way towards your credibility in this small community if you can make a couple of house calls on some of my neighbors needing medical services. The nearest doctor is all the way over in Keene now, after the majority of the country's doctors fled during the purge a few years ago."

Dr. James, said, "Sure, we can go whenever you're ready. Let me finish my tea first." He looked at Deanna and asked, "Do you want to go? I might need a nurse and you're the only one I have now."

Deanna looked at Theresa to ask if she would be okay here and Theresa headed her off by saying, "Go ahead, I'll be fine. I'll go help Ms. Barbara and Stacy while you are gone."

Deanna turned back to James, "Sure, why not. Might be fun for a change. I need the distraction anyway. How long do you think we might be gone?"

Big John shrugged his shoulders and replied, "I don't know for sure, maybe a couple of hours or so? Is that going to be a problem?"

Deanna shook her head and said, "No, I don't think so. I'm just nervous about Robert, who's likely still out there looking for us."

Big John patted his gun and said, "We'll be fine. Between your pistol and mine, we should be okay."

Dr. James set his tea cup in the sink and stepped over to put his boots on. Deanna did the same. As they stepped out onto the back steps, Big John followed them out and they went into the barn to get into his truck. Dr. James had his backpack with medical supplies so he was as ready as he could be.

As soon as the three of them slid into the truck with James sitting nearest the door, Big John started the truck up and they headed out. While they were driving, Big John told them about this neighbor they were going to see. This woman had been sick for a little while and complaining of pain. They didn't have much money and they didn't want to drive all the way to the city. He didn't know much more than that.

The farm was just a couple miles down the road from Big John's place so the trip was quick. The driveway led to a rundown looking farm that had seen better days. As they pulled up next to the house, an elderly man stepped out onto the porch and welcomed them. When they all went inside, he introduced himself as Roland and his wife as Esther. She was sitting in her chair in the front room with a blanket across her lap. Both of them looked to be in their late seventies or early eighties.

Dr. James introduced himself and Deanna as his nurse. Big John they already knew. He asked, "May I examine you to see if we can find the source of your pain?"

 Esther replied, "Sure doctor, whatever you need. We can go to a back room if you want?"

Dr. James said, "Whatever makes you more comfortable." Everyone walked back to a bedroom and it was obvious that Esther was having a hard time getting around.

She sat down in a chair next to the window and asked "What do you need from me?"

Dr. James answered, "I need to first ask you some questions to try and narrow this down." Then the examination began in earnest. Deanna told James, "I'll wait outside with Roland until you either need me or you finish the exam."

Deanna went back out to the front room to wait with Roland and big John, assuring Roland that Esther was in good hands. Deanna had never been good at small talk with strangers so she kept quiet while they waited. After about a half hour, Dr. James came back out with Esther and helped her sit back down in her chair, then wrapped the blanket around her again.

Roland was getting impatient and asked, "Is she going to be alright?"

Dr. James looked over and said, "Let's you and I step out onto the porch please." When they were outside, he said, "I am pretty sure your wife has cancer. I can't be sure without x-rays and maybe an MRI but all the symptoms point that way. I am sorry."

Roland stared out across the scrubby lawn for a quiet minute, then turned back to Dr. James, "How long do you think she has?"

Dr. James replied, "I don't know and I don't have access to the necessary imaging equipment to find out. Again, I am sorry. I suggest that you get her admitted to a hospital as soon as possible to see if there's anything more that can be done for her."

Dr. James stepped down off the porch and waited for Deanna and Big John to come out. Roland shook his hand and walked back inside. As soon as he walked in, Deanna and Big John came out and saw the look on his face. Deanna walked over and gave him a big hug then they got into the truck.

Big John asked, "Is it pretty bad?"

Dr. James replied, "Without disclosing any doctor patient confidentiality, yes, it is and that's all I can say at this point. Esther needs to be in hospital as soon as possible"

Big John started the truck and drove back to his farm. They rode in silence and when they arrived, it was lunch time. Barbara, Stacy and Theresa were in the kitchen making lunch for everyone. Seeing the long faces on them as they entered through the back door, they got quiet until Deanna, James and Big John were settled at the table. Barbara, who knew the folks they had just gone to see, knew it was bad just by the look on her husband's face.

She decided to try and cheer everyone up. She asked, "Who wants to go out to the garden and help pick some vegetables for lunch and dinner?"

That got everyone's attention. All of a sudden, the mood switched to one of excitement as none of the visitors had been near a garden in weeks. Everyone trooped out back to the kitchen garden Big John and Barbara grew for their own use with Barbara explaining what vegetables she grew and how much they had planted in order to can and freeze what they needed for the winter every year.

Ben and Stacy got animated and walked down through the rows remarking about this and that like a couple of kids. Deanna smiled and watched them go. Then she looked over at Barbara and saw the look in her eyes. She knew then that the newlyweds could have a forever home, if they wanted it.

Chapter 29

Getting Ready to go to Maine

Once some lettuce and kale had been picked, everyone headed back to the house to eat lunch. Stacy pitched in by helping rinse off the veggies and make sandwiches for everyone. While Barbara and Stacy were busy by the sink counter, Big John sat down at the table with the rest of the group and started asking a few questions.

Big John looked at Ben first and asked, "What do you really want to do and what can I do to help you get started?"

Ben thought for a minute and remarked, "Stacy and I want to eventually have our own farm to raise children in safety with minimal government interference. We just want a quiet life together."

Ben then looked over at Deanna, Dr. James and Theresa and said, "When we arrived here this morning, we fell in love with this place and decided that this is what we want for ourselves, no more running from anyone or worrying about parents' wishes and so on. We're tired of being scared, hungry and tired."

Dr. James looked back at him and nodded his head in agreement. "I am tired too. I also want to have a life where I'm not constantly looking over my shoulder anymore. No more running over mountains and through the woods, dodging militias and the government. I have a plan but I need to get to Maine in order to get the help I need to carry it out. I thought I could do that here in New Hampshire but things change and not always for the good, it seems."

Deanna just looked on quietly because she'd already decided back at Robert's hideout that wherever James went, she was going also. She thought, "He didn't say no, so that means yes."

Theresa spoke up and replied, "I'm not sure yet so I'll follow them to Maine and decide from there. I know what I want to do and I'm hoping Dr. James's friends will be able to set me up once we get there."

Big John just kept nodding as each one of them spoke. He knew what he had to do now and it was just a matter of reaching out to 'this guy' he knew about a car. After everyone finished with their answers, he replied, "After lunch, I'll make a phone call to a friend, who knows this guy with the shady cars. That'll set things in motion for you. After that, we'll just have to wait to hear from the guy with the cars. Is that okay?"

They all agreed. About that time lunch was served by a beaming Stacy with a proud looking Barbara standing behind her. Not much more was said as lunch was devoured by the hungry group.

 After they were finished, Dr. James asked Big John if he could borrow a phone. "I'd like to try and contact my friends in Maine in order to update them on what's happened and to let them know to expect me in a few days."

Barbara replied, "Sure, let me take you to the phone in the other room so you can have a little privacy."

Dr. James excused himself from the table and followed her into the front room where the land line phone was. Barbara handed him the receiver and said, "I'll be out in the kitchen if you need anything else."

James waited until she had returned to the kitchen, then dug out a worn notebook from his backpack. In it were phone numbers for his contacts from all over the country. James knew that this little notebook would be a goldmine for Homeland security if they should capture him so he kept it where could dispose of it in a hurry if needed. Preferably by burning it if possible.

He quickly searched out the 207-area code number he had and dialed it. James waited through the third ring before a man picked it up with a very distinct down east accent. He said, "Hello, who is it?"

James responded, "This is the traveling doctor calling to set up a house call. I am letting you know that I can be available to come see you in a few days, if you want to make an appointment?"

This was the coded phone message Dr. James used to contact his friends in the underground network whenever he knew he was headed their way. The man replied back, "Su'wa, we always look fowahd to you'wa visits doc. We'll keep the po'ach light on for ya. See ya' when you get he'ah," then he hung up.

James hung up the phone and walked back into the kitchen. He told everyone, "We're all set. All we need is some relatively secure transportation."

Big John looked up and said, "Give me a few minutes and I'll see what I can do." He walked out to use the phone.

Dr. James sat back down at the kitchen table, looked at Deanna and said, "There wasn't anything odd about this call at all this time. My friend just acknowledged the call in his usual way and said he'd be waiting for us. I don't think we have anything to worry about but, after the last episode, we shouldn't get complacent either."

Stacy was over helping Barbara clean up after lunch still and it sounded like they were having a great time together. Ben just sat in the corner chair and watched silently with a slight smile on his face. Theresa sat opposite him at the table. She seemed to be thinking about some serious things also because she was pretty quiet too.

Dr. James got up and asked Deanna, "Do you want anything while I'm up?"

Deanna replied, "No, I'm good for now, thank you."

James walked over to the stove and asked Barbara, "Is there anymore hot water for tea?"

Barbara looked over from where she was standing at the kitchen counter and replied, "That water is likely cool by now. You may reheat it if you want."

While James stood by the stove heating the water for more tea, which was near the archway to the family room, he caught a little of Big John's phone conversation from the other room. It sounded like he was getting a little testy with whomever he was on the phone with. After a couple of minutes, Big John put the phone down a little hard and turned around. He saw Dr. James standing next to the stove watching him.

He walked up and asked quietly, "Would you and Deanna come over here for a minute? I need to talk to you about this car business." Dr. James looked over at Deanna and motioned for her to follow him.

Deanna got up from the table with a question mark look and walked over. James put his arm around her waist and they walked into the front room with Big John. When they were standing next to the phone table Big John told them, "We have a problem. My friend of a friend is under scrutiny by the local police for some things that have nothing to do with you guys. Getting to him is going to be a little more trouble than I thought. My friend is going to do some checking around to see if we can come up with a better solution for you. The trouble is, it may take a little longer than I thought. Are you guys going to be okay with that?"

Deanna looked at James and replied, "How much longer do you anticipate? We didn't plan to be here overnight."

Big John thought for a minute, and said, "Let me make another phone call." As Deanna and James stood by, Big John dialed another number and started up a banter with, what sounded like, another neighbor.

As they chatted pleasantries back and forth for a minute, Big John asked him, "Bret, I need a favor. Do you know anyone around here that might have a car they want to get rid of? I have an interested party that needs something fairly quickly." Big John listened for a minute and replied, "I will let them know and call you back in a few minutes." He hung up the phone and turned around. Big John smiled, "There is someone who has a car for sale, sort of, if you want to go take a look? It isn't your normal car but it'll get you where you need to go quickly. If you're interested, I can call my friend back and he'll make the arrangements."

Dr. James looked at Big John and said, "None of us have a large amount of money to be able to buy a car outright. All they have is just a few dollars between them and I only have a couple hundred for traveling money. I don't see how we can do this."

Big John told him, "Don't worry about that right now. As I said before, we like to barter for things around here since the crash. How would you like to work it out in trade this afternoon? Bret and I know of someone who needs a doctor which might take care of the car problem, if you're interested?"

Dr. James looked over at Deanna, who nodded her head in agreement. James replied, "Okay, when can we get started?"

Big John said, "Let me call Bret back and we'll get things in motion. I'll let you know in a couple of minutes." Dr. James and Deanna walked back to the kitchen table to wait. Deanna briefed Theresa while James poured his cup of tea, then sat back down next to Deanna to wait.

Ben was getting restless. He decided that he wanted to go look around and stretch his legs. He walked up to where Barbara and Stacy were working and kissed Stacy on the head. He asked Barbara if it was okay to walk around outside a little.

Barbara replied, "Sure, just be careful. I am not worried about you around the farm, but we don't know who may be driving by on the road. We don't need anyone to know you are here yet until we introduce you guys to our neighbors."

Ben said, "I understand and I'll be careful." At that, he put his boots on and went out the back door to look around. As he left, Big John walked in the kitchen and told Dr. James and Deanna, "It's all set, when do you want to go?"

Dr. James replied, "Anytime, I just have to grab my bag and we can go. Deanna, do you want to come?"

She looked at him and said, "Absolutely, I'm restless and need something to distract me so let's go." James gathered his backpack and headed for the door. Big John reached over and hugged Barbara, "We'll be back in a little while. Tell Ben we went out and to keep an eye on things while we're gone."

They walked out to the barn and got into the truck for the second time today. Once Big John started backing out of the barn, Deanna asked, "How far away is this person?"

Big john replied as he started up the driveway, "They're just a few miles down the road, but we're going to have a look at that car first to see if it will meet your needs before we make any deals."

Chapter 30

The Car

Big John headed north for a couple miles, then turned west on a side road, driving for a little bit before pulling into a driveway. He stopped in front of a modest house with a free-standing two-car garage next to it. As they got out of the truck, a man stepped out to greet them and asked, "Is this the doctor I was told about?"

Big John replied back, "Yes, this is Dr. James. He is here to look at that car you told Bret you were willing to trade for."

The man, Steve, walked up, shook Big John's hand and did the same with Dr. James. He nodded to Deanna and said, "Welcome. Let's go see the car." They all walked over to the garage where Steve opened the little side door to let everyone in. As they all entered, Dr. James saw a car under a tarp and wondered, "What kind of car needs to be kept under a tarp?"

Steve walked over, jerked the tarp off the car with a flourish, almost like a showman and smiled, "There she is, ain't she a beauty?" What he uncovered was a really old Chevy Nova that looked like it had seen better days. The paint was a metallic blue that had dulled with age and the chrome trim was dinged and flaky.

Steve walked over telling them, "This car was once what we call a ridge runner. It's got a V-8 police interceptor engine and transmission in it from the days when I use to run the roads doing things not strictly legit. I haven't taken her out in several years, not since the crash. She needs a new home somewhere where she can kick up her heels again. Anyone driving it needs to know how to drive a stick and be careful around curves as she tends to lean into turns a little," he said smiling. "If you're interested, we can make a deal today, if you want?"

Dr. James and Deanna walked over to look at the car. James opened the driver's door to have a look inside. Deanna asked him, "Pop the hood please." James looked down near the door and found the hood release. There were also a couple of cables holding the hood down besides the latch so Deanna unhooked them to open the hood for a look.

Underneath, she saw the big, gas guzzling engine and started poking around checking hoses, belts and anything else that looked like it might show signs of age and potential trouble on the road. Dr. James got behind the wheel, sitting down in racing style bucket seats and started playing with the chrome gear shift that had a polished wood knob on top. He thought to himself, "Whatever this car may look like on the outside, it has been well taken care of on the inside."

He got back out and walked around to look at the tires and the rest of the car. The tires looked fairly new. They were wide all-season radials and when he looked inside the wheel wells, he could see the shocks and brakes were all in very good shape. He made his way around to the front of the car where Deanna was still poking around and asked her, "What do you think?"

Deanna looked up and replied, "This car will stick out like a sore thumb on any major highway but if we stick to the country roads, we should be fine. Let's go see what he wants for it. It might be a little cramped in the back seat for Theresa but we can figure that out later."

They walked over to where Big John and Steve were standing and Deanna asked straight out, "What do you want for it?"

Steve looked at her as if to say, "Who're you?"

Deanna had seen that look before and knew that Steve was apparently one of those who believed that this was 'mans' business and women should know their place. She waited for an answer and sure enough, Steve ignored her and looked straight at Dr. James saying, "If you can take care of my daughter and tell me what I need to do to make her well again, you can have the car as trade for your house call. That's what I told Bret on the phone and I'll stand by it. I don't have any more use for her." He looked fondly back at the car, "I can't afford to take care of the car anymore. I need all I can get to take care of Robyn, my fourteen-year-old daughter."

Dr. James looked at him and said, "I won't make any promises but I will come look at your daughter, whether we make a deal on the car or not. I would never turn away from someone in need, especially a child."

Steve nearly broke down in tears, "Thank you doc. Do you want to take a look at her now? She's right inside waiting for us."

Dr. James looked at Deanna and Big John, then back at Steve, "Sure, let's go inside so I can take a look. I need my nurse though, just in case, will that be all right?"

Steve looked befuddled for a minute, then looked at Deanna with a new light. "I am so sorry; I had no idea you were his nurse. Of course, doc, whatever you need."

Big John told them, "I'll hang out by the truck and wait on you. Don't worry about me, I'd just be in the way anyway," and he walked out of the garage to his truck.

Dr. James and Deanna followed Steve into his house and found little Robyn sitting in a wheelchair by the door. Dr. James stepped over and leaned down. "Hello Robyn, my name is Dr. James and I understand you aren't feeling so hot right now, do you want to tell me about it?"

Robyn explained in a small voice, "I fell a couple of days ago and now I hurt really bad on my lower back."

Steve chimed in, "She was pushed down a wooden step by a bully, whom I took care of. Afterwards, she complained of a sore spot on her lower back. I looked at it briefly the day of the fall and put a bandage on it for her but I think it may be infected now."

Dr. James reached into his bag and pulled out a thermometer. He asked Steve, "Do you have any isopropyl alcohol? I need to sterilize some things to get started."

Steve thought for a minute and replied, "Let me check, I'll be right back."

Dr. James put the back of his hand on Robyn's forehead and thought he detected a slight fever. He smiled at Robyn and said, "Don't worry, we'll get this figured out and have you up and playing with your friends in no time."

Robyn looked at him with a wan smile as if she were in a lot of pain and replied, "I don't have any friends Dr. James, that's why that boy pushed me down. He started calling me ugly names and pushed me down in front of everyone. That's when I fell down the steps and got hurt. No one wanted to help. They all just laughed at me sitting on the ground until a teacher came to see what all the noise was. She helped me in to see the school nurse and they called Dad. It hurts really bad now Dr. James and I don't feel so good."

In a couple of minutes, Steve returned with a small bottle of isopropyl alcohol and gave it to Deanna who was waiting for him. As Dr. James continued to question and sooth Robyn, Deanna took the thermometer out of his case and inserted it into the bottle of alcohol for a couple minutes.

Deanna touched James on the shoulder and gave him the now sterilized thermometer. Dr. James looked at Robyn and said, "Please put this under your tongue for me for a couple of minutes so I can check your temperature."

After about two minutes, Dr. James pulled it out and it read a litter over a 100 degrees. A low-grade temperature consistent with a bacterial infection. Dr. James told Steve and Robyn, "I need to examine the wound. You may be right. She likely has a local infection in that sore spot in her lower back. I'll need a place where Robyn can be made comfortable on her stomach while I take a look."

Steve replied, "We can put her in her pajamas and on her bed, if you think that'll work for you?"

Robyn spoke up, "I can go now and let you know when I am ready," as she started to get out of the chair.

Deanna reached over and helped her sit back down, telling her, "Don't get up, I'll take you back and help you get ready. Once you're ready, I'll come out and get Dr. James, okay?"

Robyn smiled and replied weakly, "Thank you." Deanna turned the wheelchair around and whisked her off towards the back of the house as Robyn squealed in delight at the fast ride.

Once they reached Robyn's bedroom, Deanna asked her where her pajamas were. Robyn told her, "They're in the second drawer of my dresser."

Deanna looked in the drawer for a minute and asked, "Which one is your favorite?"

Robyn replied, "The elephant ones," she said with a smile.

Deanna pulled out a different set and said, "Good, we won't mess those up then. How about this one that I found on the bottom? I take it you don't wear it very much, right?"

Robyn told her, "My mom got those for me a long time ago and I haven't worn them since she died a couple of years ago." Robyn looked at them with a sad face as if holding back some tears.

Deanna came over and gave Robyn a small hug, "I understand. My mother died when I was still a kid and I'm still sad about it. Let me help you out of the chair and over to the edge of the bed so you can change. I'll stand just outside the door until you're finished. Then I'll help you lay down and we'll put a sheet across your legs so Dr. James can come in and take a look at you, okay?"

Robyn nodded and Deanna helped her out of the chair holding her arm guiding her to the bed. "Are you going to be okay to change by yourself," Deanna asked?

"I think so but I'm glad you'll be just outside just in case," Robyn said with a small smile.

As Deanna waited outside in the small hallway, she started thinking back to when her mother had passed due to cancer and tried not to be too sad. She needed to keep up a brave front for Robyn now.

 After about 5 minutes, Robyn called out, "I'm ready."

Deanna stepped back in and said, "You're a brave girl, I can't imagine how much that must have hurt. Let me help you lay down and I'll put a sheet over you. Once you're ready, I'll go out and get the doctor."

Once Robyn was all set, Deanna walked back out to the front room, "She's ready for you, doctor."

Dr. James smiled and said, "Thank you nurse, I'll be right there." He looked at Steve, "I would prefer it if you'd wait here for us to finish the exam. When I am finished, I'll be back out to let you know what I've found. Are you going to be okay out here?"

Steve looked at him helplessly and said, "Yeah, I'll be fine, just take good care of her for me, she's all I have left." Steve sat down in his chair to wait.

Dr. James and Deanna walked back to Robyn's bedroom and he asked her, "Is she prepped?"

Deanna replied, "Yes doctor, I have her all ready for you to look at." Dr. James didn't say anything else as he was in full doctor mode now. All that mattered now was his young patient. They stepped in and Dr. James said, "Hi, Robyn, are you ready?"

Robyn replied, "Yes doctor, as ready as I can be."

Dr. James lifted up the bottom hem of her pajama top and quickly found the source of the problem. There was an infected, open sore on her lower left back, right above her hip. It looked like there might be something in it below the skin as it was all puckered up and oozing with pus. The red spot was about the size of a quarter.

Dr. James asked Robyn, "I need to touch it. You let me know if it hurts really bad, okay?" Robyn nodded and scrunched her face up in anticipation. Dr. James took his finger and pushed on the skin around the sore spot. When he did, more pus oozed out. Robyn let out a muffled cry of pain. He looked at Deanna and said, "We need to go talk to her father right now. Robyn needs immediate attention as soon as possible. If he can't get her to a hospital, I can try something here but I am worried about the lack of sterile operating conditions."

When Robyn heard the word operate, she cried out, "Operation? Do I need an operation doctor James?"

Dr. James looked at her and said, "Let me bring your father in here so I can tell both of you what I see, okay?"

Deanna said, "I'll stay here and comfort her while you go get him, if you want?" Dr. James nodded and walked out to get Steve. They were back in a couple of minutes and Dr. James said, "Okay, Robyn has a really bad infection in that spot on her lower back. It needs outpatient surgery, usually something that can be handled at an urgent care clinic or an outpatient medical clinic. Is there one nearby that you can take her to, or your family pediatrician?"

Steve looked at Robyn and replied, "No, there isn't. The nearest medical facility is all the way over in Keene to the east and we don't have a regular doctor anymore since the government takeover. Most of them left the country a few years ago. That's the biggest reason why my wife died a couple of years ago, there weren't any doctors around here anymore able to treat her cancer."

Dr. James nodded his head in agreement. He knew all too well about the doctor shortage in this country and thought to himself, "As soon as I can rescue my sisters, there will be one less doctor here as well."

As Steve finished talking, he started to tear up a little bit. "What can you do to help us here? I can't lose her too!" Robyn could now be heard crying into her pillow and Deanna sat down on the edge of the bed to try and comfort her.

Dr. James said to Steve, "I understand completely. I've helped a lot of other people around the country in your same situation. I can try my best but I'll need your help. I'll need to sterilize my tools and we need to put her out on a stiff flat surface somewhere in order for me to operate and clean the wound. With this much infection eating away at the surrounding tissue, there is likelihood of a scar. I'm sorry."

Steve said anxiously, "We can use the kitchen table if you like, I'll do whatever you ask in order to help her. Just tell me what to do."

Dr. James looked at Deanna and asked, "Do you think you're up to helping me with this? I'll need a nurse to hand me my instruments and help me keep her still while I work. I don't have anything to anesthetize her with nor anything to numb the area on her back."

He looked back at Steve and asked him, "Do you have any kind of strong alcohol here? We can give her just enough to relax her and I can use the isopropyl alcohol to sterilize the area with. We can use ice cubes to numb the surrounding tissue around her wound. I'm afraid that will likely be the best I can offer her at the moment, I'm sorry."

Steve looked over at Robyn and asked, "Robyn honey, do you think you can be tough enough to handle this while the doctor takes care of you? We'll do our best to keep it from hurting too bad but it will still be really hard. What do you think?"

Robyn replied, "Daddy, I don't care right now. Just make it stop hurting so bad. I'll be okay."

Dr. James said, "Okay then, let's get started. Steve, you and Deanna go scrub the kitchen table and get it ready to be an operating table. I will start sterilizing my instruments out there as well. Robyn, please lay as still as possible for now until we are ready for you. Nurse

Deanna will come get you when we are ready. Will you be okay by yourself here for a few minutes?"

Robyn replied, "Yes Dr. James, but I want to help."

Dr. James smiled and remarked to everyone, "She's pretty brave to have made it this far and still want to help with her own surgery. Pretty remarkable. Most kids would be screaming and going crazy about now."

As they all left to get started, Deanna stopped briefly at the bed and whispered to Robyn, "If you really need someone, just yell out and I'll come running. Don't worry, this'll all be over soon. Dr. James is pretty famous around the country so you don't have to worry." Robyn nodded and turned into her face into her pillow to wait.

It took about a half an hour to get everything ready for the operation. As soon as Dr. James signaled that he was satisfied that they had everything ready as best as they could with what they had, Deanna went to get Robyn. After a few minutes, she returned with Robyn in the wheelchair and the three adults carefully lifted her onto the kitchen table, now covered with a clean sheet.

Deanna covered Robyn with a blanket from her room, then started to numb her lower back with ice cubes. Steve held a cup with a straw in it so Robyn could drink the 'medicinal' relaxer. A mix of bourbon and soda.

Robyn made a face when she took the first sip but her dad said, "You can do this, darlin', just drink it down and don't think about the taste right now. You can tell me how yucky it is later when you're feeling better."

Robyn smiled and kept sipping. After she finished what was in the cup, she told her dad, with a big smile "I'll hold you to that dad. If I ever smell that nasty stuff around you again, I'll read you the riot act." With that, she lay down on the table and remained quiet. Steve held her hand and tried to keep her calm.

Dr. James reached out with his gloved hands and gently touched the skin where Deanna had been rubbing the ice cubes. When Robyn didn't flinch, he waved his hand and said, "It's ready."

With Deanna assisting, he opened the wound and peered inside with his magnifiers. Sure enough, he saw what looked like a wood splinter deep inside. He made a small incision and, using small forceps, he managed to pull out the biggest piece and put it on a small plate. He dug around as gently as he could while Deanna kept the ice cubes going. He pulled out a couple of other very small pieces and started the cleanup. This would be the hardest part. Dr. James needed to cut away the infected tissue surround this wound to prevent gangrene. The wound was nearly there now.

Chapter 31

Defending the Castle

As Dr. James cleaned out the wound, Robyn started to squirm a little bit with the pain and Steve had to help hold her down. Dr. James worked as quickly as he could to minimize the pain but he knew he had to get this wound as clean as possible before stitching her up and putting on any antiseptic and bandages. Once he left, there would be no one here to check on Robyn's recovery and definitely no one around should the infection return.

When Dr. James was finally satisfied that he had done all he could do to clean out the infection, he told everyone, "Get ready, I need to stitch her up now and this will sting some."

Robyn let out a moan and tried to grit her teeth. Deanna asked, 'Do you want something to bite down on Robyn?"

Robyn replied with slightly slurred speech, "Yes please."

Steve got up, found a clean wash rag in a drawer and helped her put it in her mouth. When she nodded ready, Dr. James started stitching her wound, being watchful for more signs of oozing pus.

Once he was finished, Dr. James let out a sigh and looked up. He asked Robyn, "How do you feel?"

Robyn just looked at him with slightly glazed eyes.

Dr. James took Steve aside and explained, "She'll need to keep this extremely clean and dry for a couple of days. You or someone you trust will need to help her with that. Change the bandage a couple of times a day until it stops seeping. Check the bandages for infection. A little clean blood is a good thing until it heals. Don't let her get it wet when she bathes for about a week. I will also leave a small amount of anti-septic cream to put on it to keep the wound from getting too dry and opening back up. If you can find some triple anti-biotic to put around it, that would be good. I would also like to ask Big John's wife, Barbara to look in on you guys, if you like? I think Robyn could benefit from having another woman around, especially now."

"We need to get out of here as soon as possible so I won't be around if she relapses after today. The most important thing right now, is watching for infection. The wound may seep a little blood over the next day or so but, if you see any red, radiating lines or any ugly green discharge coming from that wound, she'll need to see a doctor at a hospital immediately. I did the best I could here in your makeshift field hospital so keep a close eye on her for the next week or so. I will leave a phone number with Big John, in case you have any questions but know this, I will be out of touch for the next few days until we get to where we are going."

Steve nodded and sat back down with a now, sleeping Robyn. Dr. James applied the anti-septic cream and put a large, square bandage over her wound, sealing it with tape. Dr. James said, "Do you see how I put this bandage on? This is how any new ones will need to be applied. This'll need to be changed out a couple times a day until she is no longer seeping and once a day thereafter until the wound is fully closed. That should take a couple of weeks. Do you have any bandages like this? If not, I would make arrangements with someone to watch over her while you go to a store and stock up. Please try not to mention me to anyone, okay? That way we all stay out of trouble."

Dr. James added, "If you need to go get medical supplies now, we can ride back over to Big Johns and wait for you. If you want, I know two very capable women there who would be more than happy to watch Robyn for you. I can send them over as soon as we get to his place. That way you can relax and go get what you need with minimal scrutiny from anyone in your community. What do you think, is that what you want to do?"

Steve nodded yes, and replied, "Yeah, that works for me. There is a drug store not too far from here and I can be gone and back in no time. I won't need any help this afternoon and you can pick up the car later after I get back. Let's walk out and talk to Big John."

Dr. James looked at Deanna, and she said, "Go on, I'll watch her."

Dr. James and Steve walked out and found Big John sitting in his truck listening to the radio. He looked up when he saw them approaching the truck, turning off the radio as they stepped up.

Big John asked, "Well, did everything go all right? Is she going to be okay?"

Steve replied, "Yeah, it looks like Dr. James saved her but she will need to be watched closely for a while. Which is what we want to talk to you about. Do you think your wife would like to help me watch over her for the next week or so? I'd sure appreciate it and I think Robyn would feel a little better having a woman help her bathe and do other personal things."

Big John got all exited and replied, "Absolutely, that's what neighbors are for. I know she would jump at the chance to help out." Then he looked over at Dr. James and winked, as if to let Dr. James know that he would take care of Ben and Stacy.

 Steve looked so relieved he failed to notice the wink. Big John got out of his truck and walked up to the house with Steve and Dr. James, talking about how he happy he was to hear that little Robyn was on the mend, telling Steve that if he ever needed anything, just to ask.

When they arrived back in the kitchen, Robyn was still sleeping. They all got quiet and Dr. James suggested the four of them carefully pick her up and carry her to her bed to let her sleep it off. With great care, they lifted her off the table and carried her to her bed. It was a little tricky getting her in through the bedroom door but now, she was sleeping comfortably and Dr. James and Deanna felt like they could leave her in her dad's capable hands.

They walked quietly back out to the kitchen talking in low voices. Dr. James told them, "We need to get going. We have a lot of preparing to do before we can leave." He looked at Steve and said, "I assume you know Big John's phone number, right?"

Steve nodded and replied, "Yes, I' call if anything changes for the worse."

Dr. James couldn't help asking, "Do you have something other than that race car to use?" Steve smiled and replied, "I have a small grocery getter around back that I use for around here. That road monster in the garage uses too much gas for small errands around town and attracts a lot of attention. Are you sure you want to take it?"

Dr. James looked at Deanna and remarked, "We'll need all of the speed we can get in order to get where we need to go. Not to worry, we aren't planning to drive like race car drivers but it'll be nice to know we can if we need to."

After the kitchen was cleaned up and Dr. James had collected all of his instruments and supplies, they headed out to Big John's truck to say good bye. Big John and Deanna got in first. Steve took a moment to shake Dr. James's hand and to say, "Thank you for everything doc, I wish you well and a safe journey wherever you're going. If you don't hear from me again, that'll be a good thing."

Dr. James got into the truck and Big John drove them home. When they finally arrived, Ben was waiting for them in the barn. As Dr. James stepped out of the truck, he looked over at Ben and asked, "Is everything all right?"

Ben came over and said in a low voice, "Robert's men stopped by after you guys left, looking for us. Barbara put us down in the basement to hide while she convinced them that she was all alone here while her husband had stepped out for an errand. We need to talk, all of us, when you get settled in." Ben waited for Deanna to get out of the truck. Meanwhile, Big John was already halfway to the back door.

When they all trooped in and put their things away, they noticed Big John was in the front room with Barbara making sure she was okay after the encounter. Deanna and Dr. James sat down at the table and Deanna asked, "What happened?"

Theresa answered for Stacy, who looked shaken up. "They drove up to the house with their guns out and demanded Big John come out to answer some questions. Barbara hurried us all down into their cellar and we hid out there. I crept up the stairs to the cellar door to see if I could hear anything. I heard Barbara at the front door shouting at them that Big John was out on an errand and they should come back later. The man in charge told her that they are out looking for some traitors and were searching the area looking for them. He told her that if she or her husband were to see any strangers, they were to tell them where so they could pick them up. Failure to do so will make the big boss mad and he would likely retaliate."

"Barbara told them that they hadn't seen any strangers wandering around but she would tell her husband when he returned home. Then they left," she said. "I'm scared Deanna, when can we leave?"

 Dr. James stepped away from the table and walked out to where Big John and Barbara were standing in the front room. "I'm sorry for bringing you any trouble. We'll leave just as soon as we can get Steve's car, hopefully soon. You never saw us and we'll make sure we don't leave anything behind to get you in trouble with Robert's crew. Meanwhile, if we could trouble you for some food for the trip and your clothes washer, we would like to get ready to go as quickly as possible."

That woke Barbara up. That was all she needed to get back into the groove. She gave Big John a peck on the cheek and went back out to the kitchen. Dr. James could hear her asking Stacy to help her get some food ready and she would show them where the washer and dryer were.

Dr. James stood next to Big John wondering what to do next, when Big John reached out and clapped him on the shoulder. He said, "Come on, I want to show you guys something." He headed towards the back door, grabbing Ben on the way out. As the three of them went out, Deanna looked up and started to ask where they were going but James shook his head no, so she sat back down.

The two of them followed Big John out to the barn and over to the back wall behind some old hay bales. Underneath, tucked away under a tarp, were a couple of old automatic machine guns. Ben recognized them as M240's and wondered how Big John managed to get them. They looked well cared for.

Big John reached down and pulled one out from under the tarp and underneath were several belts of ammunition. He explained, "I managed to find these along with the ammo a few years ago during the crash. Some national guard troops walked off and left everything laying out as if they didn't care anymore and I happened to be in the right place at the right time. So, I scavenged up as much as I could and hid it out here in the barn. Barbara doesn't know I have this plus a few other toys I picked up."

Big John opened some other boxes and inside were a handful of M4 rifles with some ammo boxes, grenades and what looked like a couple of Javelin rocket launchers. Dr. James had no idea what he was looking at other than some military weapons but Ben knew exactly what they were. He had always been a fan of weapons, especially military ones. He had wanted to join the Army once until he found out what they were doing to people inside the U.S.

Big John grinned wide when he saw the look on Ben's face as Ben recognized what he was looking at. He closed the boxes and pulled the tarp back over, kicking a little hay over the tarp as they walked back out.

When they had walked as far as Big John's truck, Big John told them, "Up until now, I'm the only one who's ever known about his. Now that you know," looking at Ben, "should those idiots come back and try to cause trouble, we can give it to them. I'll show you around outside some more so you can see where my foxholes are and my fields of fire towards the front of the property." He walked out and instead of heading back to the house, Big John walked around the barn to the field out in front of the barn.

As they walked, Big John pointed out a small hummock just off the corner of the barn. He told them, "That's a foxhole with a camo cover that lifts up quickly. Someone can scoot under and be ready in seconds. There's an excellent field of fire towards the driveway and the road out front. There's also a quick release door on the corner of the barn in case someone needs to pull back in a hurry."

He then led them across the front yard of the house to a patch of woods on the other side. Big John pointed out a tree stand in a big tree back off the road and another camouflage blind in some bushes with a foxhole underneath. All with a good field of fire anywhere on the front of the property and the road beyond.

Big John told them, "Ever since the crash and the government takeover, I've been paranoid of local militias so I built all of this with those military grade weapons in mind. Those Javelins can be fired from either spot and even from the tree stand, although I wouldn't recommend that. You'll automatically give yourself away if you fire one from up there. Unless Robert's crew has an Abrams tank or a Bradley fighting vehicle, they won't stand a chance. Let's hope we don't have to use them."

Ben spoke up, "We should set out those M240 SAW's (Squad Automatic Weapons) and Javelins in the blinds now just in case they return today, along with some ammo and grenades. I don't want to take the time to grab them while Robert's people are trying to shoot up the house. What about the women? Do they have a safe place they can go if things go hot?"

Big John replied, "That's a good idea. And yes, there is a bunker on the backside of the barn they can get to if things go south out front."

Big John also said, "I hope we don't have to use the M240's or Javelins. I don't want to attract the attention of Homeland Security if we blow up a truck or two and the neighbors report the sounds of automatic weapons."

Dr. James echoed that sentiment as well. He replied, "Although I know nothing of these weapons, the last thing we need is federal law enforcement finding out we are here."

They went back to the barn to grab the weapons and ammo in order to set up crossing fields of fire for the front area of Big John's land. Once it was all completed, it was getting dark and there was still no sign of the militia. Dr. James had been thinking about another solution while they were busy setting everything up.

When they went back into the house to clean up for dinner, he brought up his idea to everyone. "What if an anonymous call were to be placed with the federal authorities telling them that Robert's militia was harassing innocent civilians in this area? We know, from what Robert's people told us, they're already on the list of groups that Homeland Security is trying to take down. If they were to stake out this area and capture them, you wouldn't have to worry about starting a small war with Robert."

Big John thought about it for a minute, and replied, "What about your group? You don't want to get caught by the feds either."

Dr. James responded, "If all goes well, we'll be gone by tonight so that shouldn't be a problem. My concern," and he looked directly at Ben and Stacy, "is what about you two? Homeland Security doesn't know about you but Robert does and he'll keep coming after us until he can't anymore, and that includes the both of you. What do you want to do?"

Ben sat up straight, "I want to fight. I don't like running all the time and we want to make a home here. I'm not worried about Robert or his people. They can bring it and I'll take them down myself if I have to," he said with a defiant look on his face. Stacy sat there looking on but the expression on her face said she agreed with him.

Dr. James looked over at Big John, "There's your answer. Let's wait a little longer to see if Steve calls about that car. You can make that call as soon as the three of us are long gone. With Ben here to help, you should be able to handle one truck load of hooligans for now. If they come back like they did earlier today, step out with your guns strapped on and don't let them near your house or barn. Then make the call after they leave to get reinforcements. If they try to force you, take them out, then make the call. Either way, call Homeland security and report them. Let the feds do the hard work for you. A win-win for everyone."

Big John looked around at everyone and asked, "Is everyone in agreement with his plan? I don't want anyone backing out if we say go." Everyone at the table nodded or replied yes.

Chapter 32

Trouble in Paradise

With the agreement on home defense out of the way, Barbara declared, "Everyone out of the kitchen so we can get dinner on." Stacy stepped up to help and everyone else decided to head outside to enjoy the twilight and nice cool temps. Dr. James reminded Barbara and Stacy to come get him if Steve should call. As they stood around on the back patio, Deanna decided to look at the flower beds alongside the house. Theresa accompanied her just for something to do.

Dr. James, Ben and Big John watched them go off and Ben remarked, "It's so quiet and peaceful here right now. This is what we want and we're looking forward to it as soon as we finish taking out the trash" in a noted dig at Robert. The other two smiled but remained with quiet with their own thoughts admiring the lighting bugs and moths drifting with the breeze.

After a bit of somewhat uncomfortable silence Deanna and Theresa came back over. Deanna started to ask if everything was all right and just as she opened her mouth, Stacy came to the back door, "Dr. James, there's a phone call for you."

Dr. James replied, "Thank you Stacy, I'll be right there," then hurried in behind her.

Dr. James eagerly took the phone from Stacy and replied, "This is Dr. James speaking". After a couple of minutes, James said, "Sure, I think we can manage that somehow. Let me talk to Big John and I'll call you right back. Let me have your phone number please." Dr. James scribbled down a number on the pad next to the phone and hung up.

He immediately went back out to find Big John, who was still on the back patio talking to Ben, Deanna and Theresa. Dr. James hurriedly walked up and said, "Excuse me, may I have a word?" When everyone stopped talking, Dr. James said, "Steve just called to let me know we can come pick up the car anytime now. But we shouldn't wait too long as he needs to attend to Robyn. I'm concerned about leaving with the possibility of Robert's people coming back while we're gone. Would it be okay if Deanna and I borrow your truck to run over and get that car? We'll try to make it as quick as possible."

Big John replied, "Absolutely, here," and passed him the keys. "Just put the truck all the way in the barn and park the car behind it when you get back. Ben and I will handle things here."

Deanna took the keys from him and said, "Thanks, we'll be right back." As she headed for the barn, Dr. James told her, "I need to bring my bag so I can take a quick look at Robyn while we're there. I'll meet you at the truck."

Deanna got into the pickup truck and waited for James, who got in a couple of minutes later. As soon as James closed the door, she started the truck and drove back to Steve's house. She was a little worried about finding his place in the dark.

As they turned out onto the road, Deanna asked "Do you think Big John and Ben can hold off Robert's crew by themselves?"

Dr. James looked over at her and replied, "I think so. Ben is very capable and Big John is a military combat veteran. They're much more capable than you or I."

Deanna was driving slow so as not to miss Steve's turn off and driveway. James kept an eye out as well to help her. Pretty soon, they spotted the distinctive mail box and turned up his driveway, parking next to the garage.

As they got out of the truck, Steve came down the driveway to meet them. He caught up the them in front of the truck, and said, "I'm glad I caught you here and you brought your medical bag. Can you take a look at Robyn before you go? I want to make sure she's mending okay."

Dr. James said, "That's why I bought my bag. I anticipated doing that. If you want to give Deanna the keys to the car so she can get it ready to go, I'll follow you up to the house and take a quick look at her. Is she awake yet?"

Steve looked back and said, "Yeah, she woke up about an hour ago and asked for something to eat. Something she hasn't done in a couple of days. That's a good sign, right?"

Dr. James replied, "Yes, it is; I'll know more once I take a look." Steve threw Deanna the keys to the car and told her "Go ahead, it's all yours." Steve and Dr. James continued into the house as Deanna headed into the garage.

Once in the front room, Dr. James found Robyn in the kitchen eating what looked like soup and crackers. She was sitting in a chair with a cushion behind her slurping her way through some Campbells soup when he walked up. Dr. James asked, "How are you feeling Robyn?

Robyn looked up from her bowl and gave him a big smile with red tomato soup on her upper lip. She replied, "Hi Dr. James, I'm feeling much better now. It hurts still but daddy gave me a little Tylenol before I sat down to eat. I don't feel so tired and hot anymore."

Dr. James sat down next to her and asked, "May I take a quick look while I am here? I just need to lift up your pajama top and see under the bandage for a minute, if that's okay?"

Robyn replied between slurps, "Sure Dr. James, go right ahead."

She reached down to grab her pajama top but Dr. James stopped her, "I just need to take a peek, you don't need to take the whole thing off. Let me help." Dr. James picked up the bottom edge above the bandage and lifted it enough to see.

The bandage had some blood seepage as expected but there were no signs of any pus. Dr. James said, "I need to pull a corner of the bandage loose to look underneath, it might sting a little."

Robyn said, "Go ahead doctor, I'll be fine."

Dr. James pulled the top corner loose, trying to be as careful as he could. He felt Robyn wince a little when the tape pulled away from her skin but she didn't cry out.

Underneath, Dr. James looked at his stitches and the wound. No red, radiating lines, the puckering was already starting to diminish and there wasn't any new blood. He put the bandage back on and pulled her top back down. He said, "Looking good Robyn. I think you'll be fine as long as you keep it clean and change that bandage a couple of times a day. It should be changed now as a matter of fact. Let me tell your dad."

Dr. James got up, touched her arm briefly with a smile and left her to finish eating. He walked out to find her dad and tell him the good news. Steve was standing near the front windows looking out at Deanna with the car already in the driveway.

He remarked as Dr. James walked up, "She's quite a woman for a nurse. It looks like she can handle that car nearly as well as I can."

Dr. James nodded and replied, "Yes, she learned a lot from her brothers apparently, and I am still learning more about her many talents as well. I need to tell you the good news. It looks like Robyn is going to mend just fine. She needs a bandage change now. Just remember to keep it clean for the next couple of weeks until it heals up completely. Change the bandage a least two to three times a day until it closes up. Those stitches can be removed after the wound completely closes and there is no more sign of any infection. There is still a possibility that I didn't get all of the pieces of wood out of her so she may see some tiny dark spots over time. They can be taken out like any other splinter you might get in your finger. Just keep things clean and she should be fine."

Steve started to get emotional and softly said, "Thank you doc. I don't know what we'd have done if you hadn't shown up when you did. Letting you have that old car is just a small token of what I owe you for saving her life." Steve grabbed James's hand and shook it, then looked away for a minute to get himself together. "I'll change her bandage as soon as she's finished eating, you can be sure. I'll take good care of her, no worries. She is all I have left since my wife died so I'll do whatever I have to, to make sure she's safe."

Dr. James said, "Take care Steve, I doubt we'll ever meet again so I'll say good bye now and wish you and Robyn a good life." Then he walked out the door down to the truck. Deanna was at the end of the driveway waiting. James turned the truck around, falling in behind her as they headed back to Big John's farm. Deanna needed a little bit of time to get used to the clutch and jack rabbit speed of the car but after a couple of spits and sputters, she finally got the feel of things and off they went. It'd been a long time since she'd driven a stick shift but, like riding a bike, it all came back to her.

Deanna pulled into Big John's driveway and noticed that all of the lights were out except a faint light coming from the back of the house shining through the front window. She pulled over to the side of the driveway to let James go ahead with the truck. As she sat there watching, she didn't see any other vehicles around but she tried her best to ghost the car into the barn behind the pickup truck. She waited for James to meet her at the car door and voiced her concern.

James replied, "You have your pistol. if you're worried, take it out and I'll follow you to the back door." Deanna pulled the pistol from her holster, then kept it up and pointed ahead of her as they quietly made their way to the back door. When they arrived, Deanna very softly, stepped up to the door to look in through a corner of the window pane. With no back patio lights on, Deanna figured she could take a quick peek to see if anything looked wrong without being seen from inside the kitchen.

As she peered in, she saw Barbara working at the kitchen sink but Stacy was nowhere to be seen. Deanna thought, "That's a little odd." There was no sign of anyone else in the kitchen, which might be suspicious or not. She decided to wait a little bit to make sure.

Using hand signals, Deanna signaled to James that they were going to wait a little bit out here to make sure everything was okay. James signaled back that he would step back into the shadows to wait for her.

Deanna kept low under the glass pane of the door and waited a minute before looking in again. This time she thought she saw a shadow pass by the kitchen entryway coming from the front room. She kept looking but it didn't reappear, so she ducked down again. Deanna waited another half minute and looked in again. This time, Big John entered the kitchen from the front room with a stranger walking behind him. Deanna quickly ducked down so she wouldn't be spotted.

Deanna signaled to James that she saw one possible bad guy in the kitchen. James waved at her to be careful. She poked her head up again to look and the stranger was turned the other way, as if listening to someone. As Deanna watched, Barbara saw her and stopped for a second, before continuing to wash something in the sink. Deanna noticed the hesitation and put her finger over her mouth to caution Barbara.

Barbara waited until the stranger went back out to the front room, then made a shooing motion with her left hand. She closed her fist and extended two fingers, twice, as if to signal two men. Deanna quietly stepped back down the steps and found James.

Deanna grabbed his arm and walked him around the corner away from the steps and door. "Barbara is in the kitchen under duress, and Big John is in the front room with probably two bad guys. Ben, Stacy and Theresa are nowhere to be seen. Those two guys had to have seen us drive in and are probably getting anxious as to why we haven't come in the house yet. That could be to our advantage. If I wait in the dark here, I can ambush them when they come looking for us, as they most surely will eventually," she whispered.

James replied back also whispering, "They'll only send out one and the other will stay inside holding Big John and Barbara and maybe the others hostage. If we take one out, we endanger the others. Let me sneak around the other side and see if Ben is in one of the foxholes. You go see if Stacy and Theresa are in that bunker in the barn. We can meet back here in about fifteen minutes or so. What do you think?"

Deanna said, "Okay, that sounds good. I'll meet you right back here. Don't you dare do something stupid and get into any trouble out there," kissing him briefly. James headed across the back lawn, crouching down below any windows in the dark and Deanna went the other way into the barn to see if Theresa and Stacy were in the hidden bunker.

First, she went around to the back of the barn and waited to see if she was being followed. She didn't see any sign of anyone yet. Then she scooted over towards the pasture fence and felt around on the side of the barn for the hidden door Big John had showed them earlier. Deanna knew to look for a recessed handle. In this dark, all she could do was feel along the wood until she found it. After a few minutes, she found what she was looking for.

Deanna decided to knock on the door first before just barging in, just in case someone had a gun pointed at the door. She gave three fast knocks, then four slow ones. A pattern that Theresa would be likely to remember. After a couple of minutes, Theresa cracked the door open from the inside, grabbed Deanna by the arm and pulled her inside quickly.

Stacy was there but Ben was not. Theresa gave Deanna a brief hug and said, "Am I glad to see you. Is Dr. James with you?" Deanna replied, "Yes, he's out on the other side looking for Ben. Where is he?"

Stacy spoke up, "Ben got me and Theresa in here quickly when they arrived. He said Big John and Barbara wanted to stay in the house so as not to arouse suspicion. Robert's men came back right after you two left and took us a little by surprise. We had just enough time for Big John to get us out of the house. Ben knew what to do, so he brought us here first, gave Theresa a pistol and took off again, warning us not to open the door for anyone but one of us."

"I think Ben is outside somewhere trying to find a way to take care of those two men in the house. The others took off and left them here. I'm worried about Ben being out there by himself."

Deanna told her, "Dr. James is looking for him right now so there'll be the two of them now. You two stay here and keep that gun handy. Don't open this door for anyone unless you hear that knock code I just used. If anyone tries to break in, shoot them, got it?"

Both young women nodded yes and stepped back from the door. Deanna put her ear to the door to listen for a minute and when she didn't hear anything, she cracked the door open and looked again. There was no one around. Deanna stepped out quickly, hugged the barn wall, and looked around again before heading back to the rendezvous point to meet James.

She kept her pistol out in front of her while she stopped at the corner of the barn to look around the corner. There was no sign of anyone, so she hugged the walls, working her way to the back of the house again to wait for James. Deanna knew she was a little early so she settled down to wait in the dark, watching the back door.

James crouched down below the windows to go around the back of the house to try and find Ben. All he could think about was Deanna. Was she going to be safe and would she find the others? As he left the side of the house to go out into the trees and bushes where he thought that foxhole might be, he did his best to be as quiet as possible. It was very dark once he made it into the trees. He crept along slowly so as not to walk into a tree or low hanging branch.

After a few minutes, he came up on what looked like the blind and foxhole Big John had showed them earlier in the day. He stopped and whistled to see if anyone responded. After a minute, James whistled again and an answering whistle came back. James walked up a little more and Ben poked his head out pointing one of the rifles at him. When he saw that it was Dr. James, he lowered the rifle and motioned him in.

Ben whispered, "Glad to see you doc, did everything go okay with your patient?"

Dr. James replied, "Yes, she'll be fine. She's on the mend nicely. What happened here?"

Ben told him, "They came roaring down the driveway so fast that we didn't have time to set up a defense in the house so Big John told me to get the women out the back door as fast as I could and head for the bunker. He said he'd try and stall them for as long as he could. I put Stacy and Theresa in that hideaway bunker on the back corner of the barn, went in a grabbed a couple of the A4's and some ammo, then snuck around the house to this spot. I figured this was the best hideout of the two for a one-person defense. So far, no one has returned. They showed up with six men, left two when Big John didn't offer any resistance and took off, presumably to get more men." Ben reached over and passed the other rifle to Dr. James telling him, "It's ready to go. Just let go the safety and shoot."

Dr. James checked the action and saw that there was a round in the chamber. He also noticed that the M240 SAW was set up and pointed out towards the end of the driveway with a belt of ammo in it, ready to go. Dr. James had never fired one of those and had no desire to learn tonight. He looked at Ben and asked, "Do you have a plan yet?"

Ben shook his head no. "No, I don't doc because I don't want to endanger the folks inside. They might as well be hostages right now. The only advantage we have is that they don't know we're here. Although, with you two driving down the driveway and parking in the barn, they now know that Big John and Barbara were holding out on something and they're probably getting anxious waiting on their backup."

Dr. James agreed. He told Ben, "I need to get back to the house. Deanna is probably waiting for me at our rendezvous point out back. We thought about something, and now that I know where you and the other two are, we'll see about making it happen. Do you want to help?"

Ben asked, "What's your plan?"

Dr. James told him about trying to get one of the militia members to come out the back door to look for them and they would jump him when he stepped out. "The only worry we have is the one left inside. He might do something stupid and hurt or kill Big John or Barbara. If we could hit them both at once, we might be able to pull this rescue off. Could you hit the house from the front and take out the man inside? It would have to be quick and we'd have to hit them both at the same time."

Ben thought about it for a minute and replied, "Sure, I can wiggle my way to the front of the house and see if I can get a shot through a front window. Give me a few minutes to get ready and I'll give you a bird whistle when I'm ready."

Dr. James told him, "Just be careful. I'm not too worried about you but I don't want Big John to get caught in the middle."

Ben chuckled, "I'll be careful, don't worry."

Dr. James left out the way he came in and found the back of the house again. He crouched down, making it back to where he saw Deanna waiting for him on the dark side of the house where they agreed to meet.

When he crept up on her, she was waiting. "Did you find Ben? I found the girls in that hideaway bunker so they're safe for now."

James replied, "Yes, he has an ambush set up for anyone coming down the driveway but now he's working his way over to the front of the house. When you hear a bird whistle, we'll know he's ready. Now we have to figure out how to draw one of them out here so we can jump him."

Deanna hadn't been idle while she was waiting for James to get back. She had crept up to the back door again to see if anything had changed. She found Barbara still at the sink but this time, she was by herself. When Deanna peeked in the window again, Barbara tried to use some hand signals to let her know that the bad guys were nervous and arguing about who was going to come out to find them. She kept looking back to the front room as if expecting one of them to come in the kitchen at any second. Barbara looked scared.

Chapter 33

The Ambush

Deanna stayed close to the window until one of the men checked the kitchen as if he had heard something. Deanna crouched back down below the window while Barbara went back to washing vegetables in the sink. When she saw James coming back around the corner of the house, she stepped off the back porch and ducked back around the corner of the house to wait for him.

As they were discussing how to lure the militia man outside, they heard Ben's whistle from around front. It sounded like a warbling bird whistle. James told Deanna, "We need to do something now. How about you go back up and signal Barbara to try and talk that man into checking something out back here? Do you think she'll do it?"

Deanna replied, "I'm sure she wants to help without endangering Big John. Let me see."

She crept back up to the door and waved at Barbara again. Deanna, using hand signals, tried to tell Barbara about the plan. After a couple of minutes of back-and-forth hand gestures, Barbara finally understood and nodded her head yes.

Deanna pointed out towards the back lawn and Barbara nodded yes again. At that, Deanna crept back down to set up the ambush. She and James had decided to wait in the dark with James on one side of the steps and Deanna waiting around the corner in the dark on the other side. The plan was to wait until the man stepped down off the steps onto the patio, then lure him away from the house. Once he was far enough away so that any shots fired wouldn't end up in the house, they would put him down. Hopefully, the first shot would distract the attention of the other one in the house enough so Ben could nail him as well. If Ben was lucky, Big John would be able to duck out of the way.

Within minutes, the back door opened and one of the militia members stepped out, gun at the ready, looking around for anything wrong. He stood there for a minute shining a flashlight around before coming down the steps to search the area. As he stepped down to the bottom of the steps, James threw a fist-sized rock out to the back lawn. The man shined his flashlight towards the sound and started to walk out to the back yard. Once he cleared the patio and was a few feet into the back lawn, Deanna stepped out from the shadows and shot him in the back, three times in a close pattern, just like her dad and brothers had taught her.

As soon as the sounds of the shots rang out from the back of the house, the one militia member left inside jumped up to see what happened, leaving Big John alone for a split second. That was just enough for Ben to shoot him through the front window with the rifle, putting him down in the front room. As soon as he saw the man go down, Ben ran towards the back of the house to make sure everything was all right back there.

When he rounded the back corner, he saw Dr. James and Deanna standing over the other militia member down in the back yard. He slowed down to a fast walk, announcing himself, "It's me, Ben, I'm coming in." Deanna turned around and waved at him to come over. Dr. James was cleaning his hands off on a cloth of some kind as he walked up.

Dr. James acknowledged Ben with a nod standing with a grim look on his face. He finally said, "I couldn't save him." Deanna touched his arm as if to try and console him but Dr. James was too distraught by the taking of these lives, like so many others in the past.

Ben told them, "I got the guy inside, if you want to check on him? Once I shot him, I ran back here to check on you guys. He may still be alive."

Dr. James looked up and ran into the house. Deanna stood there watching him go. Deanna had no remorse in shooting this guy dead at her feet. She knew it was a them or us situation so she wouldn't be losing any sleep over any of this. She decided to head over to the bunker to get the girls while James was sorting out the rest. She looked at Ben and asked, "Do you want to come with me to get your wife and Theresa from the bunker?"

Ben turned to head out towards the back of the barn but Deanna said, "Wait, I told Theresa to shoot anyone that tried to get in that didn't give the coded knock. Let me knock first before she shoots you."

Deanna rapped on the door with the special knock signal and waited. After a minute, Theresa opened the door with the gun pointed out until she saw Deanna and Ben standing there. Stacy stepped out from behind her and hugged Ben. Theresa asked, "Is it all over?"

 Deanna replied, "For now. The two guys inside are down but the rest may arrive any minute now so we need to get ready to move quickly."

Deanna headed back to the house at a fast pace with the rest following behind. As she entered through the back door, she saw Barbara on the floor with Dr. James, trying to patch up the wounded militia member, who looked pretty bad. There was blood all over the floor where Ben had dropped him and Dr. James was trying to stop the bleeding. Barbara was holding a towel over the bullet wound but the man was still slowly bleeding out, despite Dr. James attempts to save him. Ben's shot had taken him in the back.

Deanna stepped inside to let the others in behind her. Stacy saw the mess on the floor and got very upset. She looked like she was going to be sick and Ben held her close to keep her from seeing any more. Theresa came around them and asked, "Is there anything I can do to help?"

Barbara looked up and shook her head no. She didn't think this man had much longer to live.

Ben asked, "Where is Big John?"

Barbara said, "He went out the front door to man one of his 'defensive positions,' as he calls it and I haven't seen him since. He's fine though, thank you for saving him."

Ben smiled and replied "You're welcome". He looked down at Stacy asking her, "Will you be all right if I go out and help Big John defend this place against Robert's people?"

Stacy looked up, sniffed and wiped her eyes. "Go ahead, I'll manage."

Ben stepped out through the back door, then walked around to the front of the barn to see if Big John was in that foxhole in the front pasture. When he had crept up to where he thought the foxhole was, he whistled to see if Big John was in there. No response. He slowly crept up and found it empty. Ben thought, "He must be on the other side." Ben jogged all the way around the back of the house and out to the other blind where he had been before.

As he approached, Big John called out, "Is that you Ben? If you aren't Ben, you're going to be dead if you don't identify yourself."

Ben called back, "It's me Big John, I came out to see where you're at and talk battle plans with you. Is it all right if I come in now?"

Big John replied, "Come on in and I'll tell you what we're going to do next." Ben crawled in next to Big John and sat down.

Big John looked out towards the road. "Ben, they're coming and we know it. I'll give you the choice but, if you want, bring out a couple of those Javelins, one for each of us and let's set up this ambush. You in the pasture over there and me over here, just like we talked about earlier today. This may be a long night but if we can take those guys out, we'll all be able to breathe a little easier around here."

Ben asked him, "Are you going to okay over here by yourself? I can bring everything over here if you want?"

Big John smiled, "Ben, I was a combat Infantry soldier with the 10th Mountain Division in Afghanistan. This is like getting on a bicycle again after a long time. My old training has kicked in and I am just as ready now as I was over twenty years ago when I was a young pup like you are now. Don't you worry. You just take care of yourself over there and remember, don't do any Rambo stunts. You have a wife depending on you to survive the night just like I do."

Ben looked at him and quietly asked, "What's a Rambo stunt?"

Big John started laughing hilariously, "You've never heard of Rambo? They're a bunch of military action movies from years ago, played by Silvester Stallone. Must have been before your time," still laughing.

Ben smiled, "I'll have to watch them with you sometime, if we can find them somewhere."

Big John laughed again, "You bet'cha, I look forward to having a guy's night with you sometime soon, with popcorn and a movie. The girls can go find their own entertainment that night."

"Done. Let me go get those Javelins and I'll be right back." Ben left to go back to the barn to retrieve the rockets. He also wanted to check on Stacy and let Barbara know that Big John was fine and enjoying himself. Ben entered the back door and looked for Stacy. The militia member had been moved, but the blood hadn't been cleaned up yet. Ben carefully stepped over the mess and went to look for everyone.

Ben walked through the front room towards the bedrooms in the back. He started hearing muffled voices and found everyone in one of the rooms standing around a bed. Apparently, Dr. James had managed to keep the man from dying on the floor and they brought him back here to watch him.

Stacy saw him at the door, ran over to hug him to ask, "Are you okay?"

Everyone else looked up and Ben told them, "No sign of anyone yet and Big John is fine. He's enjoying himself out front in one of the ambush sites. I'm on my way to get more ammunition and then I'll be standing guard in the other site."

Ben was deliberately not giving out too many details in case the man on the bed could hear him. He wanted to let the man know that they were well prepared for his friends when they returned, in case he should manage to get loose and warn them somehow. Although Ben doubted this man was going anywhere anytime soon. He looked like he was in pretty bad shape laying on the bed.

Ben hugged and gave Stacy a brief kiss before heading back out. He went to the barn and grabbed two Javelins to give Big John. He wasn't sure if he wanted one in his forward outpost in the pasture. If it went wide, it might hit the house or the woods where Big John was hiding. Since he didn't have any experience with firing one, he figured he shouldn't take any chances.

After returning to Big John's foxhole, Ben told him about his misgivings. Big John got serious and said, "I'll leave that decision up to you. If you don't feel comfortable, no problem. I'll keep them here and hope we won't need them. If I do fire one, it'll make one hell of a bang out there and surely draw the authorities. Something we don't need here. Go on with you and be careful. I'll see you later or at breakfast, whichever comes first," he said with a smile. Ben smiled in return and left to go to his post.

Ben made it over to the foxhole and settled in for a long night. He scooted down into the dirt hole and sighted in the SAW. Then he pulled up the A-4 rifle and set that pointed toward the driveway, keeping it close. Now it was just a matter of waiting for their prey to come. As any hunter waiting in a blind for the animal they're out hunting for, Ben knew all about how to be patient while waiting for the game to come to him. Now that the trap was set, Ben just needed to stay awake and quiet until sunup or when the bad guys returned, whichever occurred first.

Inside the house, Dr. James had done all he could for the man on the bed. There was still a bullet deep inside of him that would take major surgery to remove. Something he couldn't do here. He had stopped the external bleeding for now but it was only a matter of time before his patient died of complications, unless they could get him to a hospital. Something that didn't look likely tonight. If the man lived through the night, then maybe.

The women got together and started cleaning up the house. Deanna told them all, "We need to behave as normal as possible when they arrive. Don't let them in the house. If we all pitch in and clean up, it won't take long to finish up. Theresa and I can take care of the dead man in the back yard, if...," she looked at Barbara and Stacy, "you two want to clean up in here?"

Barbara replied, "Sounds good to me. I don't want to get involved with moving any dead bodies, thank you very much," she said with a snap. "Come on Stacy, let's get to work out here while they deal with the business in the back yard."

Deanna and Theresa stepped over the mess in the kitchen doorway and went out the back door. By this time, the body was starting to smell as everything inside had let go after death. Theresa gagged a little bit but she grabbed the man's legs and asked, "Where're we going to take him?"

Deanna looked around in the dark and replied, "Let's take the body over behind the barn as far down in the pasture as we can manage without killing ourselves. We don't need anyone finding him when they come."

The women grabbed the body and started dragging it across the grass towards the back of the barn. This man had been heavy to begin with and now, his dead weight made him that much harder to move. Deanna wondered if there might be something in the barn that might make this easier. She told Theresa, "Let's go look in the barn and see if we can find a wheel barrow or something we can move him with."

They left the body where it was for the moment while they went looking. Neither one of them had a flashlight so that made things more difficult. Theresa found an old wheel barrow tucked away in a corner and pulled it out. "Here Deanna, I found one," she called out. Deanna walked over and said, "That'll do fine, let's go."

They went over and rolled the body into the wheel barrow. Then, with each of them grabbing a handle, wheeled it down past the back of the barn, leaving the smelly body next to the fence, far enough away from the house so that no one would see or smell it. Both of them were tired from the exertion but feeling better about things so far. Now everyone just had to wait and see what else the night would bring.

Chapter 34

The Firefight

Once the house and yard were cleaned up, Barbara suggested, "We should all try to get a little sleep now. It's late and there's no sense in all of us staying awake all night."

Deanna said, "Someone should remain on watch just in case. We got a little used to night watches while we were traveling up north, so one of us can sit up and we can relieve each other every couple of hours. I'll take the first shift, then wake up Theresa in a little while."

Theresa replied, "I'll take a nap but make sure you wake me, I don't want you playing soldier and staying up all night," she laughed. Barbara turned out all of the lights except the one over the kitchen sink. Dr. James, Theresa, Stacy and Barbara went off to bed for a while.

Deanna set up her post by bringing a kitchen chair to the front room where she could watch out the windows. The first thing she noticed, grimly, was the bullet hole in the glass where Ben had shot through it. It had already been a long night and it was starting to get a little longer.

Her watch was pretty uneventful so, about one am, she went to find Theresa to relieve the watch. She found Theresa and Stacy sharing a queen-sized bed together, still dressed but asleep. Deanna quietly walked over and gave Theresa a gentle nudge. Theresa woke with a start and looked at Deanna with eyes wide in terror. She recognized Deanna within a moment and calmed down a bit.

Deanna quietly asked, "Are you okay? It's time for your watch, if you're up to it?"

Theresa swallowed and said, "Yeah, I'm good, just a bad dream. Give me a couple of minutes and I'll be right out."

Deanna left her to get ready and went back out to the chair in the front room. She didn't think anything was going to happen at this time in the wee hours just after midnight but at dawn, it was a good possibility.

After about five minutes, Theresa came out and Deanna explained about the chair and what to watch for, which wasn't much. If anything did happen outside, she was to come wake the rest and stay under cover.

Deanna pointed out, "If our boys outside start shooting, I doubt anyone will remain asleep anyway but check on us and stay low. Dr. James is your watch relief in two hours." Theresa nodded okay and sat down in the chair to start her watch.

Deanna went back, washed up, then climbed in next to Stacy to try and get a nap before sunup. As she closed her eyes, she thought, "I wonder if I should check on James? He's just across the hall." Then she thought better of it and decided, he's adult enough to take care of himself and drifted off.

Outside, Big John was trying his best to stay awake. It'd been many years since he had stood an all-night guard duty and it was showing. He tried to move around some without making a lot of noise but it wasn't enough. He was also watching the house and he noticed when the lights went out. He thought, "Barbara must be settling the house down for the night." All he knew was that he had to find a way to stay awake. "Some of her coffee would be good about now," he thought.

Ben was also struggling a little to remain awake. He was laying down in the foxhole with little to no room to move around without disturbing things. All he could think of to do to help him stay awake was to remember the bad things they had been through so far, including the arguments with his and Stacy's fathers. His father had been a little more understanding but was against the marriage purely on their social class standing in their community. His argument was that Stacy's family was way above their social class standing in the community and he didn't want any trouble. This had disgusted Ben and when Stacy came to him with the plan to escape, he was all on board. He just didn't realize how much trouble that decision would create at the time.

As the night dragged on, with all the night watches trying hard to stay awake, Dr. James lay awake wondering if they were going to make it through the night and the next morning. He thought to himself, "This is mostly my fault for everyone being in this mess. I should've asked around about Robert before blindly believing that he was still the same guy I remember from the last trip up this way. He really fooled me but I'll never let that happen again." He tossed and turned until Theresa gently opened the door to see if he was ready to stand his watch.

As soon as Theresa stepped in, Dr. James looked up and quietly asked, "Is it my turn?"

Theresa replied in a whisper, "Yes, it's about three am and time to change the guard, if you are up for it?"

James nodded and told her, "Let me wash up and I'll be right out." Theresa left him and walked back out to the front room to wait.

Dr. James came out a couple minutes later and Theresa said, "All is quiet right now Dr. James. I just hope it stays that way."

James nodded and replied, "Get some sleep, you'll likely need it. I don't think things will remain quiet for much longer." Theresa nodded in agreement and whispered, "Good night."

James sat down in the chair for a moment, then jumped up to start pacing the floor in thought. All he could think about were his feelings of guilt over everyone being in danger right now and "What can I do without endangering my friends anymore." He couldn't see any other way beyond what they were already doing. "After our escape, Robert is not going to forgive and forget."

As the long night started to give away to dawn, Ben and Big John were really struggling to stay awake. Big John had dozed off a couple of times accidently and caught himself. All he could do was shake it off and move around as best as he could for now.

Ben was in the same way. He had caught himself dozing off and had to shake himself awake a couple of times throughout the early morning hours. But with the sun starting to rise in the east, he was awake now. He knew that if Robert was going to attack today, it would be soon. The typical cliché dawn attack. At least that was how Ben thought of it.

About a half an hour later, just as the sun was starting to show on the horizon, Ben heard the noise of a car engine on the road coming their way from the south. As it got closer, he heard more than one vehicle and he knew this was it. He lifted himself up a little bit to wave his hand in Big John's direction, hoping he would see him.

After a couple of waves, he lay back down to get ready, wondering if Big John had seen him. Ben thought, "I'll certainly get his attention when I open up on those cars." That was Ben's plan. Wait until they entered the driveway and as soon as they were directly across from him, let them have it in a surprise ambush. "I should be able to take out several of them before they get organized enough to shoot back. By then, Big John can catch them from the other side and we wipe them out altogether, I hope."

Within a few minutes, two SUVs slowed down and turned into the driveway. There wasn't much daylight yet so visibility was low for them as the driveway was in an easterly direction. Ben thought, "What little bit of sun there is, it's gotta be hitting them right in the face." After turning into the driveway, the lead SUV slowed down to a crawl moving down the driveway towards the house while the other one stayed at the top of the driveway in an overwatch position.

Ben watched from his camouflaged position in the pasture and kept the SAW tracking the lead SUV until it stopped a little way up from the house. As soon as it stopped, one militia member stepped out of the front passenger side door and yelled for someone. Ben assumed it must be one of the men they'd left behind last night.

At that point, Ben pulled the trigger and let out a burst from the SAW directly into the man and into the side of the SUV. The man went down immediately and suddenly the opposite doors on the SUV popped open. Two militia members hit the ground on the other side, looking for the shooter. Then, an explosion hit the other SUV at the end of the driveway, sending it up into a ball of flame as a Javelin missile made a direct hit from Big John's position.

Ben opened up on the lead SUV again trying to draw their attention away from Big John so he could turn around and get his SAW going from his side. Within a minute after the Javelin went off, the other SAW let out a burst to hit the two men on the ground under the lead SUV. It was all over within minutes. Ben grabbed his A-4 and crept out of his foxhole, running to the barn and then out to the SUV to take out any stragglers, if any.

Big John jerked up when he heard the cars coming up the road. As soon as he heard the second car, he grabbed the Javelin and got it ready to fire. He hoped Ben was ready and wouldn't choke on him when the time came. As he watched the driveway, he saw the two SUVs turn in. Keeping the Javelin aimed at the last SUV, he thought, "Here we go. Alright Ben, let's see what your made of."

As soon as he heard Ben open up with his machine gun, he watched the lead SUV jump a little as the bullets hit. When he saw the two men jump out and hit the ground, he fired his Javelin at the second SUV. He watched his missile hit the front grille, making the SUV go up in a ball of fire. Big John thought, "Direct hit. No one is getting out of that truck alive." He dropped the launcher and quickly grabbed his M-240 from where he had it pointed at the end of the driveway, bringing it around to shoot at the two men laying down nearly under the other SUV.

Just as they turned to look over at the burning SUV, wondering what happened, he let loose a quick burst, spraying bullets all over the area where the men were laying. He fired until neither of them was moving anymore. As Big John looked up a little bit from his foxhole, he saw Ben running across the field towards the barn. He decided to wait and see if anyone else made a move from the SUV to provide cover for Ben from here.

Ben made it to the barn without incident so he stood up behind the back corner and looked around towards the SUV quickly, then ducked back. No shots fired. Ben walked down to a small door on the back of the barn leading into where the pickup and car were parked. He quickly went through the barn and peered out from the big door. He could see the front corner of the first SUV but he didn't see any movement.

Ben ran hard to the back of the house, then crept up to the corner where he could see inside the SUV through the front windshield and around the car. There was one man slumped over in the passenger side-rear seat and not moving. Ben reasoned he must have got hit with his initial burst. As he peered out a little more, he saw the first man he had shot laying under the open passenger door, also not moving and blood everywhere under him.

Ben ran up to the front of the SUV, crouching down below the front hood to peer around the driver's side. There were two other men laying on the ground with several bullet holes in their backs and legs. Neither looked like they would be getting back up. He stood up, knowing that Big John was watching, and walked around to check all of the bodies for signs of life.

Ben walked up to the two on the ground and nudged them with the toe of his boot. Neither one moved so he put two fingers on their necks. They were both gone. Ben walked around the SUV to check the one he had shot and he was also dead. Then, with his rifle pointed at the back door, he wrenched the door open quicky, ready to shoot at the slightest move. The man inside had been hit in the back and side. He was bleeding out but still breathing shallowly.

Ben stepped away and with his gun pointed at the door, he waved for Big John to come over. While he waited, he looked up towards the end of the driveway at the other SUV only to see a smoking ruin. Ben thought, "There're no survivors there to worry about."

When the SUVs turned down the driveway, Dr. James ran back to wake everyone up. As he was going from room to room, he heard the first burst of automatic gunfire and soon after, the big explosion. Everyone came boiling out of their rooms, and Dr. James told them, "They're here, stay low and follow me out through the back door."

By the time everyone gathered together in the kitchen and started heading for the back door, the shooting had largely stopped. Dr. James said, "Stay down here in the kitchen while I take a quick look." He duck-walked over to the front window, expecting any minute to hear shots ring out and bullets hitting around him. He heard one more burst of machine gun fire from the north side of the house where Big John was, at least that's where James thought he was anyway.

Then it got eerily quiet outside. James peered out of the front window to see one SUV parked in front of the house and the other a burning mess at the end of the driveway. As he looked over the window sill, he saw the bodies and immediately ran back out into the kitchen to tell the women what he'd just seen.

Deanna said, "Let's wait another minute to make sure there isn't any more danger. We don't need to get shot running out there before we get the all clear from Ben or Big John."

Dr. James replied, "I'm going now to see if someone needs help. I agree with Deanna, stay here until someone says its safe." Dr. James ran out the back door and around to the front. As he approached the first SUV, he saw Ben standing by the rear of the car with his rifle pointed at the door. James yelled out, "Are you guys all right?" "Does anyone need my help?"

Ben looked over and waved Dr. James out. When Dr. James ran up, Ben said, "Yes to both doc. Big John and I are fine, as far as I know anyway. But there's a severely wounded man in the back seat, if you want to take a look? I'll stand guard while you check. If he makes a move towards you, jump and I'll finish him."

Dr. James looked at the man on the ground and asked, "Are there anymore survivors?"

Ben replied, "No. Sorry doc, the rest didn't make it."

Dr. James opened the door to check on the man in the car. He was still breathing, barely and looked to be in very bad shape. He needed to be removed from the car and laid out on the ground right now before anything else could be done for him.

Dr. James stepped away from the man and as he started to talk to Ben, Big John walked up with his rifle at the ready. Dr. James proceeded to explain what needed to be done.

Big John responded, "We need to pat him down for weapons first. We don't need any accidents from any fanatics." Big John stepped over and said to Ben, "Watch him for any sudden moves while I check him."

Big John reached around to the seat on the other side to look for weapons. Then he started checking for pistols and knives on the wounded man. He found a pistol and a long knife on his belt at his back, which he quickly removed. As he grabbed them, the man groaned and moved a little but remained largely unconscious.

Once Big John was satisfied that the man was weapons free, he stepped out and said, "Okay doctor, I think we can move him now without too much danger to us. Ben, keep a close eye on him while we try to get him out and on the ground."

While they were tackling this job, the women came out to see if they could help. Stacy saw all of the bodies and blood and turned away. She said, "I can't stand to see all this blood and dead bodies, I'd like to go check on the man in the house please," she said with a white look on her face.

Ben replied, "Not by yourself. Someone needs to go with you in case he tries something."

Deanna looked around at all the carnage and spoke up, "I'll go with her. You don't need me here right now and I can shoot. Stacy, come on, I'll go with you." They went to the back bedroom where the wounded man was laying and found him awake now but in a lot of pain. He watched them when they arrived at the door and Deanna immediately pointed her pistol at him.

He just looked at them with an angry, pained look as if daring them to do anything. Stacy walked up to the bed but stayed out of arm's length. She asked, "How're you feeling this morning?"

The man looked at her and snarled, "How do you thing I feel after being shot in the back by you traitors?"

Stacy backed away and walked out. Deanna followed her into the little hallway and told her, "Don't worry about him. He's not going to hurt anyone anymore but I'll keep an eye on him if you want to start making coffee and tea for everyone and some maybe some breakfast, if you're up to it." Stacy looked at her, nodded weakly "okay," then headed for the kitchen.

Deanna needed to let everyone know that this one was awake so they could set up a guard. But she didn't trust that he wouldn't try to escape and possibly hurt Stacy in the process. She decided to stay put for now until someone came in from out front. She thought, "There's no sense in taking chances here."

Back outside, Big John and Dr. James worked on getting the wounded man onto the ground by letting Theresa get in from the other side and help lift him out. Once they had him out, he was put on the ground next to the car so Dr. James could look at him.

It was obvious that this man didn't have long to live unless he got to a hospital emergency room right now but there weren't any nearby. The nearest one was all the way over in Keene, which was miles away. Dr. James did the best he could but the man died after a few more minutes. Barbara decided to head back inside to see about coffee and breakfast. There was nothing more she could do out here.

When she walked in the back door, she found Stacy already at work making coffee and hot water for tea. Stacy looked up and gave her a wan smile, "I needed to do something to take my mind off what's going on, if you don't mind?"

Barbara returned a grim smile and replied, "I couldn't agree more. Maybe if you and I work together, we can make a good breakfast to help everyone else take their minds off all this bad business too."

As soon as Deanna heard Barbara talking to Stacy, she hollered out to her, "Hey, Barbara, can you come here for a minute?" Barbara looked at Stacy but she just kept her head down and continued working on the coffee pot. Barbara walked down the short hallway and asked, "What's up?"

Deanna explained that the man in the bedroom was now awake and that she needed someone to help guard him. "Would you mind going out and letting them know that this one is awake please?" Barbara peeked around the corner of the door and found the man sleeping again but he very obviously looked better than last night. She replied, "Sure, I'll go out right now before I start cooking breakfast. Be right back."

Barbara left to pass on the news and Deanna stayed in the hallway out of sight. She didn't want to hear any more crap from this one. "I'll be very glad to see this one gone, one way or another, as soon as possible," she thought to herself.

Dr. James was cleaning himself up while Big John, Ben and Theresa were standing around discussing what to do about the bodies and trashed SUVs, when Barbara walked up to give the news about the wounded militia member. Ben immediately started for the house because he didn't want that man anywhere near Stacy.

Big John had decided to call the local branch of The Homeland Security before any of his neighbors got ahead of him. "Let them sort this out and deal with the bodies."

Theresa was standing next to Dr. James, cleaning herself up and was glad to hear that. She asked, "Do you think we should bring up the other body from last night and put him out here with the rest?"

Big John thought for a minute and said, "Yeah, we probably should. I can go." He looked at Dr. James and said, "Are you two going to be okay here if I run down behind the barn and grab that other body?"

 Dr. James replied smiling, "Yes, we should be fine here. If anything happens, we'll run like hell and yell for help."

After he left, Dr. James looked at Theresa and thought, "Here's a classic case of PTSD if I ever saw one." He asked her, "Are you going to be, okay?"

Theresa looked up at him with a haunted look and said, "I think so but there's just so much blood. I had no idea things would get so messy. I don't ever want to see something like this again. How soon can we get out of here?"

Dr. James had nearly forgotten that they were supposed to be headed for Maine by now. It was an instant wake-up call. He replied smiling big, "You know, with all of the distractions going on, I had nearly forgotten about that. I think we need to see about that immediately after breakfast, what do you think?"

Theresa smiled back, "Sounds good to me. I bet Deanna is ready to get out of here too."

Dr. James looked around and thought, "There's nothing left to do out here, time to go see about breakfast and look in on Deanna." He looked at Theresa and said, "Let's go in the house and see about some showers and breakfast. I'm starving and I could use a good hot cup of tea."

Theresa was asking herself if she could eat anything after seeing all of this but a hot cup of coffee did sound good right about now. Dr. James and Theresa walked over to the back door to see Big John struggling with the body from last night. Dr. James told Theresa, "Go ahead, I'll be right in as soon as I finish helping him."

Theresa went in through the back door and Dr. James walked over to grab a handle to help get the loaded wheel barrow out front.

 Big John said, "Thanks for the help doc, and I mean for everything. Things could have gotten a lot worse if you and your friends hadn't been here." As they muscled the body off the wheel barrow next to the SUV, Dr. James arranged the body to lie next to the other one on the ground.

Dr. James responded back, "We would likely be dead alongside the road somewhere or dead up on top of Robert's Mountain retreat. Either way, we are also in your debt. Once we've had breakfast, we need to discuss us getting out of here safely before any Homeland Security troopers show up."

Big John looked up at him and said, "I'll be sorry to see you go but I know you have to. I'll do whatever I can to help and I know Barbara feels the same. Don't worry, we'll see you to the road and make sure everyone around here knows to forget they ever saw you. But we will never forget you where it counts. There're a couple of folks around here who will certainly never forget you."

Big John said he would clean out the wheel barrow and put it back, then be right in. "Go on in doc, I'll be in shortly." Dr. James left him and went inside. Deanna was sitting at the kitchen table with Theresa while Barbara and Stacy worked on getting a hearty breakfast going for everyone.

Dr. James took an offered cup of hot water and placed a tea bag in it before sitting down next to Deanna at the table. She had a hot cup of coffee sitting in front of her. Everyone looked stressed and very tired. Deanna spoke softly, "Do you think Robert was in that other SUV that got blown up?"

James replied, "We'll likely never know because any bodies left in that vehicle are crispy fried. It'll take dental records and DNA testing to identify any remains now. It doesn't matter anymore as we're getting out of here this morning."

Deanna asked, "What about Ben and Stacy? Do you think they'll be safe enough here?"

James replied, "It's very clear that Ben can take care of himself and Stacy. They'll be fine, if they still want to remain behind. Don't worry. We'll ask them after breakfast but I'm pretty sure they want to stay." Deanna nodded and sat back, sipping on her coffee.

After a few minutes of thoughtful silence, Barbara announced breakfast was ready. "Step up, grab what you want and go sit down. Stacy will bring you guys some more coffee, if you want. Then we can all sit down and try not to think about last night for a little while. Just as she finished, and started handing out bowls and plates, Big John came in and smiled big, "I smell my favorite breakfast. Let's eat and be thankful that we are all here to enjoy it."

Stacy said, "I want to fix a plate for Ben and take it to him. I'll be right back. As she filled a plate and left, everybody got in line and Barbara dished out oatmeal and pancakes to everyone else. As they sat around the table and enjoyed their food, everyone was thinking of the elephant in the room, or the one in the bedroom that Ben was guarding.

How were they going to stop him from telling Homeland Security about Dr. James, Deanna and Theresa?

Chapter 35

Parting is so Hard

After breakfast, they sat around the table sipping coffee and tea trying to brainstorm how to manipulate the scene outside before calling Homeland Security and figure out what to do about their prisoner in the back room.

Big John told them all, "We need to make a decision quickly because the longer we wait, the more questions they'll be asking about why we waited so long to call. The bodies outside speak for themselves, but this wounded POW in the back room, is a whole 'nother matter. The best thing that could happen would be for him to pass on due to his wound but it doesn't look like that's going to happen."

With that thought, Dr. James said, "Let me go check on him now to see how he's doing. I don't have any ideas either but I can't let him die out of negligence on my part." He got up to go check on his patient.

Deanna spoke up, "I might have an idea. What if we loaded him into the back of your truck and took him somewhere away from here for a while? Provided he is stable enough to transport. After Homeland Security has left, he can be dropped off at the hospital in Keene anonymously. That gives us the chance to get out of here without being seen by Homeland."

Big John thought about it for a minute and replied, "That sounds like the best plan so far. Does anyone have any better ideas?" Everyone else shook their heads no. "Okay then, let's get to work. We need to check on the status of our POW and work on our stories. Our stories all have to match." Big John looked pointedly at Stacy.

Deanna said, "I'll go check on Dr. James while you guys work that out." Deanna got up and went to find James. She walked around through the front room and saw Ben standing guard in the hallway outside the bedroom.

As she walked up, Ben smiled, "Quite a morning so far."

Deanna smiled back and replied, "It's still early yet, and we still have a lot to work out," as she swept past him into the bedroom. Inside, she found James working on the prisoner. He had rolled the man over and was checking his wound.

Deanna came to his side and asked, "Do you need any help?" Dr. James replied, "Yes, can you hold him while I check his bandages and the wound? I want to make sure he isn't going to get worse. I'm worried about that bullet that's still inside of him."

Deanna held the man over on his side as Dr. James checked him out. Then she watched him put a clean bandage on before they settled him back on the bed. The man glared at them but didn't say anything. Deanna figured that this man has to be in great pain, which was why he wasn't putting up any fight.

Dr. James didn't have any pain medicine in his bag and all Barbara had, was over-the-counter Tylenol. Not something you give someone with a wound like that. He'd told the man this earlier but all the man did was grunt a little, as if it didn't matter.

After Dr. James cleaned up a little, they walked out in the little hallway to talk. Deanna spoke in a low voice so as not to be heard by the prisoner, "I volunteered to come see if this guy will be stable enough to take him to the hospital in Keene after we leave? We need to leave ASAP to avoid problems for everyone else here with Homeland Security."

Dr. James said, "He's as good as he's going to get, considering. If we can get him outside and into Big John's truck where he can lay flat, they might make it, providing they don't travel on any real rough roads. Too much bouncing around will cause that bullet to move around and that could kill him."

Deanna nodded okay, "I'll let Big John and Barbara know. How soon can you be ready to leave? We need to be ready to leave here as quickly as we can."

James replied, "I can be ready in just a few minutes. Let me gather my things here and I'll meet you back in the kitchen momentarily."

Deanna left him and walked back out to the kitchen. As she entered, Theresa smiled and said, "Are we ready to go? I have my bag ready; I just need to go get it."

Deanna looked at her and smiled back, "I'm glad to see you're feeling a little better. Yes, go get your bag, we need to leave very soon."

Deanna waited for Theresa to pass her on her way back to the room they had briefly shared last night. She looked over at Stacy and saw that she was still pretty shaken up but Barbara was sitting with her, trying to comfort her as best as she could. Deanna asked Big John, "Can we step into the front room for a minute to talk?"

Big John said, "Sure, come on." They both stepped over to the front window and Deanna asked, "Are they going to be okay after this morning?"

Big John got a serious look on his face and replied softly, "I'm not sure yet. Stacy is pretty shaken up and Ben looks more like a young soldier with every passing minute. I've been wondering if they'll still want to remain here after all of this. I'm more worried about Stacy than Ben at this point."

Deanna said grimly, "Okay, I'll have a talk with them in a minute to see if they've changed their minds and I'll let them tell you what they want to do."

Big John looked saddened by this but he nodded his head and went back out to the kitchen. Deanna walked back down the hall to talk to Ben.

Deanna walked up and asked Ben, "Have you and Stacy had a chance to talk this morning? We need to know your plans as we're leaving within the next few minutes. Do you still want to stay here or come with us to Maine?"

Ben looked down at the floor and replied, "I haven't had a chance to talk to Stacy much yet and I need to. I know she's very shaken up with everything but I don't know yet to what extent. Would you take over guard duty for a few minutes and let me go talk to her?"

Deanna said, "Absolutely, go ahead. I'll take the rifle and you can have it back when you return. Take your time but not too long, okay?"

Ben handed her the rifle and went to talk to Stacy. Theresa came out of the bedroom about that time with both of their bags and passed her with an inquisitive look. Deanna said, "Ben's talking to Stacy," Theresa shrugged and replied, "Okay, I'll be waiting in the kitchen."

Ben stood across the table from Stacy and asked her, "Do you feel like talking to me for a minute?" Stacy looked up and her face looked deathly white and withdrawn. She mumbled, "Okay" and slid out from around Barbara to walk over to Ben. Ben took her hand and asked, "Do you want to talk outside or will that be too much for you? We can just go in the front room, if you want?" Stacy looked up at him and said in a small voice, "Let's just go in the next room. "

As they stepped into the front room, Stacy looked Ben in the eye and said in a low voice, "I just want to get out of here Ben. I am so scared right now and I'm afraid I will always remember what happened here if we stay. I need to go somewhere safe so I can try and forget all of this. As much as I love John and Barbara, I know this place will always give me nightmares if we stay. Are you okay with that? Maybe Maine will give is the life we are looking for. I realize this takes us a lot farther away from our families but I'll do whatever you think is right."

Ben whispered to her, "Stacy, I love you with all my heart and I'll do anything I can to try and make you happy. As much as I like them, if you're not happy here, then neither am I. I'm only happy when I am with you and that can be anywhere. I trust you to know when we're there. Maybe you're right, and Maine will be a better fit for us. I hear they have plenty of open land and farms there, and they're pretty far off the beaten path from the rest of the country. If you're okay with it, I'll ask Dr. James, Deanna and Theresa if they'll let us continue on to Maine with them."

Stacy nodded yes and they walked back out to the kitchen. Ben looked at Big John and Barbara. He could tell by the look on their faces that they already knew. Ben hung his head and told them, "After all that's happened to us in New Hampshire since we walked across the border, Stacy's too traumatized to stay here anymore. We really like you because of your kindness but there're just too many bad memories for her here now."

Ben looked over at Dr. James, Deanna and Theresa and asked, "If you have room, may we travel with you to Maine? Maybe we can find some peace there finally."

Dr. James looked at Deanna as if to say, "It's your call." Theresa smiled at Stacy and said, "I think we can figure something out, right?" turning to look at Deanna. Deanna didn't look all that enthusiastic but replied, "Yeah, we can try and figure something out. It'll be tight in that back seat for three of you, if that's what you want? And, there won't be too many places to get out and stretch your legs until we cross into Maine."

Dr. James interjected, "I-95 at the Maine border is the most heavily traveled highway going into Maine and the most likely to be watched. We'll need to come up with a different entry point if we're going to make it across unnoticed. We'll need to find another way across the Piscataqua river or go across farther north, which is what I recommend. We should travel north from here on the 63, catch highway 9 northeast until it merges with the 202 east. That'll bring us to a fork where we can cross the border on whichever route has the least amount of traffic. Likely state route 9."

Deanna shrugged and replied, "As I know little to nothing of this area of the country, I defer to you to pick the best route to get us to your other friends in Maine. But no matter how you look at it, it'll be a long, stressful ride until we're well into Maine and reasonably safe. Do we all understand what we're getting into here?"

Ben spoke up again, "Look, we're at your mercy and we'll make it work, if you don't mind the excess baggage that we are. I just want to get us somewhere safe so we can start our life. We're willing to put up with more discomfort for a few more hours as long as we can reach safety. If that's okay with you folks?"

Deanna nodded her head and said, "Okay everyone, let's get ready to hit the road." She stood up and stepped over to Big John and Barbara. "I feel like we're leaving you when you need us but we don't have much of a choice with a bounty on our heads. If we get caught, you'll be taken in too, for harboring fugitives." Deanna shook Big John's hand and Barbara gave her a little hug, telling her, "We'll make do somehow. We have friends around here we can call to help out so, don't you worry. Just be safe."

Ben and Stacy walked over and did the same. Stacy gave both of them big hugs and started tearing up. "I will miss you both. Somehow, we'll get word to you when we're safe somewhere. You're like another set of parents to me and I won't ever forget you."

Dr. James and Theresa came over last and shook hands. Big John said, "Doctor, I don't know what we in this small community would've done if you hadn't shown up when you did. I know little Robyn will never forget you and neither will we. If you ever make it back over this way, we'd sure like to see you again, and not just for doctoring," he said with a grin. Dr. James smiled back and nodded his head.

Deanna looked at everyone, "Let's get that SOB from the bedroom into Big John's truck and get out of here." With Dr. James leading the way, they went back to lift the wounded militia member out of the bed. Ben volunteered to carry him piggy back out to the truck.

They all filed out the back door and headed for the barn where they laid the man in Big John's truck bed, then covered him with an old blanket Barbara had. As they stood around for a minute saying their last goodbye's, Deanna looked at Steve's car and thought "It truly isn't made for long distance travel but it'll have to do." Deanna looked at everyone and told them, "Put your gear in the trunk and let's see if we have enough gas money to make it to where we're going. How much do we have between us?"

Dr. James replied, "I have a couple hundred dollars still."

Ben said, "We have less than a hundred here."

Deanna looked at them frowning, "Theresa and I have next to nothing. Maybe less that twenty dollars between us. If you guys are willing to share the wealth, we can make it. This monster's a gas guzzler but we should be able to manage as long as we don't get into any high-speed chases." She smiled. "Let's go!"

Theresa, Ben and Stacy pulled the front seats forward and got in the back. There wasn't much leg room, especially for Ben. He put Stacy in the middle and climbed in last. Dr. James and Deanna jumped in and Deanna started the car up. The older car started right up with a muscular rumble and purred like a big jungle cat.

Deanna backed the car out and waved goodbye as they turned up the driveway. She had to stay to the left into the grass to avoid running over the dead bodies and drive around the burnt-out SUV at the top of the driveway. Once she made it out to the road, she turned right and headed north with a pang of regret. She really felt bad about leaving them with that mess to take care of.

Chapter 36

The Road to Maine

Deanna started out relatively slow as she was still trying to get used to the car. As she finally started to get a good feel for how it would handle, she started to relax a little and look at the scenery. They had just over a half a tank of gas to start with so she kept a close eye on how fast this old machine would use it up. She half listened to everyone else commenting about the woods, farms and older houses along their route but remained quiet as she wanted to pay close attention in case of any odd sounds or possible issues in this new ride.

As they continued to travel north on the 63, the conversation slowly died out as James started paying more attention to their surroundings. He was looking for road signs that would point them in the right direction. Out here in this very rural area, road signs were few and far between. He was looking for signs showing highway 9 east.

As more houses and farms started to show up along the road, James saw the first sign for the intersection of 63 and 9. He pointed it out to Deanna as they passed it. "We're almost at the turn off. It should be just ahead. Everyone, keep an eye out for any police or anything like them as we turn off."

After about another half a mile, they came up on the intersection going east and west. Deanna turned on the blinkers as she slowed down for the stop sign. She thought to herself, "Now's the time I need to practice perfect driving. We don't need any local LEO's to pull us over for the slightest of traffic stops."

There were a handful of houses clustered around the intersection but it looked like just another sleepy little village, much like Big Johns had been. Deanna looked over and noticed a local gas station up ahead after she turned onto the eastbound side of highway 9. She decided to pull in and fill up while they were here. She wanted a more accurate rate of gas milage with a full tank.

"Okay everyone, pit stop while I fill this beast up with gas to see how far we can get on full tank. This is a good time to stretch your legs before we settle in for the long drive east today. With any luck, we can be in Maine by supper time." She pulled up to the outer row of gas pumps and got out to look around. James exited out of his side and helped everyone get out of the back seat. Theresa and Stacy immediately headed in to use the bathrooms, with Ben following for security. They had decided it was best to leave the rifles in the trunk and the pistols out of sight in the car, unless they spotted danger.

Ben followed the women inside with a wary eye out for any possible danger. He wasn't worried about Dr. James and Deanna. He kept his focus on Stacy and Theresa in the store. Stacy and Theresa were starting to get pretty close and Ben thought "That's a good thing. Stacy needs a friend besides me whom she can trust."

Ben looked around when they entered to see if there was anyone else in the store. As it was near lunch time, there were a couple of people shopping but they looked pretty harmless. They didn't pay Ben or the girls any more attention other than a cursory glance and then carried on with their business.

Ben browsed the coolers while the women were in the restrooms, keeping a passive eye on the front doors. Pretty soon, Stacy and Theresa came out, with Theresa saying, "I'll stand guard while you go in, if you need to go?"

Ben smiled, and replied, "Thanks, I'll be right out." Theresa caught up with Stacy and asked her to stick close to her while Ben was in the restroom.

Outside, James and Deanna were nearly finished fueling up the car. They discovered that this car had a twenty-five-gallon tank, which was pretty good for a car like this. Deanna finished up and James went in to pay. Since they were paying cash, they decided that he would pay since most places like this had security cameras and no one knew what he looked like, so far. Deanna and Theresa, on the other hand, still had their pictures on the occasional news feeds.

Theresa was hanging back amongst the aisles waiting for Ben to come out when she spotted Dr. James come in to pay for the gas. They'd already talked about her and Deanna staying as far away from any security cameras as possible just in case so she tried to hang out in the back, keeping a low profile to avoid any cameras.

Ben came out after a few minutes and said, "Okay, let's go. We don't need to spend too much time in here drawing any attention to us." They headed around to the front and out the door without so much as a look from the cashier, who was still taking care of Dr. James.

 Once they returned to the car, Deanna asked, "Any problems?"

Theresa replied, "Nope, smooth as silk. I think Dr. James may be deliberately stalling at the cashiers' counter to keep them distracted while we use the restrooms so I would go quickly now before it gets awkward."

Deanna smiled and waved as she nearly ran into the store. When she entered, she saw James slide a look at her as she walked to the bathrooms. Deanna did all she could to walk to the back without drawing any attention. She was tall enough to be noticed, if anyone was looking. She took another quick look up front but it was starting to get busy with the lunch crowd so no one was paying any attention to her.

Dr. James tried not to follow her with his eyes as she went towards the bathrooms, wrapping up his business quickly as soon as he saw that she made it okay. In his nervousness, he decided to see if Ben and Stacy might go back into the store and buy something to further distract those up front so Deanna could exit without being noticed.

James walked out and found everyone hanging around the car. He stepped up to Ben and asked, "Would either of you be willing to go back inside and buy something to distract the cashiers so Deanna can exit without being noticed?"

Stacy piped up and said, "I'll go."

Ben looked at her and told her, "Not without me. We aren't out of danger by any means yet." He looked back at Dr. James and replied, "We'll go make sure she makes it out safely, don't worry."

Dr. James thanked them but he knew if they spent too much time parked at the gas pumps, that would also draw unnecessary attention and he was anxious to get going. He watched Ben and Stacy go back into the store and pretend to be shopping while waiting for Deanna. All he could do is try and be patient but it was hard right now with everything that's at stake.

Ben and Stacy entered the store and walked back to the soda coolers. Stacy picked out a can of Pepsi and an orange soda for them, then they slowly meandered around towards the front counter, trying to watch out for Deanna. After a couple more minutes, Deanna came out of the lady's room. Spotting Ben and Stacy, she waited a minute until they were at the front counter before walking out into the parking lot. She came around to the driver's side and got in, deciding that "Out of sight is out of mind."

Within a couple more minutes, Ben and Stacy came out and everyone jumped the car, breathing a sigh of relief that no one seemed to have noticed them as anything other than ordinary customers. Deanna didn't realize just how tense that had all been until they were headed east down the road again and she could feel the tension leave her body.

She looked in the rear-view mirror and said, "I never knew that just going to the bathroom could be so stressful." When she said that, everyone started laughing hard, even James. The tension was gone just like that and now this was turning into just another road trip, except it wasn't. Even though Deanna felt a little better now, she knew she wouldn't be able to relax entirely until they crossed the border into Maine.

Now that they were traveling on a larger highway, it was even more imperative that they maintained a low profile, or as much as they could in this old muscle car. Everyone was looking out the windows for anything suspicious or any local police who might decide to pull them over for any reason. So far, so good as they continued to head east.

Dr. James's biggest worry was when they would be passing through the southern side of Keene. There was more of a chance of someone seeing them in an urban setting than out here in the countryside. The plan was for them to follow the road signs for highway 9 east all the way into Maine. The trouble is, highway 9 merges with state highway 202, then state highway 4 going through Concord. There was even a section of I-395 around Concord that they needed to avoid.

Dr. James was consulting the road map they had gotten when they first came over the border from Vermont so long ago, or it seemed. He told Deanna, "We need to stay off the toll road in Keene. Get on the 101 to highway 10 north until we get around the toll road, then get back on 9 east until we get to Henniker. From there, we'll take 114 south to get around Concord."

Deanna replied, "Roger that." She didn't need to worry about which highways to maneuver around while trying to pay attention to this car and their surroundings. She was so glad James could read a map. She kept the car right at the posted speed limits, or sometimes a little above. She didn't want them to look any different than any other car out here on the road. Deanna knew that if she kept it rigidly on or below the posted speed, that might also draw attention to them.

After a few miles, everyone starting to relax a little and chat in the back seat. Ben, as usual, kept to himself unless asked about something. He was more about looking for bad guys than chatting with the girls or even Dr. James in the front seat. Dr. James was also relatively quiet, trying to pay attention to landmarks and anything out of the ordinary. All he wanted now was to get across the border to safety.

After heading east for about forty-five minutes, Dr. James started seeing signs for West Henniker and he knew they were getting close. He cautioned Deanna that they were close to their turnoff for highway 114 south. Within a few more minutes, they saw the sign for the turn off and Deanna turned right onto 114 south. This road was a lot smaller but she knew they had a better chance at staying out of sight from anyone important.

James told everyone, 'We're looking for a local road number 77 east down here in about twelve or thirteen miles or so. Everyone, help me keep an eye out for it so we don't miss it." The girls in back replied, "Okay" and they quieted down to help look.

After about fifteen minutes of traveling through more farm country, Theresa found the first highway sign. It said 77 east to Concord at the next intersection in a small town called Chase Village. Deanna slowed down when she saw the first sign for Chase Village.

By this time, she also noticed that this car only got about nine to ten miles to a gallon of gas and the car was already down to just above a half tank of gas. Deanna asked James, "Do you want to fill up here so we don't have to fill up around Concord?"

Dr. James thought that was a good idea and looked around to the back seat. "Does anyone need a bathroom break?" Ben and Stacy replied, "Yes please, we'd like to stretch our legs a little before heading through the big city."

Deanna noticed a little mom and pop looking gas station as they were looking for the 77 intersection and pulled in like before, on the outside row of pumps. She parked to try and obscure the car as much as possible from any prying eyes. Everyone got out and, like before, Ben, Stacy and Theresa headed in to find the bathrooms while Dr. James stayed out with Deanna to fill up the car.

Inside, there was nothing much to see but a couple of rows of snack racks and local papers near the door. The bathrooms were in the back corner and didn't look too clean. As a matter of fact, the whole place looked pretty rundown. Ben looked over at the cashier's booth and saw a young man there who looked like he was a local with a dirty tee-shirt and blue jeans on. They were the only ones in the store and Ben didn't like the way he was eyeballing them.

He looked at Theresa and whispered, "Keep your heads down and hurry up. Both of you go together and pay attention. I don't like the looks of this guy up front. I'll hang around here near the door just in case. If he reaches for a phone, I'll come get you but be ready to run if I do." Theresa nodded and kept her back to the front of the store as they walked back towards the women's bathroom.

Ben looked over at the young man and shrugged as if to say, "Women." The young man relaxed his posture a little and went back to looking bored. Ben kept an eye on him while waiting for the women. He noticed that the young man was still watching him suspiciously, which made him more nervous.

After about ten minutes, the girls returned from the bathroom, with Theresa keeping her head down so the young man up front couldn't get a good look at her face. She walked out, laughing a little to try and throw off suspicions. Stacy knew how to be a good little actress and kept up the charade all the way out into the little parking lot. It was all she could do not to break into a run for the car.

Ben followed a few paces behind, trying not to look over his shoulder at the young man inside. As they reached the car, Deanna knew from looking at their faces that something wasn't right. She waited until Ben came around to her side of the car before asking, "Is everything alright?"

Ben replied, "Not sure. That kid inside makes me nervous by the way he was looking at us."

Deanna asked for more details but Ben said, "I can't pin it down but he just watched us like we were criminals or something so I cautioned Stacy and Theresa to be careful, then kept an eye on him in case he tried to call anyone. I didn't see him pick up a phone but he could have waited until we left the store before calling."

Dr. James was listening in on the conversation and interjected, 'Do you think it's safe for me to go in to pay for the gas?"

Ben replied, "I don't know for sure doc, but maybe I should go just in case. Let me handle this but we shouldn't hang around any longer."

Dr. James gave him enough money to cover the gas on the pump meter and Ben headed back inside. As he approached, he started looking around outside. All was quiet so far. He walked in and headed for the counter where the suspicious looking young man was standing. Ben said, "I need to pay for the gas, will cash be okay?"

The young man pushed himself off the back wall and stepped up to the cash register and fuel monitor. He asked in a sullen voice, "Which pump?"

Ben thought, "We're the only car out there and he's asking which pump?" Ben fired back, "Pump 2, how much?"

When the young man punched it up, Ben gave him the money, got his change, and said, "No," when asked if he wanted a receipt. He walked back out and Deanna let him into the back seat. As she got behind the wheel again, she asked Ben, "Do you still think he'll call someone?"

Ben looked up into the rear-view mirror and said, "Let's not wait to find out."

Deanna pulled out and got back on the street headed south again and after about a block, the intersection of 114 and 77 east appeared at the only intersection in town with a traffic light. Deanna pulled into the left turn lane to wait for the light to turn, watching the rear view just in case. The last thing they needed was a local law to pull up behind them now.

As soon as the left turn light came on, she turned onto 77 east and headed slowly out of town. So far, all she saw was a bunch of quaint New England style homes on each side of the street as they headed out of town until they faded into the countryside once again. Deanna didn't relax though. Her 'spidey sense' was tingling again and she could feel that trouble was just over the horizon, either from behind them or on the road ahead. Which direction remained to be seen.

She told everyone, "Keep an especially sharp eye out from now on. I'm getting a bad feeling about that last place we just left and I'm a little worried. Maybe we can dodge a bullet by going up through the back country." She kept the speed at sedate 55ish once they were out of town, trying not to look like they were in a hurry to get somewhere. Deanna remembered what Mona had said once about looking like tourists out for a drive through the country when they were first picked up by Robert.

Chapter 37

The Pursuit

As they meandered up 77 east, everyone kept anxiously watching out the windows, especially the rear one. Deana kept an eye on her rear-view mirrors also for possible tails. So far, everything was quiet. After about five miles or so, the only thing they saw were farms, the odd house and lots of trees. It seemed that they had gone unnoticed after all. Still, Deanna had that nagging sense that not all was right with the world and so remained vigilant.

They were about six or seven miles from Pages Corner, and the intersection of 77 and 13 when she spotted a car behind them. It didn't look like a police cruiser or a sheriff's deputy so she just continued to watch. After a minute, Ben spotted it too. He didn't say anything because he'd been watching Deanna's constant looks in the rear-view mirror. He just turned a little in his seat to better keep an eye on their possible tail.

Stacy and Theresa were still chatting next to him and he didn't want to worry anyone unnecessarily yet. Deanna watched and after a couple of minutes, the car started to close the distance a little more. She was now able to get a better look at the car and it looked more like a rolling tank, rather than a cruiser or a normal sedan. Now she got worried. She glanced back at Ben and noticed that he was also watching the car.

"What do you think Ben?" She said quietly. Ben grunted a little and turned around a little to look at her. "I think they're looking for us. This might be one of Robert's remote groups. That kid at the last gas station likely called in for the bounty. Now I wish we had the rifles up here with us."

Deanna hadn't thought about any units of Robert's militia being this far east but it shouldn't be surprising. She replied, "Break out your pistol but keep it low so they can't see it and let's see what they do. Maybe we're getting paranoid over nothing. Let's hope anyway."

Deanna maintained her speed and paid close attention to the road ahead. She decided to let Ben handle the defense to start, if it was needed. She would need to pay attention to defensive driving in case they tried to run them off the road. She looked up again and noticed that they were edging closer, trying not to draw attention, or so it seemed.

Deanna kept watching every few seconds to see what they were going to do. After a few minutes, it became more obvious. It looked like they were trying to edge up to be close enough in order to make it look like a bad traffic accident on a back road. Deanna chuckled a little and James gave her a startled look. She said, "I bet they think we're a bunch of inexperienced, women drivers who would be easy to bump off the road into a tree somewhere up ahead. James, I need you to keep an eye out for sharp turns ahead so I can be ready for them when they try to make their move, okay?"

James said, "Okay, I'll look for any spot that looks like it would be an opportunity for them to try and let you know. I don't think this road has any sharp curves, but there might be something else that they know about and we don't."

Deanna took another quick look and the car had moved up a little more. They were only about a couple hundred yards behind them now and closing slowly. Deanna knew that if that heavy car rear-ended them at high speed, it would push them off the road and they would end up in a tree or overturned in a field somewhere ahead. Deanna told James, "Keep an eye out for any empty fields ahead. They might try to ram us and bump us out into a field, upside down. If they try, I'll punch it so everyone," she yelled, "find something to hang onto when I tell you to."

Stacy and Theresa had caught on a few minutes before, that something was up so they had stopped their chit-chat and were now paying attention. Stacy was looking at Ben as if waiting for him to fill them in but he had his eyes glued to the rear window and the car behind. Stacy looked down to see that he had his pistol out and in his lap.

Ben kept watching and started to notice a pattern to their moves. It seemed that every time the two cars traveled between houses and farms, and there was no one to see them, they would move up a little more. Ben continued to watch a little more before remarking to Deanna, "You might want to increase your speed a little to see what they'll do. It looks like they might try to make their move in the next couple of miles or so."

Deanna hmphed a little and stepped on the gas. The car sounded like it wanted to go, like a young colt itching to run in an open pasture. As she stepped it up, the other car lagged behind some, as if that move caught them by surprise. Then, after a minute or so, they caught back up and closed the gap even more. Ben turned around the other way in his seat to face the side window and asked, "I want to open this window so I can get a shot off, if I need to, okay?"

Deanna said, "Sure, go right ahead." Ben lowered the window and kept the pistol down just below the bottom edge. In a couple more minutes, the car crept up even closer and they were now within striking distance, should they attempt to.

Deanna stepped on the gas a little more and they kept up this time. Just as Deanna was playing cat and mouse with the car behind them, James spoke up and said, "The trees are giving way to open fields up ahead in about a couple hundred yards. Be ready."

Deanna decided that enough was enough. She yelled out, "Hang on, I am going to punch it and see if we can run away from these rednecks." After a few seconds, she hit the gas pedal and the Nova took off like a Nascar special. Everyone was feeling the G-force almost immediately. Aas Deanna held the steering wheel in a death grip, she watched as the heavier car dropped away quickly behind them. She decided to keep the speed up for a bit longer to see what they'd do.

"Ben, keep an eye on them while I try not to crash us on this narrow country road. Maybe we can make it to the next town and evade them somehow."

Ben replied, "Okay, I'm on it. No sign of them catching up yet."

By this time, the Nova was pushing eighty miles an hour on a two-lane country road and Deanna needed everything she had to keep the car on the road. She knew that the slightest mistake or distraction would kill them all at this speed. This car still had more under the hood to give her but she was more worried about some farmer up ahead getting in front of her or an animal on the road. Deanna thought, "Just a couple more miles baby and we should be in the next town."

Ben shouted from the back, "Here they come."

Deanna snuck a quick look in the rear-view mirror and sure enough, the car was trying to catch up with them. She remarked, "Well, it looks like these guys are not just some local boys out for a joy ride. We need to get serious now. They're obviously after us." Then she started thinking, "How did they know what car we were in? Did Robert's people hurt Steve or Robyn to get the information from them? Did they hurt Big John and Barbara? Maybe it was just that kid back at the last gas station." She didn't want to think about the idea that their new friends may have been tortured for information.

Deanna gave the car another goose and brought their speed closer to a hundred on this narrow, empty stretch of road. It was fairly straight so she wasn't too worried but with all of the empty fields on either side, she knew they were getting closer to the next little town. Maybe just a couple more miles?

Ben hollered out again, "Here they come but they're struggling to catch up with us at this speed. Their car is to heavy and not real streamlined for high-speed chases. If you give it a little more, they'll likely fall behind."

Deanna gave it another little boost and they were now doing just under 110 mph. The Nova was just getting its wind but the road was getting harder to stay on at this speed.

Deanna told everyone, "Watch out. We should be nearing the next little town very soon and I'll need to slow down really quick without jamming on the brakes. Keep a close eye on our friends back there, although, I doubt they'll try anything in town. We'll have to watch for them once we get to the other side of this town though. I doubt that I'll be able to run this fast on the next highway towards Concord."

Ben replied, "I see them but they've fallen pretty far behind now. They likely know that we're getting close to town also. You can probably start easing off a little."

Deanna let the car slow down to eighty and watched for signs letting them know they were getting close to town. After another mile or so, she saw the first speed limit sign and she knew they were close so she backed off to the posted limit and breathed a sigh of relief.

Ben knew that they had barely escaped this time but now he wondered, "Just how far east does Robert's Militia reach? Will we be dodging bad guys all the way to the border?"

Deanna looked down and saw the gas needle sitting at just above a half tank again. That little run had cost them almost a half tank. They really needed to lose these guys as soon as possible.

Within another minute, they were at the town limits and coasting into a little New England farm town. Deanna was running the speed limit now as they drove through a sleepy crossroads town and turned onto 13 east to Concord, New Hampshire. Their pursuers had dropped behind but Ben caught glimpses of them now and again as they were trying to keep a low profile apparently. Ben remarked, "Maybe this far east isn't as friendly to them as Keene is."

Deanna kept an eye out for any local authorities as they headed out on 13. This road was a little bigger but that also meant their pursuers also had a little more room to maneuver as well. She wouldn't relax until they were in the clear and that may not be until they crossed the border later. It was mid-afternoon now so she asked James, "How far are we from the Maine border?"

Dr. James replied loud enough for everyone to hear, "We're about another three hours or so from the Maine border so we all need to pay attention and try not to panic. I'm sure we're all thinking the same thing, will they try something when we have to stop for gas? That's when we'll be the most vulnerable. All we can do is find a very public place to fuel up so they don't dare try. When we do, we need to make sure that none of us are ever left alone anywhere from now on, even to use the restrooms."

Deanna knew by now that they had enough gas to make it through Concord but they would have to fill up again once they got out on highway 9 east out past the I-393. The plan was to stay on 9 east all the way to Maine. The backup plan was to go across on the 202 or highway 4, depending on their circumstances. Those border crossings were likely to have more scrutiny so they were only a last resort if they were being pursued.

Ben spoke up again and said, "I see them still but they're hanging back a lot more. There's probably too much traffic to try another stunt like before. We should be okay for a while."

Deanna didn't need to remind him to keep watch. She knew he'd be glued to the rear window until they were safe across the border.

Dr. James told her, "Let's see if we can lose them in Concord. Maybe we can take back streets over to the other side of the city and lose them somewhere in between. What do you think?"

Deanna looked at him as they drove up the highway, and replied, "If you can navigate, I can drive. There's no way I can find my way around in a city I don't know without getting lost."

James smiled at her and said, "Deal."

Dr. James didn't say the one thing out loud that he knew Deanna was thinking also. This car stuck out like a sore thumb and would be easy to spot. But it was worth a try. After a little while longer, they were in the suburbs and getting closer to the interstates running through Concord. They started seeing signs for I-89 and knew that things were likely to get a little intense while navigating around the main highways to avoid detection.

After a little bit more, they crossed under the I-89 overpass and headed deeper into Concord. After a couple more miles, they passed under I-93 and Deanna followed the signs for highway 9 east as James pointed them out.

Ben couldn't see their pursuers anymore but he wasn't going to get complacent now. He didn't think for one minute that they'd given up.

Highway 9 east merged onto state highways 4 and 202 east after a few more miles and now they were on a pretty good-sized major throughway. Deanna sped up to bring them up to the posted speed limits and cruised. She said to Dr. James, "We need to find a very public gas station soon. We don't have enough gas to make it all the way to the border."

"Okay, I'll keep my eye out and let you know as soon as I see something suitable," he said. About then, Ben spotted their pursuers.

He raised his voice and said, "Here they come. They're just following for now but they're close enough to watch us and they likely have guessed that we've spotted them too."

Deanna decided that they'd have to deal with this soon. The best place would be at a very public and crowded gas station. If they dared anything that public, she would find a way to manage.

She told everyone, "Here's the plan. We'll pull into the gas island next to the store and Dr. James, Theresa and Stacy will quickly run inside. Ben and I will wait for you by the car to see what they plan to do, with pistols showing. I'll pump the gas and Dr. James can pay inside like before. Only this time, no one leaves the store until either

Ben or myself gives you the word. Dr. James will keep you together in case someone sneaks in the back door to try and grab one of you. Most likely you, Theresa, because we have a wanted poster on us. Understood?"

Everyone agreed and things got quiet for a few minutes. Soon, Dr. James spotted a travel plaza alongside the highway with a truck stop and a restaurant. He pointed it out and said, "Get off the highway at the next off-ramp and go over there. We should be very visible there."

Deanna turned off on the exit and took the side road to the truck stop. She slowed down to scout the parking lot and didn't see anyone obviously waiting for them so she pulled up to the pumps and waited for their turn. As she was waiting, their tail pulled in at the end of the parking lot and pulled over to the side. The windows were tinted so dark she couldn't see how many people were inside but that big ugly looking car would probably hold six people easy.

She slowly got out and let Ben out. Ben made a big show of putting his pistol back in the holster on his thigh, all in front of whomever was in that big car. Deanna also had her holster with a pistol strapped to her leg as well, in plain view of everyone. Ben quickly walked around to the other side of the car and told Dr. James, "Get out quickly and stoop down so they can't get a good look at you. We don't want them to be able to identify you later. Once you're inside, I'll send Stacy and Theresa in as quickly as I can. All of you stay away from the doors and windows but keep an eye on us out here. We'll wave or come get you when we're ready to leave."

Dr. James said, "Okay, I'm ready." Ben opened the door and James scooted inside as quickly as he could, hiding his height and face. Stacy and Theresa looked scared but Ben reassured them that everything was under control. A couple of minutes after Dr. James made it inside, Ben helped the women out of the car and watched them run inside to find Dr. James waiting for them.

Ben returned his attention to the car watching them. From what he could see, it looked like a modified Cadillac Escalade. It looked almost like an Army HUMVEE built by General Motors back in the day. This was not something they wanted to get into a ramming contest with. Ben waited while Deanna pumped the gas and kept watch.

After a few minutes, Ben watched as a man got out of the big car and walked towards the convenience store where James and the girls were. Deanna saw him also.

She said, "Ben, go warn them that there is a bad guy coming and to find a place to hide, even if they all have to cram into the women's restroom. We don't want them to match Dr. James to any drawings that Robert's guys may have made of him."

Ben gave a quick salute and ran inside before the man made it across the parking lot. Ben was sure he'd been seen but it didn't matter now. He quickly found everyone standing in an aisle and he relayed the message. Dr. James and the women moved fast towards the bathrooms and the girls went inside. Dr. James decided to wait around a corner to see what their pursuer did. He could duck into the ladies' bathroom quickly if he needed to.

Ben went back outside and let the man pass him on his way in. He wanted to get a good look at who was chasing them. The man stared at him with a mean look as he went inside. Ben did his best to get a good look so he would remember later. His antagonist was about six foot tall and a well-built 225 pounds. He was dressed in khakis, a pull over polo shirt, with dark hair and complexion. He looked like a professional. An Ex-military mercenary most likely. A big step above the usual militia members that ran around the countryside.

Ben waited outside the door between the car and store to try and keep an eye on things everywhere. He was worried about those inside if this professional soldier decided to go looking for them. As Ben watched, the man went straight to the men's restroom. He hadn't gone anywhere else yet. Ben kept a watch but turned around to look towards the large car. No one else was stirring. After a couple of minutes, Mr. bad guy came out of the restroom and walked around to the coolers. He was searching but trying not to be obvious. After grabbing a cold flavored water, he went up to pay for it, all the while scanning the store.

Ben kept watching him while he finished and as the man walked out of the door, he raised his hand, making a pistol pointing it at Ben, "bang," he said, smiling with a dark look to his eyes, looking down at Ben's pistol. Ben stood where he was, watching him without so much as a twitch to his face, especially at the taunt. He watched until the man got back in the car and waited another minute to see if anyone else would get out. When no one moved, he walked back over to Deanna and asked, "Did you see that man?"

Deanna had just finished filling the gas tank and looked at Ben. She replied, "Yeah, and if this is the caliber of men that's hunting us, we're in big trouble. These are professionals. Robert must be desperate to get us. The fact that they didn't try to do a drive-by shooting here means that Robert wants us alive. Let's get out of here."

Ben walked back in the store and found everyone. Dr. James went up to pay for the gas and Ben hustled the girls back out to the car where they got right into the back seats, ducking down below the windows. Ben waited outside for Dr. James to return in case there was any trouble. Once he was out and ready to get in the front seat, Ben stooped in and got in the back seat next to Stacy. Deanna got in and started the car. "Is everyone ready?"

Ben replied, "I may need to go to the bathroom a little later but I can wait a little to make sure we're reasonably safe." Deanna said, "Me too. I don't dare take a chance now with these guys on our tail. Let's go see how much trouble we can get into."

Chapter 38

The Border

As soon as Deanna pulled away from the gas pumps, their pursuers edged out as well. No longer making any pretense on what they were about. Deanna figured that Robert must have paid for a hit contract on them and these 'professionals' had orders to bring them to him alive. "Although," she mused, "that might change if they couldn't fulfil the contract before they reached the Maine border."

She pulled back out on route 4/202 eastbound and headed for Maine. Deanna decided that, since they were out on a very public highway and their tail wasn't planning anything too desperate yet, she could continue with the normal speed limits to avoid hitting the radar of any local cops. They wouldn't believe their story about professional bad guys chasing them, who would disappear at the first sign of any authorities.

After driving for a few minutes, Deanna told everyone, "We'll stop at the next rest area, provided it's full of other travelers, for bathroom breaks. But once we leave, that will have to be the last stop until we are safe across the border, okay?"

Everyone replied "Okay," and settled in for the ride. Ben kept an eye on their pursuers to make sure they didn't try something on the way. He wondered what their next move would be. As he didn't know the roads ahead at all, he was worried that they may end up on another narrow, backwoods road to cross the border and they would make their move then, like the last time. He planned to keep a close watch on them just in case, even at the expense of a sore neck trying to wrench around to look through the back window constantly. "It's a small sacrifice for our safety," he figured.

About halfway between Epsom and Northwood Center, they came up on a small roadside picnic area but Deanna vetoed that as not public enough. She decided that they would just have to tough it out until they reached the next decent sized town, which would be Northwood Center. She asked, "Is everyone going to be alright until the next town? It looks like it might be about a twenty-minute run from here."

Again, everyone responded with, "We're fine for now, go for it."

Ben piped up and said, "I think I can hold on that long but it will be close. I shouldn't have had that soda."

Everyone laughed and Deanna replied, "If you need me to pull over, let me know. I don't think they'll bother us on this busy highway "

 Ben replied back, "Will do, thanks."

Ben noted that their tail was staying pretty close to them, about one to two car lengths back. As things got quiet again, James started thinking about what lay ahead of them. Like everyone else, he was worried about their pursuers and how far they would go to try and grab them. Would they follow them into Maine? James knew about the road conditions in Maine. The back roads were all tree lined for the most part and sparsely traveled. Perfect areas to try and run them off the road and capture or kill whomever was on or not on their hit list.

James had no illusions about losing these guys here in New Hampshire. This road was too public and switching to a back road would only invite disaster. They likely had automatic weapons in their car and would use them as soon as it was safe for them to do so. This car would be taken out quickly if that happened. It was best to stay right where they were unless something drastically changed.

Within a few more minutes, they arrived in Northwood Center and looked for a good place to take a bathroom break. Deanna slowed down as they entered town and started looking for somewhere safe. In a couple of minutes, she spotted a Wal-Mart and said, "How about this Wal-Mart? It's public enough and we can maybe check out some things we may need for the trip."

Ben responded with a grunt, as if he really needed to go but didn't want to embarrass himself. Stacy and Theresa replied, "Let's go, we should be safe enough."

Dr. James said, "I volunteer to stay with the car if you all want to do a little shopping. I went to the bathroom at the last stop so I am good for a while. I don't think I'll need a gun out here."

Deanna pulled into the parking lot and drove down as close to the doors as possible. She parked in a space that would be covered by any parking lot security cameras. As everyone got out, Dr. James looked out over the parking lot entryway to spot their tail also following them but staying out towards the back side of the lot.

Dr. James pointed them out without being too obvious as everyone gathered around Deanna. She told them, "Alright, you know the drill, we go in, we stay together as a group and no one gets separated, got it?" All nodded their heads. She turned to James and asked, "Are you sure you're going to be all right out here by yourself? What if they try to take you while we're all inside?"

Dr. James looked at her, "We're right here in plain sight of the main entrance and there are too many people coming and going for them to try something as bold as that here in plain sight. They probably don't have any protection from local law over here like they did around Keene or they would have tried by now. They aren't going to chance getting into trouble here. I should be safe enough as long as no one dawdles in the store."

Deanna said, "Okay, we'll be back as quickly as we can." She turned around and lead everyone inside, looking over her shoulder one last time before they entered the store. James got back in the car and cracked open a window for air. He didn't want to roll it all the way down, in case they did wander over to see what they could get away with. He knew that he was likely their primary target, with the rest as a bonus. To be killed if they resisted. He figured that if he got too hot in the car, he could just step out without attracting much attention.

Inside Wal-Mart, Ben headed straight for the men's room and the ladies followed. Deanna went first, admonishing Stacy and Theresa to wait together until she was finished. They shook their heads yes and stood together outside the restroom area. Theresa told Stacy, "You watch that side and I'll watch this side to make sure we weren't followed in here, okay?" Stacy nodded and started watching the other side of the store.

After a few minutes, Ben came out with a less stressful look on his face, and walked over to Stacy. He said with a slight smile, "That was a little close. I wasn't sure how much longer I was going to be able to hang on."

Stacy laughed a little and mock punched him. "I need to go now silly; I'll be right back." She ducked into the lady's room and Ben took up her position.

While they were hanging out, Ben watched everyone walking around the store thinking, "If I wanted to follow us, I would come through the other doors to try and avoid being seen." Sure enough, just as he said that to himself, he noticed a man enter by himself who looked like he was out of place. He didn't look like your normal, weekday Wal-Mart shopper.

As Ben watched, he entered wearing military style boots, khaki cargo pants, a button-down somewhat military style shirt with sunglasses and a ball cap. He looked like something straight out of some magazine for mercenaries or so Ben thought. The man came in and started looking around as he walked out into the store. He missed them standing by the restrooms for now.

Pretty soon, Deanna came back out and Ben waved her back into the alcove of the bathrooms. He didn't want to lose sight of the man as long as he was still hanging around the front of the store so he just told Deanna to hold with a closed hand gesture. Theresa noticed the interaction and looked over where Ben was watching and saw the same man. She quietly told Ben, "They know what you look like after our last stop, but not me so much. Step back into the bathroom out of sight and I'll watch him."

Ben quickly ducked back into the alcove with Deanna to wait. Theresa noted that the man hadn't even looked their way yet. He was looking out into the store. While they were waiting, Stacy stepped out and Ben quickly put her behind him. Theresa kept watching without being too obvious about it, as if she were waiting for someone.

After a couple of minutes, the man wandered off into the store and disappeared from sight. He likely had a radio of some sort with an earpiece so he could radio for help. Theresa waved everyone out and Deanna decided that they didn't need to go shopping after all. Everyone chuckled and they headed for the door. As they walked towards the doors, a Wal-Mart door employee asked to see their receipt. Deanna laughed and said, 'Something just came up and we didn't get to finish our shopping, maybe next time," and they walked back out to the car.

Deanna led them back to their car looking for signs of James. As they walked up, he stepped out of the car and Deanna breathed a sigh of relief. Dr. James smiled at them, "I was just getting ready to take a short cat nap, what happened?"

Deanna walked up to the car and replied, "We need to get going, I'll explain in the car." Deanna looked out across the parking lot to find the mercenary's car and she didn't see it where they had been before. Ben was also looking and when he didn't find it where he had last had seen them in the back part of the parking lot, he started looking around. The car would stand out some, since he knew what to look for.

Ben pointed them out down by the other entrance to the store. Deanna said forcefully, "Get in now, we just might be able to outfox them and get away." Everyone jumped in and she slowly eased out of the parking spot and drove out in the other direction, leaving the lot by another driveway. Since there were a lot of cars between them and their pursuers, they managed to get out without being seen.

Deanna headed straight out of the parking lot, made a left turn up a side street and drove up to the traffic light. As soon as the traffic cleared, she turned right back onto the main street and sped up a little to try and put a little distance between them. As she made her way out of town and back onto highway 4/202, she asked for ideas.

"We need to try and shake these guys for as long as possible. James, get out that map and see if we can find a less obvious route across the state line. Something our predators won't consider right away."

Dr. James got out the map and started looking. Ben kept an eye out through the back window again for any sign of their pursuers.

After a couple of minutes, Dr. James said, "I think I have something. We can go up the 202A out of Northwood Ridge and get back on the 202 in Rochester, crossing the border on the 202. It's a little farther north than I had planned but it should work as long as we can elude our tail long enough to make it."

Deanna replied, "Very good. Everyone, keep a sharp lookout for our bad guys and highway signs. I am going to push it a little bit and hopefully, stay under the local speed radar, if there is any up ahead." With that, she pushed the car up to seventy and kept an eye ahead for any local cops or possible speed traps.

Dr. James remarked, "We're nearly there. The intersection where the 202 splits off is just a few miles up." Deanna drove another few miles and they started seeing signs for the highway split with still no sign of their tail. She knew that they couldn't go much faster than she had been, so they were probably still pretty far behind by now. If they had stayed on this road, that would have changed.

Dr. James said, "The intersection is just ahead in about a half a mile." Deanna got her head back in the game instead of thinking of their pursuers and slowed down as they reached the city limits. The 202A was a left turn as soon as she turned onto the 202. She slowed down, made the turn and drove up this little two-lane highway, heading through a residential area.

Ben still hadn't seen any sign of their pursuers and was starting to de-stress a little. He turned around and looked out the front window to see where they were heading. He didn't see anything but a city street which should lead out of town to a country road in the woods, and hopefully, to freedom.

Within a couple of miles, the houses gave way to the countryside, with signs for a lake ahead and the next town up the line. There were lots of trees lining the sides of the road and no traffic to speak of. It was getting on towards dinner time out here and most folks were coming home from work or the fields. They passed the occasional car going the other way towards Northwood Ridge but none heading in their direction.

Deanna drove on with the sun starting to set off to her left for a few more miles when they passed the lake. Everyone tried to get a look out through the windows on the driver's side as the sun was going down over the lake. It was so beautiful right now. Ben just tried to sit as far back in the seat as he could so Stacy and Theresa could get a good look before they passed into the trees again.

A few minutes later, they entered Center Strafford, passing through the sleepy little New England town on their way to Rochester. It was another ten or twelve miles to Rochester from here so Deanna pushed it a little bit with no traffic out here.

Within another twenty minutes, they entered the suburbs of Rochester, NH and Dr. James told her to stay on this road until they found highway 125 north. From there, they could get back on the 202 east and into Maine. Deanna followed 202A, which turned into a city street and passed under the toll road, highway 16. In a couple of minutes, she found the turn off onto the 125 north and she headed up the four-lane highway to the 202. It only took her a couple of minutes and they arrived at the on ramp for state highway 202 east.

Ben reported, "Still no sign of those mercenaries."

Deanna took a good look in her rear view as they headed east towards the Maine Border. No sign of that big ugly car. Then she thought, 'What if they ditched it for something lower profile? Maybe I'm just being paranoid.' "Ben," she said, "Keep an eye out for any cars that look like they might be tailing us."

Her 'spidey sense' had been going off all day and it was still warning her of impending danger. She didn't think they were out of the woods yet with these guys. The border was just up ahead with a small bridge to cross. She had a feeling that crossing the border wouldn't stop these guys.

As they crossed the bridge, Theresa let out a little cheer when she saw the sign on the bridge welcoming them to Maine. Ben, meanwhile, had been watching a four-door Ford pickup truck that was following them into Maine. This was a decent sized highway for this area so he wanted to make sure before saying anything, but this truck had been with them since they had gotten on the 202 back in Rochester, as if they had been staking out the highway leading into Maine.

Dr. James told Deanna, "Our next stop is going to be Sanford, Maine, about 20 miles from here. Once we get there, we can stop for a break and I'll try and call ahead to let them know we're here in Maine and that we plan to be there later tonight. We're heading for the seacoast town of Round Pond on the north side of the Portland area. It'll be quite late by the time we get there so I want to give them a heads up."

Deanna nodded her head and drove on. The girls in back where elated but Ben was still watching that Ford truck, which still showed no signs of turning off anywhere. He was starting to get a little worried.

Ben turned around and said, "I think we got company behind us. I've been watching this Ford pickup since we left Rochester and it followed us across the bridge. It's still behind us now, a little way back. The metallic blue one."

Deanna looked in her rear-view mirror and saw the truck. She had seen it before but didn't pay much attention until now. She sighed, "Okay, keep an eye on it and we'll see what happens when we stop for gas in Sanford."

It seems Deanna's 'spidey sense' was still working for her. Now she thought she knew the reason why it was still tingling despite making it across the border. Just what they needed, another tail to worry about. This one apparently didn't have any border restrictions. But then again, maybe the others didn't either. As she thought about it, she wondered, "Are there other hunters out there crossing the Maine border after us?"

Chapter 39

Escape From the Bounty Hunters

It was getting towards late afternoon when they drove into Sanford, Maine. Deanna started looking for a very wide-open gas station to fill up at. Dr. James wanted to jump on highway 109 south to get down on the coast to Route 1 north. Deanna was starting to think this might be a bad idea with one truck appearing to be tailing them, without knowing how many more might be out there looking for them.

As they entered town, Deanna spotted a good-sized gas station right on the main street and pulled in. She didn't open her door just yet. She was trying to watch that blue Ford pickup truck to see what they were going to do. As they watched, the truck went past them down the street.

Deanna turned around in her seat, telling everyone, "I don't know if they're tailing us and they drove by to report our position, or were they truly just another traveler. I don't want anyone to let their guard down. We do like we did before. Ben, Stacy and Theresa go in first, I'll fill up the car and Dr. James will remain out here with me to help me keep watch. Once I've filled up the car, we can trade places. You guys come out here and stand watch while Dr. James and I go in to use the restrooms and pay for the gas, okay?"

Everyone agreed and they got out of the car. Deanna went around to pump the gas while Dr. James went in to pay in advance. He quickly returned to stand outside providing lookout while she filled up the car. Ben, Stacy and Theresa headed in to use the restrooms and look around a bit. Ben decided to go last so he could stand guard outside of the bathrooms. As the women went into the ladies' room, he took up a position close by so he could watch the doors without drawing unwanted attention.

As Deanna started filling the car, James started to look around. He was looking for any cars or other vehicles that had people sitting in them, looking like they were not doing anything. After a couple of minutes, a SUV pulled in and parked over on the side of the store. As James looked on, no one got out right away so he tried not to be too obvious as he watched them. After a minute or two, a man got out of the passenger side rear and walked into the store. He didn't look over at them but he stood out a little bit because he was a well-built, rough-looking man in his mid-thirties.

James motioned at Deanna and used his head to point out the car to her. She spotted it right away and nodded okay. She stood there with her hand on the nozzle watching the car. As she was on the opposite side of their car from the store, she could watch without being too obvious. It was a good thing these places had longer hoses these days.

The man walked in the store and Ben spotted him right away. He tried to keep a low profile at the end of an aisle while waiting for the women to finish up. The man walked up to the front counter and asked for something behind the counter. While the store employee walked to the shelf to get it, some cigarettes it looked like, the man turned to look around the store.

Ben turned away from him but tried to keep an eye on him with his peripheral vision. About then, Stacy and Theresa opened the bathroom door and Ben, keeping his hands below his waist, waved them back in. Theresa saw him and blocked Stacy from exiting behind her. She pulled Stacy back in, as if they had forgotten something. As Ben watched, the man at the front counter seemed to glance at the bathrooms but his gaze didn't linger long. He gave Ben a quick look, then turned around to complete his purchase.

Ben knew that the pictures being circulated on the news had been only of Deanna and Theresa but that may have changed since they had last seen any news. Ben asked himself, "What if Homeland

Security has gone to our former town and gotten pictures of us?" He thought it best to not take any chances.

The man exited the store and Ben walked past the ladies' room door, knocking as he walked by. As he stood off to the side looking in a cooler, Stacy peeked out and Ben waved her out. Theresa followed and they quickly walked outside. Ben didn't know where the other man's car was so he steered everyone off to the side of the store and waited.

Theresa tried to keep her face hidden as best as she could while they waited next to the building. Her hair was pulled down loose around her neck so she pulled it over her face a little more. Ben looked over at Dr. James to see if he should be worried and tried to get his attention but Dr. James was looking at the other side of the building.

Ben decided to go ahead and walk out to the car. In the worst-case scenario, he'd yell, "Run" and they'd all jump in the car. He motioned for Stacy and Theresa to come on and they casually walked out to the car. Ben walked up to Dr. James and asked in a low voice, "What's up?"

Dr. James pointed to the other car with his chin. "We have company."

Ben noticed the car then after Dr. James pointed it out. He asked, "Is that the car that man in the store got out of a few minutes ago?"

Dr. James replied, "Yes. Did he spot you?"

Ben said, "If he didn't see us in the store, they've certainly seen us now. They'll know what we all look like now since we're all standing together around the car like this."

Dr. James agreed, "I guess there's no help for it. We'll just have to do the best we can to avoid any trouble. I hope we can lose them before we get where we're going."

Ben shook his head and walked over to the women. He warned them about the car and reminded them that they were far from safe yet.

Ben said, "You can get back in the car, if you want. I'm going to stay out here and help keep an eye on them until Dr. James and Deanna come back from using the restrooms." Stacy and Theresa both said no. They wanted to help and stretch their legs anyway before they had to leave.

Deanna looked over at Ben and said, "I'm just about finished. We'll head in to use the bathrooms and be back out in a few minutes. Is anyone hungry or thirsty?"

Ben looked at Stacy, who shook her head. Theresa replied, "Could you bring out some water?" Deanna looked at Ben, who said, "Water would be good please." Deanna nodded and, with James, she went into the store.

As they walked in, a different man got out of the car they'd been watching, following them inside. He trailed behind them a few feet and Ben looked at Stacy. "I'm going to walk over there to make sure nothing happens. I know Deanna can probably take care of herself, for the most part, but I'm more worried about Dr. James. He's worth a lot more money, if they can grab him."

Ben reached into the back seat and grabbed his pistol. He had taken off the holster to be more comfortable while sitting in the small back seat. He strapped it on while he walked to the store. He knew Deanna still had hers on but thought, "What if she's in the ladies' room and Dr. James is in the men's room or out by himself on the floor?"

Ben knew that Stacy and Theresa would get in the car while he wasn't there and lock the doors. That was what they had discussed before in case this situation ever occurred. Ben walked in and didn't see either Dr. James or Deanna anywhere. He decided to go to the men's room to make sure Dr. James was okay.

Ben walked over to the men's room and opened the door slowly so as not to alert anyone right away. As he stepped in, he saw the man from the car in front of a stall, looking like he was mad about something. Ben decided not to take any chances and pulled out his pistol. The man looked over at Ben, saw the pistol pointed at him and backed away with his hands up. Ben called out, "Hey, are you alright?"

Dr. James yelled back, "I'm fine so far. I'm glad you decided to check on me. This man has decided that I'm to come with him, whether I wish to or not and he wouldn't take no for an answer."

Ben walked up to the man and pointed the pistol at his head. The man flinched but didn't say anything. Ben asked him in a stern voice, "Why're you trying to kidnap this man? Do you know him?"

The man hesitated and then sneered, "We know what you all look like now and we'll get you. I don't know him other than I found him alone in here. He's traveling with you all and that's all that matters to us. You don't stand a chance of getting away. Our client has put out quite a bounty on all of you and there're a lot of bounty hunters out looking for you."

Ben kept his pistol on the man while Dr. James exited the stall and left the bathroom. Deanna was anxiously waiting just outside. Once Ben knew that Dr. James was clear of the restroom, Ben brought his pistol down on the man's head, knocking him out, then stuffed him in the stall where Dr. James had been. Ben figured he should be out long enough for them to get away.

Ben rushed out of the restroom and told them, "We need to leave now."

Deanna looked at him as if to ask, "What did you just do?" But thought better of it and let it go. Dr. James had grabbed several bottles of water out of the cooler while they'd been waiting for Ben and went up front to pay for them as Deanna and Ben went outside.

Dr. James came out a couple of minutes later, jumping into the car. While he was walking out, they watched as another man got out of the SUV they'd been watching, who went into the store, presumably to find their missing crew member.

As soon as Dr. James closed the door to the car, Deanna punched the gas, spinning the wheels as they left the parking lot, turning hard onto the street. As she drove through town, she decided to take a side street down to the 109 south. Deanna said, "It's just a narrow, two-lane country road and as it's getting dark now, we just might make it down to state route 1 without being seen again."

The only worry would be driving through downtown Portland. Deanna reasoned that If she kept to the back streets as much as possible, they might get away from the bounty hunters.

Dr. James told her, "Don't worry, I know Portland. I can guide you down by the waterfront and around the downtown area using the backstreets. If we stick to the tourist areas, all we'll have to worry about is dodging foot traffic. It'll be slow going but they're not likely to be looking for us there."

Deanna kept driving on into the darkening skies, looking in the rear-view mirror for anybody tailing them. She knew Ben was also watching but she couldn't help herself. For right now, she was good with driving down this narrow road in the dark. At least out here, if she needed to pull over into some trees for a few minutes, she could do that without too much trouble from the locals. As long as she turned off the headlights, they might go undetected.

Deanna continued to drive at a steady speed, depending on the curves and pot holes. So far, no tails and no traffic. At this time of night, most rural folks were sitting down to dinner and in for the night. They hadn't seen one car since passing through South Sanford. The only thing out here was houses and farms with porch lights on, or inside lights showing through front windows.

According to Dr. James, there were no towns or villages on this stretch of road until they hit the turnpike so it should be smooth sailing all the way down, hopefully. At least Deanna wanted to believe that. She was getting tired of running. She was sure that everyone else was too. It'd be nice to be somewhere safe for a while without having to look over their shoulder all of the time.

After driving for about fifteen minutes, they started seeing signs for the Maine Turnpike, I-95. Within minutes, they saw the overhead pass ahead for the interstate, so Deanna slowed down. She wanted to check out the area under the overpass and the exit ramps before just cruising through. They didn't need to pick up another tail here. Deanna pulled over off the road just a little bit. She didn't dare pull off too much as there wasn't much of a shoulder here.

As she slowly stopped and turned off the headlights, they waited. No cars came out of the dark. Deanna drove slowly down the road until they were just underneath the freeway and stopped again. No headlights still. No cars waiting for them. Deanna started breathing again. She turned the headlights back on and followed the road until she found state route 1 to Portland. They were in Wells, Maine now. A small coastal town that depended on lobster fishing and summer tourists.

So far, no tails. They would be passing through some more towns and small cities here on this coastal road but she hoped they could elude the bounty hunters in the dark now. After about five more miles, they passed through Kennebunk, a mid-sized city but they still had a long way to go tonight.

James spoke up and said, "Hey, let's see if we can find a pay phone here in Kennebunk. I need to make that phone call I told you about earlier. We were a little busy back in Sanford."

Deanna replied, "Okay, let's wait until full dark before we stop in order to give us more cover."

James said, "No problem, we're just a few miles south of Biddeford and we can stop there somewhere."

This stretch of road was more of the same. There were lots of trees and houses off into the woods and alongside the road. Some of the homes looked pretty expensive. When Theresa said something about the differences, Dr. James told them about how this part of Maine was big on tourism and that there were a lot of rich people, most of them from out of state, who owned summer mansions along here. Some of them dating back the late nineteenth century. The disparity was between the rich 'summer folk' and the local folks who lived here all year round.

As Dr. James was playing tour guide, they arrived in Biddeford and Deanna starting looking for a gas station that might have a pay phone. As she kept driving, they saw a franchise gas station that looked a little run down so Deanna pulled in and parked down near the back of the store away from the front lights. She pulled the car in between two others to try and blend in. She guessed that this might be employee parking.

She turned off the headlights and stopped the engine. She said to everyone, "We can get out and stretch our legs here but keep a low profile. We don't know who might be watching so try not to bunch up too much. They now know how many of us are traveling together and they have a fairly good description of us after that disaster in Sanford. Let's make it as hard as we can to find us, okay?"

They all nodded their heads in agreement and James stepped out to look around. It was pretty quiet here. A few cars out on the street but none that looked suspicious. He decided to take a chance and see if there was a pay phone he could use somewhere here. James walked around to the front doors and looked in through the front window to see who was inside.

There was just a cashier and one customer, a young man looking like a scruffy college kid. James walked in and asked the cashier, "Do you have a pay phone I can use?" The young woman looked up and pointed to the back, "There's a phone way in the back by the bathrooms you can use," she said with a heavy down east accent. James thanked her and made his way back to the phone.

He picked up the receiver and dialed the number from his little book. When a man answered, James told him who he was and where they were. The man gruffly answered, "Okay doc, we'll be watching out for you. By the way, have you had any trouble along the way?"

James replied, "Yes, we have. We were chased across the border and we had to deal with a car full of bounty hunters in Sanford, why?"

James's friend Tim told him, "We heard through the grapevine that there's a huge private bounty on all your heads now. It was put out by this outlaw over in New Hampshire. He must really want you bad for that kind of money. What'd you do, kill someone?" He chuckled on the phone.

James said, "That's a story I'll wait to tell you in person," he laughed. "Anyway, we should be there sometime near midnight, provided we don't run into any more trouble tonight. I'll try and call again if we're going to be any later."

Tim replied, "Don't take any chances. Just get here when you can and we'll be here waiting."

James said, "Thanks my friend, you don't know how much that means right now" and he hung up. James walked back out distracted in thought and nearly forgot to check his surroundings. As he looked up from the back of the store, he noticed a man at the front counter who looked like a possible bounty hunter.

James froze where he was and ducked down a little behind a display to avoid being seen. As he peered over the aisle shelves, he noticed a mirror off to the side that gave him a view of the front counter but, he realized, that could work in reverse as well. He ducked around a corner and watched the mirror from a hidden vantage point.

The man lingered around the front trying to make small talk with the cashier while she rang something up for him. As he kept hanging around, she noticed that he seemed to be searching for something or someone. A couple of minutes after she had rung him up and put everything in a small bag for him, she started to get a little nervous. She wondered if she should tap the panic button underneath the register because this man was starting to creep her out.

Just as she was about to hit the silent alarm, the man smiled at her and walked out. She breathed a sigh of relief and just about the time she was going to sit down on her bar stool, Dr. James walked up and half-scared her to death. "I forgot you were back there; you gave me a fright."

James replied, "I'm so sorry, I didn't mean to startle you. I stayed out of sight as that man looked a little dangerous and I don't have a cell phone."

The young lady smiled wanly, "It's all good. I am okay now. This is why I hate this job. It's a little scary at times, especially working the night shift like this. There're some characters that come in here who make me wish I had a small pistol or something."

Dr. James smiled and replied, "I know what you mean. Do you have any hot water and a tea bag?"

She looked over and realized that no one had set up their coffee bar earlier and replied, "No, I'm sorry but we don't have anything set up right now. You just reminded me that I need to set that up now though. Thanks."

James said, 'No worries, I'll carry on then. Have a good night," as he smiled and walked out.

He stepped out and stood off to the side, looking for any cars or people that looked out of place. He waited a minute or two for his eyes to adjust to the darkness. When he didn't see anyone nor any cars in the front parking lot, he slowly walked back to the car. As he rounded the corner, he looked over to make sure everyone was still okay.

"That's odd, there's no one standing around the car," he thought. He waited another minute to see if anything was amiss. When he didn't see anything, he started to walk to the car, staying close to the building just in case. As he neared the car, he could see everyone inside, so he ran up and jumped in his seat.

As soon as he hopped in and started to pull the door shut, Deanna started the car, pulling out just as he shut the door. James remarked,

"I take it you must have seen something?" Deanna pulled around and exited the gas station on a side street, then turned down away from the main street they had been on.

Ben spoke up from the back seat, "Yeah, there was a car that pulled in not long after you went in. Some crazy looking dude jumped out and walked in as if he were looking for us. We ducked back into the car hoping we wouldn't have to run and worry about coming back for you. Are you alright?"

Dr. James replied, "Yes, I'm fine. I saw the man as I completed my phone call and managed to remain unseen but it was close. I agree, he was probably looking for us. Even the cashier said he looked strange."

Deanna asked the unspoken question. "How did they know where to look for us? Parking around the back like I did probably saved our bacon but how did they know where to look?" While she was talking, she turned in behind some stores in a strip mall. "I want to get out and look around the car while it's quiet. We may have a tag or something under this car."

Everyone got out, then Deanna and Ben started feeling up under the bumpers and inside the wheel wells. When Ben crawled up under the rear of the car, he found it. An Apple tag button stuffed up under a frame member. They didn't have much range but anyone in the vicinity who knew the tag's frequency, could find them, if it wasn't blocked. Apparently, one of the cars Deanna had parked next to at the last gas station had blocked the signal so the trackers only knew that they had pulled in there but not exactly were. There was no time to wonder when that tag had been put on the car now.

Ben crushed it and they piled back into the car. Deanna drove out to the back street behind a big grocery store and went over a couple of streets to Alfred Rd. She intended to circle around the area and get back on highway 1 a little further up in case those hunters were staking out the gas station. She turned left and followed the street to Union Street, made another left and drove back out to Route 1.

They had just barely dodged another bad situation out of sheer luck. Deanna knew that their luck was running out. They needed to get somewhere safe now. All she knew to do now was drive, drive, drive tonight and try to keep them out of trouble.

Chapter 40

Running through Portland, Maine

Once back out on Elm Street in Biddeford, they drove north following route 1 out through town. After a while, they passed under the I-195 overpass and the road changed to Portland Rd. There didn't seem to be any more tails. Deanna was a little worried about passing under the interstate bypass but there was no sign of anyone so far. She kept the car at the posted limits and cruised into the night.

Now they were traveling though the Portland suburbs and there were a lot more business and houses out here. When they'd left the shopping center in Biddeford, she told them, "Everyone keep a sharp lookout for any suspicious looking cars. We don't know where these people are and as Dr. James told us, there're a bunch of bounty hunters looking for us as we've just seen."

Everyone replied they understood and the car got quiet. Anyone who sat next to a window started looking, scanning all of the side streets they passed, while Ben kept looking out the back window for tails. No one said much for quite a while until they passed under the freeway. Deanna slowed the car down to see if there might be an ambush waiting for them.

Deanna's 'spidey sense' had quieted down as well by the time they reached Portland. It was still a small tingle but nothing like it had been before. She attributed it to their broader danger level rather than any immediate threat for the moment.

After driving for a while, they started seeing signs for the oceanfront areas of Portland and Dr. James advised Deanna, "Stay on the small road unless we pick up a tail. Portland can be easy to get lost in, especially after dark,"

Pretty soon they passed under the I-295 overpass and followed the street over the Veterans Memorial Bridge. Dr. James pointed left and

Deanna turned onto Fore River Parkway to head back towards route 1, which merged with I-295. James guided her up the parkway and around to Congress St., where he directed her to turn right.

Deanna kept driving, turning left onto Bramhall St., then immediately onto Cumberland St. east. James then said. "Follow Cumberland all the way to Washington Ave., then turn north to the freeway. We'll have to get on the I-295 for a bit to get across another bridge in order to get back on route 1 when it finally splits off the freeway. Hopefully, we can get across and back on the small road without being seen."

Deanna kept going. This car was not made for inner city driving and her leg was starting to get tired of constantly having to push the clutch in and shift gears at every red light. After a few more lights, she asked, "Hey, is anyone hungry and needing a bathroom break?"

The three in the back seat looked at Dr. James and hesitantly said "yes," as if asking his permission.

Dr. James replied, "That sounds like a good idea. Maybe we can find a quiet restaurant where we can park around back and enjoy a decent meal for a change. Help me look."

Ben kept his eyes on their back trail but now the young ladies in the back started looking for a restaurant that might be safe to get into. There didn't seem to be much in the way of quiet restaurants in this part of town so Deanna kept going. After a while, they saw the signs for Washington Ave and Deanna turned left. Then they spied a sit-down restaurant they could get into without too much trouble right off the street.

It was a southwest BBQ place and it was near to closing time. So, there should be no one else other than the staff and maybe one or two people at the bar, if they were lucky. Deanna pulled in behind the restaurant and found the employee parking. She managed to find a parking spot between two other cars. Deanna got out first and took a look around.

She didn't see anything and this being a weeknight, there wasn't too much traffic on Washington Ave this late. None that looked to be suspicious anyway. She let Ben out of the back seat and Dr. James got out to let the ladies out on his side. Deanna led the way into the restaurant.

As they walked towards the door, she quietly said to Ben, "We'll need to periodically walk out and check on the car while we're eating. We don't need any more surprises tonight."

Ben mumbled, "Copy that."

When they all entered, the hostess greeted them and asked, "Where would you like to sit?"

Deanna told the young greeter, "We'd all like to sit together where we can watch the street, if you please? And may we wash up before ordering?"

The hostess showed them a table in the center of the dining area and pointed out where the restrooms were. "I'll send out your waiter in a couple of minutes after you have settled down." Deanna nodded thank you and the young girl headed back to the door.

Everyone took turns in the bathrooms and came back to look over the menus. As everyone settled down, a young man came out and introduced himself as their waiter, then took their orders. As he went off to the kitchen, Ben got up saying, "I'll be right back. I'm going to check the parking lot and the car."

Stacy looked up with surprise. She asked Ben, "Can I come with you?" Ben looked down, then at Deanna, who nodded yes. Ben looked back at Stacy and smiled, "Sure, let's go." He grabbed her hand and they walked to out to the door to look around. The hostess just smiled and looked back down at whatever she was reading.

Ben poked his head out to look at the parking lot with Stacy standing behind him. When he didn't see anything out of place, they stepped outside to look over at the car. As they were looking around, Stacy asked Ben, "Do you like it here in Maine?"

Ben paused while looking over at the car. He didn't see anything out of place, so, after a minute, he turned to Stacy and replied, "Beautiful, I don't care where we end up as long as you're happy and we're safe."

Stacy blushed a little and smiled, "I love you Ben, I think we may've found our happy place finally."

Ben smiled back and kissed her. Then they walked back into the restaurant to sit down and eat. As they walked up to the table, Dr. James was telling Deanna and Theresa about his friends up the coast and the place where they lived.

Dr. James described his friends as typical New Englanders who didn't trust outsiders. But not to worry, they'd welcome them with warm hospitality. His friend Tim was a burly old fisherman and his wife had been a schoolteacher before they retired. Dr. James warned them with a laugh, "They have very thick down east Maine accents so they might be a little hard to understand at first but you'll be fine."

While he was talking about his friends, the young waiter came out and James quieted down. Everyone looked up at the young man as he apologized for interrupting. "Your meals are ready, if you are?" Dr. James answered back smiling, "You're fine, bring it out. We haven't had a decent meal in quite a while."

After the food was served, the young man retreated back to the kitchen out of sight. James kept an eye peeled on the server area as they ate. They were so hungry for this good food, no one was talking much. After they had pretty much devoured their plates, Stacy asked Dr. James, "Is this area really nice to settle down in?"

Dr. James looked at her and Ben and said, "Yes, it is. There're a lot of really nice people up this way and the weather is pretty good for the most part, if you can handle the cold. Down here near the coast, they can get some bad ocean storms called Nor'easters. But, if you go further north, the weather is almost a mirror of where you came from in upstate New York. There's plenty of farmland available and everyone here pitches in once they get to know you."

Stacy beamed with pleasure at hearing that. She looked at Ben and said, "This is it, the place where we'll start our family."

Ben looked at her and shook his head. "First, we have to get through the night, then we can discuss the future. But I will admit, I do like the smell of things here. I look forward to seeing more."

They were pretty much finished with their meal when the young waiter came back out to ask if everything was okay. Everyone responded with a lot of enthusiastic yeses. The young man asked them, "Would anyone like any dessert? We have some apple pie and our famous Maine Whoopee Pies, if anyone wanted anything?

Everyone but Dr. James wanted to know what a 'Maine Whoopee Pie' was. The young man grinned and tried to describe one to them. Dr. James spoke up over everyone and said, "Bring us four and we will take them to go please." The young man smiled and replied, "I'll be right back."

While he was getting the desserts, everyone got up and started putting their money together to pay check. When the young waiter came back with the Whoopee Pies in a take-out bag, Theresa and Stacy couldn't resist and had to look inside. Dr. James and Deanna settled the bill with cash, which surprised the waiter a little but he went and brought back their change.

As they were leaving, Dr. James left a generous tip on the table for their nice waiter and they walked back out to the front door. Ben stepped up to the door and peeked outside again. All was quite where he could see. He stepped outside by himself and walked over towards the car. He waited a moment and looked around. He didn't see anyone near the car but there was someone standing up the street a little way looking towards the restaurant.

Ben watched him for a minute without looking directly at him. The man was standing out on the sidewalk on Washington Ave. After a few minutes, he walked off but Ben kept watching for another half minute before rushing back to the others. He looked inside and told everyone, "We need to go now and go quickly. I saw someone out on the street looking in this direction but it was too dark to get a good look at him. He walked back down the street but we shouldn't take any chances."

They all walked rapidly out to the car and climbed in. It was all Deanna could do, to not mash the gas and squeal the tires to get back out on Washington Avenue. Now she was on high alert and her 'spidey sense' was back in strength. At this time of night, there was hardly any traffic out so she pushed it a little bit, hoping to lose anyone that may come looking for them back at that restaurant. She hoped the staff didn't get into any trouble because of them. They had seemed so nice.

She drove up the street, checking her rear-view mirror every couple of minutes. Ben was glued to the back window and Dr. James and Theresa were doing their best to watch the side streets for any unusual cars. Stacy just clung to Ben as best as she could with a scared look on her face.

She kept driving until they reached the I-295 exit and Deanna headed north towards Tukey's Bridge. As they approached the exit ramp, Deanna watched for any odd cars that stuck out.

Once they were on the exit ramp, Ben said, "I still don't see anything but anyone with any common sense knows which direction to track us now. We'll have to be extra watchful until we get across the bridge to the other side. If anyone's waiting for us, it may be on the other side of the bridge."

Deanna punched the gas a little more as they merged onto I-295 north. The bridge was just ahead. As Ben watched, he noticed a pickup truck pick up speed behind them headed in the same direction as they were. Even though they were in the fast lane, Ben thought they looked a little out of place. The handful of other cars heading across the bridge were more nonchalant but this one was coming up fast.

Ben warned Deanna and she looked in her side mirror on the door. She could make out the truck and told Ben, "I see him. Watch him in case I have to do something radical here." Ben kept looking and the truck kept coming. After a couple of minutes, the pick-up truck slowed down alongside them out in the fast lane and Ben got a look at the man on the passenger side. He looked like a local but he was looking right at their car.

As Ben and Deanna watched, the truck sped up and took off across the bridge. Deanna didn't know what to do now. They were in a one-way situation here and couldn't turn around. She had no idea if they were going to get ambushed on the other side now. She pulled out her pistol and set it in her lap. Ben noticed and did the same.

As they crossed the bridge, the pickup was nowhere to be seen. Now Deanna was sweating bullets. She would rather fight an enemy she could see, instead of something she couldn't. She knew everyone else was stressed out as well but she kept her eyes on the road ahead. They passed the midway point on the bridge and everyone started looking hard out the front windshield for the pickup truck that had passed them.

As their car made it off the bridge, they still didn't see the truck. Deana kept going looking for the route 1 exit. Within minutes, she found it and exited to route 1 north. This was Veranda Street, a business area by the ocean. James told her to just keep going because there was an even longer bridge up ahead, they had to cross.

Dr. James was becoming even more nervous as they could get jumped from any one of these side streets out here. Deanna kept going, gripping the steering wheel nervously. With everyone watching out the windows intently, it seemed like time was going in slow motion. Seemingly taking forever to get to the end of this business area and across the Presumpscot River bridge.

Once across, they were in a little less of an industrial area and Deanna relaxed just a hair. There were more retail stores over here so she felt like they were in a more public area. Less chance of being blindsided by bounty hunters. As she kept going up route 1 north through town, she got to thinking about that pickup truck that'd passed them and made them all so nervous.

Deanna tried to destress a little bit. "I wonder if that truck back there was just a bunch of local rednecks admiring this fast-looking car we're driving?"

Ben looked up from the back window and remarked, "That could be, since we haven't seen them since they passed us. But I'm not relaxing until we get where we're going." Everyone agreed and kept a lookout as they passed through this small area of stores and businesses.

After a few more minutes they came up on a park and a country club. It was a little darker out here without any retail stores to shine street lights. Everyone went back on high alert. It didn't take long to get past it but it was a little tense for a couple of minutes.

Deanna kept going without any more incidents but it was getting pretty late by now. Near to midnight and they were still a long way from Damariscotta and the small road to Round Pond on the coast. The tension was getting to everyone so no one was talking much. They only spoke to mention not seeing anything and the only sound besides the tires on the road was the shifting of a leg now and again.

After another hour of driving through retail areas, and a traffic loop that made everyone nervous, Route 1 started to thin out of buildings and the road meandered closer to the I-295 bypass, crisscrossing the freeway now and again until they reached Freeport. It was more of the same, retail stores with their night lights on, those that had them, and the occasional car still out this late at night.

Then it was Brunswick, a decent sized small city as they continued on through the night. Deanna was beginning to think that they had lost their pursuers when they got rid of that Apple Tag under their car.

Dr. James told them, "Maine is all small town and back road travel once you get off the Maine Turnpike and freeways. This far out from Portland, trying to track us without technology would be like looking for a needle in a state-sized haystack. The further north we travel on route 1, the less chance of them finding us out here in the middle of the night."

Chapter 41

Tagged Again and Out of Gas

As they all started to realize that they were fairly safe out here in the rural coastal areas this late at night, everyone started to relax. Stacy had dropped off to sleep in her seat and Theresa looked like she was trying hard not to join her. Even Dr. James was looking droopy.

Ben turned around and asked Deanna, "Maybe we should try and find a coffee shop that's still open this late. Even a 7/11 would be fine. I need to use the bathroom and I bet you could use a break too."

Deanna replied, "Good idea. Let's see what we can find way out here." They were passing through Bath, Maine as this point and as they crossed the Sagadahoc Bridge over the Kennebec River, they found a Dairy Queen on Read Island that was still open. Deanna pulled in and woke everyone up. "Get up and stretch your legs. Let's get some coffee or something. We still have a long way to go yet tonight."

Everyone woke up and got out of the car moving like zombies because they were so tired. Deanna waited until everyone was headed inside before she locked and closed the car doors. She was exhausted as well but didn't want to admit it out loud. She stretched and thought, "I want is some strong coffee and the bathroom, and not necessarily in that order." she told herself.

As they trooped in, Ben noticed that there were only two staff members here this early in the morning. "It's about two thirty right now," he noticed, looking at his watch. Ben watched as Theresa, Stacy and Dr. James head for the bathrooms so he around hung around in the order area waiting for them to finish, and for Deanna to come in. Deanna entered and walked straight up to the counter. The teenager stepped up and she ordered a large coffee to go.

As she stepped back to wait, Ben stepped up and ordered the same, with cream and sugar. Ben wasn't too worried with both of them standing watch. As soon as Ben ordered, Dr. James came out and ordered a hot tea. Then a few minutes later, Stacy and Theresa came out and ordered coffees too. Deanna sat down at a table where she could see the car and tried to unwind a little bit but her 'spidey' sense was tingling still, telling her something was wrong.

Deanna's coffee was up and she went to get it thinking, "Something's not right. Why haven't we seen anyone following us since we left Portland?" She couldn't put a finger on it maybe because she was overtired. She sat back down and continued to think back over their route while sipping her coffee. James got his hot water and tea bag and sat down with her. While the girls waited for theirs, Ben paced the floor with his coffee.

As she thought more about it, she remembered what Ben had said to them back at that restaurant. There had been a man watching them, he thought, out on the street that had walked off after seeing Ben. Then it hit her like one of those oh crap moments. She now thought she knew why they hadn't seen anyone.

She called out for Ben to come over to their table for a minute. Ben walked over with Stacy and Theresa. As Ben walked up, she looked at him, "Ben, I think I know why we haven't seen a tail since Portland. That man you saw back at the restaurant probably put another tracker on the car while we were inside and he waited to make sure he saw one of us before reporting to his boss. They've been tracking us ever since. They don't have to be within eye sight. They can follow us with an app on a cell phone that tells them exactly where we are and where we're going."

Ben started to turn around and head out to the car but Deanna stopped him. She said, "Don't rush out there just yet. They may be outside in the dark watching us right now. See if this store has a small flashlight you can borrow to check something on the car. When you step out, wait a bit, then duck down between the cars so they can't see you. Then start looking around the obvious places where a tracker might be. They didn't have a lot of time to place it so it's somewhere they could attach it quickly and get out."

Ben looked at Stacy and told her, "I'll be back in a few minutes. Stay here." He walked up to the front counter and asked for a flashlight. It just so happened that they had one out back in the kitchen. When the teenager brought it out, Ben thanked him and told him, "I'll be right back." He walked up to the doors they had come in where the car was parked and peered out into the parking lot. He didn't see any cars with people in them close by so he walked out to their car. He waited for his eyes to adjust to the dark and looked around again.

He quickly ducked down between the cars onto his knees and waited again. He didn't hear anything so he crawled down the side of the car on the driver's side, shining the little flashlight around the front wheel wells, fenders and door sills. He didn't see anything so he continued towards the back of the car. He didn't see anything on the driver's side rear wheel well either.

Ben kept his light shining to a minimum, only turning it on long enough to take a quick look and shut it back off again. He continued around to the rear of the car. This time he lay down on his back and pulled himself up under the rear of the car. As he shined the light around, he found it. This time they had used a magnetic tracker that was mounted on the back side of the rear bumper. Ben removed it wondering what to do with it. He didn't want to take it inside.

Then he thought of a wicked idea. He crawled out from under their car and he moved over to the little car next to theirs. He reached up and mounted the magnetic tracking device up on the frame next to the gas tank. Ben figured they could get pretty far before their pursuers figured out the ruse. He decided to wait until they were well on their way before telling anyone what he just did. Ben couldn't help smiling a bit over his little trick.

He got up and slowly walked inside to give the flashlight back. The teenager asked Ben, "Did you fix it?"

Ben gave a little chuckle and replied, "I certainly hope so," and walked back over to where everyone was sitting. As he walked up, Deanna couldn't help noticing that Ben had a slight smile, like a cat that ate the pet bird. She decided not to ask.

Ben strode up and Deanna asked everyone, "Are we ready to head back out again?" They all got up and headed out to the car. Deanna asked Ben, "Did you see anyone out there?" Ben shook his head no and walked out with Stacy. Deanna let everyone get in and took one last look around. No cars with people sitting in them here in this parking lot but they may be close. They could be hiding down any side street around here waiting to pounce.

Deanna decided to take a side street out of the parking lot. She pulled out and turned left on Woodbridge Rd., then left again on Old Arrowsic Road. back to route 1. As she turned onto Arrowsic, she and Ben kept a good watch behind them. She drove slowly to see if they noticed anything but there were no tails or any other cars for that matter this early in the morning.

As she drove down the road, Ben told them about the magnetic tracker and what he'd done with it. As he finished his story, he said, "I don't think the other car will be moving very soon so it may take them a while to figure out something's wrong and go check. We need to be long gone by then."

Deanna smiled a little at Ben's story but wondered why the bounty hunters hadn't set someone watch them while they were in the Dairy Queen? "Maybe they're as tired as we are and decided to depend on their technology." She mentally shrugged her shoulders a little bit and offered a little prayer to the powers that be in this area for some shadow to hide their path.

Deanna set out at a good speed down route 1 north again. She took Ben's advice and tried to get out as far as they could into the dark before his little ruse was discovered. They soon passed beyond most of the retail and businesses and soon passed through another little town asleep in the wee dawn hours.

Then they passed through Wiscasset, a mid-sized city here on the wide Sheepscot River. Deanna was a little worried about just driving right down Bath Road through the center of town, so she turned off and went down a side street towards the water. When Deanna reached the last street before the beaches, she turned up Water Street and turned right at the light onto Main Street and the bridge.

They needed to get across this long bridge and Davis Island without being seen. Deanna figured that if they could get across without being spotted, they probably could make it the rest of the way. Dr. James told her, "We're nearly to the turn off for Bristol Road. Just a few more miles."

Just as the car set out across the bridge, Ben reported, "I still don't see any lights behind us." Deanna pushed the speed limit a little faster than she had before because she was worried about being seen going across here. This old car stood out like a neon sign. As she headed across, she looked down at the fuel level gage. They only had about a third of a tank left and she didn't see any place to pull in and fill up anywhere here.

Deanna remarked smiling, "Just when I thought we had it made, we'll probably run out of gas before we see another gas station out here in the sticks. I'm glad this car has an extra-large fuel tank but we're running low. Keep an eye out for any gas station at all."

She kept driving into the early morning hours, trying to find that balance between speed and fuel economy. Just about the time the car was down to nearly empty, they arrived in Newcastle. Almost on the other side of town, they spied a locally owned gas station and Deanna pulled in, thinking, "Whew, we're nearly down to fumes."

The place didn't look open yet but it was just a little after five am with the sun just coming up on the eastern horizon. Deanna parked the car at the island right in front of the office, thinking that maybe they could hide a little in plain sight. She got out to stretch her legs and noticed the gorgeous sunrise. As she stepped out, everyone else got out as well. Stacy and Theresa oohed and awed over the sunrise, wanting to walk around a little bit to see it better. Ben barked, "Not a chance. We're not safe yet. One of those bounty hunter wolf packs could drive up any second so we do not want to get separated, period." Stacy pouted a bit but stayed close. Theresa just shrugged her shoulders and said, "Fine, there'll be others."

Ben stood out in the parking lot with his hand on his pistol in the holster. He kept looking down the street as if expecting a car load of gun toting bad guys to roll in at any second. Deanna just leaned into James and sighed, "Are we close yet?" James looked at her and gave her a hug. "Yes. In the next town over, we turn off into the countryside and hopefully lose any more pursuit."

Deanna looked around and decided that, although this town and this gas station looked a little run down, it still had a welcoming feeling to it. She smiled a little as they settled down to wait for someone to show up for work.

Long about six am, an older man drove up in an old pickup truck. He pulled into the side of the building and stepped out, noticing the car and the folks standing around. "Been waiting long?" He asked in his growly down east accent. Deanna looked at him and saw an older man in overalls, obviously a mechanic, with a cigarette in his fingers.

She replied, "About an hour or so but it's quiet here so we didn't mind waiting. We sure could use some gas to finish our trip though. Can you help us out? We're about empty." The older man walked over and unlocked the door to his shop. Pretty soon, Deanna heard the pumps come on and James went inside to pay.

She took the old nozzle off the hook and stuck in the car, then pulled the old lever. As soon as she pulled the hand lever on the nozzle, she locked the handle and waited. The pump was one of the really old mechanical ones that had the numbers that rolled over. Deanna thought she would never see another one of those ever again.

Theresa walked over to watch. "I've never seen a gas pump this old. This state must be a little behind the rest of the world," she said smiling as she looked on.

Deanna replied softly, "And I think that might be a good thing." After a few minutes, the tank was full again. She put the nozzle back up and put the gas cap back on.

Deanna walked inside to see what James was doing, noticing they were engaged in car shop talk. The man, who turned out to be the owner, was asking about their car and Dr. James was extolling her virtues like a car salesman when she walked in. James turned around and waved a hand in her direction, "Here she is, she can tell you more about that car than I ever could."

The man started to ask her about the size of the engine and a bunch of other technical questions and Deanna didn't have a clue. She suggested he just come out and look for himself. The man just about tripped over himself trying to get past them to get a look under the hood.

Chapter 42

A New Car and Round Pond, Maine

As they all filed out after the man, he was already popping the hood to take a look. Deanna was starting to get a little nervous at the apparent liberties he was taking with their only ride to Round Pond. Once he started poking around a little, he let out a slow whistle. He turned to them and introduced himself.

"My name is Mike; I grew up around here and I've had this little repair shop for a lot of years now. Once in a while, I've been known to do a little horse trading with cars when I see something worthwhile and this is one of those kinds of cars. I haven't seen one of these in years. The fact that you are running in it tells me a lot about the car and how good it is," he said with a slight smile.

Deanna took a mental step back for a moment. "How did he figure out we're on the run," she thought. After a quiet minute as everyone digested what Mike just said, Dr. James asked, "Do you have something in mind?"

Mike smiled again and replied, "How attached are you to this car? I'm thinking about doing a little trading here if you aren't."

Dr. James looked at him for a moment, looked at Deanna, then the others. "What kind of trade are you thinking about?"

Mike said, "I have a newer model car that has a lot more leg room and gets better gas mileage than this old racer. Some guy couldn't pay his bill a while back and left it here after I took out a lien on it. I never heard from him again. He was probably another one of those druggies from out of state. We've seen our fair share of those people up here over the years. Are you interested in taking a look at it? It definitely won't stand out in a crowd like this one does and I know how to keep a lid on things if we trade."

Dr. James looked over at his friends and said, "Let us discuss this for a minute amongst ourselves and we'll let you know shortly. Give us a minute please."

Mike replied, "Sure thing. I'll be inside once you decide one way or another."

As Mike walked into his office, Deanna voiced what everyone was thinking, "What just happened?"

Dr. James looked at everyone and said, "It looks like we may have an opportunity to lose our pursuers for good, if this car is a good as he says it is. Who would think to look for us in an ordinary car that looks like everyone else's out here. I have to admit he may be right; this car stands out in a crowd anywhere. Maybe we should at least look at what he wants to trade for this and think about it. We can always say no."

Deanna thought for a minute. She spoke up, "You have a valid point but we'd give up the advantage of speed, and we don't have any papers on this car. No title, the car is registered to someone else out of state and we don't have any insurance either. This would strictly be a shadow deal. Will this Mike go for that?"

Dr. James stood silent for a moment and replied, "We won't know until we talk to him. I don't think he'll report us to anyone. We paid him cash for the gas so there's no trace of us on any computers. If we do this, we'd have to insist on a no paper deal with his car as well. All we can do is negotiate in good faith and decide from there. We won't make any decision unless we all agree on it, okay?"

Everyone agreed to at least hear Mike out and make a decision afterwards. Dr. James walked back inside to find Mike. He explained their position a little without giving any details while Mike listened. Dr. James finished his plea about looking at the other car with a no paper trade deal as the only way they would consider anything and Mike looked at him for a moment.

"I kinda knew you folks might be in a little trouble when I noticed you sitting at my pump this morning acting like you were looking for some not so nice people. Especially since my gas is usually a lot higher than any of the franchises. No help for that as an independent but that's a story for another day. In your case, as long as that car hasn't been reported stolen anywhere, I can hide it on my own with a little creative paperwork with the local DMV office. I've done that before on rare occasions. What do you think, you all wanna go take a look at my trade?"

Dr. James said "Yes, we agreed to at least take a look if we could agree on the paperwork. Lead the way."

Mike stepped around him and walked outside. He waved at the others and they followed him around back to a veritable junk yard. There were about a dozen cars in various stages of repairs, with some looking like they were ready to drive off. He walked over to a Jeep Cherokee that looked like it had been left outside for a while.

Mike reached in the driver's side door and popped the hood, then opened the doors so everyone could get a good look. The engine compartment was a little dirty but Deanna noticed that under the dirt, the belts and hoses all looked pretty new. The front of the radiator was good and clean. The wheel wells weren't all rusted out nor were the running boards. This car hadn't seen too many salty roads in its past. The inside seats were still in very good condition and it was an automatic.

Mike stood back and explained, "I don't have the title to this one either. I have a lien on it to pay for the repairs I did for that feller who left it but I can cancel that easy enough. We can trade even up. I'll take off those New Hampshire plates and park it out back here for a bit before I decide to do something with it. Hell, I might even keep it for myself as a toy," he laughed.

Dr. James stood over with Mike to let Deanna and Ben look over the Jeep. Deanna asked Mike, "Can you start it up for me please?"

Mike said, "Sure, hang on." He got in, turned the key and the Jeep started right up. Deanna listened for a minute and said to everyone, "This is a pretty good car to take us where we need to go and then some. What does everyone think? Has that old Chevy finally outlived its usefulness?"

Dr. James added on to this by saying, "I don't know about you guys but I'm tired of being chased and having to look over my shoulder all the time after the last few days. This might be our last chance to get off their radar for a long while. As for you three," he looked at Ben, Stacy and Theresa, "if you decide to stay here in Maine, you could get lost here very easily and not have to worry them ever again. Theresa, that bounty on your head will disappear in time as long as you don't do anything else to attract attention."

Everyone agreed that this sounded like a pretty good deal that had just dropped in their laps. Dr. James turned around to Mike and told him, "We all agree to this and we'd like to negotiate in good faith. We'll give you the history on the Chevy and if you still want it, we have a deal."

Mike beamed and walked over to shake everyone's hands. He told them, "I already have some plans in mind for that Nova. I know some people that I'll get with later on where we can make some money at the local dirt tracks around here. If I cart it around on a trailer, I won't need to put plates on it right away." With that, they all walked back around front.

Deanna told them, "Get our stuff out of the car and hide it out of site for now while we finish this deal. We can bring that Jeep up here and put everything in quickly out of sight of prying eyes once we're done inside." She left Ben, Stacy and Theresa to carry that out and she walked inside with James.

Mike was sitting at his desk looking at something when they walked in. He turned around in his old chair and asked, "Okay, tell me the story about the car. I'll run a check on it with a friend of mine at the state police to make sure it isn't on any list of stolen cars anywhere."

Dr. James told him about how they got the car from Steve back in New Hampshire, leaving out the part about the shootout at Big John's. Dr. James told him a little bit about who was chasing them but not why.

Mike said, "That's quite a story. Here I was thinking that you guys were just some stranded tourists from out of state or something. Okay then, how about we do an even swap for the cars? No paperwork like we talked about, and I worry about anyone that might see the car before I repaint it, "he said smiling. "Everyone around here knows me and with my reputation, I'm not too worried about strangers bothering me here."

Dr. James looked at Deanna, who nodded yes. He said, "Done." He shook Mike's hand and took the proffered keys from him. As they walked outside, Dr. James held up the keys and smiled. He told everyone, "I'll go round and fetch the Jeep. Be right back."

Deanna walked over to where everyone was standing next to the Nova and put her hand on the car. She said quietly, "Well done old girl, you did your job and got us this far. Now it's time for you to rest and enjoy the rest of your life with Mike. I'm sure he'll take good care of you from now on." She almost teared up at leaving the car as it had done so much for them.

Dr. James came around front with the Jeep and parked so that the Nova was hidden somewhat. Ben loaded the rifles and ammunition in the back. He looked over at Deanna and said, "I'd feel more comfortable if we had a blanket or something to cover everything up here. Do you think Mike might have something?"

She looked at James with a questioning look and he walked over to where Mike was looking on. Mike had watched Ben load everything in the back and was wondering just who these people were. He hadn't seen anyone with that kind of hardware and ammunition in a really long time. As Dr. James walked up, he decided that he didn't want to know. Probably safer that way.

Dr. James looked at Mike's questioning look and thought, "If he doesn't ask, I won't tell." James asked, "Would you happen to have an old blanket we could get from you or something we can cover the back cargo deck with?"

Mike looked at him and had to think for a minute. He replied, "All I have here are some fender covers in the shop. I can let you have one of the old ones. Let me get it for you."

After he returned with the cover, Dr. James took it from him and gave it to Ben. As Ben was covering everything up in the back, the ladies were putting everything else in the back seat while Deanna was sitting behind the wheel getting a feel for their new ride.

Dr. James walked back over to Mike and said, "Thank you. You have no idea what this means to us. Maybe when things have quieted down, we can pop over and tell you the rest of our story someday. It is quite the adventure, I promise you."

Mike shook his hand again and replied, "Well, I hope the rest of your trip goes quietly after this. I look forward to tipping a beer with you and hearing that story someday. Be safe now." James walked back and got in the Jeep. As Deanna drove out, she waved goodbye and headed back out to route 1 north.

She looked down and noticed that the Jeep had a full tank of gas, which Deanna thought was a bonus. Of course, they had given Mike that Nova with a full tank so she guessed they were even. Now they had an everyday-looking SUV with Maine plates on it and as long as no one looked too closely, they were good.

Deanna couldn't help yawning and said, "Sorry, it's been a long night. Maybe we should get some breakfast and coffee before we get too far down the road." Everyone enthusiastically agreed and started looking for any drive-through along the way. They made it to Newcastle and Deanna left the main road the go down route 1 business, Main Street.

Dr. James told her to look for Highway 129, Bristol Road south. As they were traveling down through town, they stopped in a McDonald's and got breakfast and some more coffee for everyone, and James his tea. After several blocks, Deanna found the Bristol Road turn off and turned right. This road took them down through more retail businesses and subdivisions.

At the intersection where Hanley's Market stood, she turned left, following Bristol Road down Highway 130. They kept going down to Bristol and right after they passed a diner, James pointed out the small road called Lower Round Pond Road. As Deanna turned left, James quietly said, "We're nearly there."

He guided Deanna down through Round Pond and over towards the ocean by Moxie Cove. He told everyone, "My friends live over off Moxie Cove Road in a house near the beach. My friends are retired and living off her school teachers and their social security pensions. They also make a little extra on the side helping refugees now and again."

"They don't have much of any kind of resistance network up here like those folks in New York and other places around the country. But they do know a lot of people up here and as you've learned, trust is earned here, not freely given. We should be very safe for as long as we want to stay. Tim has a good-sized house and their neighbors are used to seeing guests. Tim always brags that they run a B&B without all of the government regulations."

After driving a few more minutes down Moxie Cove Road, Dr. James pointed out an older house almost right out of a Maine postcard. It was a large, typical two story, New England style house that looked like it could withstand the Nor'easters that sometimes came through here. Deanna pulled into the driveway and drove up to the house. This house had a nice front porch with rocking chairs, lots of windows around the house, with faded white paint and a dark asphalt shingle roof. It all looked so warm and cozy to everyone.

Chapter 43

Safe at Last

As Deanna stopped the car, an older man and woman came out on to the porch with a large, shaggy dog. Tim looked like a summer version of Santa Claus, and his wife, somewhat shorter than him, could have been Mrs. Claus. They had thick, white hair and both were on the heavy side but they looked like it should be normal for them. As soon as Dr. James stepped out of the car, Tim grinned wide, his eyes lit up and he said in a booming voice, "About time you got here, we're just about to send the staties out to look for you," he laughed. His wife shushed him with an elbow and a smile, then walked out to the car with the dog, who just ambled along, wagging his tail.

She wrapped Dr. James in a big hug and said, "We're so glad you all made it here safely. I take it by your lateness, that you had a bit of trouble on the way?"

Dr. James replied, "Yes, we did but by sheer good fortune, we dodged them and finally made it here. I'll tell you all about our misadventures as soon as we can get settled in a little bit. Right now, we need showers, clean clothes and some rest. It has been a couple of days since we have had any of those. Let me introduce you to my traveling companions."

Dr. James introduced everyone and the dog, Buster, came up and gave everyone a good sniff before deciding that all was good with these new strangers. He went back up to the porch and lay down to lazily watch everything unfold.

Deanna shook Tim's wife Rachel's hand, as she introduced herself, and asked if they could safely unload some things from the back of the Jeep discreetly. Rachel looked a little puzzled by the request and Tim walked up telling her, "Don't worry dear, I'll take care of it. Go ahead, bring everyone inside and let's get them settled in."

Dr. James introduced Ben again and told his dear friend, "Tim, I'm afraid we have some heavy artillery in the car we need to stash somewhere out of sight. We have everything wrapped in a blanket; we just need a place to put them for now until we decide what to do with them later."

Tim had dealt with this small problem before with other guests so he knew what to do. He had a place out of sight and secure so he shook Ben's hand and told him, "Grab your gear and come with me. I have just the place for them. That includes those sidearms you're carrying, you won't need them here."

Ben opened up the back hatch and grabbed the rifles, still wrapped in the old fender cover and followed Tim up to the house. Everyone else was already inside with Rachel. Tim went down the front hallway to a stairway going upstairs. He turned and told them, "I have a gun safe upstairs that no one can get into but me. Go get that pistol from your young lady friend and I'll meet you upstairs."

Dr. James walked out to the kitchen where he heard the ladies talking and laughing. As he entered, they were all standing around the kitchen when James walked up to Deanna smiling, "It's good to hear laughter again. Deanna, please let me have your pistol so Tim can lock it in the safe upstairs. He assures me that we won't need them here."

Deanna looked at him with a now sober look. She immediately thought, "How do we know this place is safe? We said that about Big John's in New Hampshire." She looked at Rachel and decided that if she wanted to be trusted, she needed to trust in return. She undid the belt buckle and leg strap to give James the pistol. She reluctantly handed the rig to James with misgivings but she secretly hoped that her mistrust was wrong.

Dr. James walked upstairs and found Tim and Ben waiting for him by a door. When Dr. James reached the top of the stairs, Tim opened the door and walked in, Ben following with his bundle with James bringing up the rear. Inside was a study with a large standup gun safe in the corner. Tim walked over and inserted the combination and opened it up. Inside were a couple of other rifles and pistols of varying models. Tim motioned for Ben to bring the bundle over.

Ben walked up and unwrapped the rifles. Tim whistled low when he saw the AR-15 style rifles and extra magazines full of ammunition but didn't ask where they got them. He noticed that one of them had blood stains on the stock. As he started putting them in the safe next to his, Ben undid his holster and gave that to Tim also. When he was finished, he stepped back and James handed Tim the other pistol. Tim stowed everything and promptly closed the safe.

"Let's go back downstairs and see what the women are doing. They're probably cooking up some mischief without us," he laughed.

 Ben thought, "I like this guy. I haven't been this comfortable around anyone since we left Big John's." He still missed the older veteran and wondered if they were still okay. Maybe he could find out in a few days once they got settled in here.

The men went downstairs to the kitchen to see what was going to be next. Since it was a little too early for lunch yet, Tim thought, "Maybe we should have a sit down and get to know everyone over coffee in the kitchen."

They walked into the large kitchen and the women were still hanging out, as if waiting for them to arrive. Rachel said, "Everyone head out to the parlor and I'll bring out some coffee shortly." Stacy and Theresa, ever helpful, offered to help her make it and bring some out to everyone. Rachel pooh, poohed and sent them all out to the parlor. She'd be out directly.

Tim led them out to what he called their sitting room, a small family room with comfortable chairs and an old sofa. He bade them all to sit and make themselves comfortable. He looked at James and asked, "So, what kind of trouble have you been getting into since the last time you were up here?"

Dr. James started his story with when he had left here the last time and went to the mid-west for some work out there. He said, "That trip was nothing special. I left here, traveled down towards the Ohio River valley and worked at different places around Ohio, Indiana and Illinois for a few months. Then I received a message about some immigrants around the New York City area that needed help so I snuck in there and worked around that area for a couple months. Then Deanna's group got me out on what was supposed to be a routine extraction but it all went sideways once we got to upstate New York."

Dr. James continued to tell him of their adventures since escaping from the Lake George area of New York, with Deanna and Theresa adding small things here and there. While they were talking, Rachel brought in coffee for everyone on a tray and sat down next to Tim to listen in. Everyone helped themselves while the story unfolded.

After a couple of refills on the coffee and James his tea (Rachel remembered), they came to the part of the story about last night and the bounty hunters. When Ben chipped in his part of the story about placing that magnetic tracker on the other car, Tim started laughing. "Serves them right, the bastards."

James finished up with the part about the car swap early this morning with Mike in Newcastle. Tim said, "I know of Mike. Good people. I'm glad he did right by you. Now that you're here, what are your plans? Doc, are you planning to take off again soon?"

James told them, "I don't want to go anywhere for a few weeks. I need a vacation after all of this being chased around. But once I do decide to get going again, I'm going south to Virginia to rescue my two sisters, then get us all across the border. With my medical background, I should be able to apply for asylum in Canada easily enough. As for everyone else, I'll let them tell you."

Deanna spoke up next, "I'm going wherever James goes. I don't have any family anymore that I'm close to and my home in New York was either taken over or destroyed by Homeland Security. I don't have anywhere else to go." She looked over at James and grabbed his hand, "Besides, we make a pretty good team."

Tim looked at Rachel and remarked, "I know all about that. Rachel is not only my beloved wife of many, many years but my partner in everything we do."

Stacy spoke up and told them about how she and Ben wanted to find a quiet place to work a farm. "We want one of our own someday so we can raise a family away from all of the people fighting each other around the rest of the country." She told them about Big John and Barbara and how they almost stayed there until Robert's men made that impossible anymore. "Now we want to find something like that here in Maine, if we can."

Tim started to say something but Rachel spoke first. She told Ben and Stacy, "There're lots of working farms here in Maine, all the way to the Canadian border. You can have your pick of neighborly, small town living pretty much anywhere from down east to Aroostook County in the far north. We can ask around if you want to start out down here and figure it out as you go. You just let us know how we can help."

Theresa sat there quietly. She waited until everyone finished talking and spoke in her turn. "I'm not sure where or exactly what I want to do yet. I want to help people, that's all I know. I thought about trying to find another refugee network like we had in New York where I could help people get across the border but after the last week or so, I'm too shook up to get involved with anything even remotely dangerous for a while. I think I'd like to find a group that works with refugees and immigrants, if there's something like that around here?"

Rachel sat quiet for a minute and said, "How'd you like to help us here? Part of what we do here out of this house, is to help people like yourselves when you need it. We get travelers like Dr. James all the time. Most of the folks we help are refugees from the lower forty-seven states looking for a safe place away from government eyes. Most of them are non-white or of another religion than the new government mandated one. We have some connections up in Somerset and Aroostook County that've helped people get across the border at times. Does something like that interest you? We're getting on in years and we could use a young person like you to do the things that are harder for us now."

Theresa sat there shocked for a minute or two. She got emotional and replied, "Are you sure? You don't know me but I would love to help you out. I'm good at office administration so I can help with any bookkeeping and other things. I can cook too. I also learn very quickly. I can start tomorrow, if you want," she said excitedly

Tim laughed and told her, "Whoa young lady, we'll get to all of that in due time. First, we need to get you all settled into some rooms and showers. Then lunch. This afternoon, I'll give all of you the grand tour and then we can relax on the porch. You've been up for a couple of days now and I just know that after a shower and a good meal it'll be sleepy time."

With that, Rachel got up and started to collect the cups and tray. Theresa jumped up to help and they took everything to the kitchen. Tim told the rest, "Okay, let me show you guys the guest shower. You can take what little you have and get in line to clean up. Then, I'll show you to some spare rooms upstairs to settle down in."

Tim led the crew upstairs to the guest bathroom and showed them their choices of spare rooms. He let everyone pick their own and he left them to it. "I'll meet you all downstairs when you're finished."

When Tim went back downstairs, Deanna looked at James and said, "Well, here we are again. Do you want to share a room with me stranger," she smiled coyly.

James grinned broadly, "Absolutely gorgeous, lead the way." They picked out the nearest room and put their packs inside. All the rooms had full sized beds, nothing fancy, just a typical old house with early twentieth century décor.

Deanna told James, "I got first dibs on the shower, unless Ben and Stacy beat me to it." She grabbed her bag and looked down the hall. Ben and Stacy were still checking out their room. She sauntered down the hall and took a long, hot shower to wash off a couple of days of cars and road smell. As she was showering, Deanna thought, "I'm looking forward to a few days of not having to worry about bad guys around every corner for a change and some serious cuddle time with my favorite doctor."

Chapter 44

New Beginnings

After everyone had their showers and changed into some clean clothes, they gathered in the kitchen again. Tim asked, "How's everyone feeling, better I hope?"

Deanna replied, "Yes, much better thank you," and everyone else just sort of nodded or smiled. Tim smiled and asked, "Are you ready for the grand tour?"

"I want to show you how we do things here in Maine. I have my office upstairs, as you've seen, but we also have what I call our communications room." He walked out into the foyer towards the front door and opened another door. Inside was a medium-sized room with computer equipment, a couple of laptops and some radio equipment.

Tim stepped into make room for everyone and explained. "We manage an outreach program that stretches throughout the state. We have contacts all the way up into the Allagash wilderness on the northern border, a handful of people in the towns along the eastern border, along with other people in a couple of western border counties around the state."

"We operate a ham radio outfit here, as you can see, for folks who don't have access to the internet in the remote areas. I also run a website for those who do, in order to provide information for folks who need our special brand of help. All of this has kept me pretty busy these last few years when I had to quit fishing and trade my commercial fishing boat in for something with a little lower profile, which I'll show you this afternoon after lunch."

Tim looked over at Theresa and asked, "What do you think? Do you think you can you learn to help me with all of this?" Theresa walked over to the tables and looked at the equipment. "I can help with the website management and computers but I only have limited experience with a radio system like yours. All we had was private CB radios in New York, but I think I could learn everything pretty quickly."

Theresa continued to poke around a little bit and Tim told her, "Go ahead. We'll continue the tour. You can come find us when you're ready" Tim invited everyone to step back out into the foyer.

Deanna asked, "Have you ever had any problems with Homeland Security up here? We always had to hide and move our stuff around in New York to keep from being discovered."

Tim replied, "This is Maine, a backwater state with a local government that has learned, since the crash, to pretty much leave everyone alone. They try their best to keep Homeland Security out of everyone's business up here. Whenever Homeland Security does decide to come up here for any reason, the state police meet them at the border in Kittery and escort them wherever they feel they need to go. Meanwhile, everyone that has access to the state-run communication system, a mobile app and a website, gets an emergency email message stating that they're here and to stay out of the way."

Deanna was incredulous. She'd never heard of anything like that before. Dr. James, of course knew all about this and remarked, "Maine isn't the only state like this, Deanna. Montana, Wyoming, Idaho, and most of the other sparsely populated states out west also have agreements like this with Homeland Security now. Homeland doesn't have enough manpower to police all of these states so they only concentrate where the largest population centers are and leave the states who want, to police themselves as long as it doesn't involve any national security issues."

Dr. James continued, "Texas has become almost completely independent of the federal government. I'm surprised they've even remained a state. Homeland Security doesn't even travel there anymore unless invited. There're other western states that are so far removed from Washington D.C., they rarely see anyone from the federal government. The U.S. is pretty close to becoming a loose group of independent states now out west. California, Oregon and Washington state are just about cut-off from the rest of the country and operate pretty much autonomously of D.C. This is what's left of the United States."

Tim whistled when James finished. "I had no idea it was that bad way out there. That explains a few things here then. Maine has become pretty near autonomous as well, being so out of the way up here. Somerset, Aroostook and Washington Counties are more Canadian now than American because they're on the border, with a long history of American and Canadian cross-border commerce and families."

Dr. James finished, "There is serious talk out west about the U.S. not being able to afford to hang on to certain border territories and offering them up to the Canadians and the Mexicans for something in return. Like in the beginning when the U.S. bought the French and Spanish territories in the nineteenth century. Texas and California may become independent countries, divvying up New Mexico and Arizona between them. California, Oregon and Washington State are close to becoming one big west coast country. Up on the northern border, the counties bordering Canada may get sold off to Canada within a few more years. Alaska is a forgotten state and might as well be a Canadian province. The only reason the feds are trying to keep Hawaii, is because of its strategic location, which may change as things continue to get worse."

Everyone just stood there quietly for a minute trying to take that all in. Ben and Stacy had no idea about any of that. They'd grown up in an insular community in the Adirondack Mountains with little to no education about U.S. history from before thirty years ago. Some of the states Dr. James mentioned they'd never heard of.

Deanna also was surprised that the United States had fallen into such a mess. She started thinking about what lay ahead for herself and

James when they decided to leave Maine to head south. She shook herself off and said, "I'm content to just live in the moment for now, at least for a couple of weeks. I need a vacation," she laughed.

Tim was a little taken aback as well about the revelations of the western United States. He knew things were bad but he hadn't known just how bad until now. He started thinking a little about things up here but decided to worry about that another day.

Tim looked at everyone and remarked, "Well, that was pretty sobering. How about we take a look around outside? It'll be lunch time once we finish the tour." Tim stepped out the front door and onto the porch to show everyone the lay of the land as he called it.

He walked out onto the sparse grass with Buster walking alongside, tail wagging. Tim walked around to the side of the house, showing everyone the basement entryway. "We have a stairwell in the house as well but this gives us more room to move things down out of the weather when we need to." He continued around to the back of the house when Theresa let out a small cry of joy. She saw the ocean just a short way from the yard. "We didn't get to stop and see any ocean on our way here and this is so beautiful."

Tim explained that he has his own dock down by the water with a boat tied to it. "We own all of the land from the road to that stretch of beach down there. It's very secluded in case I need to take the boat out for a special trip once in a while. We'll go down there after lunch and take a look around."

The rest of the backyard looked like any other tree-filled back yard. There were lots of pine and spruce trees, with a few broken things strewn around here and there amongst the trees. Rachel had a large vegetable garden and some flower beds around the house as well. Deanna thought it all looked so peaceful right now in the late morning sun. There didn't seem to be any sign of strife going on anywhere. Just flowers and insects doing their summer things to get ready for next winter.

Tim asked, "Does anyone have any questions?" Ben spoke up and asked, "When can we start exploring the area around here? Stacy and I want to get a start on our new life up here as soon as we can." He looked at Dr. James and Deanna as he asked.

Deanna looked at him and replied, "I imagine as soon as you guys are ready. If you go farther north without us, you should be able to evade any bounty hunters, since they're looking for five of us and that old Nova we gave Mike. I would get some different clothes and no one will take you for being fugitives on the run anymore. You'll just have to learn how to talk with a down east accent, like the people here in Maine, to completely blend in," she chuckled.

Ben and Stacy both smiled at that and Stacy replied, "We'll sure try. We'd like to look around starting tomorrow, if that's okay?"

Deanna said, "You guys can borrow the car, if you want. I don't have any plans to go anywhere except maybe to a lawn chair or for a boat ride." She looked over at Tim with that last remark.

Tim looked at his watch and said, "Hey all, it's about time for lunch. What say we head in and see what's cooking." Tim turned around and walked up to the house, entering in through the back door. This door entered the kitchen and as they all walked in, Rachel looked up from where she was cooking at the stove and said, "Good, your all here. We can sit down to eat soon. How was the tour?"

Theresa replied, "I wish I'd known you were doing all of this cooking; I would have stayed to help."

Rachel said, "Not to worry, you'll have plenty of time to help out around here. You need time to get caught up with everything and your sleep. I've been feeding folks for a lot of years and I still have plenty of energy to spare. Now everyone go sit down to the table. This is ready."

Everyone stopped by the sink to wash up and go sit down at the dining room table. Rachel put the big soup pot in the middle and showed Theresa where the dishes were. As everyone started to sit down, Theresa and Stacy put out some soup bowls, cups and silverware around the table for everyone. After a few minutes, everyone dug in to a New England style pea soup with ham. Rachel brought out some homemade bread to go with it.

They all remarked about how good lunch was and Stacy wanted to know how to make everything. Rachel promised to teach her how to cook like a "Mainer" while they stayed here and she'd be welcome back anytime in the future, wherever they ended up.

After lunch, Theresa and Stacy helped clean up while Tim, Dr. James, Ben and Deanna walked out to the back yard. Tim said, "Let's walk off some of that lunch and go see the boat." Tim headed down towards the boat dock with Buster at his heels.

The path went down through a few trees to the beach, which turned rocky as soon as they passed the trees. Tim said, "Be careful, the rocks might be a little slick." There was no sand around here, just rocks and water. As they came up on a rocky ledge, the path led down to a small hidden cove down below where a boat dock jutted out from the rocks.

There was a sleek looking modern fishing boat tied to the dock. It looked fast and was big enough to accommodate a half dozen people without too much crowding. Tim stepped down to the dock and said, "This is a floating dock due to the heavy tides and rocks. Just be careful if a wave comes in and the dock starts to rock a little bit. I don't want to have to fish anyone out of the water today," he laughed.

They all warily walked onto the dock and up to the boat. Dr. James, being a little familiar with sea going protocols, stepped up and said, "Request permission to come aboard captain" Tim laughed and told everyone to come aboard and take a look around.

Dr. James had seen this boat before so he stepped aside to let everyone else take a look. Deanna went straight for the cockpit to see how modern this boat was. She saw a pretty sophisticated marine radio system, an electronic GPS navigation system and what looked like a small radar console. She raised her eyebrows at all of this high tech but decided not to ask where it came from. Maybe Tim was like Mike, he acquired things a little irregularly.

After Ben came back up from down below, he said, "This boat has a huge engine that could make this boat scoot pretty fast if needed." He was smiling at the thought of learning more. Ben looked like he'd like to go for a ride right now, if they could. Deanna looked at him and thought, "I bet Ben would love to learn to drive this thing. He might not be moving too far away from here after all."

Tim was obviously very proud of his boat as he stood by beaming while everyone looked around. He sidled up next to Dr. James and quietly asked, "What do you think? Not much has changed since the last time you were up here, other than you brought some strays this time. You know you can stay as long as you like. We have plenty of room and if you get restless, I can put out the notice again that you're back and you'll have all kinds of patients. Just say the word."

Dr. James looked at his old friend and said, "I can't thank you and Rachel enough for all that you've done for us. I know that Ben and Stacy will probably not go too far away from here to set up a place of their own and you've made Theresa happier now than at any time since I met her in New York. Deanna and I will be traveling to Virginia to rescue my sisters when we're ready but we do appreciate you putting us up in the meantime. I have a lot of preparing to do before I'll be ready to go though."

Tim replied, "You know that Rachel and I would do most anything for you and you're welcome to stay as long as you need. I can help with that prepping also, when you're ready. I've made a few more connections with some people south of here down in Mass and Connecticut. I can reach out to them and they can reach out and so on, to make sure you have all we can give to help you on your way."

James said, "Thank you Tim, that really means a lot to me. I've been putting this trip off for way too long now and it's time to go get my sisters before it's too late. I haven't seen them for nearly five years now. Just the odd letter now and again. They're managing still but I'm not afraid anymore so I want to bring them up here and get across the border before we get caught, especially me with that bounty on my head. I want to get somewhere where we don't have to live in fear anymore. I heard from some other friends out west that Canada is offering asylum to doctors still."

Tim said, "I've heard that too. You know we'll welcome you and your sisters back here whenever you can get them up here."

James asked, "Tim to change the subject, I need a favor when we get back to the house this afternoon. I'd like you to reach out to your local contacts around here to see if there's any news about our bounty hunters. I'd very much like to put all of that mess behind us, especially for Ben and Stacy's sake."

Tim replied, "Absolutely, I'll get to it as soon as we get back. It'll be a good opportunity to show Theresa how everything works and start her training. I think she'll fit in with us just fine. She seems a little reserved but maybe that's because of all the adventures you've all had getting here. I hope she'll be all right given some time without any more trauma."

Dr. James remarked, "She has had a rough life even before getting caught up in my mess. Give her a little time and I'm sure she'll come round."

Tim smiled and patted him on the shoulder. About then, Ben walked up and asked, "Can we start her up? I'd love to hear her purr." Deanna walked up behind him and said, "Me too, I'd like to see how some of that fancy technology works."

Tim laughed and said, "Sure kids, I'll let you play with the new toys."

 James just sat back on the bench seat at the fantail and smiled. He was enjoying the moment while it lasted. After walking back to the cockpit, Tim inserted the key and started the engines. As expected, they roared to life and started purring like big cats. Ben stood there and listened. Deanna started checking out the equipment as Tim explained what everything was and how it integrated with the other boat systems.

After a little bit, Tim shut everything off and they walked back out to the stern where James was still sitting and enjoying the afternoon sun. Tim asked, "Are we ready to head back to the house? I have more things to talk about while doing something for the good doctor this afternoon."

Everyone replied "Yeah, sure." Then Deanna remarked in a spoiled little girl voice, "Yes dad, we're done playing for now," and they all broke out laughing.

Back at the house, Dr. James, Deanna and Ben followed Tim back to his ops center, grabbing Theresa along the way. Tim told Theresa, "It's time to start your training. Are you ready?"

Theresa looked surprised but said, "Sure." He sat her down behind a computer and logged her in. He told her, "I'll set you up you're your own account later but for now, let me show you the websites we use to find out things and monitor local activities."

Tim talked her through which websites they used and how to navigate around in them. As she was looking through some things that Tim had pointed her to, he got on the radio and made a call to a friend nearby, asking if he'd seen any strangers around the area or had heard of anything strange up near Damariscotta and Newcastle way. His friend reported that there'd been an out of state car that'd gotten into trouble at Mike's Place in Newcastle about noontime today but the local LEO's took care of it and he hadn't heard anything else about it. He joked, "If anyone tried anything on Mike, he likely pounded the bastard and left him for the cops to pick up afterward." His friend signed off laughing and Tim had a smile on his face. "That was my friend William up in Damariscotta, he's a bit of a corker."

Tim said, "It sounds like your bounty hunters may've found your old car and tried to interrogate Mike but it didn't go too well for them. I hope Mike didn't get hurt. But it does mean that they're still out there looking for you. Maybe you should think about hiding out here for a few days to see if things settle down."

Deanna was a little worried for the first time since arriving this morning. Her 'spidey sense' had disappeared after they arrived here and it wasn't flaring up now. She had a sense that they had disappeared from the world for the moment. Now they just had to make sure they stayed that way.

Deanna agreed. She looked at Ben and said, "I'm sorry, but you may have to be patient for a couple more days until we can be sure we've thrown them off our trail. Will you guys be all right with that?"

Ben replied, "I guess we don't have much of a choice, do we. I don't want to be out looking around, then end up either kidnapped or they follow us back here. I can take care of myself but I worry about Stacy. I don't want her to be traumatized anymore."

This was all pretty sobering. The happy mood was gone now. They all filed out of the room, leaving Tim and Theresa to learn all they could before supper. Deanna walked back out to the parlor and sat down. James sat down next to her on the sofa while Ben went to find Stacy and give her the news.

James asked, "What do you want to do now? I think we're pretty safe here unless those bounty hunters start torturing people to find out where we are. No one but the people in this house knows where we are right now. I don't think they intercepted my land line phone call from Kennebunk last night."

Deanna sighed, "I guess you're right. I need a good night's sleep and we can worry about it some more tomorrow. She curled up in the sofa in his arms and snuggled. James leaned over and gave her a tender kiss, holding her close for a few minutes.

Later that afternoon, Tim and Theresa came out of the ops center when Rachel called everyone to supper. As they sat down to dinner, Tim told them, "Theresa has taken to this like a champ. She's even shown me a couple of new things." Theresa blushed and smiled with the praise.

"We did find out that Dr. James, Deanna and Theresa still have bounties out for your arrest by Homeland Security but your whereabouts are unknown. As for this Robert feller, the word is out across the local message boards that a couple of out of state boys tried to assault the owner of Mike's Place in Newcastle earlier today and were apprehended after Mike defended himself and held them for the authorities. Mike was just bruised up a bit."

"That means that the hunters are still out there but they aren't going to find you. Now that the word is out for everyone to be on the lookout for more out of state hooligans, they won't be around much longer. A couple of days at best before they're all spotted and run out of the state. So, relax, enjoy the summer weather and we wait a bit. Ben and Stacy can probably start venturing out in a couple of days."

After supper, while things were being cleared off, James and Deanna walked out to the porch and sat down, giving Buster a pet and scratch behind his ears. Deanna just sat there not saying anything, watching the sun go down over the trees. James sat down in a chair next to her, allowing her some space. He knew how peaceful this place was and he also knew that the smell of pine trees and ocean were very soothing. He took a deep breath and savored the quiet as he put his hand on Buster's shoulder, gently petting him. There was no sound now other than the birds and crickets. Tomorrow would be another day.

Chapter 45

Peace at Last, End of the Journey

They all woke up very refreshed the next morning. They had slept soundly between utter exhaustion and the fresh ocean air coming through the open windows at night. As they wandered down to the kitchen, they found Theresa helping Rachel in the kitchen make breakfast for everyone. They all sat down with Tim joining them. Everyone, including Rachel, sat and enjoyed breakfast together, chatting about what they were going to do today.

Ben and Stacy wanted to take a walk out by the ocean. Theresa wanted to help cleanup and then join Tim in the ops center to learn more about her new job and their fugitive situation. She also was anxious to learn about Tim's refugee program.

Dr. James and Deanna waited until they finished. Deanna said, "We want to go walking also but not with Ben and Stacy," she smiled. "We'll find another path somewhere near here. But remember, we're not out of danger just yet until we know that all those bounty hunters have been rounded up and shipped back across the border, okay? So, be careful."

They lingered around the table a bit after coffee and tea, then they started getting ready for their morning walks. Deanna sat there looking at Theresa in her element, smiling and laughing with Tim and Rachel. She thought to herself, "Theresa has finally found a home. I just hope she can finally heal from her past."

She watched Ben and Stacy talking in hushed, excited voices. Stacy was happier now than even when they were at Big John and Barbara's place. James walked up and put a hand on her shoulder. She looked up at him and covered his hand with her own for a minute before getting up.

She smiled at him, gave him a quick kiss before grabbing his hand and leading him out the door. They walked down towards the ocean and talked about the future. Deanna asked him, "What do you want to do here besides prepare for the trip to Virginia?"

James replied, "I think I'll seek out some local clinic work in order to keep busy and you're welcome to play nurse, if you like? We make a good team and you have enough basic medical skills to assist me with the small things, while I teach you some more advanced stuff as we go along."

Deanna thought for a moment and told him, "I'd love to help you when you need me but, no offense, I don't want to spend every waking and sleeping moment with you every day. I will need some 'me time' now and again. Will that be okay with you? If you want to make this relationship a little more permanent, maybe we should think about what that might look like soon."

"I'm a Wiccan and I am not changing that for anyone. You'll have to accept that as much as I accept that you're a Muslim. Can you handle that? I need to know before we go too far down this road we're on right now." Deanna had stopped walking when they reached the rocks near the boat dock. She turned and looked at James right in the eyes, waiting for his answer.

For the first time in his life, James Naismith knew he'd met his match. He looked at her and realized that he loved her with all his heart now and couldn't bear to be without her. He said softly, "I want us to be together the rest of our lives and I'll abide by whatever makes you comfortable with me. If you want a wedding that fits your traditions, I am sure God won't mind," he chuckled. "All I know is that I don't want to go anywhere without you by my side, or in your case, likely leading the way," he laughed.

Deanna laughed with him and gave him a big hug. She reached up and kissed him deeply in front of the sea birds wheeling overhead. They walked along the rocks some more, talking about the future and how to help Ben and Stacy.

After a couple of hours, they meandered back to the house, finding Ben and Stacy hanging out on the porch, petting Buster and talking. Deanna walked up on the porch and asked, "How're you two doing?"

 Ben replied, "Fine, we're just making some plans for when we can start looking around. I hate waiting for things like this. I have no problem stalking game but waiting for news is driving me a little crazy right now."

Deanna smiled and asked, "Have you heard any updates this morning?"

Ben said, "Not yet, I'm just waiting. Do you want to go ask?"

Deanna replied, "Let's go see." As they walked in, Dr. James said, "I'll wait in the kitchen over a cup of tea. Let me know if anything has changed." Deanna and Ben knocked on the ops center door and Tim let them in.

Tim said excitedly, "I have some good news. Apparently, your bounty hunters aren't too swift. They were lazy and relied too much on technology to try and hunt you down and it was their undoing. They were all caught overnight by the state police, who used a scanner to find their tracking frequencies. They've all been rounded up and dumped back in New Hampshire with a notice that they got off easy. If they ever get caught in the state of Maine again, they'll never see daylight outside of a prison."

Ben's face lit up like a Christmas tree and he ran out to find Stacy. Deanna gave Tim a quick hug and went to find James. After she delivered the news, she said, "Have you thought anymore about us getting married? I'd like to find out if there is a licensed someone who can marry us outside of a traditional wedding ceremony. Unless you've changed your mind?"

Theresa and Rachel were listening and Theresa's face lit up as she heard them talking. Rachel got a thoughtful look on her face but kept quiet. James replied, "I have thought about it a little since our walk, and no, I haven't changed my mind. Just tell me what I need to do and let's do it."

At this point, Theresa stepped over and said, "Congratulations. I knew you guys would eventually be together for good." She hugged them both and stood there smiling, with tears in her eyes.

Rachel spoke up at this point. "It just so happens; I might know of someone who does handfasting ceremonies sometimes. He professes to be a Druid but he is licensed in this state to officiate weddings. Will that work?"

Deanna looked at her, then smiled back at James and replied, "That'll work. You may reach out to him whenever you want and set it up. We have plenty of time."

The rest of the day went quietly. Ben and Stacy continued to make their plans for tomorrow when they planned to get out and take their first look around. Deanna started working with Rachel planning the wedding ceremony to be held here on the grounds. Rachel was tickled pink to be part of that. Since James was just in the way for now, he decided to hang out with Tim and Theresa in the ops center the rest of the day.

Chapter 46

A New Future

The next morning, Dr. James and Deanna walked out with Ben and Stacy after an early breakfast to see them off on their road trip. Deanna reminded Ben, "There's no paperwork for this car, so if you get pulled over, you tell them where this car came from and they might just give you a warning. Don't argue and end up in jail. Just be careful."

Ben assured them that they would be careful and they drove off. Stacy was all excited about their first road trip by themselves since leaving home in New York. Ben had his serious look on so Deanna wasn't very worried.

By noontime, the non-denominational minister had been arranged for, the flowers were picked out, from Rachel's extensive flower gardens, and clothes were cleaned and made ready for the ceremony to be held the next day. All Dr. James had to do today was answer a few questions for the state marriage license and hang out with Tim and Theresa again, monitoring the radio and internet message boards.

Later in the afternoon, a reply came in for Tim on one of his messages from one of his contacts in Massachusetts. The message read, "Issue in New Hampshire taken care of. Threat neutralized. HS in charge of redoubt now."

Tim waved James over and let him read it. "It looks like your problem with the Dread Pirate Robert (referencing a very old movie) has finally been taken care of by Homeland Security. I doubt you'll have to worry about any more bounty hunters looking for you guys now. But you still have to worry about Homeland Security."

Dr. James replied, "I've been living with that threat for so long, it has become a silent partner now. I'm not sure what life will look like once

I'm not under their shadow anymore. It might take me a while before I quit looking for them around every corner. I'm just glad that Robert's finally been dealt with. He told us that Homeland was closing in on him, so I guess they finally caught him. I wonder if that mess at Big John's had anything to do with that? We may never know for sure."

The next day dawned and Deanna woke up smiling in James's arms. The sun was shining through the bedroom windows, on what looked like a perfect day for a wedding. She looked at him still dozing and kissed him awake. He woke with a smile and when he quickly realized what day it was, he leapt out of bed and grabbed Deanna around the waist. He swung her around a bit and kissed her soundly before letting her go to the bathroom first. "I love you madly," he cried as she laughed on her way to the bathroom.

Later that morning, the minister arrived and introduced himself as Bruce. He came in and Rachel welcomed him with a cup of herbal tea, introducing the bride and groom.

Deanna, he knew about from talking to her on the phone but James, he was a bit of an enigma. Deanna had told him that James was a Muslim but had agreed to the handfasting for her sake. Bruce wondered how a practicing Wiccan and a Muslim were going to work out their spiritual beliefs together but, he mused, "Stranger things have happened when it comes to love."

One o'clock on the back lawn found Deanna decked out in a flowered head-piece, and flowers laced through a flowery dress they managed to gather up. James wore a flowered necklace around his neck and Tim had somehow managed to find a sort of traditional Muslim long embroidered shirt with a high collar at one of the local thrift stores yesterday.

Ben and Stacy returned by noontime for the wedding as Stacy and Theresa were bride's maids. Ben and Tim were groomsmen with Rachel and Buster managing everything behind the scenes to make this all come together. Tim and Ben had made some rings from some hardwood leftovers in Tim's workshop the day before. Tim had quite the woodworking shop out back in the outbuilding behind the house.

Tim had a lot of different tools and one of them happened to a small wood lathe that they carved out the rings on, then polished with some wood oil he had to make the wood shine. Deanna told Tim and Ben when they showed them to her, "These are perfect, thank you."

Bruce waited until everyone was ready and started the ceremony. Deanna had set up the circle around the wedding area beforehand with flowers and pine boughs from the trees around the house. Everyone gathered just outside the circle, waiting for Bruce to start.

He turned to each of the four directions and spoke the words of peace.

Let there be peace in the East, so let it be.
Let there be peace in the South, so let it be.
Let there be peace in the West, so let it be.
Let there be peace in the North, so let it be.
Let there be peace through all the Worlds.
So let it be.

We gather here in peace for this sacred occasion that is the First Rite of Marriage between Deanna and James. As our Circle is woven and consecrated, this moment in time and this place become blessed. Let each soul truly be here that the spirits of those gathered may be blended in one sacred space, with one purpose and one voice.

What followed was a mix of Wiccan and Pakistani Muslim wedding traditions, as best as James could remember anyway from years ago, that Deanna and James had agreed on, based on their spiritual beliefs.

Bruce was happy to work with them beforehand to make sure all was legal as far as the state laws were concerned but, as he told Deanna on the phone the day before, "The ritual ceremony doesn't matter to me as long as you make your promises to each other, to your respective deities in front of witnesses."

So, the ceremony was a combination of consecrating the sacred circle, an offering to the Gods, and a sharing of honey (from James's traditions) that Rachel had from one of her friends with bee hives. No store bought for them.

James and Deanna honored their parents, now deceased, their ancestors, and recited their vows.

At the beginning of the ritual, Bruce had tied their hands loosely together with a sacred ribbon. Bruce now untied their hands and laid the cloth on the makeshift altar. He picked up the rings and gave one to James, who placed it on Deanna's right ring finger, as per her tradition and recited his vows "I promise to love and cherish you, to be your equal in all matters of the heart and family, and to remain by your side in all things, thick and thin until we are parted by the Gods."

Bruce then gave Deanna the other ring and she placed it on James's right ring finger and recited her vows, "I promise to love and cherish you, to be your equal in all matters of the heart and family, and to remain by your side in all things, thick and thin until we are parted by the Gods."

The offerings to the nature spirits and Gods were given and after more promises were made, the ceremony was complete.

Deanna and James lead the way out of the circle with Ben and Stacy right behind them with the rest following, Bruce leaving last, giving the final prayers of the rite closing.

What followed was an afternoon of food and fun as the new couple started to enjoy their new lives together as a married couple. After a while, as the sun started to set and Bruce was saying his good byes, James reflected on the days event.

He thought to himself, "I never imagined I would get married, especially like this. My parents must be both smiling and furious with me from the grave for not marrying someone they'd picked out. I wish they were still alive to celebrate my wedding day." He started to shed a couple of tears as Deanna walked up.

James let them fall and Deanna asked softly, "Are you thinking about your parents and sisters? I wish they could have been here for you." She took his arm and held him for a moment as he came back to reality. He smiled and told her a little more about his traditional parents and the future they had picked out for him a long time ago.

 "I miss them very much today. I didn't realize how much until I saw all of our friends go out of their way to put this wedding on in such short notice. I truly wish my sisters could have been here today to see this."

Deanna just held him close and thought, "Now the real work begins. Planning the trip to Virginia."

As they watched and waved goodbye to Bruce, they walked over to their friends and thanked them for everything they'd done to get this ready today. They all congratulated the newlyweds again and said "Don't worry about it, we haven't had this much fun in a long time. We need to find some music to dance to and enjoy the rest of the day."

With some old dance music playing on Tim's CD player, they all spent the afternoon and evening dancing and drinking, or at least everyone but James. He told them, "I may have just gotten married in a very non-traditional wedding ceremony but that doesn't mean that I've given up my beliefs. I will still abstain from alcoholic drinks and eat Halal whenever I can."

Everyone else laughed and Tim said, "That's okay, I'll drink yours for you." Rachel reached over and swatted him, making him laugh even more.

That night, after everything had been cleaned up and put away, the newlyweds went upstairs to bed. James asked Deanna, "Are you sure you want to go with me to get my sisters? I expect it will be dangerous."

Deanna snuggled up to him and replied, "We're married now, where you go, I go. Quit worrying and make love to me like we're a couple of young newlyweds." James put his fears aside and they forgot all about the tomorrows for this one special night.

This concludes the first book in the Fugitives in a New United States Series. I am working on the second book of this series that continues our intrepid couple's adventures as they travel to rescue James's sisters in Virginia and escape across the Canadian border.

Afterword

This book started out as series of blog posts because of my activism to help make the world a better place to live in for everyone, regardless of skin color, religious or sexual preferences. My friend liked them so much, he encouraged me to turn them into a book. I liked writing the story so much, I decided to turn it into a series.

The series is about the different people across the New United States struggling to survive in their new world after the economic collapse of the old world as they knew it.

I hope readers will be patient with me as I write these stories in the hopes that I can bring to life a very real glimpse of a possible future if things keep going the way they are.

Acknowledgement

I would like to acknowledge my faithful editor, Suzy Jacobson Cherry, who gave up a lot of her limited time to edit this story via Medium.com. Between the two of us, I think we may have something entertaining and thoughtful for everyone to enjoy. I would also like to acknowledge my fellow veterans, Bruce Coulter and Jack Finn, who encouraged me to turn my musings into an actual book for everyone to read. Thank you all for without you, this would still be just a file on my server.

About The Author

T. Ó Domhnaill

I am a career military veteran, now disabled and semi-retired. I write articles for medium.com and Substack.com when I have time and the odd book now and again. I am of Irish descent, part of the world-wide Irish diaspora. If you want to learn more about what I do when I am not writing books, find my website at www.crann-na-beatha.com to learn a little bit about Irish culture and a little more about me and what I do to fill my days.

www.ingramcontent.com/pod-product-compliance
Lightning Source LLC
Chambersburg PA
CBHW070657010826
48975CB00014B/1739